a stone gone mad

A NOVEL BY JACQUELYN PARK

ALYSON PUBLICATIONS

LOS ANGELES

Printed in the United States of America.
Printed on acid-free paper.

This is a trade paperback by Alyson Publications Inc.,
P.O. Box 4371, Los Angeles, California 90078.

First published by Random House Inc.
First Alyson edition: May 1996

ISBN 1-55583-364-0
(previously ISBN 0-394-55861-8)

5 4 3 2

Library of Congress Cataloging-in-Publication Data
Park, Jacquelyn
    A Stone Gone Mad/by Jacquelyn Park
        p.   cm.   ISBN 1-55583-364-0
    I. Title.
PS3566.A6736S76 1991
813' .54-dc20   91-52674

TO JANE

And on summer nights, after the young stones are asleep, the elders turn to a serious and frightening subject—the moon, which is always spoken of in whispers. "See how it glows and whips across the sky, always changing its shape," one says. And another says, "Feel how it pulls at us." . . . And a third whispers, "It is a stone gone mad."

RICHARD SHELTON, *You Can't Have Everything,* University of Pittsburgh Press, 1975

Acknowledgments

To: Ava Nawy and Jamie Geller—my first readers, who offered me early
  support,
Roslyn Garfield, Phyllis Temple, Nancy Hand, Candy McCann—good
  friends, who loaned me money when the times were lean and were
  always interested,
Steve Delco for his unstinting fascination with the writing process and
  warm affection,
Nini Lyons, who, during a dark and bitter period once, helped to keep
  me afloat, my chum of longest standing,
Robert D. Loomis—esteemed Random House editor, who kept his
  patience and faith,
William Styron, wonderful author, who initially sent the book to Bob,
Dorland Mountain Colony in Temecula, California, which gifted me with
  time, beauty, and solitude,
my former drinking buddies, their fish stories, our long tales of excess and
  illusion,
the memory of my mother, Alice Chandler, my father, James Holt Park,
the spirit of Linda Johnson Maltsberger, star-seeker, pilgrim, staunch
  friend of my childhood, the bravest person I have ever known,
her noble companion, my generous friend Tay Maltsberger,
and Jane Freeman, for every reason I can think of.

I thank you all.

CONTENTS

WHITE RIVER TO NEW YORK

Part One

VERMONT ⎯⎯⎯⎯⎯⎯⎯⎯⎯⎯

. . . Some things are not womenrain, as the Caribbeans refer to their lighter showers quickly absorbed by the sun. Some are the manstorms that change the face of the earth, that uproot the very foundations of nature, that follow us all the days of our lives. That was Mattie and me that October in 1948—there in a ripple of falling leaves while Sheila watched.

Mattie was Sheila's best friend . . .

Thus with Emily: Ella leaned against the railing on the back porch, a light wind bumping her collar, the reasonable perfume she always wore when she went out enveloped by a long black mink, its color standing in perfect consonance with the austerity of the month. It was October, leaves falling like cats and dogs even as Emily and her sister, Sheila, furiously raking up before their father returned from Boston, sat down for a break.

Several tall pines curtseyed over a second terrace that held the iron chairs, a gazebo, a flotilla of birches, and what in the spring would be roses that formed the descending syllables in the mosaic. Their house in Vermont was like a swan on water.

"Look at her!" Emily nudged Sheila, motioning toward Ella. "She's got on that coat she always wears when she goes play bridge." She began to taunt, "That's all she ever does: play bridge, play bridge, play bridge!"

"That's not true!" Sheila jerked her head in Ella's direction. "You know darn well it's not true, so why say things like that? Mother works hard at the restaurant, and she works hard to be good to you if you'd give her half a chance!"

"I do give her half a chance! I give her whole chances all the time! Anyway, you're her favorite," Emily concluded as Ella went back inside.

"Oh shut up!"

"It's true. You're always cleaning the house with her and listening to her and stuff."

"Well no one's slammed the door in your face, Emily. You just shut yourself out. You've always done that. You won't even call her mother."

"She's *not* my mother!"

"She is too!"

"No she isn't!"

"Well, what is she then, Miss Smart Aleck?"

"She's Dad's second wife."

"That makes her your mother, stupid!"

"No it doesn't! Not to me it doesn't!"

"Emily, if you'd quit thinking about yourself so much, you'd get along a lot better in this world." Sheila's face assumed a serious, self-important expression. "As a matter of fact, I was reading something the other day that said people either live in a room full of mirrors or a room full of windows: they either just see themselves or they see beyond their noses. Well, little sister, you live in a room of mirrors. You spend all your time thinking about yourself. The fact is if a woman marries a man, she automatically becomes the mother of his children whether *you* like it or not. And don't look at me like that. I didn't make the rules. Anyway, mother tries real hard with you, and for what? It's a two-way street, you know!"

"Dad says blood's thicker than water."

"Is that all you can say?"

"But he does! I heard him!"

"Dad says that because he wants us to be close."

"Oh, sure he does," Emily retorted sarcastically. "Is that why he's gone all the time? Because he wants us to be so close?" She ran her hand down the pole, leaned over, and tore some leaves off the rake's iron fingers, then stared down at the ground guiltily. Sheila's right, she thought. She knows how to love. She sees the best in everyone. She gets love and puts catsup on it and takes big bites—that's what Sheila can do. Emily clucked her tongue; she should write that in a poem: putting catsup on love.

Frankie came up. Frankie was her mutt named after Frank Sinatra, and she was mad about him. She rolled over on her stomach and almost got hold of his legs, but he sprinted off toward the Hutchinsons' cat next door as she stared glumly after him. The leaves were blowing harder. She grabbed her rake, hoisting herself up, and tapped Sheila with the end of the wood. "Did you hear what I said about Dad?"

"Quit hitting me with that thing!" Sheila said brusquely, standing up herself. "I've got two ears! What do you want me to do about it?"

"I don't know," Emily answered in a subdued voice. And she didn't. She picked up her sister's rake in a gesture of cooperation and handed it over; then in a hurt small sound she asked, "Why doesn't Dad love us more?" She stood there waiting for a reply, somewhat surprised she had said that. What was really bothering her was something else, something she couldn't tell her sister.

But Sheila, seeing Emily's confusion, softened, and she patted her shoulder reassuringly. "Oh, so that's it. That's why you've been so moody today? It's Dad, isn't it?" When Emily didn't respond, Sheila went on, "He does love us, Em. He just doesn't know how to show it sometimes. Sometimes, you know, kids have to be older than their parents. I keep telling you that."

Having expressed this about her father, Emily almost believed that was what was troubling her. She cried, "But what does that mean? How can you love someone and not show it if you really do? I don't understand that. I don't ever want to be like that. If I love someone," for a moment the force of this conviction overwhelmed her, "they'll sure know it. And I'm sick and tired of Dad's bullshit!"

"Don't say that!" Sheila snapped crossly. "Don't use language like that!"

Emily glanced toward the porch to make sure Ella hadn't come back. Then she repeated the word defiantly. "Shit!" Sheila recoiled, and Emily said it again, though with a touch of playfulness: "Shit!"

"Emily!"

"Why what's wrong with shit? You do it!"

"Say *merde* if you have to say something foul like that."

"Say *what?*"

"*Merde.*"

"*Merde?*"

"Yes, dummy. *Merde.* That's French for what you just said." Sheila turned and started toward the terrace.

"Shit!" Emily yelled after her. "I will never say *shit* again! When I'm tempted to say *shit,* I will say anything but *shit shit shit!* I will say feces or bowel movement or I make a movie in the toilet or number two or the Big Bathroom, or I'll hold up two fingers and when Frankie *shits* out front I'll say he's *merding* in the flower beds. And when I've got the runs, I'll . . ."

"*Em-uh-lee!*" Sheila ran back, slung leaves in Emily's face, pushing her to the ground. They wrestled. Emily succeeded in pinning Sheila's arms down with her knees. Sheila, heavier by pounds, knocked her on one side, and for a few minutes they lay there, all ill winds gone, laughing, ferrying clumps of foliage onto each other. It was a havoc this day, a maelstrom of red and apricot-tinted leaves swarming around as if dumped from an overhanging bucket, bringing with them brown, floaty stuff from the fields.

Staring straight up at the sky, Emily's mood changed again, as if their little frolic had never happened. "I mean it's crazy to love someone and not show it," she said as though speaking to herself. "Mattie . . ." Shocked at what had come from her mouth, Emily sat up with a crushing lump in her throat.

Sheila sat up too and eyed her sister oddly, "Mattie? What about Mattie?"

Sure enough, Emily got all fuzzy in her thoughts. Now she had really put her foot in her mouth: she wasn't supposed to say Mattie with no provocation. She was just a lowly sophomore; Sheila and Mattie were seniors. Emily wasn't even supposed to know her sister's friends that well, even though Mattie had practically grown up in this house. Five feet five of trim build, boyish hips, short curly black hair, and wide lips became stock still. Her blue eyes clouded in anxiety. Her astonishingly healthy complexion turned even pinker. Then she did what Lillian, her best friend, always said to do when you're trapped: look the person straight in the eye without blinking. Emily did that now, and Sheila returned the study. That made an interesting contrast. Sheila, seventeen to Emily's fifteen years, was shorter, inclined toward chubbiness. She had shoulder-length auburn hair, hazel eyes, and was quite as pretty as her younger sister, though to her everlasting sorrow she had inherited the Stolle nose: it was slightly humped, like a small tent flared at both ends. But her brain was excellent. Sheila, dying to be class valedictorian, often consoled herself with that. Around Emily, her common expression was indulgent if not always tolerant, in that manner of the elder daughter whose lot (so they write in their diaries) is to sacrifice and sacrifice so everyone else in the family will be happy. Sheila was a girl who wanted everything perfect. And when it wasn't, she said it was.

"Nothing," Emily stammered, on her feet now, nervously brushing leaves off her shirt. "I don't know why I said Mattie. I guess 'cause when she comes over, she cleans the icebox out.

Like the other day there wasn't any jelly left after she'd been here; and then *I* got blamed for it." She paused to see how this would sink in; then she went on hurriedly, "What I meant to say was that people who can't tell you how they feel about something—well, that's pretty stupid if you ask me." She grabbed her rake and began tackling the yard feverishly, struggling to keep control but really upset. Big mouth, she scolded herself. You're going to ruin everything, like Sheila knew Mattie was always on a diet, so why would she be raiding their icebox for jelly? Emily kept her head down and continued raking. Out of the corner of her eye she could see Sheila's feet; she could feel Sheila look at her in perplexity; and then the feet moved off only to come right back. Emily stopped raking and looked up to that face of duty and resolution, Sheila's ears no doubt tuned to their father's oft-repeated remark that she should set a proper example for her younger, more headstrong sister, whom he once had described as too sensitive for her own good.

"I want to finish this up about Dad, Emily. I want you to appreciate what he does for us, working so hard so we can go to good colleges and be happy and checking on his restaurants day and night."

"Well, I hate his restaurants," Emily growled.

"Fine. Hate as you please. But they're what buy you those sweaters you hide so I can't find them and that car you'll be wanting when you turn sixteen, and camp, and going to Macon every summer!" Sheila's voice rose in annoyance, "You just want your cake and eat it too, Emily Stolle. That's *your* problem!"

Darn but she hated that cake-and-eat-it-too routine. Anyway, Sheila was dead wrong. There wasn't cake as much as there was hurt; but she didn't know how to talk about it because it was a secret, and yet the hurt was too big to keep inside: that secret was like two pounds stuffed in a one-pound sack: its contents were leaking out through her pores; the bad parts were coagulating like dried blood, forming a hard, brittle surface on her outsides. These bad parts were the lies she was telling: lies right now to Sheila about what was bothering her, lies to Lillian as when Lillian would ask why Emily wasn't coming to the Muskateer Girls' Club meeting or why she wouldn't stop in at the Indian Bar-B-Que, and Emily, if she was meeting Mattie instead, would say she was sick. Because she didn't want to go to the Muskateer meetings or to the Indian Bar-B-Que.

When she wasn't with Mattie, she wanted to be alone. She wanted to lock her door and listen to Frank Sinatra and dream of dancing with Mattie. And she didn't want to act silly. Like in history class the other day, the teacher had asked what the explorers had found when they opened up the Egyptian tombs. Emily had called out "bones" and everyone had roared. In the past she would have welcomed that reaction, but that day she had been disgusted with herself because she was in love, which meant she was supposed to be mature, which meant the only time she could be joyful was when she was with Mattie. Then she felt not only joyful but strong as a hurricane. However, that could change overnight. For instance, when she saw Mattie with Roy Dean she felt like an ant. Roy Dean was Mattie's steady. He was captain of the football team, with muscles bigger than Charles Atlas's. And what was confusing was to go from being a hurricane to being an ant—feeling strong when alone with Mattie but turning into a runty sophomore next day at school if she saw Roy Dean with his arm around Mattie. When that happened, she had to walk by as if her world hadn't ended, she had to act like a regular Muskateer with Lillian as if she weren't dying inside. And it was just going to get worse after last night.

Last night! Her raking came to an abrupt halt, and Emily squinted in the hard gospel of the October sun until Sheila's stare brought her back to earth. Then she grinned, because once someone had told her her grin could charm the toothpaste back into the tube. "Sheila," she muttered, grinning so hard her mouth hurt, "all I'm saying is this house is too empty."

Still irritated, Sheila responded, "Well then, do something about it instead of hiding out in your room like you've been doing lately." With that, she turned to leave; but, as if having a sudden insight, she whirled right back around. "I'll bet this is what you tell Lillian and all your other friends: about how poor little put-upon Emily Stolle has things so tough! That nobody loves her! That she's all alone in this big house! I bet you spread that around like butter when you know we're the envy of half the town!"

"Why?"

"*Why!* What do you mean, *why*? Because Dad owns all those restaurants, that's why! And that new place he just got in Boston so that you have enough to get almost anything you want within reason, but you still complain. I mean there's just no pleasing you, Emily!"

The wind shuttled more leaves as Sheila turned to leave. But Emily had to get the last word. "You know what's wrong with you?" she yelled to her sister's retreating back. "You give everything a paint job! You look at things that go on right under your nose that have nothing to do with Dad's business and you pretend it's not there. You're like that striped giraffe that stood in front of the striped house hoping nobody could see it. You live in a dream world!"

"Dream world, my eye!" Sheila stormed, turning back and sawing the air theatrically. "You're the dreamer! You and Dad! But at least he doesn't mope around all the time! You're your own worst enemy, Emily Stolle! You think because he's gone a lot or Mother's at bridge when she's not working her hands to the bone or because our real mother died, you have a curse. But look at what Dad does for us! And Mother too! Do you think she likes working as a hostess for him? Do you think I like having to apologize for your behavior all the time? And look at all the starving children in Europe! And Jesus hanging on the Cross! Look at the nails in His hands and feet! And he didn't even have any water! How do you think He felt about *that*?"

A few yards off, Emily winced. Sheila's religious reasoning always befuddled her. Never mind God could have turned the Cross into a toothpick or that He and Jesus had probably worked it all out in advance. The fact was Sheila, as fervent a churchgoer as anyone in White River, used God the way a writer uses a period. "Rather than sitting around on your pity-pot," Sheila lectured righteously, "why don't you think about blind people and kids with no arms or legs or Jesus—or, in more practical terms—why don't you remember poor Rose Perkins!"

Not fair! At this moment Emily saw Rose Perkins flat out in the leaves. "Ol' Ski Nose," the kids at school used to mock her because her nose was too long. But then Rose, as if to punish them for their cruelty, had gone to Jesus, just up and jumped into Canyon Lake this past Labor Day and drowned, gulp—fact was she couldn't swim; and when the water washed through her mouth, she swallowed her tongue. John Edwards, another classmate, pulled her out, which was when Emily arrived on the scene. She had been there with the Muskateers; and when the screaming commenced, they had run over. First time she had ever seen a dead body. Hadn't known what to do. Stood there looking at Rose's tongue bent in her mouth like the end of a rubber band, her face gray as old chewing gum, her eyes open and wooden. Oh boy, but hadn't she felt like a heel for all the times she had called her Ski Nose. Besides that, she was a *really* dead person. That's what Rose's corpse had said to her: here one day and gone the next, cross over into the riddle of human existence among the dark faces flashing behind trees. For an instant it all came back. That's what your God does to us! she wanted to scream at Sheila now. Instead she blinked to restrain the tears. Death scared her. So did love. So did Mattie. "I'm sorry," she murmured quietly. The thought of Rose humbled her. She didn't want to hurt Sheila. She loved Sheila. She respected Sheila's attempts to make sense of things.

Just then Ella walked out on the porch. Emily watched her pick up some magazines and return to the house. Maybe she should run in and say she was sorry for not loving her. No, she decided. She couldn't help how she felt. Ella wasn't her blood; plus, she was dumb. Well, maybe dumb was too harsh a word, but what else can you call someone who thinks Anonymous is the name of a poet? That's what Ella had said last week. She had pointed out Anonymous in one of Emily's books as her favorite writer. Emily couldn't understand why her father had married her in the first place.

. . . I think back now to how different they were: Ella never finished high school; Dad had degrees from the University of Virginia and Yale. Ella was friendly and outgoing; Dad was moody and introspective. I met Ella a few years after my mother, Marian Carver, died from tuberculosis before she was thirty. Her parents, Amelia (my Nana) and Frank Carver from Macon, Georgia, took me in because I was only three. Sheila, two years older, was sent to my father's aging mother in Newport News, Virginia; whereupon Dad, armed with a healthy inheritance from his father, Charles Stolle, Sr., a prominent banker from Virginia, turned into something of a rover. Nana once told me he had gone off his rocker after my mother died (though she divorced him on her deathbed for infidelity). All I know is her portrait hung for as long as I can recall in our Vermont home. It told of a young woman of uncommon beauty—soulful dark eyes, soft brown hair pulled from the face, delicate hands. There were times I would catch Dad staring at it. And one night in a rage I overheard him tell Ella that my mother had been the only woman he had ever loved.

My father was a remote and brooding presence to me—tall, handsome, elegantly attired, he was blessed with wavy black hair and blue eyes, and was a lover of books and words. He was southern, which is to say courtly. He was also a womanizer and an artist to boot. Nana distrusted him because (she said) he cheated on my mother and artists were weak. I don't know about that, but I can say his early life with my mother thrilled me. As newlyweds they had lived briefly in Greenwich Village, where he studied painting and she ballet until illness forced her back to Macon and she later died. After that, Dad hit a long road that carried him to Nebraska, where he met and married Ella Framer, a druggist's daughter. From Nebraska they journeyed east to White River, Vermont, so he could go into the restaurant business with an old friend. When that friend eventually sold out, Dad became the sole proprietor. He promptly changed the name to Stolle Manor and began targeting the Dartmouth crowd just over the state line. Stolle Manor was the first of several of his restaurants that extended from Vermont to Massachusetts. He was loaded.

When I was a girl, White River was a postcard of meandering streets filled with hemlocks that swung like dancers over the roads leading out toward Hanover. The Connecticut River divided us from New Hampshire, and the White Mountains, like a king on horseback, guarded us from the rear. Skiers en route to Stowe changed trains at the sprawling depot in the heart of downtown. During layovers, they often toured the small antique and syrup shops that dotted Main Street. In October, autumn coated the trees, cider smells mixed with smells of burning leaves, and the air was as clean as the northern star. White River was an egg fertilized by Norman Rockwell, its citizens typical New Englanders who had found great refuge in common sense. In White River teachers and dentists came for dinner; phone operators called everyone by their first names; bankers knew almost without checking if an account was good; fifteen-year-old boys stammered and asked for Trojans from patient pharmacists who gently lectured on the foibles of romance. Children biked everywhere, their feet up on the handlebars, and opinions about women, FDR, Catholics, and big government were as rooted as the trees themselves.

In our family, supper was taken at Stolle Manor. My shift was five to five-thirty. I ate alone, ordering the same thing every night: roast beef medium rare, a pool of gravy sunk in a tub of mashed potatoes, salt and butter mixed in Fordhook limas, iced tea, and orange sherbert that I crammed in my mouth so fast I always got headaches. From my table near the kitchen, I smelled homemade cinnamon buns and watched Ella hostess. When Dad was around, he stood beside her greeting the guests. For the men there were handshakes. For the women he would bow and kiss their hands. Never will I forget—my father crooking his head slightly over their fingers as they glowed with pleasure. Finishing up, I'd race home and practice bowing in front of my bedroom mirror.

I met Ella when Sheila and I went "Nawth" (Nana's name for any region above Georgia). I was put in care of a conductor on a train bound I thought to the North Pole. Sheila, whom I hadn't seen since our mother's funeral, got on in Richmond. We had a funny sort of ride, two small girls six and eight years old going to meet their new mother and gypsy father. She was excited; I was resentful. Hours later we arrived at a snort of a place called White River; and running to greet us, arms stretched wide as hope, was this valentine-faced blonde with blue-eager eyes. Sheila began bouncing with glee. I fell to the ground shrieking, pounding my fists, refusing to call this imposter anything but Ella, as Dad stood passively by.

All that seems like yesterday now, all my remembrances of home. I remember Sheila being the unofficial ambassador of familial good will—a confidante to Ella, who never knew how to relate to her husband, a sometimes-parent to me, who never wanted to relate to a stepmother. Before Mattie changed my world forever, I idolized my sister. I can still see us waiting for our father to come home from a trip. If the weather was mild, we might be sitting in our backyard, Sheila writing to Tyrone Power, me dreaming of becoming a spy, a cab driver, and a poet rolled into one. My legs would be crossed like hers, as next to us the crickets carried on like small black cities, the fish ponds drinking in the halfsuns that doodled on the white surfaces. Trees old as plutonium dribbled leaves on the saltfree air, and stuff kicked up by the wind cartwheeled over a field that ended only when we closed our eyes. Leaves roughed up in the wonder of fall covered us, red-on-red in vivid autumn caskets. And then we would hear his car. This coming back was the one occasion when my father, perhaps guilty that he had been gone yet again, would show his affection. Out would come the presents—a shark's tooth or a Charlie McCarthy doll for me. "Daddy! Daddy!" I'd echo as soon as I heard the motor, running to him over the skybright, kneehigh stalks as he got out of his La Salle, a dead ringer for God! That comes to me now. So does my childhood's faith that if I never had anywhere to live, I could always move in with my big sister . . .

Sheila had accepted Emily's murmured apology and was now busily raking not far off. For a moment, Emily watched. Sheila raked as she threw softballs: with no rhythm in movement. But Emily wasn't thinking about that, or about Ski Nose Perkins either, for that matter. Right now Emily was obsessing about Mattie coming over. One P.M. Her rake hit a rock, the handle vibrated, and she stood motionless, worried sick about seeing her and at the same time guilty about how she was treating Lillian. A mental dialogue started: Go on and tell her you and Mattie are in love. You've had no secrets with Lillian since third grade. And she's never ratted on you, she never told how you took money from Dad's closet to buy bus tickets for you both to Rutland or how you "borrowed" Harold Mac's car one night and steered barefoot down Mully Hill with a six-pack between your thighs or that you cheated on a math quiz.

Of course, Lillian was no angel herself. And she was smart enough to help now, Emily reasoned. In fact, Lillian was the smartest person she knew. By seventh grade she could do calculus (which gave Emily indigestion). She had memorized all the symbols in physics. She had taught herself advanced algebra and spoke Spanish and could fix motors better than a boy. Lillian Waller Jackson even looked like a genius. She wore big glasses, the type that make owls' eyes look human, she had the sort of skin that burns in the sun and a cowlick that wouldn't stay down even if you wet it and held your hand over it for five minutes. They both were coleaders of the Muskateers; and until Mattie, they were together constantly. That added yet another dimension to the problem, Emily suddenly realized. If she told Lillian, Lillian might get jealous because Mattie was a girl!

To complicate things even more, Lillian knew all the particulars: for instance, she knew Mattie and Sheila planned on rooming together next year in college. She knew Mattie was head cheerleader and went with Roy Dean. She knew Roy Dean. She knew Emily was supposed to be nutty over Harold Mac because he had a Model T with a radio that got seven stations. She knew all these things and all these people because they all went to the same high school. So maybe telling her would be too much. And how would Emily do that anyway? How could she tell Lillian she had touched Mattie's breasts last night, and that when she had awakened this morning, Mattie's nipples had been stuck to her brain cells; and when she had looked in the mirror, she could almost see Mattie's tongue in her mouth? Oh, God! Emily started raking again, but she couldn't concentrate. What if Mattie was mad at her? What if Mattie twisted things and decided Emily had attacked her? What if she told Sheila? Even worse, what if she told Roy Dean and he came back and killed her? Emily clutched her rake so hard her hands hurt. But Mattie wouldn't do that, she argued with herself. Last night Mattie said Roy Dean had never made her feel like she did.

Emily swallowed hard; her insides burned like paper. Then why didn't I see her in school this morning? I know we only had a half-day, but shouldn't she have been in the halls, or somewhere? Maybe she's run off with Roy! Emily panicked. No, stupid! she answered herself. Mattie hasn't run off with Roy. She'll be coming over here; just be patient. But that didn't make Emily feel much better. She hated seeing Mattie with Sheila. When that happened, and when Sheila's back was turned, Mattie would give her cow eyes, or Mattie would torture her by saying, "Could you hand me that so-and-so over by the window pul-eeze, Em-uh-lee?" her eyes wiggling over Emily like a big caterpillar, and grinning to beat the band—which paralyzed her until Sheila (who had a personality change around her friends) would look at her and say haughtily, "Yes, Emily. Is there something I can *do* for you?" And her only recourse would be to stand there with Mattie ticking her head like a bomb, or walk away wondering if she looked okay in the behind.

Emily stopped to brush a leaf off her face. Maybe someday after she and Mattie had worked everything out, they could tell

Sheila and Lillian, and then all four of them could be best friends. Now wouldn't that be having her cake and eating it too!

. . . Me, I was just one fool in those days, writing my poems to "My dearest absolute love, Mattie"—then tearing them up quick as the ink dried, making up fish stories to cover my tracks. In our nearly four months of meeting on the sly, my imagination soared off the charts. You see, Mattie was an architecture of dark eyes and skin, long syrup-textured hair, wide red lips; why when Mattie walked by, the flowers sang a song. And she knew it. She was a tease. Yet when we were together, we changed: I became wiser, stronger; she more serious, with a sweetness I had never experienced. Mattie would lie on me in the woods back of my house and stick her head in my neck. She'd sew her small hand into mine and tell me my poems were great. She'd bundle herself in my jacket, tying my legs with her own; we'd laugh at nothing more comical than a leaf, a stick of wood, agreeing on things neither of us understood, kissing with more of an aching tenderness than with anything else. All this we seemed to take for granted, rarely speaking of how odd it might be. It was like we were just something else alongside each other in the river, and we swam together for a while. There were houses and people on roofs with scared faces and cattle and single bits of wood floating by separately, but Mattie and I swam in unison. It was like we were part of the same journey, never knowing how we had started, where we were going, what we were about. Yet the more we swam, the more we became whole and perfect and rare. And we never questioned our feelings, just as you never question how a rose smells. Believe me, it was that simple and that searing and that complicated. When I held Mattie, she was like a letter sliding into an envelope and we sealed each other and flew off into some deep us. At fifteen, I was put in touch with something real in myself. How can I say this: if Mattie died, I thought my world would end. That's how I saw our relationship. That's what I believed.

But we almost got caught! One evening after everyone had gone to bed, we met in the fields near our house. Around midnight we crept into our kitchen for a snack. Using a flashlight, we were about to make a sandwich when we heard a cough. It was Sheila! Sheila was coming downstairs! My heart started doing a St. Vitus; Mattie's face looked as if it'd been stuck in a socket. We made it into the broom closet just as the door opened and the lights went on. We could hear Sheila rummaging in the icebox. A few minutes, and then she walked toward the closet. I remember promising the Lord if He would make an earthquake or give my sister diarrhea I would become a nun.

Gratefully she passed on by . . .

More wind. The yard thickened with leaves, and once again Ella came out on the back porch, her long dark mink printing the air. "Sheila!" she called out.

"Yes Mother! I'm over here!"

"Is Emily with you?"

"She's by the flower beds!"

"Sheila, come out where I can see you!"

Obediently Sheila stepped into view. "I'm going up to the Turners'," Ella's voice trailed over the terrace, "and then on to the restaurant. You all don't have to eat there if you don't want. Daddy won't be home until after eight."

That's another thing, Emily said to herself. She calls him Daddy.

"Okay," Sheila responded. "See you later!"

"Be careful if you burn any leaves."

"We will."

"There's hamburg and potato salad already made up," Ella added before vanishing into the house. Sheila walked down the long apron of grass that served as the upper terrace. Two chipmunks bobbed through a copse of trees. A thrush lit on a pile of leaves and stared just as Emily picked up a stick and tossed it to the side. When was Mattie coming was all she could think.

And when she did, shouldn't she look special? Shouldn't she have on her jean jacket which Mattie always said was great looking? But Ella had just sent it to the cleaners. Damn! She watched her sister darkly, remembering once again how she dreaded seeing her with Mattie. Yeah, her hurts were real big all right. Again she checked the time. One-thirty now. Jeeze, was Mattie coming over or what?

. . . I will put things into perspective: The Hursts (Mattie's family) were neighbors, separated from our house by an enormous field. Mattie's father was a director of the bank; Mattie's mom played bridge with Ella. Mattie herself had been around our place forever, it seemed. Sheila in fact used to say they were "born" best friends. Yet when I look back now, I marvel at the propensities of youth, because Mattie and my sister were as different as night and day: Mattie was showoffy, Sheila much more reserved; Mattie was into drama, cheerleading; Sheila was president of the Latin Club; Mattie liked football players; Sheila favored bookish young men in ties. As for me, well, I've already said that Mattie's role as a graduating senior (so far as contact with a sophomore was concerned) was expected to be civil, but distracted; tolerant, but ostensibly bored.

What follows is taken from memory and my diaries. Yet even without that last, I could never forget Mattie. These many years later she remains the battery of my youth, as though a giant extension cord links her forever with my life.

It all began in early July shortly after I returned from my yearly summer's visit to Macon. I was depressed at my grandmother's worsening asthma. So was Ora Lu Hawkins, who had been caring for her for years. Nana was getting old, and there was nothing either of us could do about that.

So this one afternoon, oh maybe two days since I'd gotten back, I entered my house. Ella was playing bridge; Dad was out of town. On the blackboard in our kitchen where we told our whereabouts, Sheila had scribbled, "Gone to the drug store, two P.M." Now when Sheila went to the drug store it was like she was looking for a new car: she had to read the labels on things, do comparison checks with other brands, maybe pick up an opinion here and there. Knowing my sister, she would have skimmed the movie magazines to find pictures of Tyrone Power, she would have stared at herself in all the mirrors, saying hello to anything that moved (Sheila never wanted to hurt anyone's feelings). In fact, if Evie Freeman was working the counter, Sheila would have been stuck for an age, because trying to walk off from Evie in the middle of a paragraph was like trying to back your car out of the mud. But when she finally got away, she would probably drive her new Ford up and down Main Street like she was the Queen of Sheba, or she'd stop in the library to look up minerals and stuff to keep her A in physics. Then she might go to a clothing shop, though nothing would ever suit her: either her legs were too fat or she would think her hips were like an elephant's (that's some of the country my sister lived in).

Anyway, a soft wind was licking the trees outside when I walked into our study only to find the shades pulled and Mattie Hurst sitting on the floor, decked out in this long white gown like you wouldn't believe, reading aloud to the curtains: " 'I celebrate myself, and sing myself, / And what I assume you shall assume.' " I stood quietly watching. " 'For every atom belonging to me as good belongs to you.' "

Oblivious of my presence, caught up in some destiny of her own, she stretched out on the floor, raised the book in one hand, tapping her bosom dramatically with the other. " 'I lean and invite my soul,' " she directed toward a huge statue of an English bulldog in the corner. Then, arms raised, she sat up like an Indian delivering prayers. Her eyes were closed; her chest heaved as she continued quoting from *my* favorite poet: " 'Houses and rooms are full of perfumes.' " She stopped, picked a paper up from the floor. One hand swept into the bodice of her gown, extracted a red rose. She kissed it, put it back between her breasts.

And suddenly I found myself at her rear saying, " 'A child said *What is the grass?* fetching it to me with full hands; / How could I answer the child? I do not know what it is any more than he.' "

Silence. Even the wind seemed to stop blowing. Quickly an O-shaped mouth turned to me. "SHIT!" came out.

But by then I was too captivated by my own performance to respond in kind. From memory I recited: " 'I loafe and invite my soul, / I lean and loafe at my ease observing a spear of summer grass.' " At that, Mattie exploded: *"You,"* she cried, followed by two shock-opened eyes, "the brat-of-the-week know Walt Whitman!"

Never have I experienced a more exquisite satisfaction than when I smirked and replied cockily, "You bet I do. Sophomores have taste buds too, you know." At this point, an uncharacteristic modesty took over Mattie's attitude, which subsequently altered mine. After exchanging a few more lines, Mattie said she was practicing for drama class (at our house, she explained, because her folks had company and Sheila had said she could be alone here a while), and something clicked between us: I started rhapsodizing about Walt Whitman, calling him my all-time hero, saying I had read *Leaves of Grass* a million times and sometimes carried it to softball games (no one knew that but Lillian). I told her poetry was my most favorite thing and that I read it when I was sad, like today over my grandmother. Then I gave her a little Shakespeare: " 'Give me my Romeo; and, when he shall die, / Take him and cut him out in little stars, / And he will make the face of heaven so fine, / That all the world will be in love with night, / And pay no worship to the garish sun.' "

After that, I offered something of my own: " 'Each field of grass is calling, / Each blade that I remember, / Things to call back, as I fall back, / On these hills in bleak September.'

"I wrote that at this good-bye banquet at camp last summer. Everyone started hooting and hollering when I first got up to read it, but I had them crying raindrops at the end. It was five pages long," I boasted. "They put it in their catalog."

I can still feel Mattie's awe, her very expression that was to become the key to my heart. You see, until Mattie (well, Lillian listened to me; but Lillian was my age—she didn't really count), no one seemed to take me seriously. Sheila always said I was too dramatic. Dad was seldom around. Ella played the piano, but she wasn't into poems. But here was Mattie Hurst, senior-incarnate, appearing to hang on to every word I spoke. And thus I shared some of my most private thoughts. I told her lately I'd been having images of running around without my head so I could "rid myself of my sorrows." (My exact words as recorded on page 32 of an old diary.) Then I quoted some original verse on nature: " 'Thank God for sea and joy, arms to hold / Wreaths of all this water, and the cold / Dampdowning wind that warms, thank God!' "

I told her sometimes poetry woke me at night and I wrote things that burned in my brain. I said I wanted to die for a cause. I made up words I could barely pronounce. I invented books that didn't exist. One book I titled *Perils of the Hurricanes,* by a fictional Ralph Butcher, and explained it dealt with a problem that I wrestled with day and night. That problem was: why if God was so good and powerful was there all this evil in the world.

The more I talked, the more Mattie listened. The more big words I used, the more her eyes fell out of her head. And presently I found myself excited by something far more than I had ever experienced: I began craving Mattie's approval. I started coveting Mattie's attention. When she told me she was an existentialist, I said I was too. When she allowed as to how reincarnation made sense, I agreed. When she admitted that her heroine was Isadora Duncan, I screamed the same. (I didn't know existentialism, reincarnation, Isadora Duncan from three holes in the wall, but I wanted to impress Mattie; if Mattie had told me the moon was a green apple, I would have said yes.) And as we talked, the room got smaller, Mattie got bigger. When she told me she was going through something and I asked what, she answered "Life!" (as if to clear up any confusion), and I said I understood. I must have repeated "I understand" a hundred times. We talked about Roy Dean, Harold Mac, the monotony of football, the pressures of being a girl. She let me know she always felt she had to put on an act. She said sometimes Roy Dean bored her to tears but she had never admitted that to a living soul. Could she trust me, she asked. I answered, "Like a bank." She smiled. I smiled. She said sometimes she got so fired up she yearned to run to the top of the White Mountains and scream "*I love you*" to the world. Did I think she was crazy? Roy and Sheila would, she'd bet her last hat. But my response was that wanting to scream like that had nothing to do with being crazy and everything to do with being alive. She liked that answer. Her eyes beamed. She leaned over, extending a cigarette. I smelled her hair and perfume. I remember thinking: *Wow!*

In the meantime she stretched out on the floor, her dark hair spread like an open fan. We dropped a few swear words to show we were wild: she said fuck; I said screw. She said piss; I said goddamn. I drooped my right arm, hoping the hand veins would protrude like my father's. I was dying to bow like him too; but in a sitting position that would have looked absurd, so I just kept my eyelids down like Robert Mitchum. And when she asked how come I was so wise at such a tender age, I told her age was just a number and I had to keep up with the seniors. She said you think you're hot shit, don't you. I answered hot wasn't the word. She laughed. Then she wondered if I'd ever seen a Negro or a Jew. I replied I'd seen plenty of Negroes. Where? In Georgia, I answered. Were they really black, she asked. Yes, I said as if I were an expert, and they were nice too. (As for Jews, frankly I didn't know beans about them. But wanting to appear remarkable in Mattie's eyes, I revealed I'd seen lots of them on trains bound to Macon and let it go at that.) All this she accepted in a silence that was broken when she told me she had read Jews, Negroes, and artists lived in big cities and that that was where she wanted to go at twenty-one to be free. I agreed, at which point we fell silent by the depth of our mutual commitment to grow up and live where we pleased. Then something seemed to let go in Mattie. She grabbed my arm, swooning, "Emily, I want to burn and taste everything and *suffer!*" And my God if those words didn't almost eat me alive.

Oh, but I can still recall that time when Mattie Hurst and I stepped onto something larger than ourselves. And that's what happened. For in those brief hours that afternoon, the vast continents between senior and sophomore, emerging sophisticate and Sheila's kid sister, merged. Gone was this sassy twelfth-grader with her very own management of the universe. Behold one who spoke the poetic nature of my heart, spoke it, vanquishing every other sound or hesitation. And thus the room filled up with light and carols. I told Mattie I wanted to be a *serious* poet. And wonder, but she didn't laugh. She said I was special. She said she wanted to hear everything I had ever written and would tell me her poems too, and that we must never speak of today to anyone because if we did it would be like any other. Then from her bosom she extracted that single rose I had seen and gave it to me. She lit a cigarette. The smoke slithered in and out of each nostril.

I was fascinated. I felt unreal, older. It was like from some mysterious elevation I was observing the corpse of my inexperience laid bare in this theater with Mattie. Suddenly I had to go to the bathroom. I got up deliberately, hoping she would note the tennis muscles in my arm. Then, inexplicably confused in this house I had grown up in, I strode into a closet of winter coats and clanging empty hangers and backed out smiling lamely. The phone rang. I raced to get it. It was Sheila. She was in the library and would be home in a couple of hours. Was Mattie there? My heart sank. Yes, I said. Tell her I'll call her later, was her parting shot. I hung up and went to the john. When I returned to the study, Mattie's arms were resting on her knees, she looked wondrous, her body was a convention of small bones, when she moved her long dark hair marched about her shoulders as if trying to find a place to sit down. Her face was a chameleon of a dozen changing expressions.

Gave me moves in my mind!

The minutes twitched around the house. It was stuffy. I rose to open the window, stumbled on the rug. "Let me," Mattie said with a wise and terrible grin. She went to the window, came back, sat three inches away. Eyes, what I could make out through her hair, ate me up in the slow, lazy bites of a woman surveying the swimmers at a beach. "Am I sexy?" she finally asked.

My own eyes rolled over and played dead. They came back wicked, and stared at her. I started giving Mattie the evil eye.

The evil eye was the Look-of-Looks: eyes shimmering carefully over a body like a mountain climber, pausing to survey the terrain at certain critical junctures. The point: to determine sexual IQ. Everyone at school did it.

Thus I remember cruising Mattie's body in innocent fun, over the hourglass hips, unthinkable waist, and formidable breasts. She sat there waiting. She knew who she was. "On a scale of one to ten," I said thoughtfully, "ten being tops, I'd give you a three, max."

Mattie roared . . .

Emily didn't want to do the yard anymore. She stopped raking, lay down, opened and closed her legs like scissors, feeling pinecones through her shirt and daydreaming about a rock dropping on Mattie just as she saved her in the nick of time. But so what! She sat up forlornly. Even if she did save Mattie's life, she couldn't tell anyone about her feelings because she was supposed to be crazy about Harold Mac. Damn! When Harold Mac kissed her, she thought about Mattie. Harold Mac told her she was driving him crazy. Well she understood that because Mattie was driving her crazy. Why couldn't the same people drive each other crazy? It didn't make sense. Nothing made sense. Maybe Mattie really wasn't coming over. Maybe she should run away.

A gang of red and yellow leaves skirting the gazebo kicked up little squabbles of dirt. A branch jackknifed from one of the aging pines, and a burly wind slapped it sideways. Overhead a cloud turned into an anteater, the tip of a mountain became a dinosaur with a bird in its mouth. She loved this weather. It put flame to her feet, made her want to run and travel and live wherever she hung her hat, as her riding instructor at camp used to say. She sat up watching Sheila. If Sheila could drag a big vacuum cleaner down here she would, just to suck up every last leaf on the terrace. That's how perfect she tried to be, to get everything right. But that didn't make sense because they just kept coming back. "Sheila!" she screamed.

But Sheila, as if anticipating Emily's sentiments, shrugged and continued with her tasks. Emily seized a leaf, crunching it in her hand, and surveyed the yard. She wanted that double allowance Charles had promised because she wanted to buy Mattie a silver bracelet, but she wasn't in the mood to rake; so she lay down again. Little pitchforks stabbing her insides; little fearmouths sucking her heart. Just then Sheila's voice startled her: "You'd better get jumping or we'll be here all day!" Emily didn't respond. "Emily!" Sheila was unmistakably annoyed. "For gosh sakes, what's with you? I'm *not* going to do this all by myself!"

"Okay. Okay," she muttered resignedly, sitting up once more. "But what's the point? They just come right back. And look at that wind!"

This brought Sheila rushing over as a sharp gust scattered the leaves. Like ants they flew off in all directions, forming small tornadoes that swirled about in a mindless dance of color. "The point is," she said to Emily, looking pained but instructive, "we promised Dad. And it doesn't matter if the wind blows or the wind doesn't blow. It doesn't even matter if we get a hurricane, which is highly unlikely this time of year as you well know. What matters, and what always matters, is that we *try*. And," she paused dramatically, "we made a deal: if we finished the whole yard, we'd get double our allowance. Now let's be smart, Emily. Maybe *you* don't need that extra money. But *I* do!" Mattie's bracelet peered at Emily beside a gray thrasher that ducked under a pyramid of leaves.

"Anyway," Sheila's voice droned on like a saw, "you said if I spoke to Miss Arnold about your math, you'd finish up raking with me. And I did. And don't pester me about what she said until this is done!" As if encouraging Sheila's point of view, the wind turned into a lamb. What's the use, Emily thought, getting to her feet compliantly as Sheila began raking nearby. She didn't give a hoot about Miss Arnold right now. Here and there stray pieces of paper floated in the breeze. A small plastic bottle of suntan lotion was uncovered next to a tin can as yet another wind humped the trees. After a while Sheila called, "Did Lillian get ahold of you?"

"When?"

"I saw her third period, and she said she had to talk to you. She said it was important. I just remembered."

Emily went on raking as if she hadn't heard. She knew what Lillian wanted, probably to talk about her eyebrows. Three weeks ago she had shaved them off so they would grow back pencil-thin and curved like Lana Turner's. But they hadn't. They had come back regular. And now Lillian was upset wondering if she should shave them again or what. Either that or Lillian would be asking a million questions about where Emily had been during the Muskateer meeting last night. So what was she supposed to say: I couldn't make it, Lil, 'cause I was touching Mattie Hurst's breasts! Shit-a-brick but she was tired of lying! She stood stock still, pondering her complicated life as Sheila walked over dragging her rake. "Are you and Lillian having a fight or something?" she asked.

"What is this, Sheila?" She hated her sister watching her like a big hawk. "The third degree? Why would Lillian and me be having a fight?"

"I don't know. You don't seem to be spending as much time together as . . . Emily! Are you crying? Emily!" Sheila raced over and cupped Emily's chin in her hand, pulling her face up slowly. "What's going on?" she questioned softly. "Is this the way the funniest girl in the sophomore class acts? Tell me. Is something wrong with you and Harold Mac? Has he done something I should know about?"

Emily turned away watching the leaves bounce like colored balls, and relieved there were no Mattiemarks on her. A crow's flight behind a clump of maples spoke of an early frost.

"Has the cat got your tongue?" Sheila persisted, touching her on the shoulder.

Emily stood with her back turned, overcome with guilt. She felt Sheila's caring. Sheila really loved her. And look how she was paying her back. By lying. You don't do that to your best friend or to someone who's come out of the same stomach either. She heard, "Emily, are you pregnant?"

This whirled her about on her heel. "What?" she asked in amazement.

"You heard me. Are you in trouble? Has Harold Mac done *that* to you?"

Why do they always think when you're upset, you're pregnant? "Of course I'm not pregnant," she answered acidly. "What do you think I am?" But then she saw how genuinely affected her sister looked, and her heart broke. All of a sudden it was so tempting to tell the truth. "Sheila," she started. But that's as far as she got: she saw Sheila and Mattie studying together in Sheila's room. She saw them giggling at pictures of Tyrone Power and Turhan Bey. She saw Roy and Mattie and Chad Wells and Sheila going to the movies. She saw them from the olden days carrying each other's photos in their billfolds, writing in each other's yearbooks: "You're my forever best friend through thick and thin!" and she suddenly remembered Sheila always saying opposites attract and that even if she and Mattie were different, they were close as two peas in a pod. But that wasn't true anymore, Emily said to herself painfully. She and Mattie were the two peas: that was the atomic-bomb secret; but if she told Sheila, Sheila would die. Still, she had to say something. So Emily uttered simply, believably (because she felt this along with everything else): "I'm all alone, Sheila. I mean I will be when you leave."

"Why?" Sheila gasped. "Where am I going?"

"When you leave for college."

"So that's it. It's not Harold Mac?"

"Of course it's not Harold Mac. It's being stuck here after you've left."

"But you've got Lillian."

"I don't live with Lillian."

"Oh, honey; that's so far in the future it doesn't even count as a worry. And you can come visit. It's not like I'm going to the moon. It's just Boston."

Just Boston! How could she bear it? Suddenly despair got the better of guilt. Emily stood inches from her sister, stabbed by the pain of losing Mattie next fall. She took a deep breath, and this came out: "Are you glad you and . . ." The word Mattie got stuck; it lay in Emily's mouth like a pearl fastened to its shell; it hung off her lips, white and remarkable. She started again and finally it slipped out. "Are you glad you and *Mattie* are still rooming together?" Jesus, she panicked. Did I say that? But it was too late.

"Are you crazy?" Sheila responded in total bewilderment. "Why wouldn't I be glad I'm rooming with Mattie? We've been planning this for years."

"I dunno. People have been known to change their minds."

"Why on earth would I change my mind unless Mattie changes it for me and runs off with Roy Dean?" Now she put both hands on Emily's shoulders and looked her right in the eye. "Emily, don't wiggle out of this one. What are you trying to say? Is there something going on that I don't know about? Is that why you said Mattie's name a while back?"

Think fast! Emily was falling into a hole. She had built that hole, and now she was pushing herself in. But perhaps danger was a part of all this. "No. No. I was afraid maybe you'd get cold feet, and I didn't want you to 'cause I know Mattie, and if I visited you in college it'd be okay. But if you were living with some stranger, she might not want me in her room."

Sheila's eyes took one lengthy tour of Emily's face, and then she said, "Emily, if I could have a penny for every crazy thing that comes out of your mouth, I'd be richer than Rockefeller. Of course you can visit, whether I room with Mattie or not."

"Sheila?"

"Yes?"

Some madness struck her. She felt giddy, nearly hysterical. "Sheila, I like you a whole lot!" Then as Sheila watched, once more amazed at this sudden change of mood, Emily did a little jig around her rake. She flexed her arms like a body builder. She thumped her chest. "Look, I'm okay. I'm fine as wine. Come on! Last one finishes owes the other one half of her allowance!"

More raking. Emily singing to herself: " 'In the streets of southern France/Where the women wear no pants/And the men go around/With their dingdongs hanging down!' " She knew Sheila thought she was loony. Well, she'd blame it on her period. Everyone knew when girls got their periods, they went nuts. She could lie and say she had hers if Sheila asked.

The phone rang. Ella had turned it up and brought it out to the porch. Was it Mattie? Emily started toward the house, but Sheila was ahead of her. Emily called out in forced gaiety, "Wish I had a swing like that in my backyard!" In response, Sheila's hips playfully exaggerated a left-to-right swing; then she was up on the porch with her back to the yard. Emily waited in anticipation, wishing she could see Sheila's face. From that, she would be able to tell if it was Mattie or not. In a few minutes Sheila was back, and then Emily couldn't help it. She had to know. "Mattie coming over?" she asked as casually as possible.

"Yes. Soon's she does her hair."

"When's that?"

"*When*? What do you mean *when*?" For what seemed the thousandth time that day, Sheila eyed her sister curiously. "Since when do Mattie Hurst's movements have the slightest interest to you? Emily, for the last time, is there something going on that I don't know about?"

Fool! You're going to far! "Sheila, knock it off!" Emily overreacted. "You're paranoid! I just asked 'cause I told you what she does in the icebox, and I'm starved!" But Sheila didn't have time to respond. The phone was ringing again. "I'll get it!" She sprinted off, leaving Emily in the backyard with a familiar mood of anxiety draining her. Jiminy, she thought, looking toward the village. If they only knew!

Sheila returned with a sense of urgency. The call had been from Miss Lamer, sponsor of the Latin Club, which was having a huge tag sale this weekend, and Sheila's help was desperately needed. Sheila's attitude turned beseeching. "Finish up for me, huh, Em; and whatever extra allowance I get, it's all yours. Please."

Emily's immediate thought was what a wondrous opportunity: if Sheila left, she would have Mattie all to herself. But she couldn't let her suspect, so Emily pretended to be upset. She told Sheila it wasn't fair to dump the whole yard on her.

A flood of leaves navigated earthward, landed belly up at their feet. Emily went on: Dad's nose was going to be out of joint, she said, her heart pounding in her ears like the ocean. That made Sheila undecided. Quickly Emily shifted gears. She said she understood the importance of Sheila's helping since she was head of the Latin Club. "It's no big deal," she added magnanimously. "You've done me favors. I can handle it. You can pay me back by letting me wear your new angora next week. You don't have to give me any of your allowance."

"You're sure it's okay?" Sheila hesitated.

"Positive. When you coming back?"

Sheila checked her watch. "It's two-thirty now. Miss Lamer wants me to pick up Nell and Pris to help with layout and to hang stuff up." For a few minutes she calculated in her head. "I'll be back around six and make us some fudge. Tell Mattie when she comes her book's on the dining room table and I'll call her later. And be careful if you burn the leaves." She started toward the driveway, then spun around. "Oh, and don't try getting into my room," she offered a knowing little smile. "It's locked!"

"When'd Ella say Dad was coming back?"

"Around eight."

Emily's eyes followed Sheila's walk toward her car. The noise of the motor startled the stillness of the afternoon. But then its idle became indistinct from the falling leaves and her rake stabbing after one to bring it back like a startled red chick to its mother's belly. On the upper terrace, three birds picked away at the ground. A chipmunk scampered up a tree. On the second terrace, the fish pond, sparkling in the afternoon's film, published its own soft wind that swirled into a batch of silver spoons, turning. Storm brewing in the east . . .

Ticktock: Mattie's coming!

She was wearing jeans, a windbreaker over a green turtleneck, and her long black hair bounced like carriage whips: she looked simply marvelous. "Where's everybody?" she called out airily, her voice revealing nothing.

Shyly Emily answered her question.

"When they coming back?"

She answered that too.

"So we're all alone?"

"Looks that way."

Mattie walked toward the lower terrace, motioning Emily to follow. She found a spot out of view from the house; and when both were seated, she got a pack of cigarettes from her jacket. "Want one?" She held out an Old Gold, which Emily accepted eagerly.

Observe them now: two girls smoking, talking, trying not to act self-conscious. But when Mattie leaned back on her arms, her jacket opened; and Emily couldn't help but note the moon-shaped contours of her breasts. She blushed, suddenly scared. Everything seemed in slow motion: wind, trees responding to wind, leaves imploding like cats with arched backs: time yanked up on a string and the string not moving. What was happening? It wasn't like they had never kissed before, or hugged, or been thrilled by the other's company. But last night had been a step in the dark. They knew it. Before that, their basic arousal had been spiritual, as Mattie would say. But Emily hadn't felt spiritual when she touched Mattie's breasts. She didn't feel spiritual now. She felt raw, exposed, funny between her legs. She wanted to touch Mattie again. She wanted Mattie to touch her. She wanted Mattie's mouth, nipples, hands. Was that the fate Mattie always talked about? Mattie said they had to have been old souls traveling together through life, destined to connect in all the existences to come until they reached that N-place Emily could never remember. Nirvana! the word exploded in her consciousness. Oh, God! Mattie was fascinated with stuff like that. She said Nirvana was the perfect state when you died. But sitting beside Mattie now, wanting to absorb Mattie into her consciousness—that was Nirvana!

Emily leaned forward. Last week she and Lillian had seen John Derek in *Knock on Any Door*. He played a criminal with his collar up and a cigarette dangling from his mouth. At one point he said he wanted to live fast, die young, and have a good-looking corpse. Oh boy, she wished she had the nerve to say that: Mattie, I want to live fast, die young, and have a good-looking corpse. Emily put her shirt collar up, clamped a cigarette between her teeth, and inhaled, trying with all her might to feel like John Derek. The smoke dug a hole in her lungs. She coughed. Dammit! John Derek wouldn't have coughed! As nonchalantly as possible, she pulled the cigarette out of her mouth. In the process, some of the thin, white paper stuck to her lips, and with that came the bitter taste of tobacco. She licked the tobacco off as John Derek would have done, and then her cigarette went out. She started to light it as he had in the movie: ripping a paper match out of the book and cupping his fingers around the flame. But the wind blew her match out.

"Don't worry about it," Mattie said. "Look." She got something from the ground and held it up. It was a small, coin-sized stone, dark yellowish, flat on one side, rounded on the other. "A fitting memento of us being here, right?" She put her cigarette out and then pressed the stone into Emily's hand, saying, "Feel me on this, Emily. Feel the warmth from my hand. I give this to you with everything in me so that you will always remember this day and us sitting here and you can know you can bring me through it no matter what happens: just press the stone in your hand and I'll be with you. I promise." She squeezed Emily's hand. "I don't understand anything anymore, and I'm scared. I don't even know what I'm scared about; but when we're together, I don't care."

Close to tears, Emily could see her house burning down and risking her life to run back in her room to get the stone. Now she put it in her pocket as Mattie went on, "You can never tell anyone about this. You can never speak of last night. We make a covenant here before God that what we feel is sacred, and if we talk about it, we ruin it. I believe that."

"Me too."

Now Mattie's hand lay in hers like a small moth on a leaf. Emily's fingers closed around it like a water lily at night. Emily's brains felt as though they were going to pop out of her head. She could scarcely breathe. She heard Mattie say, "Sometimes I think this is all a dream, that we'll wake up in our beds and all this will have just been something that happened when we were asleep."

Inexplicably Emily thought of her sister. A cold wind cut through her. She said, "Sheila," and stopped.

Quickly Mattie put her hand on Emily's mouth. "No! Don't say it! Don't think about it! I know! It's all crazy!" As if to break the suspense, Mattie yelled, "Who'll you be? Heathcliff or Cathy?" That was their game. Sometimes Mattie would be Heathcliff and Emily, Cathy. Or vice versa.

"I'll be Heathcliff!" Emily shouted, relieved for the mood change. She stood up looking as fierce as possible as Mattie clapped her hands wildly and Emily stalked about like a lord. Running to a pile of leaves, she filled her arms and dashed back throwing them on Mattie. Then, lifting Mattie to her feet, she swung her in her arms: "My Queen . . . my Queen . . . I love you!" she called, giving her heart a voice. "I love you my Cathy, my Cathy!"

She held Mattie to her. She felt Mattie's arms tighten about her neck. She heard Mattie giggle. Emily released her. Then ensued a short leaf fight that ended with them on the ground, their arms entwined, rolling down the terrace, bump bump; Mattie rose, got a stick from the ground, twirling it like a drum majorette as Emily howled until her sides split. After that they chased each other and presently they were back on the ground and Mattie was giving her a gift, tongue and everything. Mattie stopped, put her jacket under their heads. She took off her turtleneck, then Emily's shirt; she ferried Emily's hands to hers (Mattie's) breasts, pressing into Emily as Emily's tongue penetrated Mattie's lips. Then Emily undid Mattie's bra, took out Mattie's breasts, stroked them, touched Mattie's denim vagina too as they slid southerly down a small slope near a thicket of shrubs.

Observe them again: two young birds breaking new ground. Between Emily's fingers, Mattie's nipples rose like yeast. Had hers when Harold Mac touched them twice? She tried imagining how he might have felt. But no. She wasn't a boy. She didn't want to be a boy.

"Take your clothes off," Mattie whispered. Naked. She put her breasts on Mattie's and compared them. Mattie's seemed fuller. She slid them over Mattie's and watched the brownround eye on Mattie's right nipple pucker. She lay full-size on top of her as a groan seemed to rise from the pit of Mattie as if a force at the bottom of a lake were pushing up, up, bringing the water from the lake with it, erupting that water into rapid, spinning waves; she pushed Mattie's breasts together until the nipples were alongside each other and from them Emily sucked two merged into one, licking the ends softly, rubbing her groin over Mattie's lower parts as time fell from the clock. Then lots of hands and fingers and tongues and their two souls flipping in and out of each other, Mattie sucking her breasts raw like eggs, wiggling on top of Emily's stomach, going back and forth to Emily's breasts like a child bobbing for apples until the front of Emily got wet. Mattie put her fingers inside going in and out fast, faster, she slid down Emily's body.

Oh, God! Her mouth was between Emily's legs. What if I smell? She forgot smells, images overwhelmed her: bright red flowers, bends of a lake, a king riding a white stallion behind the hill, glints of a record needle in the sun. Emily had been near crying. Now what? She pushed Mattie to the side, put her arms around Mattie's neck, covered her body with Mattie's, did this recklessly, impulsively. She was like a thief with her arms laden who comes back to the house she has just robbed. She would never feel this abandonment, this everlastingness again. And she was glad she was feeling it, that which has the power of worlds: to love fully and not care, to have the world stop while

she kissed and unstop when she unkissed and feel to her finger-
tips and not care to not care!

Then Sheila put time back in the clock. Finished earlier than
expected, she had stopped by the restaurant before proceeding
home. Coincidentally Charles, also ahead of his schedule, was
there and just preparing to go home too. They arrived at the
same time. Sheila first went into the house as her father got his
luggage and inspected his rear tires. Seeing the house was
empty, Sheila left and went to the back. The lower terrace
where Emily and Mattie lay was out of earshot, so they hadn't
heard the car; nor did they realize Sheila had found them and,
at first shocked to a paralysis, had watched them make love. But
then as her eyes accepted their vision, she became a scream. The
scream grew larger than the yard. It reverberated against the
trees. It hit the fish pond, struck the rakes, bounced like a ball
against the grass, then flew to Charles, who by then had left his
car and was standing in front of the house. Instantly he dropped
everything and ran. And there he saw:
Emily and Mattie. Naked. Entwined in each other. This
couldn't be! Emily and Mattie. Naked. Entwined in each other.
No, he didn't believe it! Emily and Mattie. Naked. Entwined in
each other.
True! He moved quickly. He yanked Emily to her feet and
shook her as if she were a rabbit in a dog's mouth as Mattie
cowered behind a tree and Sheila fell to the ground, pounding
it with her fists and screeching to high heaven.
After that nothing would ever be the same. And how do
people go on anyway?

. . . I remember: I lay curled up on my bed in a fetal position,
alternately numb, terrified, wanting to run away, wondering
about Mattie.
I had begged Dad not to call her parents. "Don't open your
filthy mouth to *me,* young lady," he had raged, "or it'll be the
last thing you ever do!" Then my father, ordinarily a permissive

parent who believed in children being independent and who pretty much had left the child raising to Ella, slapped me so hard my head reeled, and turned into my jailer: I wasn't to leave the room except to go to the toilet. I wasn't to lock my door. He would call in sick for me at school, and if anyone phoned they would be told I had the flu. Forget supper tonight. My meals tomorrow would be brought to my room. And don't even think about going anywhere. He would be watching, listening to my every move. If I tried any funny stuff, he'd—. He didn't have to finish that sentence: I got the point.

Later when Ella came home, they had a huge fight. From across the hall I could hear Dad thunder, "This never would have happened if Marian had been alive!" Sounds of glass breaking. Ella's hysterics. Sheila wailing down the hall. The word lesbian streaking through my walls like a bullet. "You've raised a goddamn *lesbian,* Ella! *My* daughter! Marian's child. A *lesbian!*"

I grabbed my dictionary. "Lesbian: 1. an inhabitant of Lesbos." Lesbos? "2. homosexual." I looked up homosexual: "Sexual desire for those of the same gender." Gender? Meaning sex, meaning I wanted sex with *girls!* Me? That's what I was? How crazy! All my life I'd taken showers in gym, gone to slumber parties, played strip poker with friends; and never once had I wanted sex with anyone, including with Harold Mac. The only person in the world I ever had wanted to kiss was Mattie. And Mattie always said we were spiritual.

Then I remembered she also said we didn't have a definition. So there I was—something without a definition!

Sheila stormed in later with her eyes all puffy. She told me I was a maggot, I had ruined her life, she disowned me. I should be *dead,* she yelled, which brought Dad in telling us to knock it off for God's sweet sake!

I don't need my diary to remind me of those sleepless hours as I lay in my room pressing Mattie's little stone to my cheek. Where was she? Had her parents killed her? At one point I recall standing by my window as if to climb down the tree to run to her. But then her parents might catch us or Dad would hear, so I went back to bed thinking we were like Romeo and Juliet about to die over love. But I didn't want to die. I just wanted Mattie.

Next morning Dad brought me some food. No, I couldn't see Frankie. Yes, Lillian had phoned, but I was not to call her back. I had to stay in my room until further notice and do school work. He would check back later. Shut up, Emily!

The whole day was filled with sounds of Frankie barking, doors banging, boxes being dragged over the floor, steps up and down the stairs, and me torn between desperation to see Mattie and unutterable grief over what had come to pass. Too much! Too much to bear!

That afternoon Sheila marched in with a Bible and aimed her eyes at me with their triggers cocked. She was pale, shaken, condemning. She *loathed* being there, she fumed, but she had a duty to perform. Before she performed it, I was to know I had destroyed her world. I was making *her* mother leave. Sheila didn't know what she was going to do without Ella. Dad had blamed her for what had happened, which had been the last straw to their marriage. As a result, Ella was moving back to Nebraska immediately to file for divorce and Aunt Francie was probably coming up to live until school was out. Sheila hoped I was satisfied.

My mind raced: Ella leaving! Aunt Francie taking her place! Jesus, I didn't want Aunt Francie up here fussing over me like I was a baby, which was what she always did when we visited her in Newport News. For a moment my father's older sister, his only living relative, swamped everything. I could see her bright red lipstick and matching nails. I could hear her accent, so southern-thick her words scarcely could move in it. Francine Stolle Mouler was childless, and widowed too. (Her husband, an avid sportsman, had died on the Roanoke golf course when a ball traveling at great speed hit him square on the temple.) She had never remarried, but not because she lacked beauty. Indeed, she resembled my father, tall and elegant with his same silly sense of humor. And she was okay too, the little I knew of her. But living here! Suddenly the possibility of that invasion made everything definite: Sheila was right. At fifteen I had demolished our family. I had eliminated Sheila's mother, Dad's wife. It was all my fault! What was to become of us? My child's heart broke anew. How could I make this up to them? How could I help Sheila forget what her eyes had seen? And how was I to live with myself? I felt so bad I wept openly. But Sheila wanted none of that. Well, could I go tell Ella I was sorry? No, Sheila hissed. Ella never wanted to see me again. And when I timidly sought more information about Aunt Francie, she snarled, "Shut up! It's none of your business what she's doing! You won't be here anyway!"

Where was I going, I quaked.

"You'll see," Sheila's lips curved ominously. Clutching the Bible so tightly the veins on her right hand stuck out, she declared that that "other person" (Mattie) was as dead to her as I. Then she ordered me to swear never to tell a living soul. "This is where I get my strength," she proclaimed, shaking the Bible in my face. "It is *now* my hope and my salvation. And if you possess one shred of decency, you will keep what you have done a secret. You owe me that for the sacrifices I've made for you; you owe it to the family honor. Aunt Francie will never find out; Dad and I have already decided that. Not even the man I marry will know!" As I stood there in tears, she shrieked I was a genetic flaw and she prayed on hands and knees my genes wouldn't be passed on to her children. The horror ended with me pledging on the Bible never to break my oath of silence. After that, Sheila wrote me off with one word: queer. Queer, she snapped, was the filthiest, most rotten thing alive; and that's what I was: diseased. I shouldn't blame it on my mother dying either because my mother had been hers too and she (Sheila) was normal. Obviously I was a bad seed. That might be because of my neck glands, which Sheila maintained were too large. She had read somewhere that that was what queers were afflicted with. "Look at *my* neck," she gloated. "See how little the glands are on the sides; you can't even see them. But your neck's deformed. You should be in a zoo and let people come study you. Dad's sending you to a psychiatrist. You know what that is? That's where crazy people go. And when you see yours, you should ask about getting a neck operation. Maybe the knife will slip. I hope you rot in hell!" With that, she stormed out, leaving me to obsess on my glands, terrified I was about to be locked away in a nut house. And what about that word? Out came the dictionary: "Queer: 1. crooked, not genuine; 2. odd; 3. homosexual (slang)." So it was one and the same—lesbian, queer, homo. I remember thinking I couldn't face myself in the mirror, like I was some female Dorian Gray with sin stuck to my flesh. I couldn't eat. I filled my diary with poems of agony, and wrote letter after letter to Mattie, then tore them up. No way could I imagine what lay ahead.

Later, Dad went over my lessons. And before noon of the following day, he was back with something like a list detailing all that was to happen to Emily Stolle. In retrospect, here's what it boiled down to:

First, I was being sent to a strict, hard Episcopalian boarding school called St. Joseph's Academy, in Cromley, Connecticut, about forty-five minutes from Hartford. If I passed their screening test, I could skip sophomore year and become a junior, which meant I would graduate from high school one year earlier.

Second, in about three weeks from when I arrived, I would begin seeing a Hartford psychiatrist recommended by a man Dad knew from Boston. The doctor's name was Harold Weiss, and Dad had had to pull strings to get me in because he was busy. However, Dr. Weiss would be talking to me every other week until I was cured. To give me the chance to develop my own trusting relationship with him, Dad had given the reason for my leaving home (he told the same thing to St. Joseph's) as his pending divorce from Ella, which he said had caused me lots of emotional stress. Also, he had told them I had always been, quote, a "difficult" child; hence I needed a more controlled environment. If I worked hard, maybe I could quit the psychiatrist in a year. But if I didn't cooperate or flunked my courses or in any way, shape, or form gave the school a hard time, or if the psychiatrist sent him bad reports, that was it: Dad was washing his hands of me forever.

Third, my aunt: he needed her to help because of Sheila, he said; so Aunt Francie in fact was coming up until June when Sheila graduated from high school. At that point, Sheila planned on getting a job at a summer resort and in September she would be starting college. Our house was going on the market in June. Also in June, Aunt Francie was returning to Newport News. Then came a real shocker: henceforth Newport News would be a kind of base for me, a pretend-home as Dad put it even though I wouldn't have to be there that often because I would be away at school. Before I could grab my breath on that one, Dad said I couldn't come back till Easter. "That's how it has to be," he stressed when I looked stricken. "You've put us through a dozen lifetimes, kiddo; and your sister and I need space. You'll be staying at that school Thanksgiving and Christmas. I've given your aunt the same reason as to why you've been sent off in the first place."

Fourth, Dad: Not only was the house to be sold, but as soon as he could find a buyer for his restaurants (something he'd been thinking about doing for some time, he said), he was moving to the West Coast. Until June (except for some business trips to California), he essentially would be in White River with Aunt Francie. He would continue sending me money until I graduated from college, about the time my grandfather Stolle's trust monies started. And I could be assured of the following: After he left White River, he would regularly visit Newport News during school vacations if I were there. He would write and call. He would be in contact with my doctor. He would always be concerned for my welfare and wish me the best. In other words, I was still a debt he assumed. He went on and on but it was getting too much for me to absorb, especially the part about losing my home. After all, I was just a kid. I was devastated. And beneath everything, like a thread caught on a barbed wire, was that subject I dare not mention: *Mattie!* What had happened to her?

Fifth, Mattie: I didn't have to ask, for Dad told me that Mattie no longer lived in White River. She had been sent to an aunt's in Philadelphia, where Mr. Hurst was from and where she would be staying until her parents moved there too, in a few weeks. Of course Dad had related the whole story. But he wasn't going into it except to emphasize that I should forget she had ever lived and make no effort to contact her by letter, phone, or otherwise. As to her parents pulling up stakes—they had decided emotionally they were unable to remain in White River. Mr. Hurst had put in for a transfer to a Philadelphia bank (actually a better career opportunity for him, Dad was kind enough to add).

Sixth, Lillian: I could see her long enough to say good-bye in my room that day. I should explain I was sick, which was why I wasn't allowed to leave the house. Through Lillian I could spread word that I was going off to school to better prepare myself for college and also because of his divorce.

Thus began the onset of the Big Lies with Lillian. There was yet a long road ahead for us to travel, but suffice to say she was plenty upset. Nothing made sense to her about this, including my not being able to come home until Easter. I'm sure I didn't make sense either. But I said what I had to, vowing to write and phone. All that. Frankly my heart was shattered and my mind so clued to Mattie that I wasn't thinking too clearly. I tried to be brave though, and I entertained with as much enthusiasm as possible our intentions to meet at Lil's Aunt May's in Maine this summer. Also, Lillian said that if I passed that screening test, she was going to try to skip a grade too, so we could go to college together as planned.

That was it. Five days after the sky caved in, I was in Dad's car on the way to Cromley. What a miserable, miserable trip. I can still see him, stiff as a board on his side, and me huddled as far to the passenger window as possible without falling out. The only sound was the radio or one of us moving. Once when I sniffled he told me to take my medicine and I only had myself to blame. I kept my little stone in my hand and tried feeling

Mattie through it, telling myself over and over that fate would join us before too long. Six hours later we turned off the highway at a sign that said ST. JOSEPH'S ACADEMY, A PRIVATE COLLEGE PREPARATORY FOR YOUNG WOMEN. I felt like a stranger from another planet . . .

ST. JOSEPH'S

St. Joseph's was a fusebox of colors when Emily and her father drove through the gates: trees bleeding from autumn's spear, clouds grazing in blue pastures, a succession of greenrich hills that led up to the main campus. They went by stables, tennis courts, immaculate brick buildings with flags in front. Girls were everywhere, talking, having a fine time. And here came Emily Stolle, the foreigner!

At a rotary a sign pointed toward Administration. They followed that into a circular parking area; and before she knew what was happening, Charles was out of the car and opening her door. That's when it all hit. "Please, don't make me go in there, Dad. Please!"

"Cut it out, Emily!"

"But I don't want to." She crouched as far back in the seat as possible.

"Are you going to make a scene or what? Get out, or I'll pull you out!" He looked annoyed, so she obeyed. And in a minute they were entering the mossy, three-tiered structure marked Wilson Hall for their afternoon's appointment with Dean Lucy Stevenson. She came out to greet them as they went into the reception area. She was tall and slender, with friendly eyes and silver hair pulled severely from her face. She shook Emily's hand warmly. Emily had never seen a woman shake a girl's hand before, but she had never met a dean either. And this one must be important, she thought as she positioned herself awkwardly in a chair listening to the dean call for someone to get her trunk out of the car and transport it to her room. She fastened her attention on a picture of the ocean while her father and this total stranger discussed *her* life. Before long, the dean turned to her with a smile and delivered the rules:

All off-campus dating had to be chaperoned. Dating allowed only from seven to ten Saturdays, three to five Sunday afternoons. Mandatory socials with Xavier's, an approved boys' school ten miles away, every other Friday. No smoking. Three hours' compulsory study each weeknight. Regular church attendance. Lights out at ten-thirty except at eleven on Saturdays. All visitors must be on approved list. A grade less than C meant automatic restriction until grade was pulled up.

"That's it," Dean Stevenson chirped as Charles looked satisfied, and Emily decided she was in prison. "I know this sounds bewildering to you, dear," she turned to Emily, "but you'll grow to love it here. Why, we have girls who can't stay away once they graduate. You'll see."

She didn't want to see. She didn't belong here. Her heart was pounding right out of her. She moved forward, clutching Mattie's stone, hearing the dean explain she would be taking the qualifying exam to enter junior class at nine A.M. tomorrow. "You're to report to the counseling office here," she drew a circle on a map and gave it to her. "Now don't worry about the test. I've talked to your high school, and you have a very high IQ. A high IQ means you have natural abilities, so we expect you to perform very well at St. Joseph's, don't we, Mr. Stolle?"

"We certainly do," Charles cleared his throat. "Emily knows that."

"Do you know that, dear?" A smile never left the dean's face.

"Uh . . . yes," she faltered, feeling her father's study. "I mean, yes, I'll do my best."

"Of course you will, and that's all anyone can ask. Now you should plan on going to summer school to make up for credits missed during sophomore year. Your father wants you to graduate as soon as possible, and that's fine; we encourage our girls to work toward the highest standards and to enter college as soon as they feel equipped. Do you understand, Emily?"

"Yes."

"Yes *ma'am,*" Charles corrected her sternly.

"Yes ma'am," she repeated.

The dean continued. "Your courses will be strictly college prep. You've had French One, so you will stay with French Two, take French Three this summer, and Advanced French your last year. We require four years of a foreign language, plus three of Latin. You were already taking Latin Two, correct?"

"Yes ma'am."

"So you'll finish that up and be ready for Latin Three next year. Now as for math," she raised an eyebrow and peered at Emily, "I understand that's not your favorite subject."

"No ma'am. English is."

"Well we have a marvelous English department, and a school quarterly that can use your talents. Your father says you like to write."

"Yes ma'am."

"Fine. There's certainly a place for you on *The Crimson Poet;* that's the student publication I was referring to." She thumped her desk decisively. "But you have to get the math in. I see you were in Algebra One before you got here."

"That's right."

"You'll need to complete Algebra Two this summer, take geometry in the fall, and complete your math requirements next summer. How does all that sound?"

She wasn't sure what to say, so she responded, "Fine."

"Good." The dean clucked sympathetically. "It must be a little overwhelming coming into a place like this now. But don't you worry. There's a lovely girl coming over soon to show you around. Hilda Sharp—she's been with us for three years, and she's what we call your Big Sister. She'll show you to your room. We have a nice one for you on the second floor of Willard Dormitory. You won't have a roommate because you're a late arrival, but the girls are very friendly and they'll make you feel right at home. Now Emily, your father says you'll be staying over Thanksgiving and Christmas. Is that right, Mr. Stolle?"

"Yes it is. We spoke about that."

Dean Stevenson addressed Emily again. "You'll have plenty of company, dear, so you're not to be concerned about that. Many of our students are from foreign countries, and they're not able to be with their families during the school year. Then we have other girls whose parents travel a lot. For all of them we provide plenty of activities and movies, things like that." Finished, she got up and walked over to the chair. At close range, her eyes were a startling blue, her teeth even and extremely white. Motioning Emily to rise, she put an arm around her shoulder and escorted her to the reception area. She should wait there, the dean said, while she spoke to her father.

Emily sat on the couch holding her stone, feeling small and helpless. In about fifteen minutes Charles emerged, and together they walked to his car as he delivered his parting remarks. "We just arranged how they'll get you to the bus in Hartford when you start seeing that doctor."

"Did you tell her?"

"Tell her what?"

"Why I'm going?"

This annoyed him. "Don't ask me that again. I'm not a liar. I've given you my word. She thinks you're just upset about your stepmother leaving. Now pay attention to me. They'll take care of getting you to the bus terminal and picking you up. The doctor's address and phone number are in that large brown

envelope in your trunk. You're seeing him, wait a minute—"
he pulled a paper from his pocket— "November eleventh at two
sharp," he read. "You got that?"

"Yes."

"Don't yes me like a flat tire. Do you understand what I'm
saying? Is it in your brain?"

She answered patiently, "Yes, Dad. I know. It's November
eleventh at two."

He appeared satisfied. "That's right. Your trunk should already be in your room. There's twenty dollars in that envelope
for bus tickets and cab once you arrive. And here's another ten
for good measure." He pulled a bill from his wallet and handed
it to her. "That's more than enough, and I'll be sending you
money every month, which you're to budget. You have that?"

She nodded and stood by the car studying her shoes as the
tears welled up. "Dad," she cried. "Dad, if my grades are good,
can I come home Christmas?"

He glowered, "We've already been through that."

"I know. But it's Christmas."

"You should have thought of that."

What could she say? She *hadn't* thought of that. She didn't
know this was going to happen. She heard him say, "No, for
the last time, no, you can't come home before Easter. You've
put us through holy hell, and Christmas is much too soon. Why
don't you think about that?"

"I am. I just . . ."

He seemed to be restraining himself. "Look what you've
done to us. Look what you've done to your sister. I . . . oh,"
he took a deep breath, "no use beating a dead horse. You just
get yourself fixed up with that doctor and we'll see you in the
spring. That's it." He opened the car door and stuck a leg in,
seeming drained and exhausted.

And for a moment Emily realized the pain she had caused,
but all she could think about was being abandoned, and she felt
desperate to keep him there. "Where will you be?"

"What do you mean where will I be?"

"How will I know? How will I find you?"

"You'll find me at home or in California, but mostly home until your feet are on the ground. I'm not leaving the country. You'll hear from me. We've talked about this till I'm blue in the face!"

The tears were openly streaking her cheeks. "I'm scared," she said in a tiny voice. Couldn't he tell her heart was breaking? Didn't he know she was sorry? What did she have to do, kill herself, run through fire, climb up on a cross and let them pound in the nails?

"Quit blubbering," he answered sharply and reached in the car for a tissue. "Blow your nose." He gave it to her and she obeyed. "It's costing me an arm and a leg to keep you here, Emily, and send you to that doctor; but I'm willing to do what I can provided you meet me halfway."

When she just remained there silently, he continued in a softer voice. "Look, maybe I haven't been the best father in the world, but when the roof caves in, family's all you've got. That's why I'm not running out on you. Don't you see? Don't you understand that? Don't you realize the ramifications of what you've done and that if you don't get your life together it's not worth a plug nickel? I want you to think about someone else besides yourself and give your aunt a chance too. Francine's doing us all a favor by coming up to Vermont, and she loves you. If you'll accept that and try a little harder than you did with Ella, maybe you'd get something in return that I guess you've missed all your life. But for God's sake, Sheila didn't have her real mother either. I don't see why you had to be the one to sink to this . . . this," he sputtered emotionally. "Oh just get *normal* for pete's sake. Why your mother would roll over in her grave if she . . ." Reality appeared too much for Charles. "Never mind!" He got into the car now, gritting his teeth. "Just thank the gods we're not in the poor house and you can get this chance."

"Dad, I'm so sorry."

"Talk's cheap. Just give us some action. Action speaks louder than words." He turned the key and gave one final shot before closing the door. "Work your tail feathers off and get this

49

sickness out of you. Remember who you are too. Your people came over on the Mayflower. You've got something to live up to. Meet as many of those Xavier boys as you can. That's the ticket. And be honest with that doctor. I'm counting on you for that. Don't think you can pull the wool over his eyes." For an instant, as if able to rise above his anger again, he grabbed her hand, squeezed it, and, within seconds, Emily was watching her father drive down the hill and out of sight.

Hilda Sharp was waiting when Emily got back to the dean's. She was a bubbly girl in a blond pageboy, with bangs and big dimples. She seemed to take to Emily right away.

Hilda was from New Haven, she announced as soon as they got outside. Her father was a lawyer, and Yale was one of his clients. Her own ambition was to marry a boy who had graduated from there. She also wanted a convertible. She had just seen a yellow one, and it was about all she could concentrate on. Did Emily drive? Yes. So did Hilda. How old was she? Fifteen, Emily said, going on sixteen. "I'm just sixteen," Hilda exclaimed excitedly, adding she liked Emily's sweater, and she could hardly wait till she was eighteen. As they walked, she pointed out different buildings on campus, including the one where Emily would be tomorrow morning. "Stevie . . . that's Dean Stevenson . . . told me you had to take the placement exam, and I'm supposed to get you there. Don't worry about it. It's no sweat. They don't let you in here unless you've got brains running out of your ears. Then they push you so you'll get into a great college and make them look good." Soon Hilda's talk lapsed into more earthy pleasures. She could hold smoke in her lungs for over a minute. Could Emily? Emily wasn't sure. "Well," Hilda instructed seriously, "if you smoke, you've got to keep your windows open 'cause they've got stoolies coming out of the woodwork around here; and if they pop into your room, they sniff around like rabbits. Student council members," she explained, when Emily looked blank. "They think they own the place." From that, Hilda launched into a description of different teachers. "Some of the single ones go into New York a lot"; the Xavier boys—"They're so stuck on themselves they can't walk a straight line"; Cromley—"If you blink, you'll miss it. I'll show it to you in a few days." All considered, Hilda seemed far more interested in talking about herself than in asking questions, which actually was a relief because Emily didn't feel conversational at all, though she did manage to get in that she was coming to St. Joseph's late because her folks didn't approve of a boy she had been dating. That remark drew Hilda's immediate sympathy. She took Emily's arm and said her parents had interfered with her life too and that you just had to put up with them until you were on your own. "The best way to get them off your back," she concluded briskly, "is to make the honor roll."

At the dorm Emily was introduced to Mrs. Tweedy, the housemother, a matronly woman who, like Dean Stevenson, had a bun of silver hair and bright blue eyes. Then she was taken to her new home. It was a large room with a good view of the woods, on the same floor as Hilda. Some pennants decorated the wall. There was a large walk-in closet, two bookcases, a desk with a green blotter, and a Yale rug. Several girls came in to meet her, and then it was getting on to five-thirty. Hilda invited Emily to join them for dinner; but she was exhausted, she said, and wanted to unpack. Would she get into trouble if she didn't go? Hilda said no, that she would cover for her and see her in the morning.

As soon as the room was empty, Emily began unpacking. But before long she got tired. She sat on her bed holding her little stone, rubbing it over her face, hearing Mattie: "You'll always be able to bring me back through this stone, Emily. You'll never be alone." She lay back, missing Mattie from every part of her, realizing this was the first time since the tragedy that she could think of Mattie without worrying about Sheila or her father barging into her room. She began seeing Mattie clearer than anything. How was she to get through this year without her? I just have to, she answered her question. Mattie's missing me too. When she finds out where I am, she'll call. Thinking that, impulse struck. Up to now, Charles had monitored the phone.

But now he was gone, and the temptation to talk to Mattie became irresistible. She got some change from her purse and went to the phone booth at the end of the hall. Her plan was to get the number from the operator. If the Hursts answered, she would hang up because she couldn't risk Charles finding out. But if Mattie answered, she would breathe urgently into the phone, using their code names Cathy and Heathcliff. She would give Mattie her number and tell her to call back as soon as possible and she would wait here all night if she had to. True. Wild horses couldn't have dragged her away if Mattie were going to phone. Thinking that now, Emily became so mesmerized by the prospect of actually talking to Mattie that she barely heard the Philadelphia operator report there was no listing for a Gordon Hurst. Oh, right, she remembered: the Hursts weren't supposed to move for a few weeks, and she didn't know the aunt's married name. Dejected, she hung up and went back to her room to finish unpacking. Then she got into bed clasping her little stone and assuring herself that somehow Fate wouldn't let her down.

Early next morning Hilda yelled through the door that it was time for breakfast. Emily felt like burying her head under the pillow. She didn't want to see anyone. She wasn't hungry. She was going to run away. But she had no choice. Later as they walked to the dining hall, Hilda told her she reminded her of a lost puppy dog so she was going to adopt her. What's more, Hilda enthused, her friends liked her too!

Emily did well on her placement test that morning and wrote Lillian that she was now a full-fledged junior and Lillian should go ahead and try to skip a grade too. She had promised to do this, and she missed Lillian; but her heart wasn't in it, her heart was with Mattie. She felt too the pressure of staying in close touch with Lillian because of everything that had happened, and also because Lillian was her main contact with the old crowd. But it was a contact that would prove troublesome, particularly when they spoke by phone. Then Lillian pestered her to come home before Easter. That forced Emily into some fiction about her aunt not wanting her around that much, and that her father had promised if she made the honor roll he would give her lots of presents so she had to stay at school to study or to work on her poetry, some of which might be published. It occurred to her that probably some of this sounded odd, but she didn't know what else to say. There were questions too about Sheila losing weight, and Lillian thought Sheila was acting funny. All this Emily had to play down, which bothered her. So did the natural wave of homesickness she had at being away from everything she knew. But by far the hardest subject to deal with was Mattie. During one conversation when Lillian said she had heard Mattie Hurst had left town because a boy from Dartmouth had made her pregnant, Emily had had to restrain herself from defending Mattie's honor. Fairly shaking, she had allowed, with some heat, that Mattie was Sheila's friend, not hers, and she didn't know beans about it, but Lillian shouldn't believe everything she heard.

On balance, Lillian seemed to accept Emily's explanations, but that only added to her great shame. For theirs was a friendship based on trust. Until Mattie, they had shared everything. But now it was different: As much as she might want to unburden herself, she couldn't pass on her emotions about Mattie, she couldn't tell Lillian how her heart stopped when the phone in the dorm rang and she wondered if it might be Mattie, she couldn't describe how some song she and Mattie had loved brought her back to their former glory, she couldn't speak of her heart's aches and pains when Mattie didn't write, nor could Emily explain her child's faith that she and Mattie were old souls traveling through time together, as Mattie had put it, and that the crooked finger of Fate would surely sign them as one. And even if she could tell, wouldn't that be violating a trust? So she made up lies to support other lies, hating herself for doing it, trying to sound brave because she didn't want pity and she didn't want anyone, least of all Lillian, to suspect the truth.

Thus a contradictory set of feelings formed in Emily's mind during this period. One feeling was an unrelieved longing for Mattie. The other was pain and guilt over what she had done. But that she blocked as much as she could because it made her feel bad when she needed to feel good. And also, thinking about

Mattie blinded her, like the sun, to any other reality, to any other emotion but how happy she had been with her. Invariably all this took its toll: Emily was a changed girl at St. Joseph's. No longer the class clown, she was now becoming more serious and, well, lonely wasn't the right word: she had friends, and Hilda included her all the time. What Emily felt was larger than lonely. It lay at the core of her being—the burden of having a deep and powerful and mysterious secret that soon found outlet in her favorite class, English.

The English teacher was a young woman named Ethel Necessary who also sponsored *The Crimson Poet.* And when she learned that Emily wrote poetry, she encouraged her to try short stories. Soon, writing became a sort of therapy, a release for all the things Emily couldn't tell a soul. Her stories were a fantasy world inspired by her relationship with Mattie, and it brought Mattie much closer. The characters, devoid of sexual distinctions, loved each other more for their minds than their bodies and were fated through eternity to be together. Their tales were of situations where love conquered all; the words they used were words taken from conversations with Mattie. It was a private world where no one was ever hurt but was just happy being with whom they loved. Sometimes in writing, Emily would feel Mattie's presence and find herself carrying on private conversations with her, which was a great comfort. In addition, she reread *Romeo and Juliet* and imagined finding Mattie just as they were each about to die. There was a poem too by Yeats that she read in class which conveyed a special meaning. It was called "Leda and the Swan," and it told of the girl Leda, who had, according to mythology, been impregnated by Zeus, the swan. Emily took this poem as something written especially for her. In her imagination she could see the girl turning into a swan and flying away forever, leaving its baby abandoned just as she felt, completely alone now. "That's me," she wrote dramatically in her diary one night. "I don't have anyone. I don't have any roots."

Ah, but she did, she later consoled herself. She had her little stone. The stone was her root: the stone was Mattie.

Then came a day in November when Emily was on the bus going to meet Dr. Weiss.

All the way to Hartford she practiced what to say. "Hello, Dr. Weiss. I'm Emily Stolle. How are you, *sir*?" Then she would shake his hand, firmly and with authority, just as Dean Stevenson had done. The goal was for him to think she was one of the most normal girls he had ever seen.

For the occasion she was wearing her best skirt and blouse; and she had combed her hair a hundred times. Now she tried pretending this trip was for fun. But what a joke! She didn't want to be doing this. It was embarrassing. She had told everyone at school she was visiting a sick relative, which would be the case all year; but she hated lying to them too and it had made her feel funny on the phone last week when Charles reminded her she should work her tail off to get cured. Cured of what? What was her disease? That's where she got confused. She was sorry she had hurt anyone, especially Sheila; but she hadn't meant to fall in love with Mattie and ruin the world. It had just happened. Some stupid psychiatrist couldn't change anything!

She took a small mirror from her bag and ran a comb through her hair again. Then she stared out the window with resolve. If she cooperated, maybe she could quit going to him sooner than later. She held that thought all the way into Hartford. Once at the bus station, she took a cab to the large building on Tremont Avenue right in time for her appointment. She paid the driver and went in, heading for the elevator. At the third floor, she walked left to suite 331. Soft music that seemed to come from the walls greeted her as she entered; and for a moment she wavered, until a door just ahead opened and through that walked a man of medium height, with bushy black eyebrows and hair, a beard, no tie, and baggy trousers. He was carrying a toothbrush, which he held like a pipe. The toothbrush was red with a green ribbon strung through the end.

"Hello," he said, looking at her intently. "I'm Dr. Weiss. You must be Emily Stolle."

"Yes, I am," she answered, all confidence gone. Why did he have that toothbrush?

"Did you have any trouble finding me?"

"No. I took a cab."

"Of course. Well, fine." He propped a reassuring hand on her shoulder and smiled. The smile was a light in a dark room, and it made her more at ease. He ushered her into his office, and there she stood as he placed his toothbrush beside the phone and flipped through a notebook.

Be careful, she warned herself. Even if he's not looking at you, he can see you. He has eyes everywhere; he's trying to decide if you're crazy or not.

He glanced up and told her to go over to the couch and lie down.

The couch? She didn't move.

"Yes, that's what I mean," he spoke softly. "Just go over and lie down."

Slowly she did. She got there and froze. Why did he want her to do this?

"Go on. It won't bite. That's how we operate in here. You relax and let your mind run free."

Now she sat on the edge of the couch, unable to go any further, as he began explaining the "ground rules," as he put it. The ground rules were they would meet at the same time, same station, on alternate weeks. If something came up, she was to give him as much notice as possible; otherwise her dad would be charged, and he had told him that. Also, whatever she said between these four walls was confidential. But she should know monthly reports would be sent to her father regarding her general progress in areas he deemed important. "Any questions?" He smiled again.

She shook her head.

"Well, then, I know there's been a split in your family, which must feel like rotten eggs. Why don't you talk about that?"

Yes, she should. That's what Charles had given as her reason for coming. But he made her nervous. One of his eyes seemed bigger than the other. She fidgeted and said nothing.

"Go on," he prodded after a few minutes.

She looked at him curiously. "Uh, it wasn't any fun. That's for sure."

"I see," he responded quickly. "I guess you've got lots of feelings about that and about being away from your home, don't you?"

"Yes, I guess I do."

"Of course." He picked his toothbrush up and held it in his right hand, which caught her attention because she wondered if he was about to set it in his mouth. If he did, she would die laughing. But he just kept it in his fist that was curled up on his desk now and continued speaking in a calm, measured tone. He told her the more she expressed herself, the clearer her feelings would get, that trying to find the words at first can be like a bottle of catsup. "You know when it's new sometimes it's hard to get out of the bottle. Right?"

"Uh huh." What was he getting at?

"So you shake it and shake it and then when it starts it just goes everywhere. You've had that happen before, haven't you?"

"Yes," she answered in a puzzled voice.

"Well, Emily, it's sort of like that here." He told her that that was the way analysis was, that you had to get into the flow of it and then things just happened. The mind was like a camera. The memory was the film in that camera, recording all the thoughts and impressions of a lifetime. Most people were naturally curious about themselves, which was why she shouldn't expect him to ask the questions. "My job," he continued, "is to get you to explore yourself. Think of me as a wall. Your problems are tennis balls you're to bounce off me. Some of the balls might be hard, some easy, and on some I might not always make it to the net. But that comes with the territory. If I can give an answer, I will. But I'm not God. The hard work is to find it inside yourself. There's no magic here. Now please just get comfortable on the couch. Just lie back. You'll see."

She did, staring up at the ceiling with her hands folded over her chest thinking this must be how it would feel in a casket. A blue flower in the wallpaper seemed to drip as her eyes smarted from looking at it. What was he doing? Hours seemed to pass, and the quiet became unbearable. She drew her wrist up discreetly to check her watch. 2:20. Goodness! She couldn't take this any longer! "I don't know what to talk about," she blurted out nervously.

"Talk about that."

I just did, bird brain. She became silent again. Yet oddly the longer she lay there, the more tempted she was to say something about her feelings, since at least he had expressed an interest. Maybe she should pretend he was a priest. Hilda, who was Catholic, said when she went to confession she talked into a little wooden door that a priest was behind and told him all the bad things she had done and then she was forgiven. Emily turned her head enough to make out the doctor's feet on his desk, and saw he was writing on a long, yellow pad. Was that a letter to her father? She better say something *fast*! She cleared her throat and began talking about school, the great food, her classes, and especially boys and how she danced every dance at the Xavier get-togethers. She loved being with boys, she said. She wanted to have twins when she got married and be a housewife. She went on and on about that and how happy she was to be an American. Then after a while Dr. Weiss said that was it. He told her where to get a taxi, and she left. And for a while that's pretty much how their sessions went.

After a month with still no word from Mattie, a quiet desperation crept into Emily's heart. Maybe she was sick or worse; otherwise Emily *knew* Mattie would have contacted her. She had to do something.

By now she was aware the Hursts had left White River, because during a talk with her father, Charles inadvertently had said their home had been sold. So on a whim, Emily got hold of the Philadelphia operator and, sure enough, they had a new number, which she wrote down along with their street address. She savored this information as if Mattie had been reborn. At first she considered sending her a letter. Then caution reminded her that Mattie's parents might know she was in Cromley and see that on the envelope. Best to call. She did. But recognizing Mrs. Hurst's voice, she hung up in a panic. Then she determined she wasn't able to go through such anxiety again. Enter Lillian. Emily would get her to phone Mattie and have Mattie call her in the dorm. But wouldn't that look weird, she debated herself. Maybe. But she could handle it. Lillian was smart, but she was also gullible: if Emily said the roof was caving in she might run out of the room. Thus armed with a course of action, she phoned Lillian one evening in November with an "emergency."

Now "emergency" between them didn't mean either was at death's door. Emergency was another word for prank, as in the old days summoning Lillian to her home under the ruse of having a heart attack; then when Lillian rushed in, stricken, Emily would fall over laughing. However, between joke and death there was another level. And in this case, she told Lillian, the matter at hand was clearly urgent. She had a favor to ask. And if Lillian would do it, Emily would pay her five dollars. Before explaining though there was something else that she probably should have told Lillian earlier except it didn't make her look so good. She paused.

"Well, what is it?" Lillian broke in.

"Lil, if Sheila's acting funny it's because she associates you with me and she and I are on the outs. She blames me for the divorce because I gave Ella a hard time and finally she couldn't take it anymore so she left. That about killed Sheila. You know how close they were. I've already told you the divorce was one reason they sent me here. Dad thought Aunt Francie wouldn't be able to handle me. You know how I am."

She sure did, Lillian responded, all ears.

But now for the TNT: "I've got something to tell you. You swear you won't tell?"

Naturally Lillian swore. What was better than a secret?

Then commenced the tale of love gone wrong. Using all the sincerity she could muster even as she felt like a louse for telling such a whopper, Emily revealed that Mattie had caught Sheila with Roy Dean in the backseat of Roy's car at the drive-in before she left town. Apparently they had been seeing each other on the sly for some time. This had destroyed their friendship. So Sheila had suffered a double whammy: losing her stepmother and then her best friend, which was probably why she had seemed funny lately. And no, Emily knew nothing about Mattie's supposed pregnancy, she told a still-curious Lillian. She hadn't called about that. She had already told her she didn't know anything. She had called because she wanted to patch things up between the two for Sheila's upcoming birthday and get in her sister's good graces again. That's where Lillian came in. Would she call Mattie and get her to call Emily and then Emily would try to talk Mattie into making up with Sheila?

"Huh?" Lillian sounded dumbfounded.

Patiently Emily went over the whole sorry mess again. (It had been absolutely the best she could come up with, and she had thought about this long and hard.) "You won't ever mention this to Sheila, now will you, Lil?"

"No. I've already promised. But why can't you phone?"

" 'Cause Dad and Mr. Hurst had a falling out too, and if he heard my voice, he'd hang up."

"But what if Mattie's not there?"

"Call me right back and we'll set another time. You have my number here. If you get her and she can't call now, pick a time when she can and that's fine with me. Either way, let me know." Her heart was pounding so loudly she was afraid Lillian might hear it over the wire, and she pushed herself to sound reasonable.

"Oh, I don't know, Emily."

"What do you mean you don't know?"

"I can't call Mattie Hurst."

"Come on, Lil," she said in her most persuasive voice. "After all I've done for you you're going to fudge on this one? This is peanuts. I'm giving you five dollars for peanuts!"

"It's not the money. I don't care about the money."

"Then what?" she asked impatiently. Getting this close, Emily felt she couldn't go on living if she didn't speak to Mattie.

"It's embarrassing. I don't know her that well."

"What's to know? I'm not asking you to move in with her."

"But she's supposed to be pregnant."

"That doesn't mean she can't talk on the phone."

"But I'd feel stupid."

"Why?"

"I just would."

"Look, she'd be glad to talk to you. You're from White River."

"Maybe that's not a good thing for her right now."

"Lillian, listen to me. I called you because you're my best friend, and this is urgent. It's for a worthy cause. Mattie's hurting as much as Sheila is. She'll welcome this."

"Why don't you just write her?"

"No. No. It takes too long. I want to give this as a present right away."

In the end, Lillian agreed, albeit reluctantly. She got the number, they hung up, and Emily stayed by the phone scarcely able to breathe with suspense. In a few minutes Lillian called back to say she had reached Mattie.

At that news, Emily's heart turned into a bird and flew out of her chest. She sat down in the booth, so faint she could hardly stand. "Did she answer?"

"Yes. And she didn't sound too happy. She made me promise I'd guarantee you wouldn't call. So you won't will you? I gave her my word."

"No, I won't," Emily answered tensely.

"How come she sounded so strict about that?"

This was irritating. "I told you. It's complicated because of our parents. You know how *they* can get."

"Well, it must have been some argument."

"I don't know. I don't care about that. Did you give her my number?"

"She's not going to call. She's going to write. I gave her your address."

"Why isn't she calling?"

"I didn't ask. She's going to write."

"When?"

"I don't know. What's wrong with you?"

"I've got a cold."

There was a moment of silence as Lillian digested the ramifications of having a cold. Then she said, "Listen, I don't get what's going on, but you don't have to send me any money. It's no big deal."

"Lil?" she asked in a small, awkward voice, restraints temporarily shattered.

"Yes?"

"Did she say anything else?"

"Like what?"

"Anything."

"I just told you what she said. We only talked a minute. She said she'd write. You sound really upset."

"I'm upset I have to wait to make this work out for Sheila." They talked a bit more, then hung up. One week passed and no letter came. Emily was in a state. Should she go ahead and write and send that through Lillian? No, that would really look fishy. Then she thought of Hilda. Hilda was going home this weekend, and she could mail it from New Haven so the Hursts wouldn't be suspicious. And so Emily wrote this letter:

December 10, 1948

Dearest Mattie,

I got worried thinking maybe you were sick and that's why I hadn't heard from you.

Anyway, I want you to know I miss you more than anything in the world, and I still love you, Mattie. I haven't changed my mind about anything. Remember the little stone you gave me? Well, it's with me all the time. I do just what you said to do: I touch it to bring you back through it so I'm not so lonely. And I haven't told anyone about us and never will. What I was thinking was maybe I could come up to see you sometime. I could get a bus. Or maybe we could run away and find jobs. When I'm twenty-one, I get my grandfather Stolle's trust, and we could go to France like we used to talk about. I can't stand not seeing you, Mattie. The hurt is so deep. It was terrible what I went through. What

you must have gone through too. But I keep believing in
Fate and that like you said it was spiritual and we're fated to
be together. Do you still believe that, Mattie? I do. But
sometimes I think we have to help Fate along. That's why
I'm writing, to say I hope you're okay and that I want to see
you. Please, Mattie. Write me right away. I understand if
you can't call but please send me a letter. I'm enclosing this
stamped envelope with my name and address on it to make it
easy for you. Mattie, I believe in that reincarnation, but I
don't want to wait until another world before I see you
again.

Always and forever my love,
Emily

Five days later an answer came. In her haste to get inside the
envelope, Emily nearly ripped it open.

December 15, 1948

Dear Emily,

I've started a dozen letters, but I didn't know what to
say. But here goes:

You must know your father told my parents everything,
and they sent me to my aunt's. When my folks came down, I
moved in with them, which is where I am now. It's been so
awful, but I don't want to go into that now. I'm just trying
to pick up the pieces of my life and go on. I'm going steady
with someone now, and we're already talking about getting
married after we graduate in June. That's the most important
thing on my mind.

Now I need to say something Very Important. When your
friend Lillian phoned I asked her to make sure you didn't
call me back. I didn't tell her why, and she never asked; but
I'm sure she thought it had something to do with my being
pregnant. I know from my parents that that rumor started,
and actually they were relieved because they thought that
was better than what actually went on. Anyway, I thank you
for respecting my wishes. I was sure you would. And if you
care about me now you will not call or write ever again, for
that would just cause more problems than I can bear. What

happened is water under the dam that I don't understand and you probably don't either. But we must go on. This letter must be the Absolute End. Regardless of anything, I believe you are fair and will do what is right. And I *know* you are strong. Please be, because if you try to reach me you risk ruining my life. I will never forget you if that is any consolation. But life is a learning experience. I believe I have learned enough to last me a jillion years; but I'm trying to find that silver lining. And I will. So will you, Emily. I'm sorry about everything.

Be kind when you think of me, as you can know I will be when I think of you.

As always,
Mattie

She was in the mail room when she read this, and her initial reaction was overwhelming. She felt weak. She leaned against the wall, struggling for composure, and for a long time stared at the page, focusing on the words "as always" as if to find in them some hidden significance. Of course they meant Mattie was forever Mattie; but Emily, so needy, took them to signify Mattie would be forever what they each had been to the other. Even so, their relationship was over. Mattie never wanted to hear from her again.

Now Emily left the mail room and walked to a clearing near the phys ed building. It was chilly, but her body was like wood. She sat down on a bench and, safe from view, reread the letter. From a distance she observed two girls approaching, so she got up and went on until she came to a private area and that was when she let go, the hurt began touching her everywhere; and she broke down. After that she got her matches from her jeans and burned the letter up, stamping the ashes into the ground. She then took her little stone that was always with her and ran her fingers over its flat gray side, bringing it to her lips for a forlorn kiss. Next, she bent her arm back and threw it with all her might so that it would become as lost as Mattie. No longer were they Fate's responsibilities. Perhaps in another life they would meet again, but not in this one. Balling her hands into fists she dug them into her jacket and blinked back the tears. She would never wreck what they had had by the cheapness and futility of words. Mattie was her secret, her memory of light and gladness to keep forever. It would be impossible to love like that again.

She turned and made her way to her dorm. No matter what, Emily vowed, she would be as strong as a lion. She owed that to Mattie's faith in her.

Mattie's letter, coming just days before her next appointment with Dr. Weiss, was very much in mind when she got to his office; and this time their session would prove to be quite different. She had arrived with her grief all balled up inside like hard wax, but when he began with his customary "How're things going?" she broke down, sobbing uncontrollably. The doctor, after calming her, seized that moment of vulnerability to stray from his usual nondirective approach and encouraged her to talk. At first she resisted, but then, needing to, she divulged she had just heard from a girl she had had special feelings about. From that came this exchange:

"What do you mean, special feelings?"

"I liked her a lot."

"Friends?"

"Yes, friends."

"More than that?"

"I don't know what you mean."

"Did you ever kiss her?"

"No."

"Did you ever touch her in a bad way?"

Damn his dirty mind! "Of course not!"

"Well, what happened?"

"Nothing. But I liked her. It was bigger than like. It was spiritual."

"So what happened?"

"She moved to Philadelphia." She caught herself. What if he told her father and her father knew they had exchanged letters. She sat up on the couch and looked over at him. He was leaning forward on his desk, seemingly very intent on their conversation. "I thought you didn't ask a lot of questions, Dr. Weiss."

"I usually don't. But I don't want to lose this. It's the first time you've shown any real emotion in here."

She lay back down and didn't speak.

After a few minutes he pressed, "So that's it?"

"Yes," she replied softly, wanting to change the subject.

"But I asked you what happened when she moved. What did she write you about?"

"Dr. Weiss, this is all between us, right?"

"Of course."

"I mean you don't tell my father everything I say, do you?"

"We've been over that. I just send progress reports as to whether you're cooperating or not and what I think in general."

"Do you say I'm doing okay?"

"Yes. Yes. Don't worry about it. I don't tell him specifics, and I never will. That's all confidential."

"You promise?"

"You've got my word."

Satisfied, she answered, "She wrote me it was over."

"What was over?"

This confused her. "She said she was getting married, and she didn't want to hear from me anymore."

"Why would she say that if you were just friends?"

"I don't know." She felt trapped.

"Were you more than friends?"

"No. I just told you." She bolted up again and glowered at him.

"Easy, Emily. Back down. It's okay. It's okay to still have a crush. You do, don't you?"

She wasn't going to get into that. She shook her head vigorously.

"Well, even if you do, it's no great shakes. Crushes between girls don't amount to anything unless you get stuck in them."

This aroused her curiosity. Lying there, arms folded defiantly on her chest, she wanted to know what "stuck" meant.

"Stuck," he answered, "means you can't go from those feelings into normal ones. You stay attracted to girls all your life. Your maturity doesn't develop. But that's not you. That doesn't look like you. You're going to dances and dating and having a fine time with boys. I just think this letter touched off something in your past. It was like this girl was a symbol of what you left behind. But you're not stuck. Let's make that clear."

Boy was she glad he couldn't see her face. She wiped a tear off her cheek and sniffled into her hand so he wouldn't hear her. What was he talking about stuck and not stuck and calling it a crush? She knew what a crush was. She had had a crush on Harold Mac a million years ago, but that was because he looked good and drove a swell car and everyone else thought he was wonderful. A crush was just a dent. Mattie was more than a dent. Mattie was deep in her bones, and for a moment Emily yearned to bravely confront him, this expert, and say she was too deep for crushes and she couldn't turn her emotions off and on like a faucet. Besides, she had been just the opposite with Mattie, not stuck, but free as a bird, developed beyond development. Once more she wanted to challenge him, but he was a grown-up and she was a kid and these were perilous times if she wanted to be able to quit seeing him, meaning she must stay on the good side of her father. She lay there with her mouth locked, feeling stuck to the couch. And when he asked if she had ever kissed a boy, she said yes so enthusiastically it startled her.

"Did you like it?"

"Sure I did." She could hear him rustle some papers, and all of a sudden she sat up again and asked the one question that had been stuck in her head ever since she saw it in the dictionary. "Does this mean I don't come from Lesbos?" It just popped out and shocked her, and him too judging by his look.

"From *where*?" He peered up from his yellow pad.

"Lesbos." Her face reddened. "I read it in my dictionary under lesbian."

"Why were you looking at lesbian?"

" 'Cause," her face felt hotter than a stove, "I wasn't. I just saw it in the dictionary." She floundered. She didn't know what to say.

"And thought maybe you were one?"

"No," she swallowed in more confusion. She knew something then as she had never known it before, she knew it from his look—that she never wanted to be that word.

"Let me make this very clear," he said firmly. "You're *not* a lesbian. Don't worry your little head about that. Lesbians have a far different style about them than you, my girl. Just let Mother Nature take her course. Mother Nature's a pretty stubborn little lady, you know, a real nag when it comes to getting her way, to making things go according to plan. And the plan is for you to meet the right fellow someday, and when it's time, to have a houseful of kids. Besides, you're way too pretty to shrivel up like a prune. That's what happens to girls who don't find husbands. They dry up." He smiled almost tenderly and said she didn't want to dry up, did she? Her eyes got big, and she shook her head emphatically. Well then, he said, and ended with a comment that if two girls were to ever try any monkey business all they'd be able to do would be to get on top of each other and flop around like dying fish.

Dying fish! Her and Mattie dying fish! For days the image haunted her.

Christmas was just around the corner. She thought of spending it with Nana, but since her father only allowed one visit to Macon a year, Emily decided to wait until the summer, when she would have a whole month. She ended up going to Hilda's; and there, to cover her embarrassment at not being at her own parents', she talked about how much her father loved her but said he might have to travel during this time, which was why she hadn't gone to White River. Over the phone holiday greetings were exchanged with Charles and Aunt Francie as planned. Her aunt, kind soul, had knitted her a lovely sweater, her father had sent her one hundred dollars for clothes, she in turn had bought them little things, including a scarf for Sheila;

but Sheila never spoke to her any time she called. After a few days, Emily returned to school, saying she had unfinished work to do for the quarterly. Thanksgiving had been spent there, and it hadn't been bad at all. Besides, that visit to Hilda's had been more a painful reminder of why she couldn't go home than anything else.

Lillian had traveled to Florida with her family for the holidays; but before she left, Emily called her. It was the first time they had spoken since that famous ordeal over Mattie, and she was curious to see if Lillian sounded the same (which would mean she believed her). She caught her in a great mood, having just gotten the news she could graduate from high school the same time as Emily if she kept her straight-A average and went to summer school. As to anything else, Lillian sounded fine and surprisingly asked no questions, not even about Mattie and Sheila. It was as if she finally accepted Emily was away and any mystery about that was best left to the gods. More tellingly, perhaps Lillian realized there were lines around Emily's life that were not to be crossed. In any event, before the new year, Emily received this letter from her, which would prove prescient:

December 28, 1948

Dear Stollie,

Well, here I am in sunny Florida at these friends of my folks. Their place overlooks the ocean which is really neat, and the light bulb of my future is blinking in my brain. I've decided I want to spend my life around the water, whatever that takes. I walk the beach here every day wishing I could be a sailor. Of course, that goes over with Mom like a lead balloon. You know how she's always riding me to do something *Important.* We'll see.

Wish you were around so we could pop a few. But Easter'll be here before we know it. We best start thinking about college! I was wondering about maybe a school in New York. Can't you see us painting that town red, white, and stinko? Mom said fine so long as my grades hold.

How about August for the Maine trip? Fits in with

summer school for both of us. Isn't it *great* they're letting me skip?

Talk to you soon. Have a happy!

Love,
Me

P.S. Forgot to tell you: Harold Mac's going steady with Sue Stacy . . . hmmmmm

Tempus fugit. It was second semester now. At Dr. Weiss's she was avoiding all allusions to Mattie as if to eliminate any inferences from that. She kept remembering his look when he had said *lesbian* (or at least the way she thought he had looked, which seemed to suggest lesbian was so vile a word it didn't belong in the dictionary). And she went to great lengths to play up the importance of boys in her life. She did the same at St. Joseph's. The fact was, something extraordinary was happening to her. Slowly, ever so subtly, Mattie was casting a net: Emily was becoming Mattie in a way. She was tucking her sweaters in to pamper her bust line as Mattie used to. She was standing as Mattie had, legs slightly apart, one hand clasping an elbow. She was actually feeling like Mattie. It was as if Mattie had become a movie, and Emily had left that movie with Mattie in her. Without even realizing, she had assumed Mattie's manners, style, ways of holding herself. She bought a dark turtleneck like Mattie's. She switched to Mattie's brand of Old Golds, deciding Luckies had a bitter taste. Increasingly, she viewed the opposite sex as her route to success. And in a move that was truly ironic, she began dating Fred Trim, captain of the Xavier football team, who drove his car with one arm hanging out the window and sucking on a butt the size of a fingernail just as Roy Dean used to. She grew her hair longer, whipped it dramatically over her shoulders. Mattie was running through Emily like ink soaked in a blotter. Mattie breathed in her when she talked about reincarnation and existentialism, concepts she really didn't understand; but they impressed others. For example, when Emily told Hilda she was an existentialist because existentialists believed everyone was connected so if you did something evil it affected everyone else, like a chain reaction (which was, Emily maintained, the basis of her moral beliefs), Hilda said that made more sense to her than Catholicism and she was going to be one too. That's how it went. When Emily danced, she leaned into her partner as Mattie used to with Roy. It was like if she became Mattie, she hadn't lost her. That was the unconscious sense of it.

And then it was spring break, which brought bum news indeed: Lillian's father had had a heart attack; and she and her mother were taking him to the Mayo Clinic. She wouldn't be home for Easter.

A bitter disappointment! After all these months, Emily had been counting on Lillian to ease her reentry as she returned for the first time to the scene of the crime.

She was wearing her royal blue dress with wide sash and petticoats when she boarded the Yankee Doodle. It was an outfit suitable for church and special occasions, one Ella had bought her a year ago that Charles said made her eyes look huge. She thought he would approve because Charles, for all of his permissiveness, still had his old-fashioned ways. For instance, he didn't really like girls in slacks. For another, his favorite quote was "A whistling woman and a crowing hen are bound to come to no good end." And Emily ached to please, not only so he would love her but also to make sure he would let her go to Maine this summer and to college with Lillian when she graduated. She had promised Lillian to bring those subjects up during this trip.

With her was a box of chocolates wrapped in cellophane with a bright red ribbon, a favorite of her father's and of Sheila's too. *Sheila!* Just thinking about seeing her sister gave her brain death. She put that thought aside and began looking out at the scenes flashing by as the train cut through the farmlands. In the old days on Sunday drives she and the family would play Cows. That was a game where the winner had counted more four-legged creatures on her side up to the first graveyard. Now from childhood's habit she began doing that; but then, deciding she had outgrown such play, she leaned against the window and fell fast asleep.

She could see Charles as the train pulled into the depot. He was on the platform under the sign that said White River. Immediately she got her suitcase and moved to the door; and when the train stopped completely, she was the first one out, walking slowly toward him as he leaned down for the obligatory kiss. "Hello Emily," he said quietly. "Good trip?"

"Hi Dad," she replied with equal reserve. Now that she was actually here she wasn't sure what to do. "Yes, it was fine." She extended the box of candy. "Look what I brought for everyone." This surprised him; but before he could speak, she was taking papers out from her purse. "See what my English teacher wrote!" she exclaimed proudly, pointing out a large red A on the last page and the words "Shows excellent understanding of Poe's genius." "I got two other grades like that in English last week. She says I'm real talented, Dad."

"Well, that's wonderful."

"She wants me to be editor of *The Crimson Poet.* That's our school quarterly. What do you think of that? You want me to read you something I wrote?"

"Oh, not just now. Not out here."

"What do you think of the chocolates?"

"It was very thoughtful. You didn't have to do that."

"Well, it was nothing," she smiled brightly. "I think maybe I'm going to be a teacher, Dad." They were just standing there as Emily rattled on, seemingly oblivious to her surroundings, pained for recognition. Charles was in tweeds and gray shoes. He looked serious and quite thin, but his hair was thick as always, and he was still the tallest man she had ever seen.

"Is this all you have?" he motioned to her overnight bag.

"Yes," she giggled. "I stuffed everything in it but the kitchen sink." She waited to hear she looked nice. She wanted him to comment on her longer hair and pretty dress and how big her eyes were; but, barely glancing her way, he started toward the parking lot. "How's Frankie?" she called after him as she tried to keep up with his steps.

"Spoiled rotten."

"I can't wait to see him."

"Well, he's fatter. Your aunt treats him like a king. Listen," he stopped now and faced her. "Speaking of your aunt, just remember she's finicky; so as soon as you get home, take your stuff right up to your room; and be neat. She's at the market now getting food for dinner. And your sister's spending the night at the Baylors, but she'll be along tomorrow. She and the older girl . . . what's her name? . . . Peggy," he answered himself. "Peggy Baylor's getting married, and her mother's taking her and Sheila to Boston for a few days to do some shopping for the wedding."

"Yes," she reassured him, not certain how to act about her sister. "I'll be neat as a pin." Charles was at the car putting her bag in the trunk. She asked, "Did you sell all the restaurants?"

"Sure did," he closed the trunk smiling faintly. "Deal went through a couple of weeks ago in fact. A fellow up in Maine bought the whole kit 'n' caboodle. I went into the Manor the other day and barely recognized it."

"You like it?" she asked, trying to sound grown up and smart.

"Doesn't matter. It's not my worry any longer, thank the good Lord."

She watched him get in the car and did the same. Sitting wordlessly in the front seat now as he inserted the key. What to talk about? Oh, she remembered; he had been out west. "How's California?" she asked as they drove out of the parking lot.

"Great. I'm thinking that's the ticket for me, that's where I'll be heading after this year."

"Really?"

"Yes. After the house is sold and your sister's settled in what she's doing this summer before college. See," he slowed down in front of Stolle Manor, appearing more relaxed. "They're painting the front." She was suddenly overcome with emotion.

"They're going to keep the name for a while," he said. "Good for business." He coughed and his voice stiffened, "Now listen, Emily. The only point I'm going to make about your visit here is that I don't want it to get complicated. You understand?"

She nodded.

"Good. Well here's the way it's going to be. You're home, and I know you have feelings about that, and so do I, and so does your sister. There's no sense kidding you. But just tow the line. All this will be water under the dam if you get off on the right foot. The right foot means minding your p's and q's and not mucking things up. Just go along with the plan as you see it. And be nice to your aunt. She's really looking forward to having you here."

She was barely listening as they pulled into the driveway. Frankie, dozing in the afternoon sun, looked up. Two ears stood erect. He quivered as she yelled his name and suddenly he was bounding into her arms. Still holding him, she followed her father into the house. At the foot of the stairs, she peered into the living room as Charles set her bag down and walked off to his study. Except for new draperies, it looked just the same: rose furniture, logs stacked neatly as magazines by the fireplace, flowers everywhere. For a minute she could almost hear Ella at the piano, eyes closed, a bar of light widening over the wooden desert of the baby grand that Charles used to say had been in the family for generations. She put Frankie down, got her bag, and started up. At the top of the stairs she paused anxiously at Sheila's room; then she went on to her room and pushed the door open. A late sun layered her horse statues and pictures of Van Johnson she had been too depressed to remove when she left home. She opened her closets; she pulled out her drawers. Everything was just as she remembered. And then the facade broke: the tears came. She went to her window and stared out at the backyard where in another lifetime her soul had caught fire: Mattie lying on the grass. Maybe she shouldn't have come back.

"Whoa, Em-uh-lee!" Aunt Francie's voice broke the trance.

"Come on down, suguh-foot, and let your Aunt Francie see herself!"

Pull it together! She wiped her eyes and in a few seconds was at the landing. "Precious pie!" her aunt beamed from the bottom. There she was, tall with dark hair slightly grayed, flawless skin, thick white powder, heavy rouge, lipstick that never came off even when she ate, her nose bearing the Stolle hump that Sheila despised, that her father bore too, wearing a polka-dotted dress with white hoop earrings and dozens of matching bracelets above blood-red fingernails. "How pretty you look!" She clapped appreciatively as Emily descended cautiously. "What a nice color on you! Look, Charles!" He had come from his study as she approached. "Isn't that the sweetest dress?" Her father grunted uh-huh. "Lamb, how you've grown, I declare! Come here and give your auntie big love!" Aunt Francie's arms stretched into a huge V; a gigantic smile swamped her face. Big love was southern talk for affection beyond the limits of human expression. It translated into an embrace so powerful the breath was sucked from the body, which is how Emily felt in her aunt's clasp, smelling the perfume she always associated with southern women.

"Gracious," Aunt Francie held her now at arms' length as Emily struggled to hide her emotions, "are they giving you enough to eat in that Yankee school of yours?" Aunt Francie's head tilted like a dog's at a shrill note. "Lordy, child, but you're skinny as a bird's leg."

"Oh, I'm just fine, Aunt Francie."

The older woman murmured, "What a girl won't do nowadays for her figure." She delivered a final squeeze to Emily's shoulders, reiterating how happy she was to have her home, and began setting the table. "Why don't you help out?" Charles mumbled under his breath. But Emily had already sprung into action. She got the napkins, set three down, put knives on top of each. This brought her aunt scurrying over. "Napkins go under the *forks,* sweetness!" She caught something on her niece's face. "Oh, that's all right, honey," she soothed. "No one's ever gone before the firing squad for setting the table wrong."

Emily smiled weakly and glanced toward Charles sitting on the sofa in the next room, reading the paper. She elevated her voice to make certain he heard her speak of school, Xavier, Fred Trim, being editor of the school magazine. Lest he forget the chocolates, she told her aunt she would bring them downstairs later on. Then she repeated she had made not two but *three* A's on her English papers.

"We have to write a theme a week," she said self-importantly.

"Well, I declare," her aunt responded.

"I can do mine in no time flat!"

"Well, that's mighty good, suguh!"

"And you should see me fence!"

"I'll just bet you're a dandy!"

"I am! I made first team!"

"Oh precious, but aren't you a force for good!" her aunt tittered. Out of the corner of her eye, Emily saw her father scratch his chin thoughtfully. Then her aunt asked, "You ever hear from your stepmother, child?"

She shook her head slowly.

"You ever write her?"

She shook her head again. This wasn't a subject to make her look good.

"Well, your sister got a letter the other day, and she's doing real fine since she got engaged to that lawyer fellow." She hollered in to Charles, "Whoa, brother! Didn't Sheila say she'd heard from Ella?"

From the man of the house came something indistinguishable. At that, Aunt Francie turned to Emily with a martyred affect. "I mean *nobody* ever tells me anything, but say as you will, I *liked* Ella Framer a heap. She just seemed like a fish out of water if you ask me. And I can relate to that. That's the way I feel up heah in the Nawth: like a fish out of water!"

"Now Francine," Charles called in indulgently, his voice giving every indication this was a time-wearied discussion.

Aunt Francie turned to her saucily. "I just say that to torment brother. I tell him he's given his allegiance to the damn Yankees and the wicked state of California, and it's left my burden to reinforce the Confederacy. The *Christian* Confederacy that is, praise the Lord!" So stated, she got bowls and glasses and placed them about. "Sheila's going to be *so* excited to see you, honey! I just know she feels terrible having to be stuck up there with those friends of hers; but one of them's getting married, so what can she do?" She looked pityingly at Emily.

Hope soared. "Why?" she asked as controlled as possible. "Did she say she wanted to see me?"

"Well, of course she wants to see you! She's your sis-tuh, lamb. Now look here, I've got to go check on the roast, so you just go on and make yourself comfortable. I can take care of the rest."

She walked outside with Frankie and watched dusk holding the yard. An opera of crickets serenaded her near the porch. In the heavens a comma of a moon punctuated what had been all day a flawless blue sky. She sat down in a rocker, full of nostalgia. Here she was, back in White River. A stranger-aunt was making dinner. Her father, who had seldom ever taken his meals at home, was now inside waiting for dinner. What a strange world. After a while her aunt came to fetch her, and she went back in as Charles approached the table. "You sit right here, Emily," Aunt Francie pointed opposite her. Then, bowing her head, she intoned, "Bless us mighty Lord for these Thy . . . ." She looked up and gazed intently at her niece. "This is *your* day of honor to be home with us, sweetness. Would you like to say grace?"

Quickly she turned to her father. She had the sense he might be upset that one so diseased could be called upon to invoke the sacred. You have no right, she could imagine him thinking, to take the name of the Lord thy God . . . "No," she blushed, "That's all right, Aunt Francie. You go ahead and do it."

Again the older woman bowed her head, "Blessed be mighty Lord for these Thy perfect gifts, and we reflect upon Thy goodness as we eat them. Amen!" Aunt Francie, beaming heartily, offered Emily a roll and leaned down to scold the dog. "You know better than that, don't you, Frankie?" Her finger ushered him toward the living room. "No begging at this table!"

Frankie knew no such thing. He edged himself into a space between Emily's feet; and when she could, she slipped him scraps. For a time they ate silently. Then Charles asked, "How's that dean? I can't remember her name, I've talked to so many people at that school."

"Dean Stevenson?"

His fork stopped midair. "That's right," he said. "That's the one."

"She's okay, I guess. I don't see her that much."

The fork landed in Charles's mouth, and he glanced at his sister. "When I first took Emily down to that school, this dean had a sign in her office that said, 'Be charming, not alarming.' I thought to myself, well now, if that doesn't say it all."

Aunt Francie winked at Emily. "Well, she *is* charming. Aren't you, dear?"

Charles concentrated on his meat quietly. Embarrassed by the silence, Emily blurted out, "What do you think about me making such good grades, Dad?"

It was then her father really looked at her. His eyes narrowed as if seeing her the first time that day, as if suddenly he found it necessary to touch the past, to remind her that indeed the past was not past but was here, like this house, surrounding them, containing them, and she must never think otherwise, she must never take anything for granted, least of all his regard, nor should she believe she hadn't chipped away at him, nerve by sinew by bitter bits of his soul. Because what came through his lips was jagged: it flew as a dagger directed, "That's splendid, Emily," his eyes nailed hers. "And I wrote you that at the time. But we never did worry about your *intelligence,* did we?" He let that blade sink in as Aunt Francie, seemingly unaware of any tension, got up and went into the kitchen, leaving Charles glaring at his daughter. But as if realizing his tone, his face changed, his voice resumed a civil pitch. "I'm glad your grades are good, Emily. That's why I sent you the hundred dollars for Christmas."

"I know, Dad," she answered penitently. Her knife hit her peas, knocking a few to the floor. She stared down: small insidious balls staring at her. Big jerk! She leaned over, picked them up, and stuck them in her pocket so Charles wouldn't see, just as Aunt Francie popped her head in to say the pie crust had burned and she would be out in a minute. Silence. Eating. Then Charles, cutting a piece of steak, said, "You wrote you wanted to go visit your friend Lillian Jackson in Maine this summer?"

Oh, wow! What a relief *he* had brought it up. "Yes, I did," she replied sedately.

"When's that?"

"After I see Nana in August."

"When's your school over?"

"June fifth, but then I'm doubling up for summer school."

"Can you handle that?"

"I have to if I want to graduate early."

"That's *not* what I asked." He put his knife down and looked at her. "Are you able to handle the pressure of so much school?"

"Well sure; my grades are great." She couldn't get that in enough.

"What about math?"

"It's okay. I'm holding a B. I'm really trying, Dad." He continued eating. "What I was thinking was I could spend a little less time with Nana and then go on up to Maine for a couple of weeks and get back to St. Joe's Labor Day."

Charles patted his lips with his napkin and took a sip of wine. "Your aunt'll be in Newport News then. I figure the house will be sold. So you should stop by to see her after you leave your grandmother's." His eyes glazed as he stared past her. What's he looking at, she wondered. Can't he just get to the point? "Your sister's taking a job on Cape Cod before she starts college. Waitressing or something." He sighed. "I can't keep up with everyone." She watched his Adam's apple. It was big, and it moved up and down with his swallow. It looked even bigger than it used to, maybe because he had lost weight. He swallowed, and it bobbed again. Involuntarily Emily touched her neck as Sheila's descriptions of her bad glands came to mind. She felt a twinge, but then reminded herself that Dr. Weiss had never said there was anything wrong with her neck, so she needn't worry. She felt her father's sharp eyes. "Are you sure that aunt of hers wants you there? It *is* her aunt, isn't it?"

"That's right. Don't you remember . . . " She stopped herself. Her father hadn't been home that much. "Well, maybe you don't; but I've been up there before. Her aunt likes me. You can talk to her if you want."

"Your aunt can call." He took another bite as his Adam's apple danced with the swallow. Emily waited hopefully. "Well," he concluded slowly, "I've no objections. You seem to have done a solid enough job at school, and that doctor," he lowered his voice as Aunt Francie came in, "gives you thumbs up. Where is it? Around Portland?"

Here was a chance for real conversation between them! "It's near Freeport where L.L.Bean's is, that great store that's open all night. You ever been there?" Her father nodded and kept on eating. "It's right near the coast, you know, near where all those islands are. There's a whole lot of them out in the ocean, Dad; even Rockefeller has one, a real big island that's only got one house on it, and it's all his, the whole thing. Maybe we'll be sailing and run into him. Wouldn't that be something? Lillian says her aunt has a new sailboat!"

She stopped and waited. Charles grunted and poured himself a glass of wine. Aunt Francie murmured, "That's nice." The conversation drifted to local politics, one of Charles's cars that needed work, the weather, a new catalog Aunt Francie had sent for. All the while Emily sat between them fidgeting inside. She was trying to decide when to bring up the next loaded issue— going to college with Lillian. She was pleased, so pleased about Maine. But New York was even more complicated, and she couldn't predict how her father would react. She watched him. His cheeks were flushed. He seemed in a good mood, talking easily with his sister.

Now, do it! So the words rushed out one on top of the other, "Dad, Lillian's going to be graduating when I do so we can go to college together, which we've planned on since we were kids. She wants to go to New York and study something that will let her travel on the ocean and they've got the best schools there for everything you'd ever want. Dad, she's the smartest person I've ever known. Do you know she can read a book in an hour and memorize it? And she made herself a radio!" She paused to allow her father to digest this startling information.

Aunt Francie interrupted, "I swanny this dog is like a goldfish! He'd eat till his stomach split open!" She began clearing the table, scraping leftovers into a dish. "Frankie-wankie," she called as he dashed eagerly after.

"Help your aunt," Charles interjected.

"Leave her alone, brother," Aunt Francie turned before going into the kitchen. "She's a guest. I don't like anyone right under my feet."

Emily went on with her father. "I've decided I want to be a teacher, Dad. There's got to be lots of schools in New York for that, right Dad? So what do you think about me wanting to be a teacher?" In the next room she could hear her aunt's step-step.

Charles stuck a toothpick in his mouth and after a thoughtful study uttered the immortal words: "I think New York's too much for a young girl."

"Dad, I'll be seventeen."

"That's pea-squat, Emily."

"It's seventeen," she defended that age as if it were her country. "It's almost old enough to vote."

"Seventeen doesn't know ding from a monkey tree, young lady."

"But they have rules. You live in a dorm. You could talk to them."

"It's not the rules. It's the city. It's the environment of urban living. I should know. Your mother and I tried it there a while." His expression softened.

"But Dad. I've been working so hard to prove myself."

His face darkened, and he pushed away from the table. "I'm talking about your level of maturity, Emily. You go to a big school like what they offer in New York and you're just a drop in the bucket."

"But Lillian's going."

"I don't care if the queen of England's going. I'm still paying the bills around here!"

Something was driving her past all the caution signs, through the red lights, careening her around the corners. "But we've been planning this since we were . . . "

Slam! His hand flattened his napkin. "Look, can it, will you! Do I have to remind you that your sister had counted on the same thing with *her* friend? Now don't get me started on this with your aunt around. I told you . . ."

"Y'all want chocolate or vanilla with your pie?" Aunt Francie opened the kitchen door and stood there with a frying pan in her hand.

Charles patted his stomach and stood up. "Not me, Francine," he smiled apologetically. "I'm stuffed."

"Charles, you're not going to eat my apple pie?"

"I'll give you a raincheck."

"What about you, lamb?" she addressed Emily.

"I'll have some later, Aunt Francie."

"Um," her aunt muttered and closed the door.

Charles stared down at his daughter. "Now get that hangdog look off your face." When she just sat there, he went on. "Listen, let me chew on this a while. Okay? I've always believed in giving you girls a free hand, but that's before all this trouble started. What I'm leaning toward is a small women's college in Virginia near where your aunt'll be if you get in a jam, and you'll receive lots of individual attention. And talk about social life—why when I was going to the university they used to cart those girls in by the busloads. You ever hear of Belle Adams?"

She shook her head.

"Well it's a fine school a couple of hours out of Washington. It might be just the place for you."

"But will you think about New York?" she pleaded.

"We'll see." His sister came back in. "Great dinner, Francine." Then he questioned his daughter as nonchalantly as if they hadn't just had one of the most important discussions of her life. "So what's doing on your dance card tonight?"

"Nothing," she stared solemnly into her plate.

From across the table her aunt threw her two cents in. "Aren't you going to call some of your little friends, honey?"

Little, she thought resentfully. Who says they're little? Her aunt tried to baby her. "Not tonight," she responded respectfully. "I'm kinda pooped."

"But don't they know you're home?" her aunt persisted.

"I wrote a couple of cards that I'd call tomorrow."

"Where's Lillian?" her father piped in.

"Her dad had a heart attack. They took him to the Mayo Clinic."

"Oh yes, I heard something about that. Well, if you change your mind and go out, let your aunt know. And don't paddle in too late." He started to leave, but before he got to the door he turned around and added, "I'm going up Rutland way very early tomorrow. But you two have fun. I've got some work to do in my study."

Emily helped clear the table. Then she lay on the dining room rug playing with Frankie. She didn't know what to do with herself. Her aunt looked in wearing a floppy hat with feathers. "I'm going down to the church. Do you want to come too, Emily?"

"No ma'am. I'm going to listen to the radio."

Aunt Francie left and Emily set the box of chocolates prominently on the hall table so Sheila would be sure to see them. If she could have put a big sign to her sister saying the candy was from her she would have. She could hear her father typing in his study. Should she go in and ask once more about New York? No, her second thought advised. Get Aunt Francie to convince him. She considered that momentarily. Yep, good idea. She got up and put her jacket on, suddenly intent on taking a walk. Outside she could feel ghosts tugging at her, tugging her across the field to Mattie's former house. In moments she was standing in front of it, almost seeing that girl who had changed her life. She felt everything, and she felt nothing. She felt distanced, and she felt Mattie's arms around her. She felt real, and she felt unreal. All the opposites right under her skin—good and bad, pain and pleasure. A bicycle was in the yard, and leaves were piled by the garage doors. Same paint, same porch and large bay windows. But Mattie wasn't there, Mattie would never be there again. Something overwhelmed Emily, an emotion so deep it was almost a physical sensation. Life sure wasn't a bowl of cherries, she thought. It was a big question mark. And this house was Mattie's casket holding the bittersweet death of their love. Except that love would never die. *Never.* That's what she wrote in the little notebook she always carried for emergencies. She cut across Birch Lane toward Lillian's. A light had been left on in the hall, and she peeked in but couldn't see a thing. She wrote "Kilroy was here" and shoved the paper under the door, knowing Lillian would recognize the handwriting. After that she crossed Main Street and shortly was walking by the high school toward the wooden bridge where she and Jimmy Black, her fifth-grade sweetheart, used to promise to love each other forever. That love remained unsullied until Jimmy, in a fit of nonperfection, showed her *his* and demanded to see *hers.* She had refused, so he made fun and joked hers was stupid anyway; he knew because he had seen his cousin's and it had a big crack down the middle just like a girl's brain. Jimmy's sister was a nun. He used to say nuns didn't have vaginas. He pronounced them "virginnies." The memory of that made her laugh. Just then she heard a car that sounded like Harold Mac's and, not wanting to run into anyone familiar, she darted behind some trees.

By nine-thirty she was back in her room with Frankie, chewing gum and devouring *Silver Screen.* Tomorrow she would see her friends and face Sheila; but for now she just wanted to be alone.

She woke from a sound sleep. It was after nine, and at first she didn't know where she was. Then she felt a small lump at her feet. Frankie. She brought him up, nuzzling him to her chin as his heart raced happily. He wasn't her dog anymore. Well, this wasn't her house either.

For a while she lay in bed thinking about yesterday and how she wanted to talk Aunt Francie into making Dad let her go to college with Lillian. Downstairs she could hear a door slam, and then the phone began ringing. She had to get up, but she didn't want to. She was afraid to see Sheila.

Aunt Francie was fixing breakfast when she entered the kitchen. She motioned Emily to the table and loaded her plate with eggs. Charles had already gone and wouldn't be back until tomorrow night. "He left you this five-dollar bill, honey."

She took it from her aunt's hand thinking that with her father gone she should make hay while the sun shone. But first she must tell about the chocolates. They were on the hall table by the door. Had Aunt Francie seen them?

"Yes."

"They're from me. I forgot to bring them down last night. I bought them as a present."

"Well, thank you."

"Be sure and tell Sheila."

"But honey, you can tell her yourself. She . . . "

"Aunt Francie," Emily butted in.

"Yes."

"Will you see if you can talk Dad into letting me go to college with my best friend Lillian Jackson?"

Her aunt was wiping the stove dry. She glanced over at Emily and murmured, "Well, I don't know, dear."

"Please, Aunt Francie. It would mean so much to me. He listens to you. Me and Lillian, we've been talking about going to college together since forever." She went on a mile a minute, about what a good influence Lillian would be and that she, Emily, was going to become a teacher. She imagined the word "teacher" was magic, that it made people take her seriously, that it meant she paid her bills and was moral and a good citizen. She said it to Aunt Francie several times, how she was interested in teaching poor children to help them with their self-images. "Self-image is important," she beamed, pleased with her grasp of psychological facts. "We studied about it in phys ed. If you don't have a good self-image, you're in real trouble!"

"Yes, that's true," her aunt agreed.

"So Lillian and me, we help each other with our self-images." Neatly she sewed everything into one package. "When you're going off to a big place like a college, it helps to know someone; it makes you feel better about yourself. So will you say something to Dad?"

"Emily, doing your best at all times is what talks the loudest."

True. He hadn't given a definite no; her grades were good. Her mood lightened.

Aunt Francie said, "I was trying to tell you your sister phoned."

"Oh, nice."

"She'll be coming over this afternoon to get some things before she leaves for Boston. Right now she's helping with a wedding party. Emily, I declare," the older woman raised her voice. "Aren't you excited about seeing your blood sister?"

"Why yes, ma'am."

"Well, you could have fooled me. In my day sisters were closer than pie. It's what I always longed for in my own family, but I just had poor brother to pick on." She stepped a bit toward Emily, and a piece of grime fell from her rag. "He loves you so much, lamb. You know that, don't you?"

She knew nothing even resembling that statement. "Yes ma'am. I love him too."

"He has such high hopes for you."

"I know. I have high hopes myself."

"I'm sure he'll send you where it's best. Charles has a heart of gold. But I don't bother with those kinds of decisions."

"But if you get a chance maybe, would you, please, Aunt Francie?"

"Yes, yes. Precious, it's mighty good having you home. And

your home's in Newport News too. I just want to say that before you trot off and get yourself occupied."

"Yes, ma'am."

"Honey," her aunt questioned, "are you pleased to be here?"

Oh, she longed to be. She wanted to mean her words. But it was all changed. Mattie's ghost was everywhere; and she would never be back again after this trip.

"Why yes, I am," she answered, caught off guard.

"You know you can tell your Aunt Francie if you aren't, if something's bothering you. It'll just go in one ear and stick to glue."

"Yes, ma'am. I believe that."

"Emily, is something wrong?"

"No. Why do you ask?"

"You just seem so serious for a girl your age. Boys don't like girls too serious, you know."

She shifted uneasily. "I guess I just think a lot."

"But thinking makes worry lines. That's not right. I told your sister you looked pretty as a peach." She ran some water in the sink.

That must have pleased Sheila a whole bunch. "Why? Did she ask about me?"

Her aunt wheeled about in surprise. "She didn't have to ask. She's your *blood,* sweetness!"

The logic escaped her. She stood up, patting her stomach, grinning awkwardly. "I'm gonna call some of the kids and go over to their house if it's okay."

"You'll be back before your sister leaves, won't you?"

"When's that?"

"The Baylors are picking her up at three, and she said she'd be here before that. I'm sure she'd come sooner if they didn't have their hands full."

"Okay. I won't be gone that long. I've got the rest of the week to see everybody."

Her aunt stood by the sink now with a kind expression.

"Well, that's nice you're seeing your friends. What did you end up doing last night?"

"Just walked around."

"Walked around? Where?"

"Downtown. Over by the high school and stuff."

Aunt Francie's eyes got wide. "Gracious, child. Why would you just walk around?"

"Aunt Francie, I haven't been back for a while. It's not so easy, you know," her voice quivered and she looked away.

Her aunt studied her face. "Lord, Emily. What is it that's so painful?"

"Nothing. I . . . I just need to get used to being here again." She left her aunt to ponder that information and hurried to phone one of her friends.

She needn't have worried about any strange questions from her old gang. Actually it was fun getting caught up on the latest gossip and talking about school, though the anxiety of having to see Sheila later was bigger than anything else. Emily also felt she had outgrown the Muskateers. A little before three they all parted, promising to meet after dinner for the movies. When she got home, Sheila's car was in the driveway. She braced herself and went inside. She must be upstairs she decided, seeing the rooms were empty. She went straight to the kitchen and looked out the window. Aunt Francie was working in the garden. Frankie was napping by one of the chairs. Nervously she took out a cigarette, lit it, took in two quick, deep drags, then fanned the smoke as she exhaled. Next, she got the box of candy and started up the stairs. At Sheila's door, she paused. No, she couldn't do it. She moved on to her room, then decisively turned around and came back. She had to get this over with. The door was slightly open, so she stepped inside. Sheila was at her dressing table brushing her hair, but she heard Emily and saw part of her in the mirror. Quickly she turned around. Her body seemed to shudder. "What are *you* doing in here?" she gasped unbelievingly.

"I came to . . . "

"I thought the door was closed."

"It wasn't completely."

"Get out of here!"

"Sheila," Emily stepped forward shyly, extending the box. "Look what I have."

But Sheila didn't care what she had. Sucking her breath in sharply, she barked, "Listen, I promised Dad I'd muddle through this as best I could if Aunt Francie were around. But this is *my* room. You've no right to be here!"

Blindly, Emily waved the box of candy. "I brought you this. It's your favorite chocolates."

"You did *what*!" Sheila's eyes blinked rapidly, and her chest heaved with emotion. "You idiot, I don't want your candy!"

"Please take it," she cried desperately. "I'm so sorry."

"*Sorry*! You're so *sorry*! God in heaven!" The color drained from Sheila's face, and her hand gripped her hairbrush so hard the knuckles went white. She seemed to be struggling for control. "Leave me be," she finally spat through clenched teeth. "I'll be gone in a minute, and I'm not coming back until you've left. I'm telling Aunt Francie I have to stay longer in Boston."

But Emily couldn't move. She stood there as if waiting for a miracle, so trapped in her own need to be loved that she had lost all perspective. At that moment, if it would have done any good she would have thrown herself at her sister's feet and begged for forgiveness. Couldn't Sheila see how much she hurt too? How hard she was trying? What must she do to make everything all right again? "I'm sorry," she repeated in a small, constrained voice.

This brought Sheila to her feet with hot, awful eyes. "Get out of here you, you piece of garbage! I don't care about your sorries! They don't mean *that* to me!" She snapped two fingers together for emphasis, and her other hand banged the table with her brush. "Maybe you can fool Dad and that doctor you go to, but you can't fool me, you . . . you . . . *queer*! Now get out before we have a real scene and Aunt Francie hears!" Brandishing her brush, she advanced toward Emily, who hurriedly backed away, and then the door was slamming in her face. She ran into the bathroom and bent over the toilet bowl. The intensity of that encounter had made her nauseous, and she vomited a bit. She heard Sheila descend the stairs. She stood up and placed the box of candy on the shelf and sat back down until a loud, insistent honking galvanized her. She raced to a hall window, where she saw the Baylors waiting in their car for Sheila. She raced to a rear window and saw Sheila hugging Aunt Francie good-bye before rounding the corner of the house to the street. She returned to her room and lay down feeling dead. Nothing had changed. Nothing would ever change. So what had she expected? The phone rang. Please, God, don't let it be for me!

In a minute she heard, "Whoa, Emily! You up there?"

She made herself stand and open the door. "Aunt Francie, if that's for me, just say I'm about to get into the shower."

Her aunt was a quarter of a mile up the stairs now, calling out, "It's Nell Ridge, honey. She wants to know if you can come over for dinner before the picture show. I think that would be real good. I've been so busy I haven't had time to get to the store for something I ran out of."

It would look too funny if she didn't go. "Okay," she answered.

She went back to bed shivering with misery. She hated herself. But she wasn't queer. She couldn't be. Her grades were too high, she was too popular. Besides, the other day Fred Trim had told her she was "food for the eyes." He wouldn't have said that if she were an abnormality. And Dr. Weiss would have let her know if there were something wrong. She just couldn't be queer because of Mattie. Mattie had been a foreign experience.

She got her mirror from the bureau and stared at herself long and hard. Who was she? She felt empty. She never wanted to come here again.

. . . I left two days later. My excuse was I'd forgotten my math book, which I needed for a huge exam when I got back. When

I told Dad this, I also let him know what had happened with Sheila. He said I had to be more patient and that once she saw I was a card-carrying member of the human race, she would come around.

The night before I caught the train, something happened between me and Dad. It was one of those evenings to die for—a jam session of moon, stars, millions of fireflies exploding in the warm spring air. And I was just sitting on the porch after dinner lost in thought, at one point recalling how me and Lillian used to trap those bugs in jars and how the jars had smelled when we let them go, when Dad unexpectedly walked out. He had had some wine and seemed surprisingly mellow. Without comment he launched into a joke about this man who went into a bar with a banana in his ear. The bartender shouted, "Hey buddy; you've got a banana in your ear." The man said, "What?" The bartender repeated, "I said, you've got a banana in your ear." The man cupped his ears with his hands and repeated, "What?" This riled the bartender, who bellowed at the top of his lungs, *"You've got a banana in your ear!"* To which the guy retorted, "I can't hear you. I've got a banana in my ear."

Now one thing about my father and me: we had the same sense of humor; and in this case it saved the day. The joke made us hysterical. We started laughing, which broke the ice and led to our first regular conversation since I had gotten home. I talked about school, becoming a teacher, my studies. He seemed interested. We touched on the psychiatrist, and he commented he thought we were doing a good job together. That really got me. Impulsively I found myself getting up and walking to Dad, who was leaning against a post. And then I did what I had never done before: I rested my head on his chest. For an instant he tensed. Then his arms tentatively surrounded me. It wasn't big love, but it was something. As quickly, he stiffened again; his muscles seemed to lock in place as if a bolt had jammed his spinal column and he broke off, mumbling he had had a long day and needed to hit the sack. I better do the same thing, he suggested, since we had to be at the station early the next morning. With that, he departed, leaving me alone, my body still warm from his embrace.

But how that moment thrilled me. I woke up at dawn crazy about my father, thinking maybe things were going to work out. Aunt Francie had made sandwiches and left a note saying she would see me in Newport News this summer. Then Dad and I were driving to the train. I remember wanting to hug him, wanting to hear he loved me and that he thought everything was going to be okay. But he was reserved and in fact discouraged any conversation. At the depot he gave me money, he said he would be in touch. There were the quick pecks on the cheek, and then he left.

I was wearing that same blue dress as when I arrived. It was wrinkled because it had fallen off the hanger the night before. But I smoothed it out with my hands as the train picked up speed . . .

Stay busy. That's how to forget your problems. Excel. Then Dad will let you go to New York.

Those mottoes were to become Emily's guiding principles once she returned to St. Joseph's: she joined the swim team, she won a part in a summer production of *Little Women,* she was, as hoped, named editor of the school quarterly and afterward proudly penned in red block letters:

ANNOUNCEMENT

EMILY STOLLE HAS BEEN DULY APPOINTED
EDITOR-IN-CHIEF OF *THE CRIMSON POET;*
ST. JOSEPH'S ACADEMY, CROMLEY, CONNECTICUT,
FOR THE ACADEMIC YEAR 1949–50.

She sent one to Lillian and another one home. Nana's she decided to hand deliver this summer because her eyesight was failing.

She also wrote Lillian a few days after Easter:

April 19, 1949

Hey hotshot!

Guess your dad's okay or you'd have called. Tell him hi.

Here's news fresh off the press! Dad okayed Maine but New York is up in the air. He wants me to go to a women's college in Virginia. Vomit. Says I'd be just a number in New York. We'll see. Best I could get was he'd keep an open mind, so you keep your fingers crossed. It'll really be the pits if our plans fall through. But if it ends up you're there and I'm stuck in Virginia, virgin-city, U.S.A., we can still see each other because we'll be older. Anyway, I'm being optimistic. If my grades stay high, I don't see how he can refuse. But you never can tell about a parent.

It was rats not having you home, but good seeing everyone. Guess Nell & Tom are really serious. And what a two-ton shocker that Caty Bird's getting married! I didn't see Harold Mac, and no big loss. I've far outgrown him. All the boys down here are going to Yale so that leaves him scratching in the dirt.

Did you get my note???

Did you know I can chug four beers (!!!) and not barf? Write!

> Kisses & near-misses,
> Emily the Great

P.S.   Tell Nell I'll send that stuff on horses soon as I get it.
P.P.S. Did you hear why the little moron took some toast to Times Square? Because he heard there was going to be a traffic jam!!!

Me getting to go to
college with you

Me not getting
to go

On Saturdays, girls could date unchaperoned provided they stayed on campus. And that's what she and Fred Trim were doing every weekend by now—they walked around or hung out in the student council. But at some point all his good manners and affability would be set aside, and Fred would turn into a sex maniac, obsessed with her body and getting inside her pants and did she have hair on her pubic, let him see, and making her nipples hard so he could take pictures of them. Die. Begging her to touch his penis. Said girls didn't realize how tough it was for guys. Said when he got excited an energy built up in it like a volcano; and if it wasn't released, it would fill up with poisons and give him a brain hemorrhage.

But Emily didn't want to touch his penis. She didn't want to be the one who had to release his poisons. She had heard that semen if it dropped on any part of the skin could get under it and travel round to the vagina and make her pregnant. She also didn't want Fred to fondle her. But she let him feel her breasts on the *outside* of her garment because she didn't want to lose him. Fred, bound for Switzerland this summer and Yale in the fall, was considered a catch. But he bored her. Xavier boys thought they were hot stuff. All they wanted to talk about was sports or their opinions and taking her clothes off. They didn't seem interested one bit in her own intellectual points of view or in poetry or her tennis muscle or the fact she could stand on her head for fifteen minutes straight and swim twenty butterfly laps without losing breath. Yet boys were a girl's rite of passage. Ask anyone. Ask Dr. Weiss.

After summer school she went to Macon. Ora Lu was living with Nana now to give her better care, which gave Emily lots of free time. She began dating young men from the "good" families of Macon. They were all wild as geese, and she did her best to stay popular without smearing her reputation: she wore engine-red lipstick, heels (even though they made her walk funny), and a white peasant blouse that showed off her figure.

Her favorite beau was Brad Jones, son of a local bigwig, who thought he was Marlon Brando and who, like Fred, was obsessed with her vagina and his penis and their possible future together. But there wasn't any future she declared, the unmistakable message being that sex before marriage was taboo. He could, though, touch her covered breasts. Period. Things ended when Brad called her a prick teaser because she wouldn't let him take her bra off. No problem. It was time to leave for Maine anyway.

But first she had to stop over at Newport News. Charles, fresh from having wrapped up the final sales on his properties, was there; and he took that opportunity to say he was still inclined toward a smaller college near to where Aunt Francie could keep an eye out, since he would be in California. Belle Adams fit the bill. And with her grades and his Virginia connections, she was bound to get in. Then came the carrot: if she did well and continued to mature in mind and spirit, she could transfer as she pleased after her first two years.

"Does that mean I can go to New York with Lillian?" she asked with a heavy heart, seeing his mind was set.

"Yes," Charles answered, then insisted on driving her and Aunt Francie to see the school before she flew to Maine.

She went, but sadly. She didn't feel like listening to him and her aunt discuss her life as if it belonged to them. She didn't want to live in Virginia or enter some prissy girls' college. She wanted to be in New York drinking in bars and being free. But at age sixteen life was just one jail sentence after another. So she sat quietly in the backseat, by turns sulky but always respectful. Nothing was fair.

Actually, though, the host town of Fricksburg was like a page from a history book, charming and filled with small cobbled streets, intimate shops, parks dominated by statues of Civil War heroes. Like Cromley, it too was built around the single industry of a school. The campus itself was a larger version of St. Joseph's: hilly, woodsy, big buildings with flags streaming in the breeze. Charles liked what he saw. Aunt Francie seemed pleased to have Emily in the same state. And she, itching to leave for Maine, stoically tried to reserve judgment. They all agreed she would apply when she got back to school.

Twenty-four hours later she and Lillian were excitedly hugging each other at the Portland airport. From there, they rode by limo to Freeport for the fifteen-minute boat crossing to the aunt's summer place on Bussell Island. Before they caught the ferry, Emily delivered the bad news. "I can't go to New York till I'm a junior, Lil," she said solemnly.

Lillian's face dropped a mile. "How come?"

"Dad wants me to go to this stupid girls' school in Virginia. Belle Adams."

"Why?"

Emily shrugged. "I think 'cause he went to the University of Virginia and he's maybe trying to live through me. You know how parents get with their kids, like you always say your mom's pushing you to be a doctor."

"Yeah, but that's 'cause she dropped out of med school when she married Dad. I don't see how your father . . ."

Emily got confused. She knew why Charles was being so selective, but she couldn't tell. So she interrupted, "It's just a hunch. But it's not the end of the world. He promised I could transfer junior year."

"But that's not the same thing," Lillian protested. "We were *always* going to be freshmen together."

She had a sudden inspiration: "So why don't you come with me?"

"To Belle Adams?"

"Yeah. For two years, and then we can go to New York."

"No, I don't think so, Stollie. I want to be in a city. I've been thinking about it a lot lately." Her eyes quizzed Emily's face curiously. Then she said, "I don't get it. Your dad used to always let you do what you wanted."

"That was before the divorce. Ever since Ella left, he's been really weird."

"Maybe he's afraid of losing you. Parents get like that."

"Maybe."

They didn't question that logic. They just started off like that, happy to be together, yet sad too: they were growing up. And because of certain realities—Lillian's returning to Florida for Christmas with her folks, another spring visit to the Mayo Clinic in the offing for her father, to say nothing of the miles that separated them now—they wouldn't see each other again until next summer up here. But they had a great time together.

Not a day passed that they didn't ride the ferry. They fished and sailed, and once Lillian's Aunt May let them drive her car to Ogunquit for lobster. Then on Emily's last day, something memorable happened. They had taken the sailboat out, and the wind died. "Becalmed," said Lillian, sounding like a pro.

"What's becalmed?"

"When there's no wind."

Soon the talk turned to the future. Lillian said, "I've been thinking I really want to get on with it, you know, Emily. I mean in a way it's probably good they sent you off to school 'cause now we're graduating ahead of time; and if you hadn't of gone, I wouldn't be doubling up on courses and going to summer school to keep up with you. But it's good; it gives us an edge in terms of what we want to do. We've got to start thinking about that, you know. It's important. You still want to be a writer?"

"Sure I do."

"What about getting married?"

"What about it?"

"I don't know. Do you want to?"

"Well sure, when it's time. But I'm not about to rush it. I like boys though," Emily added quickly.

"Well, God knows we *both* like boys." They laughed. "But seriously, everyone back home, that's all they talk about."

"Yeah, well, that's who *they* are. Betcha the Muskateers never see New York."

"Right," Lillian agreed.

"They'll just stay in White River till they drop dead."

"Yep."

"Get fat and have a hundred kids."

"Hmmm."

"I don't want that, Lil. I don't want that even a little bit."

"Me neither."

"So we'll get married when we've finished up with everything, and it won't be to some jerk. It'll be to some great guy, you know, like Hemingway!"

"Hemingway. Yeah!" They agreed *he* was something, all

right. At sixteen, smoking, popping a few cold ones, Emily and Lillian believed they knew more about life than most kids. Big shots. Wavelapping on the main. After a while Lillian asked, "What do you want to write, anyway?"

"Poetry. Maybe a book."

"Wow! A *whole* book?"

"Sure. That's nothing. I'll take lots of English classes first. Or who knows? Maybe I'll stick to poems. I've got to think about that."

Lillian pondered this in silence. Then she said quietly, "I just want to live."

"Me too!" Emily exalted. "I can't wait for people to quit telling me what to do."

"I'm not talking about that. I'm talking about *really* living."

"What's *really* living?"

"I'll tell you. Remember when I wrote you from Florida last Christmas about being a sailor?"

"Yes."

"That's half what I mean. Not necessarily to be a sailor but to be around the water 'cause of how it makes me feel. Like Thoreau," she added self-consciously. "Remember how Thoreau went to the woods?"

Emily loved conversations like this. She stretched out contentedly on the seats and lit another cigarette. "Sure," she answered jauntily. "He got down to the nitty gritty."

"That's right. That's what I'm saying. I'm not too good at spilling my guts but you're the only one I could ever say this to. I mean I've always felt there was something special I was marked for. It's scary."

This really got her. They had spoken like this before, but now, only one summer away from high school graduation, a new level of significance permeated any mention of the future. Emily sat back up and flipped her cigarette onto the water. It floated, and then a wave gobbled it whole. She looked at Lillian, who had gotten quite serious as she spoke of her pressures to please her mother. "I feel like I owe her for all she's done for me. It hasn't been easy since Dad got sick and she's had to sock money away for my education and still keep up with the bills. But she wants me to be a doctor. She thinks my brain is special."

"It is. So's mine. Between us our brains could probably sink a ship."

"Yeah, well, I don't know." Lillian emitted a little chuckle. "Mom just thinks I should *do* something. Ever since I was born it's like she's been waiting for me to finish up *her* work at med school; and now that college is getting closer, that's all she talks about. But I don't want to go to med school." She shook her head sincerely. "I can't even stand the sight of blood."

"So don't go. You've got rights."

"Not if she's footing the bill."

"Oh come on, Lil. She's not going to stick you like that."

"She's from England. They can be pretty stubborn. And she thinks so long as it's her money, she should have a say. Like the other day I just happened to have mentioned I'd love to study the ocean and she said that wasn't academic enough, so I said, What's academic enough? and she said lecturing and writing text books if you refuse to be a doctor. I mean shit-a-brick, you know. That's not what I want. I want to do stuff that helps me understand things."

"What things?"

"A lot of things."

Emily said helpfully, "So take philosophy."

"For what? To teach? I just said, I don't want to be tied down to a desk. I want to travel, get my own boat and take off solo."

"You're kidding."

"No, I'm not."

"But why solo?"

"I want to see if I can bank on myself. Like Thoreau."

"So how do we go to the same school if that's what you want? I don't want to do that."

"Emily, they've got schools in America that let you study more than one thing."

"They do?"

"Sure. We can find one in New York. I just have to get one that Mom'll pay for." She frowned.

Emily reached over and patted her knee. "Don't worry, Lil," she said sympathetically. "You will. You'll work it out. I believe in you. I say shoot for the moon, just aim and fire. You can do it. You can do anything you want."

Lillian's response in a moment was, "Is Walt Whitman still your hero?"

"Of course he is."

"Well, mine's Amelia Earhart. Yes," she suddenly said louder. "That's it! That's who I want to be! I want to do *everything*!" She stood up shaking her fist dramatically and yelling out toward the horizon, "Look here, world! This is *me*, Lillian Waller Jackson! And you better get ready, goddammit, because I'm going to take you on! I'm going to blaze new paths and sail the world and go where no one has ever been!" She looked down at Emily with a wonderful smile. "That's our bond, Stollie. We dream big, and we should never forget that." Bending over, she scooped up some water and flung it on Emily, squealing with delight. "I baptize you in the name of this fucking Atlantic, just like when we cut our wrists and took the blood oath!" That roused Emily, and soon they were in a water fight. There on that huge ox of the ocean with the sun squandering itself on the briny deep, they reconfirmed their relationship—laughing, splashing each other, embracing as the boat rocked gently on that perfect day. They swore they would always be family, no matter what. And Emily's heart swelled with tenderness and pride for such a friend. Then, with all the wonder of the youthful heart, Lillian exclaimed, "I love you, Stollie. And everything's going to be rosy. I feel that in my bones. Being here like this makes me know this is the realest I can be, and the most honest too, because it's just me and it. The ocean tells the truth. And we should always try to be like that with each other."

Not long after Emily got back to school, her father called to say Dr. Weiss had given her a clean bill. "I talked to him this afternoon. He said last week when he saw you, you seemed to have made excellent progress. And he feels there's no compelling need to continue." He cleared his throat and went on. "I take it you've leveled with him about everything. Right, Emily?"

"Right, Dad," she lied, knowing exactly what he meant.

"Good. I don't want to get into that; but from what I can make out, you seem to be on the right track. What do you think?"

"I'm fine. I feel good."

"So now I can quit shelling out those big bucks, and you can get on with your life."

"Yes, I think so."

He seemed pleased, and she wanted to keep him that way. The conversation turned to California, where he was settled in now, and her trip to Maine. She tried to relax, but she felt strained. Charles's monthly phone contacts, made regularly over the last year, were usually a litany of his questions followed by her answers, like math problems where she always labored for the correct response. Even his letters were stilted: sermonic, with the word Daddy typed and over that the same word in script, or sometimes there was just an empty space. He meant well; but in this case, the equation of father and daughter didn't get any easier. She heard him ask, "So have you applied to Belle Adams yet?"

"I'm going to next week. I got some literature on it from the counseling office."

"Good. I'm calling a friend in Richmond who has some connections to state government. But you shouldn't have any problem. Your grades are darn good."

"Yes they are," she agreed. "I'm not worried. And I'm going to make the honor roll when I get in so I can transfer out in two years. Right, Dad?"

This seemed to vex him. "We've already been over that, Emily. You should know by now I live up to my part of a bargain. You just start out with a healthy attitude and meet lots of nice fellows and you'll be in good shape. Get a solid foundation and you can go where you please to graduate."

"I will."

"Before I forget it, are you going to your aunt's over Thanksgiving?"

"Do I have to?"

"Why do you act like it's such a chore? Your aunt bends over backward to do for you."

Uh oh. "I don't mean to, Dad."

"Well, I don't care. I won't be coming myself until Christmas, so you can stay there or spend it with a student. Just let me know. But stay in some kind of touch with your aunt. You hear me?"

"Yes."

"And plan to come Christmas."

"Okay." She hesitated. "Dad?"

"What?"

"Is Sheila going to be there then?"

"I don't know. Your sister's got her own life now in college. You just worry about yourself. The rest of it will come out in the wash."

A few more comments, and she hung up thrilled. She had always dreaded those secret trips to Hartford and having to put on airs with some man she instinctively felt funny around. So that, and hearing she was "officially" normal, was part of an overall positive beginning senior year. She made swim and fence teams and loved her long hours at *The Crimson Poet*. Fred Trim never phoned, but there were plenty of other boys to choose from.

There was one unnerving incident that semester. It involved a girl who had come to St. Joseph's this year. Her name was Stits Winder, and her humor played to the galleries, which Emily was to discover when she happened into Hilda's room one afternoon. "You know what you do if a dam breaks, don't you?" Stits was regaling an audience of several girls. "You stick your finger in the dyke. Get it? Not d-i-k-e! It's d-y-k-e!" she spelled. "Ha ha ha ha." Then, hunching up her shoulders, she did what she called an ape walk: lumbering about like a truck driver as she scratched her crotch and slobbered and everyone rolled on the floor hysterical.

But what was this word Stits kept saying? Dyke and queer. (Emily had a fit inside when she got that connection.) Dyke this one and queer that one. Queer gym teacher because Miss Ross's hair was short, and she played baseball. (Women were supposed to play softball, Stits explained.) And queer Dean Stevenson. Stevenson! someone gasped. "Maybe," Stits stressed. "She's not married is she? Neither is Ross or Necessary and some others too. Bet they go into New York a lot. What do you think they do *there*? They got queers coming out of the sidewalk in New York!" Everyone's eyes got big as swimming pools as Stits, obviously an authority on this awesome subject, said queers could be regular as rain. "That's why you have to watch yourself. They can be everywhere, like the air you breathe!"

She paused for *everywhere* to tickle their collective imaginations. Then she went on: "They're like vampires. They can't have kids so they have to recruit. And that could be you, miss," she looked right at Anne Hawk, who turned into a quiver of fear. "That could be any of you in this room. You could be in the shower and one comes in and sees you naked and jumps you and then you're queer too. I know 'cause my sister told me there was one in her college who looked like anyone but she could change into a queer. She was like a werewolf based on this chemical in her body that made her go after girls, and she finally got one and made her queer. My sister said the first queer was ugly as a mud fence with big gobs of hair hanging from her armpits and the other one got ugly too." At that, Stits recommenced her ape walk to everyone's hoots and howls, including Emily's.

Yet she was sick at heart and driven by insecurities. Was it fate that had brought Stits to St. Joseph's in the first place? Had she laughed hard enough? Did Stits suspect *her* of something? And what if she had some secret chemical in her body that, without awareness, might turn her temporarily into a werewolf? Not an animal with fangs or hair, but driven at a full moon by unconscious impulses she too could go mad: she would wake up and find herself attacking some girl. My God!

Then would come memories of Dr. Weiss. Surely if she were like a werewolf he wouldn't have told her father she was okay. That was the proof.

But just in case, Emily began acting even more boy crazy. And any time the word queer came up, she went out of her way to make fun and sometimes do the ape walk too.

Before Christmas word came that Lillian and her mother had compromised. "I've decided to be an archaeologist," she wrote Emily authoritatively. "I've done some research, and it's now my second interest next to being a sailor because they let you explore and dig up stuff from the ground. I'll get to travel, and Mom's happy cause she says an archaeologist is more important than studying the ocean. I feel good about it. I've applied to three schools. My favorite is Womack College because it's in New York, so maybe you can transfer there junior year and take English."

In February not long after Emily got her acceptance into Belle Adams she received an excited call that followed up on that earlier letter. "Guess what!" Lillian's words tumbled out in a fury. "I'm going to be a doctorate!"

"A *what*?"

"A doctorate, stupid. I'm getting a Ph.D."

"Whoa! Slow down!"

Emily could hear her suck in her breath. "What I'm saying is I got into Womack and it's connected to GAI, Gunther Archaeological Institute, in New York too. So I'll be going to Womack four years, then two more at GAI, and that's when I'll be a doctorate. It's B.A., M.A., and Ph.D. I'll be *Doctor* Jackson. What do you think? I'm gonna have it engraved on a seal and send it to everyone I know: Lillian Waller Jackson, *Doctorate.* And guess what else?"

"What?"

"I'll be traveling all over. Both of them, Womack and GAI,

they send you on a million field trips for credit for maybe a year at a time, Peru, South America, Brazil. Everywhere!"

Emily's heart fell. "So where does that leave me if I come to New York and you're in Outer Mongolia?"

"Oh, we'll cross that bridge when we get to it," Lillian sputtered. "I won't be gone all the time. Just you finish up at Belle Adams and come on to New York."

"Maybe I could go to Womack too."

"Columbia's better in English. I asked one of my counselors. We don't have to be in the same school anyway. We'll get an apartment together. Won't that be something? We'll stay loaded for weeks!"

"Yeah. And go to a racetrack!"

"And nightclubs. Who's to stop us?"

"And your mom's okay about it?"

"Mom's happy as a lark about my being a doctorate. She says it's real prestige. I told you, Stollie—it's all working out."

"Great."

"So you'll be up in August?"

"For sure. After summer school I'm going to my grandmother's and then I'll see you in Maine."

Thus the year wound down smoothly. Her Georgia visit was different this time though. Instead of dating a lot, she helped Ora Lu look after her grandmother. Then after a brief stopover in Newport News, she was in Maine. Her parting with Lillian two weeks later was sweet but sad too. Now more than ever they were about to set forth into the wild blue yonder of adulthood.

September 1950, Emily entered Belle Adams College.

COLLEGE YEARS

. . . I wasn't to see much of Lillian the next four years; we were each too caught up in our own lives. However, in the background (though neither of us could know the effects of this at the time), she continued to exert her quiet but critical influence on my life . . .

Belle Adams was a more sophisticated version of St. Joseph's, and Emily a far more seasoned performer than the other freshmen. At least that was her thought when she met her new roommates, Claire Tremble, Lois Dugan, Bobbe Chase. They had never been away from home, but she had. She knew about dorms, housemothers, student council members who ratted if you broke a rule. She was accustomed to huge dining areas and girls cloned in tailored shirts with small eyes of white collars peeking over their cardigans. She was used to having her own mailbox and her name engraved on her checks. Taken as a whole, she had already made the adjustments to institutional living. And the good news was she would be much freer at Belle Adams: Charles, pleased with her grades and the reports from Dr. Weiss, had given her blanket permission to leave any weekend she chose. The leaf of adolescence was finally falling, bringing her closer to Liberation Age, twenty-one. The girl Aunt Francie drove to Fricksburg early September 1950 was vastly changed from the sad child her father had dumped in Cromley two years previous. She was actually looking forward to college.

Her major was liberal arts, with a concentration in modern poetry. Her professors were the smartest people she had ever met. They could memorize entire class rosters by looking at their students once. They had impressive initials after their names, and there were decidedly more of them than at private school. In truth, there was more of everything here—more students, more work, more of an emphasis on conformity. In the 1950s women mainly went to college to find husbands. And clearly the state of Virginia did not disappoint. There was the Quantico marine base sixty minutes from Fricksburg; the University of Virginia (U.Va.) in Charlottesville; and Washington, D.C., a two-hour drive north. Of these, U.Va. was the most popular. Ninety miles east, it was the playground for the bored and horny. On weekends, it swarmed with women students screaming their heads off, tossing beer cans out the window, determined to lose their minds for twenty-four hours straight. All week they had been cooped up with "their kind," so the logic went. Now, surrounded by men, they could hang loose. And loose they hung. They got to Charlottesville and hit the ground running. They made out in showers, on beds and tabletops, sprawled along corridors, wherever they found space. They got crocked and danced till their legs gave out as the earth turned into an elevator and some frat brother jumped about with a lampshade on his head, his pants unzipped, eager for love—or love's shadow.

The nation's capital was something else. Belle Adams's girls stayed at the local Y for five dollars a night under the special arrangements the YWCA had with area women's colleges. From the Y they came and went as they pleased. Where they pleased were the cocktail lounges of the hotels, notably the Sheraton, the jazz digs along Fourteenth, the fancy pubs off Dupont Circle, and Georgetown. In Washington the military replaced God. They were everywhere, glittering like eyes in a peacock's tail. And Emily, who soon found U.Va. boring, started going up with friends. An officer in spitclean boots and ribbons was much more impressive than a fraternity boy.

And the past? The White River house had been sold by now; Frankie had been given to neighbors, and her own bad memories she repressed as much as possible. She had to in order to keep her balance. She had to believe that what had happened with her and Mattie had been an aberration, something that had attacked her when she wasn't looking, a happening so random and so unwarranted that its chances of recurrence had about the same odds as a building falling on her when she walked down the street. In large part this distancing was helped because Emily didn't see her father that often, or her sister, either, who, by-the-by, was engaged now to a law student attending a college near the University of Vermont, where Sheila was a junior. The fiancé's name was Sam Hoffman. He was from Fargo, North Dakota; and Sheila spent most of her free time with him in places far from Newport News. If ever her visit to Aunt Francie's overlapped with Emily's, however, they avoided each other as much as possible. And when that wasn't possible, they maintained a tight-lipped civility so as to keep Aunt Francie in the dark.

As for Emily's evolving personality, it still bore traces of Mattie, particularly around the opposite sex. But she had another side too. Emily was becoming a curious mix of flirt and tomboy. Around boys she was more passive and dressed to the hilt. With girls, though, she was witty, loud, she took pride in her physical stamina, she wrote poems, some over thirty pages long, that no one, including herself, understood, and reveled in (even helped perpetuate) the rumor that she was a genius. To that end she used big words, sometimes affecting a limp which she called gout because it sounded mysterious. Hearkening to her old days with Mattie, she identified herself as an existentialist—which meant, she said, "one who believes in existence as the basis for truth." She also wore sunglasses in the dorm, relied on long cigarette holders to appear dramatic, let it be known she expected to die young like Keats because she was gifted and intense. All this commanded popularity. Her first Christmas she received four invitations to various classmates' homes. She chose to spend it in Roanoke with Bobbe Chase, who drank like a fish. Then she joined her father and Aunt Francie in Newport News. No sooner there than Alice Means, an old Macon friend of her grandmother's, phoned that Nana had died of a coronary arrest brought on by a violent attack of asthma. Charles told her she should represent the family since she had been the only one really close to Amelia Carver, and she left immediately for the funeral.

December twenty-ninth Emily stood at Fair Oaks Cemetery as her grandmother's body was about to be lowered into the ground. Next to her, Ora Lu was shaking and sobbing. Emily squeezed her hand; ashamed, the old woman, rather than sit beside her in Macon's ivoried congregation, had stood in back, her kinky white hair topping off a body dark as the inside of a hole. For over forty years she had fetched and carried for "Miz Meelie," never coming through the front door of the house, never eating at the same table (though they had been closer than sisters), never forgetting her black place in the scheme of things; and she wasn't about to change today: she wouldn't sit in the white folks' church or ride in their hearse either. The open-aired cemetery was more democratic, though. And now Emily pressed her hand again and stared at the coffin. For a moment she saw her grandmother, not caked in death but vigorous, lifegiving: arms akimbo, imperial eyes above the familiar black chiffon over a long soot-colored slip and dark stockings that fed into the most serious black shoes Emily had ever seen. Why, she thought guiltily now, hadn't she stayed with her longer this summer?

When the burial ended, she said good-bye to Ora Lu and her son Tyrone, who had brought his mother here, as well as to some of Nana's friends. Then she returned to the Meads, who had been too infirm to attend. She spent the night talking about the old days in Macon. In the morning, after saying she was leaving for home, she checked into a downtown hotel. As if to keep Nana close, she was about to relive a girlhood ritual. Now she walked to the courthouse near the movie theaters where once upon an innocent time she would see her beloved cowboy matinees. She stood waiting for bus number 1. When it came she rode to Four Corners, where she used to buy her Fudgsicles—nothing better than swallowing them whole and chewing on the stick! From Four Corners she changed to number 7, which motored past mansions that swaggered with moss and wrap-around verandas, then straight to "Niggertown," the last leg before Nana's and the part of the journey she had always found fascinating. As a girl she would take a window seat and gaze intently at the children outside, "darkies" they were called then. Usually barefoot and dressed in faded cloth, they would squat by the side of the road giggling and playing marbles while their elders scrambled onto the bus—matrons in churchgoing hats, men who might have boarded just to be doing something. They all sat in the rear talking quietly among themselves, seldom looking a white person in the face as they passed. Nothing sealed the separate worlds of the South as much as this, but it made no sense to Emily. She didn't understand why Nana forbade her to call a black woman a "lady" or to offer her seat to one if the bus were full. Years ago she had done just that to a woman so frail it looked as if a good wind could have knocked her sideways. The driver, Emily suddenly remembered, brought the bus to a full halt and ordered her to *sit back down!*

Now, as the bus lumbered through these familiar sights, she watched anew. It was unseasonably warm, and people were milling about on the road. Through the window she could see the leggy hi yallas, their bosoms swinging in the breeze of sex as they walked, a pile of laundry on one hip and a dancey-eyed baby on the other. String-skinny dogs lay next to flies that gloated on swoons of manure, and old-timers in baggy overalls still slapped each other's hands as they talked gleefully, knee-grabbing in the way she had always seen them, as if their whole bodies, caught up in some splendid variance of their own and with almost a philosophical deference to the facts of life, had no will or imagination left, just yes-yessed through time with their hands out, talking slow as molasses, laughing from some secret white folk would never know. She could see the unpainted porches, the rockers from which the denizens of this neglected culture still spat their tobacco and swapped their southern lies. In the summers it would get so hot the bugs would roll over with their legs straight up; and on the paved streets beyond, one could fry eggs. She got lost in reverie until she recognized Nana's street. She pulled the cord and got out at Coz Lane. She walked half a block and then was in front of the house that shortly would pass into strangers' hands. There was the stately magnolia where Nana used to deliver her rules for ladyhood: Ladies never sat less than six inches from the back of their chairs. They took small bites. They walked on the balls of their feet *first*. They didn't mention body parts (to the opposite sex they never admitted to having any). They refrained from burping, sweating, breaking wind. They had no interest in sports, politics, science. To Emily none of that was important, but she would listen politely. She never talked back to Nana.

Now she walked to the backyard and stood quietly as the lawn parties came alive in her head. It was here that many of the civilized ladies of Macon would gather to speak of the white race, their husbands, and God according to the Baptist Church. They would sip sweet tea as the wind drew small parentheses on the surface of their drinks, and "Little Missus Emily," as the society page would dub her, would sing "Big Rock Candy Mountain," basking in adult approval, clapping, sucking on ice cubes to keep her brains from melting. Memory's eye resaw all this. Memory's eye closed, and she walked back to the front, feeling as if she had lost something irretrievable. Never would she move through Nana's rooms again or sit by Nana's large bay window eating her favorite tomato sandwiches that dripped mayo and salt. Nor would she read *Mary Marie,* the book about a girl whose parents divorced and when she was with her father she was Mary, and when she was with her mother she was Marie, and what Emily had wanted was that they would all be together forever. Much of her childhood's longing was done here; and in a way, Nana's death ended an innocence. Yet something precious about this claimed her still, as if her spirit belonged to these lyrical trees, these smells of lilac and hyacinth, this lure from the same muddy red banks that called her now: the South of the doomed and the durable, the South of the bleeding hands and feet. The South was a switch illuminating some raw need in Emily, and as quickly it seemed to answer that need: she felt at home here. Was that why she was so overcome at this moment? Was it because her mother, and now Nana, rested in Georgian soil that she felt she too must remain in the South?

Refreshed, she returned to the hotel. Next morning she bought three lilies and went by cab to Fair Oaks Cemetery. She had the driver wait as she climbed the small hill to the graves of her grandparents and Marian Carver. It had been raining; but as she placed a lily on each slab, the ground still freshly disturbed from yesterday's burial, the sun peeked out from the clouds. She lingered a bit, then took the taxi to the airport for her flight to Roanoke where, with friends, she welcomed in 1951 before returning to Belle Adams.

She met First Lieutenant Gary Vento the second semester of her freshman year at the Sheraton cocktail lounge one February weekend when she came in with two other girls. He was drinking with some friends at a nearby table. As often happened, they all began talking; and before she realized what was going on, he had wedged in between her and one of her friends and was asking her where she was from, how did she like D.C., did she come here often—the usual. What was unusual, however, was his looks. Distinctively handsome, dark soulful eyes, the kind of skin that never burns no matter how much sun it swallows.

An Italian, he defined himself proudly as though he were the last of a breed. He told her he was stationed at Fort Eustis, Virginia (which happened to be only twenty miles from Newport News), and he was in Washington until Easter on official business. It didn't take him long to reveal that General Patton was his hero, war was the fire in his belly, he had selected the army because its colors were green for the grass, brown for the earth, red for the blood a soldier sheds for his country. He had white gloves, lieutenant bars, ribbons, his shoes were as shiny as the stars; and all she could think was how impressive that he had chosen *her*. So when he invited her to dinner, and alone, she accepted happily. He was an officer and a gentleman and she would meet her friends back at the Y.

They went to an Italian restaurant near the White House. They sat at a booth, drank, and he mainly talked while she listened. Did she know how pretty she was, he asked at one point, leaning forward to trace her cheek with his finger.

Hoping she wouldn't do something imperfect, she replied, "No, not really," as he continued to stare at her intently.

"Well, you should."

She just sat there smiling.

"You going with anyone in particular?"

"No. Not really."

"What does that mean?"

"It means we all go down to U.Va. a lot and have fun, but there's no one special."

"Ah, U.Va.," he sighed. "Big party school, I hear."

"You heard right."

"You a party girl?"

Mouth quick-as-a-trigger lapsed into slow motion. What should she say? She didn't want him to think her a dud. But she didn't want to give the wrong idea either. "No," she inched out on the conversational tightrope. "I don't really like parties that much."

Teasingly, "What *do* you like?"

Her mind went blank. "I don't know."

"Come on. Don't kid a kidder. What do you *like*?"

Should she say books or any of that junk? She answered, "I like lots of things."

"What's one?"

"Traveling."

"What's another?"

"Coming up here. I like Washington."

"What about Charlottesville?"

"It's okay."

"So why didn't you go there this weekend?"

So many questions. "Because I prefer it here. I like cities."

"But the point I'm getting at," his eyelids drooped a little, "is it's destiny. It's got to be."

"What is?"

"You. Me. Meeting like this. I wasn't going to the damn Sheraton tonight. But a little bird told me to and I did and there you were alone. That's destiny."

"I wasn't alone. I was with my friends."

"You know what I mean. You didn't have a date."

"Well," she replied with spunk. "Just 'cause you don't have a date doesn't mean you're alone." She sat back, surprised at her answer. Was she being too cocky?

"Fair enough," Gary smiled, leaning over to light her Chesterfield. She inhaled and waited for him to do or say something so she could react. The waiter came with the house salad. Gary ordered steaks; and after the waiter left, Emily just kept sitting there with an attentive expression. Nervous. Once her cigarette ash got too long and fell on her lettuce but luckily Gary had turned to order more drinks and she was able to put the lettuce on the seat beside her before he noticed. She was never sure of herself with a man, never secure about her looks or personality or how to balance on that fine line between sexy and respectable. She didn't want to go to bed with him. She just wanted him to want her. She fretted about that now as the food came and the room spun a bit, the beer-balloons inflating her brains, smiling at him as he ate and spoke and she watched his hands, the delicate forest of hairs just beneath the knuckles. Better not get too smashed, she thought, dying to get back to the Y to tell her friends.

Gary was talking about Washington again, his favorite city. Did she know the architect who designed Paris had designed this town too? "It's called the quatrefoil plan," he explained. "The whole layout is built on circles with four areas converging in them. That's why you've got all these fountains and rotaries all measured from the Capitol. It's beautiful, but man, it gets hot here." They discussed the weather, a bit more about college and the military. When the check came, Gary paid and asked if she wanted a night cap. Of course, she answered. They walked past the White House up Pennsylvania Avenue to his car, a long green Buick with an American flag on the antenna. From there, they followed M Street to the Key Bridge that led to Alexandria, and in no time were pulling into a place called The Fox-Hole. Gary cut the motor off and asked if she had ever read *The Red Badge of Courage.* She reminded him she was an English major.

"So you've read it. Right?"

"Right," she answered.

"Well do you remember that main character . . . what's his name . . . Harry?"

"You mean Henry."

"Yeah, Henry. That's it. Henry saves the day. Do you think he had guts?"

"Well, yes," she wavered. "Didn't he?"

"Hell, no. That wasn't guts. That was a good case of adrenaline. Ol' Henry was smockered scared, so he grabs the Confederate flag and charges to the front. And that's the ball game. You know," he rubbed his chin thoughtfully, and gave her a searching look, "battle tests a man like love tests a woman. You savvy?"

She said she was, but she wasn't sure. He got out and opened the door and led her inside. A baboon in a plaid jacket was singing into a mike with his eyes shut. "Probably thinks he's Sinatra," Gary snickered. They took a rear table and ordered drinks: sat there close as could be now, Larry's thigh right up against hers, his watchband clasping his olive-complexioned wrist, his breath smelling of Dentyne. She could see his nostrils flair as he breathed. Then, putting one arm around her shoulders, he picked up that earlier talk in the parking lot and said, "You know, I got this philosophy that women do the loving in the world and men the fighting and it's the same for both. It takes courage and sacrifice on both sides."

Nothing particular to say to that so she just sat there. His arm was still around her, and the other hand held hers. They had a few more drinks as they listened to the band in its madness and the baboon seducing the mike again. Later he drove her to the Y and parked nearby. Gary loosened his tie. Then he pulled her close, sliding beneath her so that she ended up straddling him with her dress hiked above the knees. He brought her face to his; his mouth covered hers tight as a suction cup, his tongue opened her lips, his hands caressed her breasts. Before she realized it, he had removed her bra, her breasts were falling into his suction, his tongue was visiting each nipple as his fingers crept toward her crotch. That sobered her. "No!" she cried, managing to get off.

Quietly he watched her rehook her bra and straighten her skirt. When she finished, he took her hand and brought it to his fly. He unzipped his trousers and placed her hand inside. She let him do it, what the heck, her head was swimming again and he was so gorgeous. Besides, she had never touched a penis, she was curious: it was out of his pants and hidden in the folds of the night. It came to as he guided her fingers to the top, then down to his balls that were soft and willing. He squeezed her hand over them and moaned. He brought her hand back to his penis again, moving it gently up and down until something oozed from the crack and it melted, but she didn't want to see the wet. He released her hand and cleaned himself with a handkerchief. Then he stuffed himself in his pants, rezipped, and leaned back with his eyes nearly closed. She waited quietly, not sure what to do, feeling some of his liquid on her fingers, which she rubbed in the seat. She said, "I best be going in now." He didn't answer except to ask if she was a virgin. Her yes seemed to please him. As he walked her to the door of the Y, they arranged to meet the next Saturday at Figaro's, the same Italian restaurant where they had had dinner tonight.

Thus it began. Not long after their first meeting, Emily asked Gary if she could wear his lieutenant bars. He gave her a set that she displayed constantly. Those bars in fact became far more important than he. They were a proof of her value. They gave her an almost palpable sense of well-being. They meant she was attractive and worthwhile, and she wanted everyone to see them. She wore them on sweaters, pajama tops, jackets. She wrote Lillian about them. When Gary, in exchange for a small snapshot of herself, gave her a flattering one of him, she immediately mailed it to Lillian with instructions to send it right back; and when Lillian did, Emily put his picture on her bureau and basked in her friends' reactions. She made up stories of Gary's great love for her. Knowing news would travel to Charles and Sheila, she wrote Aunt Francie about this dashing young officer she couldn't wait to bring to Newport News. Yet for all this, she never really trusted Gary's feelings, she never really relaxed in his company. But those were small prices to pay for his attentions.

For a succession of Saturdays they met at Figaro's. He would be there first; and when she approached his table, he would rise and extend a flower, saying a rose for a rose or something corny. But to Emily such a grand and dramatic manner was thrilling. They would sit and eat or drink, perhaps later meet friends. But the evening always ended up the same: in Gary's car parked near the Y making out. It was a time when a girl could decline intercourse and get away with it. She could say she had her period or was afraid she might get pregnant no matter how careful everything was or, better, she wanted to wait until marriage. And that's what Emily did even as Gary protested he was falling in love, implying too she was lucky to have him because he could get any woman he wanted. He also said intercourse made a girl a woman.

The problem was she wanted to want sex more than she actually did. On their second date, she came when he fondled her breasts (the extent to which she would allow familiarity). She knew it was an orgasm because she had experienced those same heartstopping sensations with Mattie. Yet with Mattie one orgasm had led to another; right up to Sheila's screams, there had been a series of bodily explosions so potent as to part mind from flesh until all she was was flesh. Yet with Gary after she climaxed she craved being left alone. And it wasn't that he lacked sensitivity. But when she came, alienation followed even as she tried not to feel that, forcing herself to relieve him as he wanted. Later, in the safety of her own bed, she would refuse to entertain any sexual comparisons with Mattie. She was just inexperienced, she told herself. In time it would all work out. And funny, but the more she rejected the ultimate act with Gary, the more he seemed to want her, as if to say: No problem. I'll break you down. I've got all the time in the world.

Then a couple of weeks before spring break, Gary asked to drive her to Newport News, where she was spending two days before joining friends at Myrtle Beach for a summer-job interview. He was going back to Fort Eustis that same day, so he could swing by and pick her up around noon, April seventeenth.

April seventeenth, and she waited for Gary in the lobby of her dorm. It was now after twelve-thirty, and she was starting to get anxious. If he didn't show up, how was she supposed to get to Newport News? She flipped through a magazine as two girls walked by with suitcases. "Emily!" one called with a friendly smile. "Haven't you left yet?"

"Nope. My ride's late."

"Well, have a good one!"

"You too." She watched them exit through the front door just as her name came on the loudspeaker. She had a phone call. She grabbed her purse and dashed into the reception area. It was Gary, running late. He would be there in about forty-five minutes.

She hung up and went into the ladies' room and stared in the mirror. It was that cheap glass commonly found in carnivals, and it stretched her face like an accordion. She edged in closer to get a truer perspective and noticed her hair was flat on top. She fluffed it up and put on more lipstick; then she examined her eyes. Last week Claire Tremble, who was always paying her compliments, said she had the deepest eyes she had ever seen, that the Greeks believed the eyes were the windows to the soul; and if that were true, considering hers of deepest royal blue, she must have some terrific piece of cake under her skin, she thought now, trying to make them profound and deep, going from pensive to smiles and watching her eyes change with those different moods. She noticed lipstick on her front tooth and removed it, then rubbed her lieutenant bars with the same tissue to make them sparkle. Finished, she went back to the lobby and began a letter to Lillian. Her father had died of a heart attack recently, and she and her mother were in Maine over spring vacation.

April 17, 1951

Dearest Lil,

It was good talking to you, and I'm so sorry about your dad. I'm waiting for Gary now to pick me up to take me to Aunt Francie's, and I just wanted to tell you again how tough I know it must be, especially since I lost my grandmother over Christmas. But it's probably for the best since you said he never really got over his first attack. Please give your mom my best. I bet you must feel a big load on your shoulders, but it'll be okay. Is your mom really going to live with her cousin in England or stay in Maine or what? Well it'll work out. I'm thinking about you!

Listen, way to go about being picked for that expedition to Mexico this summer. Sort of makes my job in Myrtle Beach look stupid. Can you see *me* waiting tables!! But it pays twenty-five dollars a week, plus tips, and it sure beats summer school. My friend here at school knows the man who owns the place right on the boardwalk. So hopefully that's where I'll be. Gary and I are okay, and he'll probably come down. That is if he ever picks me up today!!!

I really hope you and I can find some time to see each other before long, but it gets so damn busy. I was thinking the other day, Lil, it's really happening—we're really growing up, and I can't wait till we're in New York together. You know, in spite of everything you're still my best friend in the world!

Tell your aunt hi, and remember me to your mom. My heart goes out to both of you with your dad gone and all, and I send best love,

Emily

She had just signed off when Gary walked in. He was wearing a khaki shirt open at the neck, under a dark green sweater vest. His hair was longer, and he looked terrific. Too bad, she thought, no one could see them as they left together, his arm casually slung around her neck.

From the time Gary picked her up he was unusually attentive: holding her hand, saying he had missed her more than ever this week and how she made every woman he knew look like peanuts. Why, he hadn't been able to look at another girl since they met, he declared, taking her picture from his shirt pocket and giving it a kiss. Then, his voice becoming quite serious, he said his orders had just come through. That's why he'd been late; he had had to stop at the Pentagon before he left Washington. He had known it would just be a matter of time but thought he would have made it through the summer without getting shipped out. "You join this man's army and you stay on call," he said. "I'll be leaving in two days, first to Seattle to tell the folks good-bye, then San Fran, then it's a straight ticket to Korea!"

She had a sudden pang of disappointment when he told her this. But then as they kept talking about fate, things like that, writing each other, meeting when he returned in about a year, it occurred to Emily his going wasn't such a bad idea at all. She had his lieutenant bars and his picture. She could meet him at the airport when his tour of duty ended. She could see him coming down the ramp in his officer's hat and ribbons and her running into his arms: *My* lieutenant! Now *that* was something!

She heard him say he had joined up to see action and that her picture would protect him. He would keep it right over his heart when he went to battle. "Remember what I told you the first time we met? I said men do the fighting and women the loving and that it all boils down to the same objective—keeping each other alive." He left Emily to ponder the profundity of that remark as his fingers began routing their way from her hand toward her knee, moving like a deer approaching a highway—a few paces forward, then stopping to sniff for danger. Before long, his hand was breathing over her kneecap. At first that distracted her, his hand lying so close to fingerbowl-heaven as they kept talking of this and that; but as time passed and it stayed put, she relaxed and began visualizing their reunion again. She could hardly wait for Aunt Francie to see what he looked like!

Around six they stopped for food and drinks; and by the time they were back on the road (and now not that far from Newport News) dusk had settled into the heavens. Suddenly Gary brought up Old Needle Point. When he found out she had never been there, he couldn't believe it. He said, "It's only about twenty minutes from your aunt's. You've *got* to see it. Do you know they call it the diamond of the East Coast? It's got a hotel on it called the Chambers, where Edgar Allan Poe used to read his stuff on the deck overlooking Norfolk. I've even dreamt of honeymooning there if I ever met the right girl." When he said those words, he looked right through to her soul, his eyes softening.

"You like Poe?" he asked. She nodded. "You know that poem 'Annabel Lee'?" She nodded again. " '*She* was a child and *I* was a child,' " he quoted dramatically, " 'In this kingdom by the sea, / But we loved with a love that was more than love— / I and my Annabel Lee— / With a love that the wingéd seraphs of Heaven / Coveted her and me.' You didn't know I liked poetry, did you?" he laughed, seeing her surprise. "Well there's a lot you don't know about me. Did you know that no matter how calm, cool, and collected I might *seem* talking about Korea, I'm not kidding myself: I might be just another statistic coming back. You can't tell when your number's up. Boy, it sure hurts like hell leaving when things are so good between us." He looked at her again, and she didn't speak; she wasn't sure how she felt.

"Emily," he squeezed her hand, "we're like that poem. We could love like that—you know, with a love greater than love." He slowed the car down and fastened his eyes on hers for as long as possible without driving off the road. "Listen, I told you I've got two more days in this neck of the woods, and you can't count the second, I'll be all tied up at the base. So spend the night with me, darling. Let's go to the Chambers Hotel. Give us that. Don't worry. I'd never try anything you don't want. You can trust me. You know that. That's my word as an officer. Okay?" He glanced over to give her an honest look. "I just need to be close to you tonight." Were those tears glimmering in his eyes? The car speeded up. He talked a little about how much he cared for her, the fun they would have. Ahead she saw a sign, NEWPORT NEWS II MILES, and a road veering off to the right. But he passed on by.

"Gary! You just missed the turn!"

"I know. We're going to Old Needle Point. It's just thirty minutes from Newport News. I'll take you there in the morning."

"But I can't do that," she protested. "My aunt's expecting me."

"So call her. Tell her you had car trouble." His hand was back on her knee, pressing the flesh persuasively: Come on knee, the hand seemed to be saying. We've got lots to talk about. "You afraid of me, Emily?"

"No, of course not," she huffed, as if such an emotion were beneath her.

"Well good, because you know damn well there's no reason to be." His hand continued talking to her knee, caressing the kneecap, lightly touching the skin just below the hem. And she didn't pull away. She could have. At the Cork Rotary she could have jumped out or yelled or hit him over the head with her purse. But there was no need. Gary wasn't a rapist. He had never taken advantage. Besides, he loved her. He said every woman was a peanut next to her. And maybe she loved him too. Maybe Gary was who she'd been waiting for and here was her chance to find out for sure. At that moment, Emily felt this was true. The beers from the dinner made her head sweet. She felt almost motherly as his hurt, wounded-deer–like expression touched all her best instincts. Okay, her knee said back to his hand. I'll do it and get it over with for god's sake!

Twenty minutes later Emily was phoning her aunt from a booth at the Chambers Hotel as Gary checked them in. She told her aunt the car had broken down and she was spending the night at a friend's in Portsmouth. She would see her in the morning.

She hung up and returned to the lobby. Everything was taken care of and he had ordered room service, Gary said as they followed the bellhop to the elevator.

But did that bellhop know they weren't married? Did she look like a whore?

The bellhop had just walked out when Gary emerged from the bathroom saying he had left his briefcase in the car and would be right back. She went to the toilet herself, came out, and surveyed the interior. The room was small, with blue and white striped wallpaper, golden tassels on the green rug, a Bible on the bureau, and a coin massage machine beside the bed. She went over to the window and looked across the bay at the jewels of Norfolk lighting up the sky. A full moon lay on the water. To the left of that was a pier surrounded by boats, and in the distance a huge barge passed noiselessly. So beautiful, but she didn't feel beautiful. I must have been crazy to come here, she thought.

She turned the radio on. Dick Haymes was singing about Laura, and she quickly turned it off. She didn't need any mood music tonight. She heard Gary opening the door. He entered with two bottles of champagne. He said he'd taken them from the bellhop to save the guy the trip. He set his briefcase down and came over with glasses, stopping to dim the bedlight and turn off the lamp. For a while they watched the moon travel the water outside. They smoked, drank, Emily brought up Alger Hiss, whom she had been reading about in *Time* magazine, Gary's favorite source of news, which she always tried to read before seeing him. Increasingly she was getting nervous about being in this room, so she kept drinking and running her mouth as if Alger Hiss could keep them out of bed.

But suddenly Gary was up and bending over her, resting his forehead on hers. "My," he bantered, "aren't we the little chatterbox tonight." Before she could respond, he had pulled her to her feet and was straining his pelvis against hers, then backing her toward the bed.

"No, please," she said faintly when she felt the edge. "I don't want to." He was kissing her passionately, trying to get her sweater over her head. "No," she protested again. "I'm tired." But then persuaded by the drinks and not wishing to make him mad, she gave in, raising her arms meekly over her head like a child.

"There's a good girl," he murmured softly, slipping the sweater off, unhooking her bra as her breasts filled the room. "Gorgeous!" He sat her down on the bed, running his fingers over her nipples. "I could eat them alive." He knelt and moved his mouth from one to the other as her body said no, yes, maybe so. Jesus! Could her grandmother see from heaven? She pushed his head away and got herself to the center of the bed. Saying he liked a girl who gave him a hard time, he followed, attempting to remove the rest of her clothes. "Just let me feel your body against mine," he coaxed when she kept resisting.

"You won't do anything I don't want?"

"No. I've already told you."

"Promise?"

"Yes. What do you want? A contract?"

"I just don't want to go all the way."

"Fine," he answered, sounding a little tense. She sat there feeling about as sexy as a dish rag, but no longer fighting him. He said, "I'll be right back." He got up and she slid under the covers.

She could hear his cuff links hit the glass counter. She could see the shadow of his body as he took off his shirt and sweater vest, stepping out of his trousers and placing them delicately on the back of the chair. She heard him fumble with something and looked away, wondering what to do about her half slip and stockings and underpants. Maybe they would just hold each other like he said. He was back and under the covers now, all naked inches pressing into hers; he started undressing her. After saying once more she didn't want intercourse, she let him. He was all business, not talking, all to the task driven, all running his hands over her white river of skin, and her thinking, Well, he promised, but not sure she could trust him, trying to feel that mix of power and powerlessness which is the contradiction of sex.

He was sucking her breasts again and she got hot. Oh, go on, do it; who would know? She forgot to worry about a rubber and how she felt after orgasm, she found herself surrendering to the pleasurable sensations in her breasts, thinking, I'll come, he'll come, we'll come together and be done with it, then sleep and in the morning rise whole and perfect to eat cornflakes in clean bowls and stroll in the curing light, watching the holy keeper of the seas, the wind, blow the gulls seaward, and this fear and cheapness I feel now will be over!

Reality! His hand was near her middle, moving to her pubic hair, settling there momentarily as if to get its bearing and then slowly opening her up; his fingers were trying to get inside her vagina. She didn't want that. She clamped her legs together with great strength. He said, "It's okay." He said it again, more harshly, "I told you, dammit; I have something on. Here!" He brought her hand to his penis and she felt the thin protection. "But what if it breaks?"

"It won't."

"But I heard they can."

"That's crazy. Not if you know what you're doing. Relax!" Gingerly she did, and he was able to slide two fingers inside. "You're dry as a bone!" He took his fingers out, spat on them, reinserted them, repeating, "Just relax. This is going to feel great."

"I don't want to do it." She felt like crying.

"What do you mean? What's wrong with you?"

"There's nothing wrong with me." Was there something wrong with her? No. It was just the principle of the thing. "You promised you'd do what I wanted."

"Goddammit. I told you. I've got a rubber on."

"But you said . . . "

"I said shit!"

"But you did, Gary. You said if it . . . "

"Okay! Okay! I don't want a fucking lecture!" He pulled out and began feeling her up once more, kissing her armpits, caressing her breasts, again trying to go inside but licking his fingers before he reassumed that objective. "You really are a virgin, aren't you," he exclaimed when he got back in her. That seemed to excite him. Now he was on top of her, spreading her legs with his, raising up enough to open her with his fingers. He got his penis in just at the very edge; at which point, as if aroused from a stupor, Emily sat up with a mighty exertion, and his penis slipped out of her vagina. "Fucking A . . ." He was on his knees now, tearing the rubber off furiously. Grabbing her hands, he put one on each side of her breasts and pushed them together. "I want you to do this!" he growled. "At least *this*! I'm going to stick my cock through you here, and you press on it. Got it? Press hard!" At that, he squeezed in like a hot dog supported by two buns and started pumping for all he was worth until the movement assumed its own rhythm. She lay open-eyed, applying as much pressure on herself as she could until his semen shot on her skin and he rolled off to the side. Now they lay completely unentangled. Was this it? After a while he began snoring.

She got out of bed and tiptoed to the toilet, carrying her underwear. She locked the door and ran the tap lightly so as not to disturb him, washing herself hard, breasts and between her legs, to get all the semen out even though she knew he hadn't penetrated. Still, she was so paranoid about getting pregnant, and so ignorant of all the things involved, that if she could have taken her vagina out of her like a shelf and turned it upside down to drain every possible drop of wetness out, she would have. Satisfied, she dried herself, then put her underwear back on, pants, bra, slip, wrapped herself in a large bath towel, and returned to bed. There before the champagne steered her into oblivion, she had a vague idea of inviting Gary to supper tomorrow at her aunt's and making him some goulash.

The shower woke her. She was in bed alone. Nine A.M. the clock radio said. Before long the bathroom door opened, and Gary moved soundlessly over the carpet. She partially opened her eyes and saw him by the desk stepping into his trousers. She closed her eyes again listening to papers rustle, his movements back and forth, the floor creak. Should she say something? After what seemed hours she heard the unmistakable click of the door. That brought her straight up in bed. She looked around the room. His bag and valise were gone. She stood up and, draping herself in the towel, rushed to the door near desperate to run after him; but when she looked out, the hall was empty. She closed the door and stood beside it, crushed and uncertain. Maybe he was having coffee. So should she get dressed and wait?

Oh, don't be stupid, she answered herself. If he were coming back, why would he have taken his things? To hell with him. She walked around looking for a note. Found none. Went to the window and stared out on a clear day: boats, and gulls chasing them like food; below, some workmen putting chairs around the pool. Idly she watched until she realized her head was aching, so she got some aspirin from her purse and sat back down, for the first time wondering what the hell she was going to tell Aunt Francie. Oh, she'd just say they had had an argument or he had been called to an emergency and she had taken a cab. She got a cigarette but didn't have a light, and then in the trash she saw a book of matches that she pulled out. It read "Sheraton Hotel, Washington, D.C."; and there was a smudge of orange lips on the cover. Well, it wasn't hers. She didn't wear orange, it had to be someone else's. Now that figures, she thought in disgust. Lying about his great devotion, saying she made every other woman he knew look like peanuts, and then luring her here under false pretenses. The bastard! No wonder she had been tense in bed. She must have sensed his true colors. Just then something drew her attention. Her snapshot. She pulled it from the trash; then she ripped it up, ripping up her own hurt as she did and starting toward the shower as she determined to put the best face on this she could. She could say Gary had been called to active duty. Who would know? She still had his lieutenant bars. There wasn't any law against wearing them and telling people he had been shipped out to Korea.

She finished showering, got dressed, closed her bag, and walked to the elevator. As she waited, her anger began redefining itself in the nagging truth that she had been dumped. But that shortly turned to rage, and she consoled herself by saying it was good to have found out the truth now.

When the elevator didn't come, she took the stairs. Seconds later as she stood in the busy lobby, with everyone else coupled and having a fine time, she felt more abandoned than ever, even embarrassed to be alone in this strange hotel on a bright Saturday morning. Crazily she wondered if Gary might have told someone. She thought of breakfast but decided to leave right away. She went up to the bellhop for a cab. He pointed her to the front. Outside, a porter came over and asked, "You want a taxi, miss?"

She nodded, and his sharp whistle brought one almost immediately. When she got in, she told the driver Newport News. And as Old Needle Point faded in the background, her near-predicament hit her again. Thank God she had some money on her. But what if she hadn't? Then she would have been stranded and would've had to call her aunt. This made her feel sorry for herself. She started to get angry again, when the driver turned halfway around, smiling, "Nice day, isn't it?"

"Yes. Yes, it is," she answered, just to say something.

"Almost as pretty as you," he stated gallantly.

Well now, but wasn't that a shot in the arm, didn't those nice words ease her burdens? She pulled a mirror from her purse and looked at herself: good skin, eyes, wide pink lips. Surely the driver wouldn't have lied. She began to perk up. And why not?

She had friends; she was about to get a summer job at the beach. Besides, Gary wasn't the only fish in the sea. Not by a stretch, she reassured herself as she struggled with a new wave of anxiety. Oh, quit worrying! He's a rat! And better to have found that out now instead of later. She stared out at the rolling Virginia countryside as the driver turned on the radio and the warm oceanfed air revived her spirits. In the morning sun her lieutenant bars sparkled bright as a skate's heel.

Two days later she and her friends were hired as waitresses at one of the most popular restaurants in Myrtle Beach. From there they returned to Belle Adams and Emily completed her freshman year, signing on for the swim team and newspaper staff come September and delighted that her request for a single room had been approved. Things were going well all right. Already the knowledge that she would have privacy next year was giving her a new sense of independence and heightening her enthusiasm for college. To make things even better, she decided to resume her weekends in Charlottesville because Gary had soured her on D.C.

In June she and four other girls rented a huge place on the South Carolina coast. Emily worked a rotating shift at the Seaview Inn. She wore tight red shorts, a well-contoured tee shirt, a waitress cap that looked like propeller wings, and heels. She got orders confused and once dropped her tray when a drunk pinched her on the ass; but she made it through without getting fired. Her nonwork hours were full of sun, blaring radios, cookouts, dancing at the Pavilion, getting sloshed, and making out enough to fit in without going all the way: just dirty ol' American fun with the he-men wanna be's who prowled the beach in search of sexual desserts. From time to time she wore her lieutenant bars, still dishing out the fable of a young, handsome officer who was crazy about her. But privately Gary was old hat now. There was just too much going on to mourn his loss.

Some of what was going on was the tide of students who flooded Myrtle Beach that summer. They came, primarily southerners from the state schools, to raise hell and make a pack of money. They were party goers, tanned, healthy, gung-ho Confederates. And for the first time since Nana's death Emily began thinking about transferring to a southern college her last two years. In particular, she was drawn to the University of North Carolina in Chapel Hill. The students she met from there were friendly. According to them Carolina boasted a great English department in a wonderful town, and Thomas Wolfe (one of her literary favorites) had graduated from there. All that added up to good reason to go. But what about living in New York with Lillian?

What about it? That question was answered when Emily got back to Belle Adams soon after Labor Day and Lillian, just returned from Mexico, called to say she had been picked to be on a team for yet another archaeological mission to Mexico leaving Womack next June for over a year. "Do you know what this means?" Lillian was practically screaming into the phone. "It means everything! Don't you see? There's not even that many females in this school, and I'm the first one, the first girl, I mean, who ever got that from here! I bucked the tide! They told me they never thought they'd see the day when a girl would be on one of these things. Isn't that exciting? It's like it's all happening just like I wanted. There's me and another one too, I mean an older woman; but she's been doing it for years. She's the one who helped me get it because of a paper I did. She was married to the man who was head of the department and he died and she had some pull and then I got backing from another prof. So I'm going. I've got to. You understand, don't you? Even though it means I won't be here when you get to New York." She stopped, as if hearing this for the first time. "But I can still find us a place near Columbia," she went on, "if that's where you're heading. And when I get back, I'll move in with you."

What was happening to Lillian was impressive, and Emily said so, secretly relieved since this unexpected news decided her future as she wanted it right now. From that point on she set her mind on UNC; and before she hung up, she told Lillian she would come to Columbia for her master's after she graduated Carolina, the same time Lillian would be starting her doctorate at GAI.

"So this way it's even better," Lillian said. "When you come up then, I'll be grounded in New York clearing core courses, so it's worth waiting for."

The next day Emily applied to Carolina. She wrote her father, who, not surprisingly, was pleased and told her so when he phoned a week later. But there was another reason Charles called. "Emily," he said, "your sister and Sam have moved their marriage date up to the Saturday after Thanksgiving, and I expect you to be there."

Oh, shit! "Dad," she wailed. "Sheila doesn't want me at her wedding."

"It doesn't matter. *I* do. It'd look too darn funny otherwise. I wouldn't have a notion what to say to Francine."

"But do I have to be Sheila's maid of honor?" she asked in horror.

"No, no, of course not. Some friend of hers from her school's doing that. All you have to do is be there and look pretty. Your aunt and I are staying at Sam's parents', but I can get you a room at a hotel. And it's nothing fancy, believe me. Just family and a few friends is all who'll be there."

Further protests fell on deaf ears. It wasn't often, Charles reminded his daughter, that he asked much of her. But he was asking this. And if she refused to come, she could expect no further assistance from him. "Appearances are everything," he reinforced his basic stand about society with that rocksouthern point of view. "And blood is thicker than water. I'll go to my grave saying that. Your coming to your sister's one wedding in her lifetime is a step in the right direction."

She pushed her luck. "If Lillian can get away, is that okay with you if she comes too, Dad?"

"Lillian Jackson?"

"Yes. Please, Dad. It would mean a whole lot to me. It would make everything so much easier."

He must have thought so too. For after a moment's reflection, Charles said yes. She was just to let him know so he could make the room reservations. And Emily should send her sister a wedding gift too, he reminded before bringing their conversation to a close.

. . . I talked Lillian into coming even though she could only stay one night. And on a crystal-clear Saturday in November, we met at the Fargo airport. It was great seeing her. I wore a Mickey Mouse hat with floppy ears that set the tone for our reunion. And as I look back now, I'm surprised I didn't spill the beans because of how Sheila affected me.

I remember waiting to congratulate her in the reception line. Not just because she was a newlywed, but because Sam had won a big job with a law firm in D.C., where they were moving. I felt happy for her, though I was a basket case inside. I must say though, when it came my turn she was cool as a cucumber until I reached for her hand—then she visibly recoiled. Lillian was right behind me and must have noticed. But she never said a word.

Back in our motel room I felt like a rotten apple. That's how Sheila always made me feel after Mattie. And there Lillian and I were, talking into the wee hours about This and That and our Sacred Ambitions—you know how it is when you're smashed or getting smashed and life is a butterfly and you're the flower it sucks (or is it the other way around?). Deep down I ached in my heart of hearts to unload my sorrows, especially when Lillian asked me what was wrong. There we were, alike in so many fundamental ways, except she had courage and I was a chickenshit. At one point I recall she told me to "stay the course." She talked like that when she'd had a few. She'd say, "Stollie, just go with your dreams!" Drunk or sober it was Stollie this and Stollie that. Oh boy, if only Stollie had had a crystal ball!

Morning came, bullying the stars from their sockets. In hours we were to leave in separate planes. I recall as we parted she told me this was how it would probably be with us—leaving and coming back together, but we would always be connected.

I spent that Christmas in Newport News listening to Aunt Francie yap about buying a summer place in Hawaii, where she had friends.

Early in January my acceptance letter came from Carolina. And then I was in the winding-down months of sophomore year . . .

Two young women, opposites and from different parts of the globe, exerted a definite influence on Emily's final semester at Belle Adams. One of these was Claire Tremble.

Claire Tremble, a former suite mate, had been a girl Emily had never run thick with, three reasons being Claire didn't smoke or drink, and she verged on homely—hips too large, blond hair so thin if the wind blew too much scalp showed, and a gap between her front teeth. But she was bighearted and a whiz in math and had helped Emily pass trig. In gratitude, Emily had gone out of her way last year to be nice, even to the point of getting Claire dates, which had never panned out. Claire's father, an army general, had been assigned to France this year and had taken his family with him. That, as far as Emily was concerned, was the end of Claire—that is until February when, to her astonishment, she got an invitation to summer in Cannes at the Trembles' vacation cottage. Two upperclasswomen Emily barely knew were supposedly coming also.

Now just the idea of being there was mindboggling. To Emily, France was a land of rebellion. It was where expatriates sat around in cafés wearing black turtlenecks and discussing Life. They were all poets or bohemians, and they never slept. They wore shades and spoke French fluently and stayed pleasantly high. She could easily imagine being part of that scene. Maybe if she went she could take a side trip into Paris alone. At the very least, she could say she had been to France, and if someone asked her what she had done this summer she could casually remark, "Oh, I was *abroad!*" Just the way that sounded gave her goosebumps. Besides, she didn't want to waitress in Myrtle Beach again, nor spend a month with Aunt Francie in Hawaii. So she decided to keep her options open, and wrote Claire asking if she could let her know in a couple of months. Claire replied that was fine and hoped she could come.

The other young woman of note was a redhead who hit the Belle Adams campus that year with the subtlety of a firecracker. Greeneyed, longlocked, Gretchen Stryker, a transfer from the University of Maryland, was hard to ignore. Leggy, breasty, blowing kisses from hips and lips, Gretchen's figure cut a perfect 8 in the wind, and her skin contained enough cream to lighten a cup of coffee. She drove a bright maroon convertible, with the top down even when it was chilly, and blustered that her parents had stuck her in a girls' school to calm her wildness. Because Gretchen was a science major assigned to a different floor in the dorm, Emily didn't get to know her until February, when the coach made them captains of rival swim teams. It wasn't long before their fun there carried over to their social life; and soon they were partying with the same crowd in Charlottesville and trekking up to D.C. to a hot bar called The Red Tongue that featured the best Dixieland this side of New Orleans. What they had in common was a desire to test the limits. Gretchen's lack of inhibition fascinated Emily. In turn, Gretchen found Emily brilliant and profound and told her so in those words. Now to someone as ego-starved as Emily, such utterances constituted a marching band.

Came April: Jill Rogers from Emily's floor asked her and Gretchen to go out with two naval cadet friends of the ensign she was seeing. They agreed. But when the six assembled at The Red Tongue one Saturday afternoon and Emily and Gretchen had their first look, they realized they had made a huge mistake. Bob, Emily's date, had terrible acne. Gretchen's was okay but seemed awkward and stuttered when he talked. At the first opportunity Emily and Gretchen met in the ladies' room and almost ducked out by a rear exit. But that wouldn't have been fair to Jill, so they stuck it through. Before midnight they all went back to the midshipmen's hotel. Soon they ran out of beer, so the men decided to get more. At just that point Jill discovered she was out of "women's merchandise" (she wouldn't say the word Kotex in mixed company) and had them take her to an all-night pharmacy. Gretchen and Emily were invited to come along; but, glad to be rid of them, they feigned indigestion and fatigue. Ol' Blue Eyes, with a glass of champagne in his vocal cords, was crooning on the radio as everyone left. And when the door closed, Gretchen, a little tipsy, grabbed Emily, tipsy too, and, cheek-to-cheek, they began waltzing around the floor. Startled at first, Emily quickly relaxed. Girls danced together all the time in the dorm.

Of course, this wasn't the dorm; this was a hotel room. This wasn't rattling and rolling to the thunder of an audience; this was slow dancing in the big city. This wasn't some cutup with a goofy smile; this was sexy-Gretchen: Gretchen's breasts were introducing themselves to Emily's, Gretchen's red open bulb of a sweetready mouth was breathing in Emily's ear, Gretchen's Tabu was tickling Emily's nostrils. And while all this merged, a swarm of butterflies opened their wings in Emily's stomach and floated, dipped, twirled, as one song blended into another until presently they were standing motionless in that hotel room, eyes closed, arms enlaced, swaying like flowers in a summer's zephyr, before voices at the door tore them apart.

The evening went on as usual; but from then on quietly, surely, a different energy lay between them. Back on campus, their contacts seemed infused with a new awareness; in swimming, if their bodies brushed together, Emily got more butterflies, and a few times clowning about in the dorm, if Gretchen asked her to be a partner in a gymnastics routine and then balanced herself on Emily's hands with her feet in the air, Emily felt something she refused to name. But she blocked any comparison to Mattie.

Before the end of April, Gretchen invited her home to Cleveland for the summer. Without hesitation, Emily said yes, assuming Charles would give permission. That same day she wrote Claire she wasn't able to come to Cannes.

Friday of that week they were lying on Gretchen's bed listening to records. It was around ten P.M. Gretchen's roommate was away for the weekend, and the background music to *A Place in the Sun* came on. In one of that film's more charged moments, Elizabeth Taylor summons an entranced Montgomery Clift to come-to-mama; the kiss that erupts when he does is an earthquake. And right then Gretchen made like Elizabeth Taylor. Supporting herself on one arm, she leaned toward Emily, whispering throatily, "Come to mama," and followed that up with a wet deep one to the lips—a kiss like quicksand sucking Emily, absorbing Emily, pulling her in and climbing from her toes up to her ankles past her knees to her waist as she struggled to liberate herself, and then that kiss was almost to her nose when, with herculean effort (as if realizing she might drown) she grabbed the rope that fear finally flung her and yanked herself free. Now she stood by the bed, shaking in distress. Words formed, but then vanished on her lips like bubbles. Immediately she bolted to the hall and down that to the stairs, taking two at a time until she was in her room, whereupon she locked the door and leaned against it, near collapse. Then she rushed to her basin and washed her mouth, spitting furiously as if to expel that kiss from her being: her soul lay like a charred leaf in her body. Minutes passed before she heard Gretchen rattle the door. Outraged, Emily ran over. "Go away," she muttered fiercely. "Leave me alone!"

"Emily, let me in!"

"No, goddammit! Shut up before someone hears you!"

"I don't care. Let me in."

"Gretchen, I'm warning you. I'll scream if you don't leave. I swear I'll tear this whole building apart if you don't get the hell away. I mean it!"

Silence. Then Gretchen's retreating steps. Emily lay on her bed tormented with questions: Why had that happened. Why had she let Gretchen kiss her?

Because *you* wanted it, a voice taunted. She hated that voice. She wanted to drag it out and kill it. She fought it and argued with it and blamed what had happened on Gretchen. Yet even as she did, another voice inside her was saying to quit fooling herself. And so, suddenly it was too painfully obvious: ever since that dance their emotions had been building to this. And thus for all her work, pain, trouble, and distancing herself from the past, the past had overtaken her; for here it was again, that hated curse that was following her. She lay in her room thinking about werewolves and bad neck glands and all the words Sheila had called her. So this was the way it was going to be. So she would never get this behind her. She would never marry and have kids and be like everyone else in the universe!

Just then a light went on in her head, and she sat up. Intercourse, she thought. I've got to go to bed with a man. That was it. That was the only thing left: to find a man and do it, far away where no one would know if it turned out like Gary. Just do it. Prove she was normal, because everyone knew queers couldn't have intercourse. So she would phone Claire and tell her she had changed her mind; and before she came back, she would pick up a stranger in Paris, city-of-lovers, and do it: fuck.

She called Charles the next morning and got permission to go, provided the Trembles wrote him a note confirming her visit.

And that was no problem, Claire enthused when Emily finally reached her that evening. "I just got your letter saying you can't come and here you are saying you can. That's great. When do you think you'll get here?"

"As soon as I go to my aunt's for a couple of days when school's out to get my stuff ready for Carolina. I'll let you know."

"Okay. We'll pick you up at the airport in Paris."

The dwindling days of the semester ended in a blaze of shopping trips, studying so she would keep her average, getting her passport, all that. She quit the swim team and ignored Gretchen completely, including a note Gretchen slid under Emily's door begging her to talk. Emily knew this was causing pain, but she couldn't help it. By now the desire to absolve herself from any responsibility had muddled things so completely in her head that she was convinced if Gretchen hadn't asked her to dance that night, nothing would have happened between them. Somewhere deep inside she knew this was unfair. But she couldn't allow herself to explore her emotions. She was too busy blaming Gretchen for the whole sorry situation.

In early June she flew to La Guardia and there caught a plane to Paris. She came prepared to relax and happily was able to do just that. The two others Claire had invited (it turned out those girls were dividing their time between France and Switzerland) had already arrived and proved to be much friendlier than Emily had thought. Claire herself seemed more mature. General Tremble was funny and welcoming. But it was Claire's mother, actually her stepmother, whom Emily enjoyed the most.

Mrs. Tremble took Emily under her wing as soon as she learned she couldn't cook. She trotted out her prized recipes, showed her how to measure food in bottle tops, and make breads. She regaled her young guest with tales of growing up in the Midwest before meeting The General, as she called her husband. An ardent Christian Scientist, she spoke of the miracles of healing, her own personal witnessing of a broken bone that had mended under the sway of Mary Baker Eddy, and a flight of hornets driven away by the power of will. Emily especially liked the emphasis on the mind being stronger than the flesh and that if one concentrates, she can turn bad to good. On the lighter side, she played cards, soaked up the sun, attended the small parties thrown for the military. Her school-tuned French worked to good advantage. She wrote postcards to everyone she could think of, exchanged letters with Lillian, her father, Aunt Francie, and, able to be more reflective given the many miles between France and the United States, she even sent Gretchen an awkward, stumbling sort of apology, something about "Hope you're fine; sorry about everything," but received no reply. As the days passed, she became more excited about Carolina. And in the back of her mind, she prepared for intercourse.

Now, naturally intercourse involved penises. And who couldn't see them detailed as they were under the skintight swimsuits the Cannes men wore on the beach? Some went longways. Some pointed out like the barrel of a gun. Some looked stuffed. Some sagged between the thighs like eggs in a basket. How, she would wonder, can all *that* get inside, she being small, as Gary had said. She held a mirror and looked there and touched herself and felt the opening squeeze over her finger. Would it expand like a snake's mouth when it devours an animal? Terrible image! She tried romanticizing intercourse. It would take a long time. Her body would quiver like the strings of a violin. It would happen in a gorgeous room overlooking the sea. God's breath would flutter the curtains. Music would play in the background. And before that she would have met her tall, dark, handsome Frenchman in a bar as he flashed his sterling silver Zippo and stared meaningfully into her eyes: *Voulez-vous coucher avec moi, ma chérie?*

Oui, she would practice her French in front of a mirror, holding her cigarette just so: one arm supporting her right elbow with the Chesterfield perched between two fingers. The more she fantasized this man, the more he resembled Gary; so she drew him shorter and reminded herself she would be in Paris. Her Frenchman would clasp her and say *Je vous ai attendu toute ma vie.* She would hold him as Hemingway's women hold their lovers. His penis would burst inside her, burying forever the vestiges of Mattie, Gretchen's kiss. There in the dominion of his arms, she would become Woman, made whole by the redemption of his body as good conquered evil, as the mind triumphed over flesh. And if she had doubts, she would console herself with what she had heard at St. Joseph's: if you weren't normal, the penis could only get so far inside the uterus before it hit a wall. That made perfect sense.

Fine. But the thought of actually going through with this was terrifying. So she tried to romanticize the upcoming venture, reminding herself she would be losing her virginity in the most beautiful place in the world, Paris, city-of-lovers, where everyone spoke French, language-of-lovers. At this point all visions of being an expatriate were cast aside. She didn't have time to sit on the Left Bank discussing life. She was leaving Cannes the end of August to be in Chapel Hill shortly after for orientation; so she gave herself two nights to find a man. And then at the appropriate time she made her good-byes and left for Paris by train.

She checked into a small hotel near the Champs-Élysées and then hit the streets. Her plan was to act at night, which seemed a better time to have sex. As she walked, she peered into various windows until she saw something that looked nice. And when she finally entered, she carried a paper, pretending to read it so no one would think her a whore. The first night she had several chances. Two were from men old enough to be her father. Another was from a man so large he scared her. She quickly left for still another place but got cold feet and hurried back to her hotel and there put herself through the paces: Why was she making such a big deal of this? Women picked up men all the time.

With the clock ticking in her ear, she decided to try a small bar near her hotel the next evening. And before she even went in, she had resolved to go to bed with the first person who asked unless he had two heads. Before long, opportunity knocked in the form of a young man in his late twenties who bought her a drink. He was presentable enough—slight, nondescript features, but harmless, with long black hair and nice eyes. He wasn't from France. In fact, he hailed from Arizona. Boring. But the clock was still ticking, and he didn't intimidate her. His name was Jean Battle, he said. He was in Paris to study art. What was her story?

Her story was she was looking for *truth.* She said that because she figured that's what you say to an artist. Apparently it hit the spot, because he was looking for the same thing. And so it began, a new intensity, his eyes squinting as if to photograph her, an enveloping intensity as the night wore on. "Sometimes," he observed seriously, "you can't tell truth when it's staring you deadass in the face. But if it's truth, that's it, that's a fact, you know it's truth, you can't hide from it, you pull that shit and it'll get you every time 'cause truth clicks with this way deep." At the word *this* he thumped his chest and his eyes brimmed feelingly. "Like now, here, you and me," he went on. "This is truth, us meeting like this. Isn't it something, two birds flying the coop three thousand miles from the fucking U.S. of Asparagus. Hell, I wasn't even going out tonight!"

Hadn't Gary said the same thing, she remembered, eying him carefully. Maybe all men say the same thing. Maybe it's just the best line around. But so what? She wasn't going to marry him. She was just going to get laid. Could she? Oh, my God! She piled on the drinks, and they talked a while more about truth and so forth. When you're drinking, of course, truth gets even more important. The conversation turned to books. He loved Hemingway. "What's that one he wrote about the guy who blows up the bridge?"

"For Whom the Bell Tolls," she replied. By now the floor was waving at her.

"That's it; that's the one. The bell tolls for *thee.* Remember that? That's real pretty." She agreed it was, and he said, "Remember that guy who slept with the girl in the sleeping bag? Maria. Right? Remember he told her the earth moved?" When she said yes, he made his point, "Well it's moving for us now." He continued in that vein about how the earth moves little or big depending on the amount of truth in the air and in this case it was like a volcano. He said he couldn't get over how they had met, two Americans in Paris, which he seemed to take as an act of God. Meanwhile she was listening, but her head was busy as a beehive. For instance, where were they going? She didn't want him in her room when she left for the airport in the morning. The floor began waving at her again, so she excused herself for the john, where she threw some wakeup water on her face, and when she came back, he lowered the boom. Did she want to go somewhere private?

"Sure," she answered, as if that were a novel idea.

"Well, I've got friends at my joint, so what about where you're at?"

"No. I've got friends with me too."

"Okay. I know a nice place up the street," he suggested, which turned out to be not far from her hotel.

Thus it was that in a rented bed in the city-of-love, Emily finally met her criteria for being normal. She met it amid sounds of cats howling up from the street and an orphaned flute wailing in from a nearby window. She met it under a light bulb that wept its one teardrop of a cord not far above the bed where she lay stripped, waiting for truth and deliverance. Then he emerged from the toilet all penis, that's what she saw. He was rubbing it as he came to the bed, holding it. She saw it clearly. First time, and it seemed too big. From somewhere she remembered hearing you get larger when it goes inside, but she didn't want to be thinking at a time like this. He didn't have a rubber on, and she said that. Cooperatively he turned back to the chair where his trousers had slipped to the floor. He bent over; and when he did, the hair shot out from his crack like stubs of dark grass between the pavements. She shut her eyes, not wanting to see, and then he was back asking her to touch his dick. She ventured a hand forth and felt it, moving her fingers up and down as he said to do. He told her to look at it, she did, it was getting harder, he was moaning with pleasure and then laughing that he better put its clothes on, so he dressed it in rubber and got on the bed, crowing Let's see what you have, sounding bolder than in the bar. He pulled the covers down, and there she was, naked. He felt her all over and was quite slow loving her breasts up. She tried to come, she didn't care if the coldness followed, she just wanted to feel the glory before they fucked, but it wasn't happening even as his fingers entered. He pulled them out and mounted her doggy style, but having her ass in the air was humiliating, so she rolled on her back while he rubbed his penis over her body and she tried to concentrate on Mrs. Tremble's words of good being stronger than evil, thinking maybe she wasn't coming because she was high, dammit!

His tongue was in her ear, his tongue was moving over her breasts again. In his passion he bit a nipple, she made a noise. "Sorry," he mumbled. "I love tits. You got great tits." He turned her over on her stomach. Under his tongue's flame, her buttocks warmed. His tongue sank into the fleshy divide. She shifted away, not wanting him there. He brought her back to his mouth and traveled her length into the valley of her lower spine, turning her over again to glide his tongue south past her equator into her sex office where the red secretary with the wrinkled face-of-feeling waits before the tiny oval, but she didn't want his tongue in her vagina. She put her hand over it. His face pushed it off. She returned it. His tongue then tried penetrating between her fingers, but she resisted so he quit and sat up, opening her legs, saying, "Nice, that's real nice; tell me you want my cock in your cunt." But she didn't want to say I want your cock in my cunt, so she murmured something and surrendered to images of submission as his penis slipped through the vaginal lips, yes, she let him, it was in: she lay with eyes closed waiting to feel the glory, thinking of how she and Lillian used to fill rubbers with water and float them out windows, gray and smooth and plump like white balloons. "What's wrong with you?" he asked harshly, spoiling her trance. "Move. You're like ice!"

She began making obedient noises of love, writhing, contorting as he pumped in and out. She felt, but she didn't fly, she wanted to fly. Suddenly she remembered Gretchen saying men think they're such hot shits you can fake it and they'll never know, but she didn't want to fake it. She was here to be a woman, and she was going to be one if it took every last breath of her; she wanted it inside as deep as it would go; and it was inside, deep and going deeper past whatever barrier that would have stopped it if something were wrong with her—in and in, his penis now was unsoiling her, purging the infidel yawn of her vagina which Mattie's touch had defiled, cleansing the cavity that Mattie's fingers had wasted, eradicating Gretchen's kiss, sanctifying, rectifying, signaling the glad tidings of correction.

"Come on," he moaned in her ear. "Get with it." She

strained down as if to have a bowel movement, urging herself on: feel, I've got to feel. She was crying. For God's sake what a dumb thing to do! But where was the lightning bolt, the flash of stars? *Feel!* She strained again as his hands gripped her rear end; and then he was pumping inside with the rhythmic precision of a sewing machine needle, fast, faster, fastfastfast, God!

He pulled out shaking like a fish on a hook and lay beside her breathing heavily, the broken neck of his penis slumped on his thigh; and when he took the rubber off, stuff oozed from the hole. She lay beside him, small and uncertain. Was that it? Where was the glory? "Did you come?" he asked.

"Yes," she blushed.

"Was it good?"

She didn't want to talk. "Yes, it was fine."

"This your first time?"

That peeved her. "Of course not."

He reached for her, tried to force her head between his legs. "No, no, please," she stiffened. "I'm tired."

"Just suck it off a minute for crissakes. Suck my dick."

Her body, refusing, was a rod of steel. She had nothing to fear from him. He was a small man. No, she said, she didn't do that.

"Well I'll be . . . Shit," he snorted. He stood up and looked at her quietly. The lights were out, but there was enough illumination to see him distinctly. He seemed about to speak, but instead turned and went into the john. She felt just awful now. That didn't seem right.

Jean Battle was out of the john and dressing now as she lay there quietly. In a moment he had finished and was by the bed. Did she want him to take her somewhere, he asked, not unkindly. Since they were both Americans he felt an obligation to not just leave her here. If she liked, he would wait.

Thanks, she said, but her hotel wasn't that far away.

An awkward silence followed; then he said good luck and went out the door. It closed, and she began thinking about Gary. What was it about her and hotel rooms? She got up with the sheet pulled to her chin and walked to the window, where dawn was just spreading itself thin in the heavens. She looked out at the street and then came back to bed and sat down. Wasn't she supposed to feel differently? She had just lost her virginity. Wasn't something supposed to change?

Oh, be sensible. She hadn't come to Paris to fall in love. She had come to be a woman, and now she was in every way. Besides, she had had too much to drink to have experienced those exquisite sensations the poets write about. All that would come when she found the right man. The important thing was his penis had gotten inside her. That's what counted. You're cured, Emily!

. . . Was I?

I was. I believed that. Intercourse had made me pure. How ironic.

It comes back to me now, my sitting on that bed in Paris puzzling over this great riddle of my life. At fifteen I had lain with Mattie. I had had a dog, a name, I loved Walt Whitman. But when Mattie touched my body, I lost all that: I became a queer. When you're queer, that's all you are. And now a penis had given it back, four inches of standup perfection had penetrated my guilt. I was normal, I conformed to pattern. I remember breaking into laughter and staring at myself in the mirror. Didn't I feel better? Wasn't I brand-new? Hadn't a massive burden been lifted from my soul? I dressed and walked into the taintless streets of Paris, a virgin who had lost her virginity, God's child. In hours the big bird would be flying me to America. Look out, Chapel Hill! . . .

She landed at La Guardia after midnight and stayed in a nearby hotel. Next morning she called Aunt Francie to make sure her trunks had been sent and in a few hours her plane was touching down at the Raleigh-Durham airport, where she got a limo into Chapel Hill. Her instructions sent before leaving Belle Adams were to report to Ritter Dorm. There she reclaimed her trunks and met Joan Smith, her new roommate, a tall, lanky blonde with a Texas accent who was majoring in theater. Theater students, Emily would soon learn, lived in their own little world. Thus for the nearly two years she and Joan would share a living space, their paths would seldom cross.

Her first days were taken up with orientation and registration. She signed up for all the English classes she could get and the usual extracurricular—swimming and writing for publications. Her assigned Big Sister gave her the royal tour: Franklin Street, the main drag, past Kay Kyser's home, Thomas Wolfe's old dorm, toward the tree that Betty Smith had written about, which grew not in Brooklyn but in the backyard of a house not far from campus. Of all the towns she had lived in since White River, this was the prettiest. Chapel Hill was a postcard of towering magnolias and dogwoods, windy paths that tongued through a sprawling arboretum that pointed toward the Durham highway. Boys were everywhere, catcalling, acting like they had never seen a girl before. Competition for dates was stiff since men outnumbered the coeds two to one (females weren't admitted to Carolina until junior year). Emily's first date was a cheerleader named Bo Thorn who tried to get fresh after a movie. But since Paris, she felt she had nothing to prove and didn't let him do anything.

At the end of her first week, Aunt Francie called with terrible news. Charles was dead. A car accident in fog south of Monterey, California. "Your father was so stubborn, Emily," she wept over the phone. "I'll just bet someone told him not to drive, but if his mind was made up he wouldn't have heard a word they said. You could tell that man the sun was shining and he'd argue till he was blue in the face. But I guess that doesn't matter anymore."

. . . I got a flight as soon as I could to Newport News, which was where the body was being flown from California, and I couldn't help but think about Nana. Her death had come on a Christmas when I was new at Belle Adams. And Dad's had come in the fall when I was even newer at Carolina. What was that all about?

Aunt Francie and a six-months-pregnant Sheila were already at the funeral parlor when I arrived, and I went straight to his casket. He had on a blue suit and much rouge, with his hands clasped in front like my grandmother's. Only the hair moved, from a standing fan. That's what sticks in my head: hair moving on a corpse. Where was he? I was wondering that as Sheila came up beside me, crying. Her crying got me to crying. And then some courage stirred in my bosom, and I reached for her hand. I held it. My hand became a human letter writing in hers the unvoiced script of common blood, and for just those moments we were sisters again.

Not long after, I got this letter, which I've always saved:

> 3206 Q Street, NW
> Washington, D.C.
> September 15, 1952

Dear Emily,

To be honest, writing this is one of the hardest things God has called me to do, but on one level that isn't important because we're orphans now. Not that I don't have my own family; but parents are the blueprints, and ours are gone forever. I miss Dad's being alive, and I want his death to mean something. Therefore, I herewith am making a gesture that he always wanted. Ever since he was called Home, I've felt a need to extend myself in sacred sincerity. And so I am inviting you up over your Easter break. I'm sure you know from Aunt Francie that Sam is with the same law firm and that we're living in Georgetown now. I would have asked you for earlier, but we're going to Sam's family over Christmas, and I think it's best you spend time with Aunt Francie before she goes gallivanting (she's threatening to move to Hawaii!). By Easter I'll have gone through my pregnancy too, and the azaleas will be in bloom, which always puts a good light on things.

I trust all is going well for you. You'll be hearing from the lawyers about Dad's will. He remembered us both, but most of his money was left to the University of Virginia because he told me that Granddaddy Stolle's trust is more than enough for us. Yours starts when you're twenty-one, so you should be preparing to set something aside for the Rainy Days of Life.

Good luck in joining a sorority. That's so important for a girl nowadays.

Sheila

On the simplest level, Sheila's letter made me happy. It meant the past was over, I supposed. It signified our hatchet was buried deeper than we could ever get to again and now, theoretically, we could go on. Yet I remember feeling unsure, scared too, when I thought of being a guest in her home. Still, I was determined to go, determined to show my sister I was completely normal . . .

Chapel Hill in the 1950s was easy on the blood pressure, was a town to go back to just to see how things *should* be. It was a lighthouse in the southern Sahara, a place where middle-aged men could be boys again. They came, those former frat brothers, a bit more winded when they climbed the stairs. On football weekends they gathered in the stadium with blankets and jugs of gin, swapping stories of sexual conquest, dreaming of when Choo-Choo Justice had clobbered Duke. They played tackle on the fraternity lawns, blubbered over the pretty girls and Tarheel songs, and wore their own Greek pins for all to see. Nothing was more vintage American than Chapel Hill. Here marriage was the Star of Bethlehem, and being white-protestant-southern was the name of the game. So was pledging the *right* sorority if you were female.

Sororities were the red meat of a coed's fantasy, the bone marrow of her aspirations. Catering to looks, money, connections (the greatest of those was looks), they provided the surest route to the most eligible men on campus. And Emily, aware that the road to approval was paved with the proper affiliations, was to become during this time nearly obsessed with fitting in.

Competition began during rush week, a period of five days in early September when young women, desperate to be popular, flitted from one sorority to the next, calling upon everything ever learned about grace to impress the judges. The judges were active members called Sisters. Their task was to separate the girls from the dogs. They had razor-sharp eyes that could spot a mole or a crooked seam across the room, and they were sticklers for posture and attire. No beauty contest could have masked more rivalry, because to be rejected was to die, was to carry an empty dance card in the ego, was to be ugly, Jewish, or just plain Jane. Brains didn't matter; body beautiful did. Alas, many were called, but few were chosen.

Emily was. She received four bids, from which she selected Alpha Mega because it had the best reputation. The next step was initiation. At initiation an inductee, called a pledge, was required to lie in an open casket with a sheet up to her neck. Around that casket the regular members, draped in long white gowns, chanted the secret mottoes that were never to be disclosed to outsiders. This was the occasion when vows were exchanged. The Sisters would ask questions like "Will you love your sorority through all time?" Automatically the answer coming from the casket would be yes. On cue the girl would then sit up with arms extended and proclaim herself reborn into Sacred Fellowship. But Emily felt stupid saying she was reborn and would love her sorority through all time. She felt it disrespectful too to lie in a casket, with Nana and her father barely cold in the ground. She did it though, to get her pin. To keep that pin she had to promise to attend all sorority functions, to eat a certain number of meals with her sisters per week, to pay all dues regularly, and to live in the House at least one semester. The one she chose was the final semester of her senior year, deliberately delayed until then because she actually preferred the more casual life of the dormitory; and with her roommate gone so much, she had lots of privacy. She used that privacy to study, which had never been a burden. She loved her classes.

She loved walking to them with the leaves crackling under her feet, feeling like a scholar. She liked the faculty, some women, mostly men in suede jackets smoking pipes, calling their students by their last names and often inviting the English majors to small dinner parties. Thus life began at Carolina—working hard during the week, following the crowd on weekends.

In the fall, weekends meant football. Football meant crowding into a stadium on Saturdays drunk or getting that way and screaming along with the all-gorgeous cheerleaders who cartwheeled and cavorted in front of thousands of glassy-eyed fans who would no more have missed a game than jumped off the Brooklyn Bridge. The boys came with images of immortality, playing out their fantasies on the gridiron. The girls came with images of pleasing the boys. They whooped, hollered, jumped up and down frantically, waved pennants, cried when their team lost, died and went to heaven when it didn't. Afterward was party time: shades of U.Va. with one notable exception— you *had* to get pinned. That fraternity pin was the romantic equivalent of an athletic sweater with a 10 percent symbolic markup. It signified an engaged-to-be-engaged status, and a coed without it was like a ship without a sail. Emily got her sail early on from a Sigma Nu named Pete; but she gave it back soon after she met Carl Bentley.

Carl Bentley was a med student from the University of Pennsylvania and a friend of someone involved with Sally Onx from Emily's dorm. On a weekend when Pete had to go home, Emily agreed to date him for the Tarheel–Georgia Bulldog game. Carl marked the end of Pete, and for good reasons, one being his looks. He was tall with curly dark hair, large Cary Grant dimples, soft brown eyes, a manner almost old world in its gentility. Carl didn't bow as her father had over a woman's hand. But he was deferential: he stood up whenever a woman came in the room, he was quick to light her cigarettes and open the door; and he pretty much let Emily run the show. She liked that, along with his reserve and sense of humor. She also liked that he was going to be a doctor and that others seemed to look up to him. They hit it off so well that even though Sally and her friend broke up that weekend, Carl extended his stay. And once back in Philadelphia, he called and wrote. Then in two weeks he returned, asking her to wear the ring of his fraternal organization. She took it, pleased to have it. It wasn't strictly a frat pin, but it had clout, it entitled her to "belong" in a way Emily felt was important. And she was flattered. In his thoughtful, serious manner, Carl was to become just what the doctor ordered. Twenty-eight, an ex–naval officer, he had seen the world and wasn't threatened by her energy or what he called her refreshing originality. Plus he wasn't pushy about sex, even saying a girl should save herself for marriage. But for Emily the icing on the cake was the distance between them, which gave her the best of two worlds—someone she was truly proud to be seen with, yet someone who wasn't around a great deal. Carl's schedule was so demanding he couldn't get away more than twice a month. When he did, he preferred to do the traveling. So he would drive down in his 1948 Caddy convertible or hop a plane. All this meant she never had to worry about dates or going out when she didn't want to. Perfect.

They spent Thanksgiving at a friend of Emily's. And it was there in a fading November that Carl told her (exact words) he was "truly smitten." Yes it was early, and no he wasn't trying to rush anything; but he just had never felt so strongly about a girl before. By then Emily had told him she was planning to get her master's at Columbia. Carl's reaction was to try to change her mind. Instead of going there, he argued, why not apply to the University of Chicago; Carl's father, a prominent surgeon with many connections in that city, could get him his internship and residency there. Not wanting conflict when this subject came up, Emily would put Carl off by saying it was too soon to talk about this but she would think about it. Her heart was still set on living with Lillian, though.

Aunt Francie met Carl over Christmas and pronounced him "wonderful." A few days later he flew on to Chicago, where he picked up a late model Ford his parents had given him as a present. In turn, he let Emily use his old car, which she could keep until she finished school. A little insurance policy, he had joked at the time. He liked knowing she had something of his. She liked it too. She went wild with joy. She drove that car back to Chapel Hill, loaded it with friends, and cruised Franklin Street honking, blasting the radio that was strong enough to pick up Atlanta.

During this period she and Sheila had been writing. In early December Sheila had a baby girl she and Sam named Kathy. Emily sent gifts with a note that said she was looking forward to meeting her new niece. Sheila wrote back confirming the Easter invitation. And when Emily later asked if she could bring Carl, Sheila said fine.

As Easter approached, Emily found herself getting more and more anxious about staying at Sheila's. But Carl would be the buffer. Regretfully he wasn't going to be able to be there the whole week. But at least he would get things off on the right track: Sheila would see them together and know that Emily was cured. That's how she figured it.

When the time came, she met Carl in Washington, each in their separate cars; and from the moment Sheila opened the doors to admit them to her Georgetown home, everything seemed to go well. Sheila and Sam liked Carl. Emily was on her best behavior, making sure to make her bed and wash the tub after each use and to pick up her clothes. But was there something in her sister's body language when their eyes met? If so, it centered around the baby.

Little Kathy, barely four months, had taken a great shine to her aunt. When Emily came in a room, Kathy squealed and lifted her arms to be picked up. But if Emily obliged, Sheila always seemed to have an excuse to take her back. And once when Sam mentioned that Kathy looked like a baby picture of Emily's, Sheila got visibly agitated and said if their daughter resembled anyone on *her* side of the family, it was Charles.

The day Carl left, he and Emily took a late meal downtown. When she got back to Sheila's, Sam had just walked in, excited about having two free tickets from a client to *The King and I.* Would Emily mind looking after Kathy? Not at all, she answered. But Sheila went into a tizzy and began berating her husband about expecting Emily to sacrifice her vacation. Over Emily's objections Sheila called a neighborhood babysitter; and as things ended up, Emily spent the evening with a teenager as Kathy slept peacefully in the next room. Of course the thought passed her mind that Sheila was trying to keep her away from her niece.

She got her answer the next morning. Sheila was bathing Kathy when Emily came into the bathroom just as the phone rang. Emily got it and came back to say Sam wanted to talk to her, whereupon Sheila, instead of leaving the baby with Emily, picked her up, dripping suds and all, and rushed to the phone. When she returned, Emily, choosing her words carefully, said that if she didn't know better, she would think Sheila didn't want her alone with Kathy. No answer. Emily said it again. Still no answer. And then she said it a third time but, sensing something was in the air, with increased tension, finally blurting out that she loved her and the baby and would Sheila please say something.

That did it. The word love did it. The word love does it every time—either breaks a wall or builds one. Sheila stood up and in a voice riddled with sarcasm she said, "Love. What do *you* know of love, Emily? And what's love got to do with anything anyway?"

She had seen that look before. It came with the territory of history: Sheila in the backyard that October's day, Sheila in the bedroom that Easter afternoon when she had come in timidly with the candy, Sheila at Aunt Francie's the few times when no one was around. And here by intent and message nothing had changed save the baby splashing merrily in the tub now and looking up as if waiting for a kiss. Oh God, Emily thought wildly. Out came a flood of apologies for everything she had ever done, including being born. She had come here, she said, to be friends. She wanted another chance.

"Oh please," Sheila murmured in disgust, going back to the task of washing her daughter. But Emily kept on until once more Sheila was on her feet, asking if she had any idea what it had been like all these years bearing her grief alone. "But at least you weren't around that much," she said. "At least at Aunt Francie's I wasn't there when you were that often and I didn't have to be reminded. But when Dad died I tried, I thought . . ." Her chest heaved. The baby played with a toy duck. "You're right," Sheila said, confronting her squarely in the eye. "I don't want you with my baby. I'm afraid to leave you with my own flesh and blood. How do you think that makes me feel? But how do I know what *you people* might do?"

"What do you mean *you people*? What's *you people*? I don't know any *you people*!"

"Oh, for goodness sakes, Emily!"

"I love Carl."

"Carl! Why don't you tell him. How can you lead him on?"

"I'm not leading him on."

"Yes, you are. He seems such a nice man and you're wrong not to tell him. I don't mean the whole horror," she added quickly. "I've never told Sam. But at least to let him know you shouldn't have children, to make up something . . . " This pushed her to the edge. Sheila's face seemed to enlarge, taking the eyes with it; her nostrils widened. "Don't you think I've wondered what *I* might have passed on to my baby? I told you that years ago, and the fear is never far from me. My God, I've prayed long and hard over this, but I can't, you see, it's out of my hands, I can't change what's happened, it's in the blood line. You've tainted the blood line, and I don't know what you would do with Kathy. My God, if I have to choose between you and my baby, it's her hands down!"

Oh Lord, Emily thought, she actually believes . . . "Sheila, she's only four months old. You think I would do something to a baby?"

"It doesn't matter. She's a *girl*! God strike me dead before I forget what you did. You could marry your Carl and have a house full of children, but to me you . . ." Shuddering as if to ward off a sudden chill, Sheila turned her back, muttering in a low voice, "If you so much as lay a finger on my baby in some foul, diseased way, I'll . . ."

She didn't have to finish. Emily whirled about and walked

from the room. She packed. The last thing she heard as she left the house was the cuckoo clock.

. . . Me? Molest her baby daughter? My niece? *My God!*

What a trip that was back to Carolina. I was in such turmoil I turned to my best friend, booze, my companion in grief. With a six-pack and the radio on high, I blew my brains out on rock and roll. And when the alcohol finally stepped through my head, I tried reaching Carl. I guess I just needed to hear he loved me. But he wasn't in. Back at school I surrounded myself in the familiar as the angel of mercy, time, licked my wounds. Eventually I succeeded in burying my pain. I was good at that. Weeks later I received this letter from Sheila, which speaks for itself in terms of our future relationship:

3206 Q Street, NW
Washington, D.C.
April 27, 1953

For this cause God gave them up unto vile affections: for even their women did change the natural use into that which is against nature: And likewise also the men, leaving the natural use of the woman, burned in their lust one toward another.

Dear Emily,

I quote from Romans 1:26–27 because I accept Christ as my personal Savior. He is my Redeemer and my Strength, praise His holy name, I walk with the Crusader of Nations, which gives me the will to carry on. What this means so far as you and I are concerned is: I am able to forgive myself for my sin of discourtesy when you were here; I am also able to forgive you, Emily, for its root cause dating from that black day which even now my lips will not speak of. I forgive just as Christ forgave the world, even though the Bible says homos are an abomination.

All these feelings have come to fruition since your visit. Surely you will never know the burden of these feelings that I have carried for so long, burdens far greater than my strength could have shouldered had it not been for my Absolute Lord. And while I regret my outburst before you left, certainly that anger is proof of my continual anguish. For as surely as nails pierced the Flesh of the Risen Christ, so have the nails of your transgression imprisoned me. My pain has been a bottomless pit feeding upon itself, reminding me of the iniquities of my own flesh and blood. And that has brought me with even greater fervor to the Word.

All this leads me to the conviction that you shouldn't plan another trip here until my baby girl is grown. It is not that I refuse to accept you are cured as I suggested when you were here. Dad himself told me that that psychiatrist had given you a clean bill of health, and my own eyes saw you with a man you obviously care about. I would also like to believe that you agree with Dante who wrote that homos would burn in eternal fire. Yet my heart still quakes over the past. Furthermore, disease *is* disease. In other words, cancer can come back. But if all else fails, God the Helper remains. God hears the prayers of every sparrow, rest assured. And though you've done well in college and pledged an admirable sorority and, as I say, seem to have captured the attentions of a good man, should ever you be tempted again to unnatural acts, remember the Cross alone can make the difference.

Let me conclude by saying I struggle with other things from our common past. Dad used to say you were extraordinarily sensitive, as if somehow that sensitivity gave you permission to lord what I was supposed to perceive as your "finer instincts" over mother and me. But I too, believe it or not, am a human being. And I have suffered mightily from your so-called "sensitivity." There was a time when I had hoped our children might someday be close, that we might grow as sisters in our twilight hours. But that hope was dashed long ago. Ever since, my own friendships with women have been affected, and I will ever be on alert for my daughter in her own close attachments. How do you think that makes me feel, Emily? Or that my own sister has cheated my children of an aunt and me too of my blood ties? How I had wanted things to be different for Dad's sake and for my own inner restoration. But your visit brought me to the realization that I just can't have a homo in my house, or even one who *used* to be a homo. Sam will never know. Nor Aunt Francie. The only one who knows is I, who walk in the Lord and continue, despite this letter, to pray for your immortal soul, to pray that you come home to the Living Christ.

This doesn't mean I don't want ever to hear from you, Emily. It just means I can't think about it anymore, any of it. Not now. Not at this time. And when that will change I have no way of knowing.

King of Kings,
Sheila

My reaction to that letter: as I've said, I buried it.

In June I made dean's list. That summer I took two more English classes. Twice I drove up to see Carl, and he came down more often. The point I'm making is I stayed busy. That's what impresses me when I look back. It was almost as if time were a treadmill I felt I had to outrun in order to stay free of the past: I didn't want to think about it.

In August Lillian, back from the wilds, invited me to New York. So I flew up for my first visit ever. It wasn't long before I was submerged in the exhilarative sensations of Manhattan. She took me everywhere: the subway where we went from one end of the city to the other, two Broadway plays, the Empire State Building, Fifth Avenue, Macy's, and much more. We went to Greenwich Village too, which proved a wash. Frankly I had mixed emotions, knowing its reputation for homosexuals; but privately I was deeply deeply curious. Anyway, it started to pour as we left the train, so we ended up having lunch and taking the subway right back to her dorm. So much for the queers of New York City!

We toured Columbia before I left. Students were all over, and vastly different from the ones at Carolina, especially the women, who seemed far more intense. They wore jeans and sneakers, and smoked openly. Many of the men had long hair. They all looked fascinating. And I felt I belonged here. I told

Lillian that, sitting on a bench at 114th Street and Riverside as we ate a hotdog that afternoon and watched the small boats that strummed the Hudson. We spoke of getting an apartment nearby after we graduated because Columbia was so close to GAI, where she expected to start a year from this fall. There we were, connected in ways yet to be discovered: two young women off to see the world, sharing the brave young dreams of their hearts. Imagine . . .

Emily's idea of the perfect life was now inextricably wrapped up in New York City, and this vision was right with her as she began her senior year. She saw herself with the potential of becoming a real city girl. That meant that once she was living in Manhattan she would stay up all night, drink in every bar that pleased her, sit on the stools like a pro, smoke on the street, run around with famous people. New York was fizz in a bottle of life, a nerve-ending on the very spine of creation. She had a call.

Fine. But what about Carl? More and more he was after her to come to Chicago in June. She could live in the dorm of whatever school she got into, or he would find her an apartment. If things worked out, they could get married. If they didn't, she could go back East. All this put her in a bind. She didn't want to lose Carl. And so what if his kisses didn't take her round the bend, or when he touched her breasts and she had an orgasm she was visited by that same withdrawal that had always beset her following sex with men. Love was a mighty river, and in time that coldness would give way to true romance if she would just be patient. Besides, if she didn't marry Carl, she might turn into an old maid. Single women past twenty-two ran that risk—becoming crabby because they didn't get enough sex, masturbating in their rooms with the shades drawn, and drinking alone. Bachelors were footloose and exciting; old maids were prunes. But Lillian wouldn't be a prune even if she stayed single because Lillian, who always said she didn't have time for marriage, was in a different category so far as Emily was concerned. In other words, there were women, and there was Lillian, whose career aspirations justified a different sort of existence. But Emily wasn't like that. She wasn't as independent or as brave as Lillian no matter how much she admired those qualities. Not for her to explore and travel the world. She lacked her friend's noble calling. Hence would ensue Emily's mental dialogue:

- Maybe if I could just live in New York long enough to get the fever out of me, Carl would wait.
- But Carl doesn't want to wait, would come the rebuttal. You'll lose him.
- So maybe I shouldn't risk it. Maybe I should just forget New York and go on to Chicago.
- Otherwise you'll lose him, her inner debate would continue. You'll never find anyone like him again, so giving and tolerant and understanding.

Eventually Emily applied to both the University of Chicago and Columbia. But without telling Carl, she also urged Lillian to look for an apartment for them in New York.

The end of 1953 found Emily and Carl celebrating at a party in Chapel Hill. And before January died on the calendar, Emily had moved into the sorority, which was where she really got to know Lu Hestor.

Lu Hestor, arguably the one *real* individual in the Alpha Mega house, was an art major from Birmingham. She was a class act—a timber of sharp, clean bones; huge brown eyes; wide brow; black shoulder-length hair; thin and small-breasted with a kind of queenly, even aloof air. The fact that she bordered on being a loner made her distinct in a place where nonconformity was considered obscene. But by appearance alone she was sorority material. Her mother's serving on the sorority's national board was an extra bonus. Plus she was gifted: two of Lu's paintings hung in the art building. Another decorated the living room. She had won numerous state prizes and been written up in various publications. All this warranted special recognition—notably, she was excused from sorority events when painting. On a more practical level, the entire attic had been converted into a live-in studio for her; and it was here that Lu spent a great deal of her time. Emily didn't know her that well even though they had been pledges together, but that was because they had lived in different dorms before Lu moved into the House this past September. She did find her interesting, and their exchanges had always been friendly. Lu went with Ralph Litz, a Sigma Chi and campus activist who traveled the state debating different college teams. Theirs was considered a "modern" relationship: usually they dated only on weekends to give the other the freedom to pursue separate interests.

One night about two weeks after Emily began living at the sorority, she woke up starved. She lay in bed obsessing on the chocolate cake in the icebox. Sue Ann Looney, the regular cook, was so good she could make you get down on your knees and lick okra.

Her roommate, Toby Scar, was tossing in the next bed, so Emily got up carefully, grabbed her cigarettes, and descended the stairs. In the kitchen she had some cake, then she decided to make a sandwich. A huge Beefsteak tomato awaited her. She pulled that out, along with bread and mayonnaise, and was just readying the vegetable for major surgery when a sound like a *ping* drifted through the air. The piano? Must be my imagination, she thought. She piled three slices on the bread Dagwood style, heaped that with salt and mayonnaise, and took two bites. Then she heard it again. This time there was no mistake. It was the piano.

Sandwich in hand, she proceeded down the darkened corridor to the study at the end of the hall. The light was on, the door slightly ajar. She peeked in, and there was Lu Hestor bent over the ivories, her fingers persuading the gentlest tune. She slipped in quietly and stood just at the edge of the carpet, and after a few minutes was just about to leave when, as if sensing a presence, Lu whirled around wide-eyed. "Good grief"—she jumped—"you scared me half to death!"

"Uh, oh, I'm sorry," Emily mumbled, embarrassed to have

been caught staring and suddenly remembering the hair on top of her head was flat from having fallen asleep with it wet. "I didn't mean to startle you." She ran her hand through her hair self-consciously.

"What time is it?"

"A little after one."

"Can you hear me upstairs?"

"No. I didn't hear anything till I got to the kitchen."

"Is the hall door closed?"

"I don't . . . no, I don't think so." Damn. But Lu was already up and out, and before Emily could leave too she was back saying it had been open and if they heard her upstairs there'd be hell to pay because you weren't supposed to play the piano after midnight. "But I ran out of sheep to count and this relaxes me."

"You have trouble sleeping?"

"Sometimes."

"You ever try using a fan?"

"A what?"

"A fan. You put it in the window, and it catches the wind and blows it on your face. That's what I do. It works like a charm."

"Well, I didn't know . . . Oh, watch out!" Emily's eyes followed Lu's to her foot. And there making its debut on the bright green rug was a large chunk of tomato and mayonnaise that had oozed from the bread. As Emily bent to pick it up, another tomato, along with two loose cigarettes from her pajama-top pocket, followed suit. Jesus! What a slob! Lu apparently found this funny. "Wait a minute," she laughed. "There should be some Kleenex in one of these drawers." Emily heard her at the desk, and then Lu was beside her offering a tissue. "My good deed for the day."

Murmuring thanks, Emily picked up the mess, rubbed the mayonnaise into the rug, walked to the waste basket, and threw it all in. That elicited a protest that she couldn't leave it there. The maid would find it and have a heart attack. Now Lu got the tomatoes and then, in a mock-scolding voice, she told Emily not to move or she would break something. With that she ran out, leaving her to contemplate the absurdity of this. And then Lu was back and sitting at the piano bench again. "Well," she chuckled. "You should have put on that show when you tried out for this sorority and they'd have made you president."

"I know," Emily grinned sheepishly. "Can't you see it?"

"Not really."

They laughed. "Thanks for your help."

"Any time. You want a cigarette?"

"Sure."

"You got any left or did they all drown in the mayonnaise?"

"Nope. I'm okay." She pulled one out of her nearly empty pack and walked over for a match. They both lit up. Lu took a deep drag, set hers down in an ashtray, and struck a few chords on the keys. "What's the name of that song you were playing?" Emily asked.

"Oh, it's a no-name. I made it up."

"Really?"

Lu nodded slightly.

"I didn't know you wrote music."

"I don't. I dabble. That's what I do best. I'm a good dabbler."

"That's not fair. You paint. I think you're a wonderful painter."

Lu smiled.

"I mean it. I love the boat in the dining room. It's like a photograph." Hastily she corrected herself, thinking maybe it was an insult to compare a drawing to a photo. "I mean it's real, the lines and everything, like you could almost get inside it. That's what I like. That's my taste in painting. I don't get it when they throw colors on a canvas and say it means something; but then what do I know except about poetry." Why had she said that?

"You like poetry?"

"A lot."

"You write any?"

"Sometimes."

"That figures." Lu squinted at her. "You look like a poet."

Well, now. Emily dropped into a chair and leaned forward eagerly. She was dying to hear what a poet looked like. In anticipation, she forgot her flat hair and tried to act intense. "I guess that's a compliment."

"Sure it is. Poets are great. So let's hear something you wrote."

"Oh no," she blushed. "I don't have any in my head right now."

"Sure you do."

"No, I don't. I don't write much anymore."

"Why not?"

Emily shrugged. She wasn't used to talking about this, but seeing Lu's interest she offered, "There's no time."

"So make time."

"But . . . " She stopped, suddenly confused. This wasn't what you were supposed to say to a real artist.

Lu persisted, "Why don't you make time?"

" 'Cause who cares about poetry?"

"Who cares who cares? Plenty of people care. Who cares about painting?"

"That's different. You can hang a painting in a gallery and let everyone see and talk about it. You don't do that with poetry." She grinned again, and she hoped cleverly. "That's a small craft done by exquisitely tormented minds in small dungeons with the lights dimmed." She inhaled through her nostrils and blew the smoke out, watching Lu very carefully.

"You don't say," she teased. "Do you have to be more tormented to write poetry than to paint?"

"Oh. I'm just kidding." Emily changed the subject. "I hear you're going to Rome on an art scholarship."

"Who told you that?"

"Joan Franke."

"Oh, that Joan. I happened to mention it to her once, but that's it. She's dying for me to get it so she'll have a place to flop if she ever makes it to Europe. But it's no sure thing by any means. The competition's really stiff. And Ralph isn't too keen on the idea."

"Why not?"

"Men. You know. I'd be gone a year."

"Couldn't he go over?"

"That's not the point. He wants to start his own business in Charlotte and he wants me with him."

"What kind of business?"

"Public relations."

"You going to?"

"We'll cross that bridge when we come to it, I guess."

"Well that's like me and Carl. He wants me to come to Chicago with him and I might or I might go to Columbia."

"Take English, right?"

"Yep. Teach a little poetry someday. I don't see why we have to be the ones who always fold up our tents. Carl gives me a lot of room but I don't know how it'd be if we lived together."

"Agreed."

They smoked more, and for a while spoke about the difficulty of balancing men and art and the double standards between the sexes. Emily felt oddly energized at such a late hour. Lu was wearing a faded denim shirt with the sleeves rolled up, no makeup, and she looked like a cool million cash. For some reason Mattie came to mind. Mattie used to love her hands. She would tell Emily that hers were the most honest hands Mattie had ever seen. And when Emily, wonderingly, would ask why, Mattie would say, "You look at your hands, Emily, and you just *know* they can do anything you want them to." Mattie's words. Funny, Emily thought now, rubbing her hands together, hoping Lu might see that same strength that Mattie had always admired. For a moment she could almost hear Mattie, "I love your hands, Emily," she used to say. "They have such character."

Lu was back at the piano now, singing a little ditty. When she stopped, Emily asked if she had written that too.

"No. Wish I had. It's an old camp song."

"Where'd you go to camp?"

"Outside Birmingham." Lu's nose wrinkled in remembrance. "For eight summers straight a gang of us who hated Helen

White—she was the head counselor—used to throw firecrackers into the fire when her back was turned and make her hair stand on end."

Oh boy, Emily thought, totally relaxed, sitting there now with her distinctive hands and relating some of her own camping experiences. Once she'd been eyeball to eyeball with a rattler for ten minutes when she'd mistaken it for a garden hose, she reported. "One false move and . . ." Her finger slit her throat for emphasis as Lu laughed appreciatively. "Another time on a hike a girl was bitten by a rattler, and I cut her skin and sucked the blood out." She stopped, suddenly embarrassed. Sorority sisters didn't talk about sucking blood, did they? But Lu's unabashed attention was flattering. And shortly the conversation veered from snakes to books and so forth. Now regard Emily: showing off, French inhaling, getting them Pepsis from the refrig amid a steady flow of chat. And before long, morning was squeezing itself in through the blinds.

It was ten days since she had moved into the sorority.

From that night on they were virtually inseparable. They took meals together, they waited for each other after class, they hung out in Lu's loft talking about anything that entered their minds. Lu sketched Emily an image of a single rose; in turn she wrote Lu a poem about sunsets. Frequently they took long drives in Carl's car, and a few times when Carl came down, he and Emily double-dated with Lu and Ralph. But the best times were just the two of them. Emily felt fingertip-alive. She never wanted the semester to end.

Of course in the background, time, that drumbeat, was marching on. And the larger shape of her life was beginning to define itself. One of those definitions came mid-March in the form of a letter from the University of Chicago. Already admitted to Columbia, Emily assumed this to be her acceptance into Chicago's graduate English department. So imagine her surprise when she opened the envelope to learn she had just made their alternate list with no clear status in sight until summer. Her first reaction was relief. She had only applied here to placate Carl. And now she had the perfect out. That same day she called him at med school. "Chicago fell through, Carl," she said, sounding far more regretful than she felt. "They put me on their wait list, and it could be as late as August before I know whether they'll take me or not. So I'm going ahead with my plans for Columbia."

He argued, "If they put you on a wait list, there's every good reason to think you'll get in."

"But I don't want to hang on a thread until then. Lookit," she bargained, "when do you have to be out there?"

"You mean for my internship?"

"Yes."

"Last week in May or thereabouts. I'll get the word next month."

"Okay. You go on to Chicago, and after graduation I'll drive your car out, stay a couple of weeks, and then fly to New York. I'll come back to see you Thanksgiving and Christmas; and after I finish Columbia, I can move out there and teach." She said that last to keep her irons in the fire, and in the end Carl was mollified.

When she spoke with Lillian later, she knew she had made the right decision. Lillian had found them an apartment with another woman named Greta Steiner. "Remember that woman I told you about that I met a couple of weeks ago at a party, who's a foreign correspondent?"

"Yes, I guess so."

"That's Greta Steiner. She called me yesterday 'cause she knew I was looking for a place and she is too; she travels a lot, but she wants somewhere to be when she's in town. Anyway, she has a friend who's moving the end of May and wants to dump his apartment. It's a hundred fifty dollars a month."

The price shocked her. "A hundred fifty dollars a month!" Emily exclaimed.

"That's a deal. This is a three-bedroom I'm talking about, right near where I took you when we went up to Columbia. Remember that little park off Riverside Drive by the water?

That's where it is. On 113th. It's a minute from Columbia and it's good for me too when I start GAI."

"Have you seen it yet?"

"No, but I will. And Greta says it's a deal."

"Okay. If you like it, take it."

"You'll have to send up fifty dollars for June and another for security deposit."

"I'll get it off tomorrow. Now Lil, I probably won't be there until the end of June. I'm driving Carl's car out to Chicago and staying a couple of weeks."

"Fine," Lillian said.

They talked a bit longer about this good news. And as they did, Emily couldn't help but recall her sister's old words: "Emily Stolle, all you want is your cake and eat it too. Well, that's impossible. Nobody can have her cake and eat it too."

Yet wasn't that what she was getting, she thought as she hung the phone up—a chance to live in New York and still keep Carl as security?

It was May, and increasingly the thought of saying good-bye to Chapel Hill seemed unthinkable. Of course Emily looked forward to New York. But there were times the idea flickered in her heart that she would have been happy to have stayed forever in the sorority house with Lu.

Lu, though, was going to Rome. Early that same month she was notified she was one of the lucky winners of the art scholarship and should plan to leave for Italy in June. This news brought a sense of urgency. And soon Emily and she were discussing reunions in Europe or New York, or the four of them—Lu and Ralph, Emily and Carl—getting together somewhere. And then shortly before finals the gears shifted.

On a Friday Lu returned to the sorority so upset with Ralph she had made him bring her back early. They had been visiting his mother in a Raleigh hospital. And before they got to Chapel Hill, Ralph, who had never been happy about her leaving the country, announced that if she didn't give up her scholarship and marry him he wanted to break up. Bad enough. But what really got Lu's goat was that if the shoe were on the other foot, he wouldn't have done the same for her. "It's always the girl who has to give in," she fumed irritably. "But that's how it is with a man. You're just supposed to quit breathing when one comes along."

Emily suggested a ride, so on a lovely spring evening under a home of stars they made their way to the stadium down a dirt road where they parked and listened to the radio, talking quietly. After a while Lu said, "I'm really going to miss you, kiddo."

Something caught in Emily's throat. "I'm going to miss you too," she agreed. "But we'll see each other in Rome or New York."

"I know. But it won't be the same thing. It'll never be like this again." Then inexplicably Lu took Emily's face in her hands. From the light of heaven she could see Lu's expression so fine and solemn. Her heart ached with emotion. These were their days of youth and glory, when they had felt so much. And suddenly, before either realized what was happening, they were kissing. Not a planned kiss, but one that just came along, at first a spark which evolved, as a rose smells, deeper, richer, taking Emily with it, lifting her as on a balloon into endless sun and blue skies as she flew higher and higher and finally in happy triumph sailed over the city.

Until headlights from an approaching car pulled her from the glue of Lu's lips. They separated. Quickly Lu began smoothing her blouse. Stunned, Emily sat a moment before turning the key and then without a word she drove them to the highway heading toward town. Within seconds it seemed they were in front of the library. There was sorority-sister-consummate Joan Franke. She recognized the car and began waving frantically. Dammit, I don't want her here, Emily thought, pulling over as Joan bounced into the backseat chattering like a magpie: Hi guys! Where you been? Whatcha doing? Where's Ralphiebabe? Is Carl coming down tomorrow?

What was Lu thinking?

They rounded Pine Lane and were at the sorority. Ralph was standing on the sidewalk talking to two sisters. He saw them as they parked and instantly approached, acting as if he and Lu had never had a problem.

"Hi babe," he said cheerily as he opened the passenger door and brought Lu to him for a hug. "We still on for tomorrow night?" he directed to Emily, who was also out of the car now. He was referring to Carl coming down. The four were supposed to be going to a movie.

"Yes," she replied. She caught Lu's gaze, and her face burned.

"What time's his plane getting in?"

"Four."

"So how about Chuck's Steak House at six?"

"Fine."

Ralph hugged Lu again and said, "You gonna help me at Wake Forest tomorrow, babe?"

"Of course," Lu's voice was barely audible.

He explained to Emily, "We've got to be there before nine to prep for the Charlotte debate, so we'll catch you and your guy later."

"Okay." Her heart raced like a jackrabbit. "See ya," she called with bravado. With barely a glance at anyone, she turned and followed Joan's steps toward the house and from the porch saw Ralph's arm wrap around Lu as he led her down the street. She felt so sad. She went inside for a few beers, filling in for some hands of bridge and half expecting Lu to return. Before eleven she was upstairs, grateful her roommate had left for the weekend. She put her fan on and lay in bed thinking about the evening. Any warning signs in her head were ignored. She didn't want to interpret that kiss. She wasn't into searching, analytical questions or making comparisons or examining the contents under the lid. She just wanted to feel what she felt, knowing that Carl was her umbrella just as Ralph was Lu's.

She woke up with a traffic cop in her brain directing a flood of inner voices, one voice warning of danger signs, the other denying their importance. Both voices accompanied her to the dining room as she looked anxiously about for Lu. Where was she? "Anyone see Lu?" she asked as Millie Cox came in and answered, "She and Ralph left a half hour ago. She said to remind you they'd see you and Carl at Chuck's around six."

Oh, that's right, she remembered. She's helping him with the debate. She ate and did a lab makeup, trying to stay busy. But every nerve in her body had a pin in it, as though she were standing on the edge of something and the wind was blowing: wind with an ill wind brewing in it. What was happening?

You kissed her, one voice said.

So what. It didn't mean anything.

But look how you felt.

Didn't feel. I was drinking: the good voice turned that kiss into no more than a handshake. But she was still jumpy.

At four she was at the airport waiting for Carl. She saw him before he saw her, watched him walk down the corridor—great-looking guy that women noticed. Wouldn't it be easy to have him protect you, Emily?

But what about the fireworks? The bad voice said: there's no fireworks.

Who needs fireworks?

You do. You had them.

When?

You know when.

No, she didn't. Didn't want to think about it. Wouldn't think, and so the traffic cop directed that decision around some rotary of self-justification as Carl waved and she suddenly was running into his arms, leaning into his chest as all the Matties of memory have done with all the Roys, leaning as women do on their men, the stronger, more decisive, guardian sex. Let him look after you now; be traditional, Emily, the good voice said. Give in; he loves you. And something in her almost broke into tears as Carl held her and she remembered having held Lu as tightly last night. Good, decent, true Carl. He had come all this way for one final visit to Chapel Hill. Tomorrow he would be flying back to Philadelphia and then on Monday driving to

Chicago. And he loved her. Said he did. Said so now. "I love you, honeybun."

She loved him back. Said so. Didn't say honeybun, but repeated the magic three: I. Love. You. And she wanted to, tried to, right there in the Raleigh-Durham airport she longed to feel in his arms the magic of what she had felt with Lu, her heart a wheel of fire.

You can't feel that with him, one voice said as another urged patience: Give me a year at Columbia, she had assured Carl, and then you'll really see how much I need you.

They had some drinks, and then he checked into a motel. The frat house was too noisy for him tonight.

She spotted Lu almost as soon as they entered Chuck's, oh my, sitting way over on the side with Ralph. Emily walked up to the table, the soul of casual. Hi. How ya doing? Hey Carl, how's the ol' doc? You ready for the big debate, Ralphie—Lu giving her a Mona Lisa smile.

Or was she? Maybe I'm crazy, Emily thought. Maybe last night was a dream. But then why did Lu look like the cat that swallowed the canary? When their eyes met, why was she blushing? And what was the story with her and Ralph? Whatever problems about her going to Rome, he seemed to be joking about them now, saying he guessed he would have to trade her in for a new model after she left, ha ha ha; asking Carl how he handled a girl as independent as Emily, more ha ha ha's. So on and so forth while Lu raised her eyebrows and Emily's voices ran into red lights: couldn't think, didn't want to, really felt uncomfortable. But she got through the dinner. Great steak!

Later at the movies Ralph and Carl took outside seats, leaving them to share an armrest. They were both wearing short-sleeved blouses, so it was flesh-on-flesh: Lu's on Emily's, which released a cloud of balloons to her throat. Hard to concentrate; just feeling that arm excited her. Lu was pressing into her arm. Was she? She was. Emily pressed back. Looking down she saw Ralph holding Lu's left hand, Carl was holding her own; and she and Lu were squeezing their arms into each other's. Crazy world. But when she noticed Ralph's hand perilously close to Lu's right breast, she had to leave, she couldn't stand it, what was she to do, sit there and watch *that,* feel Lu's breathing skin with Ralph playing with her hair. That kiss came back, the sound and scent of the evening before, the way Lu's mouth had opened under hers, her sweet searching tongue, Lu holding her face so tenderly and in such a manner that no one, not Carl, had ever made her feel. "I've got to leave," she whispered urgently to Carl. "I've got cramps. They're killing me." She said something similar to Lu and pulled Carl up. Then with a few more words they were outside. He drove her back as she doubled over in what she hoped he saw as stomach pains, but she was cheating him and said as much when they parked near the sorority; so they made out a little until, not wanting that, she said the cramps were really getting to her. Could he ever forgive her? Sure. "I'll make it up to you in Chicago, Carl. It won't be that long," she kissed his ear with meaning. After agreeing on breakfast, she went inside, took a sleeping pill, and was out like a light.

The next morning there was a note under her door from Lu. She had to go to see Ralph's mother again in the hospital. She would be back at five, she wrote. Meet her in the loft.

Emily got through that day by blocking all her voices. Early that afternoon she took Carl to the airport. He gave her phone numbers of friends he'd be staying with on his drive to Chicago and they talked about meeting there. Before he left, she kissed him hard, real hard. At five she was in the loft. In a few minutes Lu rushed in. How was she feeling? she asked Emily, running up to her and catching her arm. She'd wanted to call but couldn't get to a phone.

"It's okay. I wasn't here anyway."

"I figured."

"Oh, Lu. I . . ." She stopped. Lu was standing right in front of her, like sunlight. And: Emily didn't want to speak. She didn't care. She couldn't contain another distraction in that room. No Carl, no voices. Just them. She put her arms around Lu and held her, and Lu said, "I don't understand."

"It's okay," Emily murmured, pressing her closer in friendship's finest hour. "It's going to be all right. We're just upset about the end of the semester and everything. Don't you think?"

"Yes. Yes. That's it."

"And all the pressures. Right?"

"Of course. It's too much. I can't handle it all, Ralph, and leaving."

"Did you get it worked out with him?"

"Yes, but . . ." She stopped and lit a cigarette. Her hand was trembling.

"What?" Emily nudged gently.

"I don't know. I can't think." They sat a while and talked; and from that came the decision to get out of town for a couple of days. Why not? They had been working hard. Soon the semester would be over and they would be miles apart; so what was wrong with taking a breather, say Pine Bluff about a hundred miles south. Ralph would be in Charlotte; Carl was leaving for Chicago. Emily said, "Why don't we just hop in the car tomorrow and drive toward Pine Bluff. We can take our books and study and get out of this rut. When's your first exam?"

"Wednesday."

"Me too. That gives us two nights."

"I've got to see my adviser at noon tomorrow."

"Okay," Emily said. "That leaves us plenty of time." There was only one voice she was listening to when Lu agreed, one voice calling from the end of the trail: Do it.

Driving out of Chapel Hill, Emily would remember thinking they had crossed a line and it was too late to pull back. Lu must have felt something of the same, for there seemed a new tension in the air. Where once had been ease and an extraordinary sense of familiarity there was now a palpable, almost painful self-consciousness between them. They talked; they didn't talk. Lu couldn't seem to get comfortable, she stared out the window, appeared to sleep, flipped through pages of a history book as Emily changed the radio dial a million times. And something else that, in itself, was unusual: they each mentioned Ralph and Carl more than ever before. Thank God, Lu burst out, that Ralph finally said he understood how important her scholarship was to her. They bought some beer and played music as the car passed through the signatures of rural Carolina: tobacco fields, dirt farms, small Esso stations.

Late afternoon they stopped at a motel outside Pine Bluffs. She left Lu in the car and went inside. A wetlipped, busty woman came out a side door smiling broadly. "Yes, suguh. What'll do you?"

She wanted a room, she answered politely.

"Just you? Oh," the woman glanced out the window to where she had parked, "you got your friend with you?"

She blushed. They were students at the university just getting ready to graduate, she volunteered quickly. It was exam time, and they were here to crack the books because the sorority house was too noisy.

"I see," the woman kept smiling. "How many nights, honey?"

"Two," she replied, then threw in, "got to get back to the boys you know."

The woman knew. She winked. She checked her listings and said, "Oh sorry, all's I got is a double. We've got a bunch of golfers coming in town. They've sewed up everything tight as a tick."

Asking herself, should she leave? No, she answered. You walk out now and tell Lu all they have is a double bed so you'll have to get another motel and that will really look funny. Anyway, so what about a double bed? We're just friends. "I'll take it," she said. "I have a bad back." She stopped. The woman waited. Then Emily realized she hadn't made much sense. "I mean," she sputtered, "I can't sleep in a twin bed. It cramps my back."

"Well, I don't have any of them anyways. Just doubles. Two

or one to a room depending, but the only thing I've got tonight is just one double, like I said."

"That's okay. That's fine," she signed her name to the roster. "I could sleep through a barn burning. How much?"

"Ten dollars a night. You say you're here two nights?"

"Yes." She put a ten-dollar bill on the counter. "You want both nights now?"

"Don't matter. You can take care of tomorrow in the morning if you like. We're not going nowheres." She gave an even broader smile and handed Emily the key. "Room one fifty-eight, right around the corner," she pointed toward the right.

She went back to the car acting without a care, nervous, but refusing to let on. There was a spring to her step and a big smiled plastered her face. When they got to the room, she ignored the accuser-bed and started blabbing about how they had sure been lucky to find something without reservations. Weren't they? Lu mumbled guess so and opened her suitcase as Emily walked to the window feeling like small hot wires were being sucked through her body. For a moment she wished they had never come here. It was just too uncomfortable whatever this was between them now, she didn't have a name for it, she didn't want it to have a name and if their self-consciousness was because of that kiss then to hell with it: she wasn't going to think about it. So she put her feelings aside, which was what she always did. Now she stared out the window wishing they could just go to sleep and wake up to a new day. In the background she heard running water. Then it stopped and Lu was announcing she was going to the pool. Without further ado she left. The minute the door closed Emily began berating herself: Dammit, forget that kiss. It was just sentiment getting a little out of hand. Lu wouldn't have come here if there were any problem. Relax.

She washed her face and put on fresh lipstick. She looked pretty all right. In about ten minutes she was seated in a lounge chair next to Lu, feeling more confident as they watched some kids dive from a high board. It was a fine afternoon, and gradually they seemed more comfortable. Later at dinner over drinks things were even better. But when they got back to the motel, the atmosphere turned prickly again. Each made it a point to say several times she was exhausted. Then they undressed separately with the toilet door closed. Emily put on the TV. The unit was part of the bureau, and to see it well you had to be on the bed, so that's where they got—as far to their opposite sides as possible. At a commercial Lu commented in a strained voice: "Wouldn't it be fun if Ralph and Carl were here."

"Yes," she answered. "Wonder what they're doing."

They carried that subject on a bit, something they rarely did when they were together. But the fact was Ralph and Carl had come on that trip too. And when the girls finally got under the covers, they moved in with them, this time they weren't on either side as in the movies, they got between them. A reporter was showing his slides of China. He looked right at them, his eyebrows raised as if to say, Two women in the same bed. Wonder what they'll think of next! After a while Emily turned toward Lu, whose eyes were closed. She said, "Well, guess it's time to call it a day." Lu grunted her assent. Emily leaned over and flicked off the light. She lay in the dark room now. Then she said, "Good night."

"Good night."

A few minutes passed of unbearable silence. Emily sighed, "Boy, am I beat."

"Hmmm," came from her bed partner.

Emily turned on her side and tried to sleep. She counted the sheep and the collies that herd those sheep and the women calling their men to supper and the farmhands with the farmhand kids, animals, and so on. But sleep eluded her until finally she drifted off. Then consciousness, like a nerve fighting to come back to life, overtook her. And presently Emily's desire claimed her mind. Now with the wind twisting the draperies into puppets' legs, fueled by emotions she refused to name and driven like a nail by a hammer, she turned her head toward Lu just as Lu scratched her head. What did *that* mean?

She stared straight up, caught in the web of Lu's breathing. She felt on fire. The dark tempted her to take Lu in her arms, repeating all the reasons they had come here in the first place. Hadn't they kissed two nights ago? Hadn't they held each other yesterday in the loft? What about their arms pressing in the theater? Didn't all that mean they wanted to be together, and hadn't they correctly interpreted what "together" meant—that they loved each other, that their love proclaimed their unbridled independence in the world? So what would it matter were they to pursue the flickering pilot light of desire down to its last red unfinished sexual ember? Were they to kiss, would the world stop? Don't cheat us, Lu!

What to do? Lying there. Undecided. The appeal of Lu's body. The wickedness of that appeal. The attempt to dispell that wickedness by reaching inside for images of purification—being young again, fresh, things like that. And in the exquisite innocence that lies at the very core of desire, to be wanted, she saw herself loved by Lu. For that was their one true emotion wasn't it? It didn't matter, their discomfort today. Wasn't love in back of everything? Wasn't being here Fate? In this grip of truth, Emily knew she wanted Lu, that nothing meant anything so much as feeling that. And after a moment Carl and Ralph left that bed. A tenderness beyond expression sprang from her breast. And suddenly she found herself beginning that tortuous journey toward intimacy, starting those infinite miles across the landmines and riggings of caution, until directly she was in her backyard moving toward Mattie, who was Lu, who first was startled. But Lu didn't leave when Emily began kissing her slowly, less slow, touching Lu's breasts to the nipples soft as the center of artichokes, which hardened between her fingers. A line from a poem: "My heart stirs for a bird"; her heart stirred for Lu, their bodies like threads unwinding from spools of clothes. "Do you want me?" she whispered. "Because I want you, Lu. I want you more than I've ever wanted anything." Oh Lord, Lu was wrapping her in her arms, Oh Lord, gripping her flesh, Oh Lord, sweeter than wine the smelling licking loving, Oh Lord, Emily be nimble Emily be quick. Jump the prayer of Lu's body, naked, kissing her lips, shoulders, breasts down Lu's stomach into the pipe between her thighs and all lightness becoming and becoming all light: she was Lu and Lu was she as if they were the same body, passing that body between them—hunger.

She awakened to voices, "You taking them three up there, Sue Lynn?" "Yes, 'um, and them two on the east wing gots a busted latch." At that the maid's cart click-clicked past the door. Emily stared at a light fixture and then turned to Lu who, with her back to Emily, was as far to her side of the bed as possible. Emily's feet found her pajama bottoms and brought them up. Her hand discovered her top on the floor. Clasping these, she got out of bed and went into the toilet where, as in Paris, she studied herself in the mirror. The skin near her spine hurt. Lu's fingernails! Feeling pleasure in the memory of their passion, and embarrassment too, she dressed quietly and decided to surprise her with some food.

Down the road she found a crowded diner and after a wait got some juice, coffee, buns and was in such a rush to get back she almost left her billfold on the counter. In the car she carefully balanced the coffee so it wouldn't topple, and started back thinking of all the great things they would do today. Wonder if they could reschedule their exams and stay a bit longer. She almost missed the turn, but there was the motel, and she pulled in.

The first thing she noticed when she walked in the room was Lu's suitcase packed and open on the bed. She herself was in the john. Emily set the food down and waited nervously. Why was the bag packed?

She didn't have long to speculate because the door opened and Lu walked out. Without acknowledging her, she crossed over to the suitcase and began throwing a couple more things in. "What are you doing?" Emily found her voice. "Lu," she repeated in alarm. "What's wrong?" She walked to her.

"Leave me alone!" Lu bit her words off a rod of fire and spit them at her. "Get away from me!" She slammed the suitcase shut and backed off with it.

Was she joking? Lu!

No joke. "Goddammit!" She slammed her suitcase shut and started toward the door. Her hair was in a ponytail, which made her face thinner and more severe. Her eyes in this rope of white were huge and distraught.

"I don't understand."

"I don't give a fuck what you understand. I'm going back to school. If you won't take me, I'll call the police!" She was so upset her hands shook. "I can't get a bus in this dump! I don't know where the hell we are! Just get me back to Chapel Hill! I'll be in the car! Hurry up, goddammit to hell!"

The door slammed. Emily sat down weakly. She lit a cigarette, took three deep drags, put it out, took herself into the bathroom where, suddenly nauseous, she threw up in the bowl. In that manner she packed and left the room.

The trip back—no words for it. Three hours of the radio pitched to high fever whenever she tried to speak. Once she managed to tell Lu she loved her. At that, Lu threatened to jump from the car. "Shut up!" she screamed as if she were at the end of a football field. "Shut up your rotten sick mouth. I don't want to hear it!" A needle of pain stuck in one end of Emily's body, inched through it like a hook on a worm until it got to her other side. The radio was drowning out all sounds of life again, and that's the way it went until Carrboro, a suburb of Chapel Hill. "Pull over!" Lu ordered tensely.

She had no willpower, pride, self-respect. All this trip she had begun admitting the sorry ordeal of what they had done. She was a sponge sopping up the sins of the world. She was a doormat letting last night wipe its dirty feet on her body. That's how she felt as she pulled to the side, stopped, and for the first time held Lu's eyes. "We're almost there," Lu said in a flat tone. "And they're going to ask questions. Just say I had food poisoning and we had to come back. I'm not staying. Ralph will be back today. I'm going in and do some stuff and then go over to Sigma Chi. If you bother me before that, I'm warning you, I'll tell them what happened!" And when Emily in a trembling voice asked what that was, Lu screamed she had attacked her. She knew that! Who did she think she was kidding? She had gotten her into that hellhole and forced herself on her! She was a rapist! That was the drumbeat driving into Chapel Hill. Rapist, rapist, rapist! She parked a little off from the House, and Lu quickly got out. Emily waited a brief time; then, leaving her suitcase in the car, she went in too. Fortunately the place was fairly empty, and Lu was nowhere in sight. Emily went upstairs, praying her roommate was gone. Her prayers went unanswered. "Oh, hi," Toby said in surprise when Emily walked in. "I didn't expect you back today."

"Yeah, well, Lu got sick."

"Too bad. She okay now?"

"Yes, she's better I think."

"Where'd you go?"

"Toward Asheville."

"All that way?"

"We never made it. She got sick."

"You don't look so hot yourself."

"Oh, I don't know," she lowered herself to the bed, covering her face so Toby wouldn't see she was crying. "I just need a little rest."

"You sure?" Toby hesitated.

"Yes. I think maybe I'm coming down with something."

"Well, I'm on my way out so you can have the room to yourself. Your sweater's in the closet. Thanks a mil."

The door closed, and Emily sat up, holding her head in her hands. It was clear what she had to do. She walked out in the hall to the stairs leading to the loft and started up, heart pounding, feeling like Gretchen Stryker. At the door she counted ten before knocking.

"Yes. Who is it?"

"It's me."

The door flew open. There stood Lu white and terrible. "I *warned* you!"

"I'm sorry." Tears were streaming down her face. "That's all I wanted to say."

Lu made a clucking noise and banged the door so hard it vibrated. Emily ran back to her room. There she put the sketch

Lu had done for her in her suitcase along with school notes and her textbooks and started downstairs. Millie Cox saw her as she descended and rushed over in greeting. But Emily, saying she had to get to Greensboro to see a friend of her sister's, scurried out the door. She couldn't worry how this might look. She had to get out of here.

Curiously that drive made things clearer. For alone now, Emily was forced to look at herself heart and soul. And what she saw made her sick. She was vermin, the lowest of the low. Lu had been right. She had taken advantage. She had brought Lu to that motel without telling her of her past. She should have been on guard to protect them both. She should have seen the danger signals, the kiss and embrace and her own eagerness to be with her. But she had been too confident since Jean Battle, too sheltered by Carl's attentions. And what she must accept now was she had a disease. Most people have diseases that can be seen. They have leprosy or paralysis or TB. They have symptoms that reveal these disorders and warn the world of their contagion. But her disease was invisible because of her lies and the way she looked. Even so, its effect was no less than cancer. Her disease, as surely as any malignancy, ravaged her and ruined those it touched as well. Perhaps Lu had been a reminder of this, that she must ever be vigilant around women. Perhaps the pain she bore now was her just debt for all the hurt she had caused. This realization brought up Sheila, Charles, and the hideous depravity and weakness of her flesh. Shame rose in her breast. Shame's wings spread throughout her body, defiling every nerve and tendon, filling her with self-loathing but with a new determination too.

She passed a Catholic church and impulsively pulled into the parking area. For some moments she stared at the building, recalling all she had ever heard from Catholic girls at school: that Catholics go into this confession room and tell all the terrible things they have done to a priest who then wipes the slate clean. All that was required was they be sorry. And that she was. So she decided to do that too; just talking to someone would help. She turned the motor off and went inside. She stood at the entrance looking about for a room that fit that description, but saw nothing. A woman was standing in the aisle, and she almost went to her to ask where you go to confess, but she lacked the nerve and instead sat down in a rear pew feeling dirty, looking at that Cross and feeling dirtier and dirtier. For a moment she saw her father leading the family into the First Methodist of a Sunday. She would be the last one, busily engaged in making faces at her friends, like when her father sang so loudly it would embarrass her. Beside her, Sheila would be praying as if God belonged only to her, and looking very serious about the whole business. Emily had never felt like that, but now she wished she could pray all this horror out of her soul. She wanted to feel clean. She wanted God to touch her as He had Moses, with some burning bush of certainty, offer her salvation, bathe her, affirm her.

It was right then that Lu stirred in her mind. She felt Lu's burning lips, she smelled her body, she tasted her hair, she relived Lu touching her, the vivid blinding-white of ecstasy. There amid the statues, candles, holy witnessing here in this sanctuary, this heart's harbor, one truth emerged from the mud of her guilt, one reality: and that was that she missed Lu, missed Lu more than she felt shame for having touched her, missed her deeper than she was sorry that she had broken any promises never to be with a girl again, missed her more than any victory she might have found with Jean Battle's penis. That was the fact that danced on the head of a pin.

But this recognition was only a flutter. And when the flutter was out, candle blown, she cursed herself for succumbing yet again to temptation. That longing for Lu was but the death rattle, the last sting of the Beast.

Now, she swore softly, she would never again be involved with a woman.

She left the church feeling stronger, but back on the Raleigh highway she became emotional. She passed a picnic area and pulled in, got the sketch from her suitcase, and tossed it in the trash. It was six now, and it occurred to Emily she better find a place to stay and study for her exams that were coming in the next few days. She started up again, passed a gas station, and for some reason stopped and tried to get hold of Lillian. But after eight rings she resumed her travel, amazed she had done that. For what? In her present state what would she have possibly said if Lillian had been in? She felt sort of crazy.

At a market she bought some beer and downed two just to put an edge on her anxiety. She was near Raleigh now, so she started looking for a motel. She found one on the outskirts of town, paid, went in her room and sat on the bed, overcome by feelings of loneliness and despair. Last night she had been in another motel with Lu and now twenty-four hours later she was in a similar spot but under totally different circumstances. There was a small icebox in the room. She put her beer inside and then hit the books, but she couldn't concentrate so she took a quick shower, vowing to focus on the immediate and fighting fatigue and a deepening depression. She couldn't go on like this. This pain was too much like Mattie, immobilizing and consuming, and she couldn't hold it all in. She must go back to Chapel Hill, take her Shakespeare test tomorrow, finish up the others this week, then skip graduation and get the hell out. But for where?

Hours passed in this manner, and during that time she made her decision. Lillian would just have to understand she couldn't come to New York right away. She remembered the Columbia catalog had stated admission to graduate school was good for one year. So she would first live with Carl until she was cured, then move to New York. She had no other choice. Obviously Jean Battle hadn't been enough. She had to have more sex with men, and since Carl loved her, it would be better with him than with someone she didn't know. So that was the solution. She would sleep with him until she was completely normal. Once more she told herself this didn't mean she was giving up New York. She was just delaying it. It shouldn't take that long. All this made her feel better. She dropped off to sleep with her Shakespeare book open on her lap and a beer can in her hand.

She woke up in a great deal of emotional pain and began

obsessing about the calls she had to make. She took care of the easy one first. She reached her aunt, who was planning to attend Emily's graduation before flying to Hawaii, and she told her not to bother because she was leaving for Chicago right after exams. "No, that doesn't *necessarily* mean wedding bells with Carl," she heard herself use that light tone she always reserved for her aunt. "I'm not sure what it means exactly; we'll have to see. But I'll be in touch."

She put the phone down and sat on her bed trying to summon the energy to plot her future. This was getting to the complicated stuff. Let's see, she mentally calculated. A two-day drive to Chicago would have her there the first week in June; and to really be healed shouldn't she live with Carl a year? She frowned at that and cut the time in half, making a commitment to stay with him through Christmas. Seven months. Then she would go to Columbia. But when? Her basic reason to be in New York anyway (aside from craving the excitement) had always been to live with Lillian. But as she had matured, Columbia had entered the picture. Along with that had come the goal of getting a master's degree to eventually teach in a good school. And if she started Columbia in January, she wouldn't finish until the next January—a lousy time to find a job. Plus she didn't want to enroll midyear. That left June. And that's when she would begin. As for Carl, she was going to him with noble intentions. And if she fell in love along the way, she would return after she finished grad school. Thus at eight A.M. she put in a call to Columbia admissions. A very helpful woman found her application, changed it from September entry to June 1955, and told her to send a follow-up confirmation letter, which Emily said she would do.

And now the hardest part. Lillian. She found her at the dorm before nine, the best time. Then nervously, but driven by a singular need to take control of her life, Emily blurted out rapidly: Carl-was-pressuring-her-to-live-with-him-before-she-went-to-New-York-and-she-had-given-in-because-he-needed-her. She would be sending her fifty dollars a month to hold her room and *definitely* would be there right after Christmas. She knew it was late and please not to be mad, et cetera. "You are, aren't you, Lil?" she asked remorsefully, pausing for breath. "You're pissed off, aren't you? Aren't you?" she repeated when Lillian didn't respond immediately.

"No, I don't know, Emily. I'm disappointed. I don't see why you couldn't have told me sooner."

"Oh Lil," she answered tearfully. "I didn't know this was going to happen. I didn't know Carl was going to take it so hard. He's starting his residency and he let me use his car and all . . . I'm just trying to do the right thing." She could feel herself about to cry. "Please hold my room. Promise me. I swear. I swear on the Bible I'm coming." She stopped, not knowing what else to do.

Lillian said, "All right. Calm down. You'll have your room. I'll put your name on it."

"Is it going to be okay with that Greta?"

"Yes. Sure. She doesn't give a hoot so long as you pay your third. She's gone most of the time anyway. But Emily, listen, if you want us to spend any time together, you better get your ass up here because I'm leaving next summer."

"For where?"

"Peru."

"Peru?"

"Don't sound so shocked. I told you after I finished my core subjects at GAI I'd be traveling, and I just found out this week it's Peru."

"For how long?"

"Could be over a year."

A great temptation seized her. To hell with it she wanted to say. Go on to New York. But the need to be normal overpowered any other consideration. So amid more apologies and protestations of her deep feelings for Lillian, she hung up and called Carl's house. His mother answered and said he wasn't expected until late this afternoon. Emily left word she would try again at seven.

Now she lay back on the pillow and counted the peels in the wallpaper. She was exhausted. After a while she got up, dressed, and tried to review for her finals. Around noon she drove back to Chapel Hill, where she took her test blindly; then late in the day and bracing herself, she returned to the sorority. She had already decided Lu would be avoiding her too, so there wasn't much chance they would meet. But the minute she walked in, she was hit by another shocker. Lu had run off with Ralph the night before. "She's getting married," Joan Franke rushed up excitedly. "She's giving up her scholarship and everything for love. Isn't that wonderful!"

"Didn't you know?" Peggy Hill asked. "Didn't she say something when you two were away?"

"No. No," Emily repeated dumbly. "I didn't know. What about her exams?"

"She's taking them this summer and getting the rest of her stuff then too," someone else answered. On and on it went. Somehow she found the strength to handle her end. And as soon as she could, she called Carl and told him her plans.

And when he assured her he loved her, she wept she loved him too. At that moment she felt she might. She let his love run all over her, and loved him back as best she could. Carl's devotion was clear, clean, healing. His cure would get her through the difficult days ahead. In her heart Emily knew he was the answer to everything.

. . . I was wrong. The "answer" raised more questions about me and Lu. I missed her. Dammit. I didn't want to miss her: the more I missed her the more I threw myself at Carl the more I missed her. That was the catch-22. I'd find myself lying in Carl's arms thinking about her. Then I'd panic and use his penis as an eraser. There was just this gaping hole in my gut I couldn't fill with him. But I tried: I decorated the apartment, I cooked, I waited for him when he worked late at the hospital, we fucked a lot and I faked my pleasure in bed. It was weird, you know: him loving me and me loving someone else while trying to make him her in that way the mind casts illusions. Carl wanted so much to have me stay forever. A part of me wanted the same thing. It was like we were rooting for the identical goal: Come on, Carl! Don't quit! You can do it, baby! You can make me love you! But underneath it all, I was rotten lonely.

Then three months after I came to Chicago, this letter arrived from Joan Franke. Joan Franke had been the Perle Mesta of our sorority, the one always needling us to "keep the spirit alive." Now she wrote that Lu and Ralph were living in Charlotte. She had spoken with her, and Lu sounded wonderful. Well that did it, just hearing that name did it. That same week, when Carl was working, I got ripped, I contacted Information and phoned. She answered. I said the name Lu, pulling out my little reels of memory. There was a nine-months-pregnant pause. Then *bang* right in my eardrum.

Yes, it was dumb I phoned. But I was beside myself wondering if time had healed the wounds and we might be friends. Or maybe I just needed to know she was alive. But it made things worse. And when Carl came home later, I was like a zombie. He began with his questions, and what the hell. I broke down and out it came. "Carl," I cried. "Do you remember Lu Hestor?"

"Of course, I remember Lu. What's she been up to?"

"Carl, we were more than friends."

"What's that?"

"I said we were more than friends. Remember that time we went away when you were on your way to Chicago? Well we went to a motel and made love. That's what happened, Carl. That's why she left school before graduation. That's why she gave up her scholarship and got married and I came here to live with you to get her out of me. I thought that would happen, but it didn't and she isn't and I can't handle what I feel anymore, Carl; I'm still in love with her."

He looked at me like I was loony. "You're nuts."

"No, I'm not nuts. I'm trying to be honest."

"You're telling me you love a girl!"

"Not a girl, not any girl. I love Lu Hestor."

"That's impossible."

"It's not impossible. It's true."

"But she's a girl. If you love a girl, you're queer. And if *you're* queer, so is the pope!" That tickled him. He started to laugh. Then he wanted to make love. I got angry; he was trying to take my clothes off. I yanked his hair and screamed, "Goddammit Carl; I don't want to make love! I want you to hear what I'm saying! I've just told you the most secret thing in my life and you won't take me seriously!" I was becoming hysterical and I kept shouting I needed help.

So he took me to a priest he knew from the hospital and told him the whole story. The priest put a ball on a string and dangled it in my face. He told me to watch that ball swing from left to right while he counted to ten in a singsong voice. Then he said in sum what Mrs. Tremble believed about the mind being more powerful than the body—and I should will this devil-woman out of me, which I could do by focusing on good. "Repeat after me," he said sternly, "I don't love Lu Hestor."

"But I do."

"Just say it."

"I don't love Lu Hestor."

"Say it again."

"I don't love Lu Hestor."

"Say it is foul and sick to love your kind, and it incurs God's wrath."

"It is foul and sick to love my kind, and it incurs God's wrath."

"You will burn in hell if you don't change."

"I will burn in hell if I don't change."

"You love Carl Bentley."

"I love Carl Bentley."

I was nodding off when the priest, by snapping his fingers, brought my mind out of its tunnel. But I didn't feel any different and said so. Then he had us kneel on the floor and pray and repeated my sister's words about God hearing the prayer of the smallest sparrow. After that he asked me to come back.

I never returned. I thought the whole thing was stupid. But I kept trying with Carl. And when the coldness came after climax, I fought it. And when I got bored, I fought that too.

I tried to shape myself as one shapes a sonnet: so many words to the line. But I wasn't a sonnet. Desire wasn't a line. And after a while I gave up.

Not on men though. Quite the contrary. Carl had proved sex was easy with them; why, if the penis could get inside me so often and I could blast off like a rocket when he touched my breasts, I was over women.

Throughout this time I was sending my rent check to Lillian, and often when Carl was gone I'd call. By autumn I had the exact date in June she would be leaving for Peru. I knew she was keeping her apartment, and we had already talked of living there together when she got back. But since she was to be gone more than a year, I was planning to move into the dorm as soon as I started Columbia. My future was all set. In December I called Lillian and said I was flying into New York on January second.

She was leading a seminar that day and wasn't able to meet me, but she said to take a cab to her place and the key would be with the super. Greta was off on assignment in Europe for a few months, so we would have the whole place to ourselves.

My last night with Carl was the best sex we'd ever had. I've often thought of that. It went on for ages and felt good. At the end he cried, I cried, but in his heart-of-hearts I think he knew I should leave. As for me, I believed the right man was out there, waiting. I was convinced of that. The past was past, and I was moving on. That's what comes to me now. That was the attitude I brought to New York . . .

COLUMBIA

... From the time I hit town, Greenwich Village was dominant in my imagination, was the skin that covered my earliest sensations in Manhattan, was there, beating, like a heart, coursing blood and vitality through the main arteries of New York, pulling me as one is pulled to the ledge of a tall building, scared but compelled, repulsed by the very thing that trances her. That's how I felt. I read *The Village Voice*. I studied the area on the little map I carried. I told myself I was curious because my father had briefly lived there and artists still did. But the main draw was the queers. I was dying to see a real one: what it looked like, wore, how it ate. I wanted to watch it go into a store and buy something, put it under a microscope and count its cells. I wanted to be a fly on the walls of Greenwich Village, Empire of the Queers, and then retreat to my uptown harbor thinking, "There but for the grace I might have gone." And though Lillian mentioned taking in a Village restaurant a few times, I always had an excuse. Fortunately she didn't bring the subject up that much. I was to learn that like most New Yorkers, including my friends later at Columbia, she tended to stay on her own turf. But even if that hadn't been the case, Lillian would have been the last person I would have wanted to see a queer with. Just thinking about that made me paranoid . . .

Emily arrived in New York with two huge suitcases (her trunks had already been sent). And from the moment she walked into what was to become her home for the next five months, she felt free as the breeze and more independent than at any point in her life. The apartment was one of those railroad affairs popular with students at the time. It was spacious, with rooms streaming off either side of a long corridor and a bucketsize bath at the end. A big sign on a door indicated her bedroom, and on the covers Lillian had put a six-pack with a yellow ribbon on top. From the window she could see the Hudson.

The first order of business was to feel like a student again. So she changed into jeans, turned the radio sky-high, got her cigarettes and beer, and was dancing around the rooms when Lillian came home. They had their usual excited reunion.

She soon learned she had moved into a mini-UN. There were Israelis from the upper floor in the building who visited. There were graduate students who popped in, drinking, dancing the night away, arguing politics. There were musicians, revolutionaries with glints in their eyes, vagabonds, intellectuals, friends of friends ripped on booze or hard living who might wander into the apartment at any hour, for the door was seldom locked. The center of all this activity was Lillian. She was a bundle of energy, and Emily could only marvel at her ability to attract so diverse a group, to say nothing of her stamina: Lillian taught, and at the same time worked on a combined M.A.-Ph.D. degree. She also played drums at a jazz joint uptown, wrote grants, studied celestial navigation and foreign languages while still finding the energy to engage in fleeting affairs with guitar-playing anorexic sorts in beards who gave her love (or that "other" four-letter word, she would wink at Emily). But she wasn't near to settling down. She was too busy.

With Lillian gone during the day, Emily had a chance to familiarize herself with the Upper West Side. There were stores to poke through, the Columbia campus to stroll soaking up the good vibes of the life to come. This was an area of immigrants, politicans, rich, poor, Columbia-dominated and all rubbing shoulders with Harlem ten blocks north. Bars like The Gold Rail on 110th Street were interesting to sit in. So was The West End, a home-away-from-home on Broadway that attracted students and other forms of life. To make herself look smart she would have a copy of *War and Peace* with her. She would sit at the bar pretending to read it, making sure the title was visible, her mind on everything but Russia. Sometimes she sat out on the benches that straddled Broadway and talked to the old people who practically lived there. She loved their accents, the sensation they gave of another world. This was Walt Whitman's New York, she would tell herself. He had done what she was doing. This thrilled her. It couldn't be noisy enough for Emily. There weren't enough cars or passengers on the subway or cabs honking or people milling everywhere. New York was the eye of creation. That's how she felt. She loved the anonymity of the city, the fact she could smoke and drink where she pleased; and it wasn't long before she was eager to get back to school, into a dorm with her own room and days of English courses. Before that, she took a temporary part-time job at an ad agency in midtown. For fifty dollars a week she greeted clients from a spacious desk in front of the elevators: she smiled, fetched them coffee, typed, and answered the phone. Afternoons off she went to the UN or windowshopped on Fifth Avenue. For perhaps the first time in her life she was really enjoying her own company. Yet sometimes she was plain scared of ending up alone. When that happened, she missed Carl terribly. One night during a party at Lillian's, she phoned him. It was their first contact since she left Chicago. He told her he had met a girl and was thinking about getting married this summer. She hung up, and in a rush of insecurity wondered if she might have made a big mistake in having left him.

. . . I remember those days now with special nostalgia. I remember my fun with Lillian. I remember too I still thought about Lu, especially when someone asked about Carolina or a certain song came on the radio. Once Lillian caught me in a sad mood and asked what was wrong. I slipped and said I missed Lu. Then, panicked, I tried covering her name up with Lynn. Lynn Hestor had been my first love I told her, but it hurt too much to talk about. Lillian didn't press. Weeks later she got home from work one night all excited because her arrangements to Peru had been finalized. For some reason I was alone in the apartment. We decided to go up to the roof for a few celebratory drinks. It was a gorgeous night. The sky had laid an egg above the city, a red moon. And we were stretched out on a blanket feeling the sweetness of the occasion until out of nowhere she said, Wasn't it funny the way Mattie Hurst had just dropped off the face of the earth.

Well my heart turned into a jumping bean. I don't recall what I answered, but she must have detected something in my tone because all of a sudden she said in the tenderest voice imaginable, "Stollie, if you ever need me," here her sound trailed into a mawkish imitation of Lauren Bacall, "you just whistle. You know how to whistle, don't you?" long pause. "You just put your two lips together and," another pause, "blow."

That did it. We cracked up, which lightened my mood; and I quickly changed the subject . . .

At the end of May, Emily moved into Miller Dorm. Her room was a large single overlooking Morningside Heights, and at night the hall was quieter than air because everyone was studying. Down the way lived a young woman named Carol Coin, who was to become her closest friend at Columbia. Carol was a political science major from Baltimore, a Barnard graduate so she knew the ropes. Not without looks—she had strong Germanic features, hazel eyes, nice brown hair she sometimes braided, and an upbeat personality—she was the sort of student who becomes president of things, a joiner, an achiever, frequently a practical joker, also stubborn. Never mind, she had a following. And as Hilda before her, she liked Emily instantly when they met in the downstairs cafeteria.

After Lillian left for Peru, Emily started hanging around with Carol and her crew at The West End bar. They were bright and idealistic, full of opinions about the world's ills. Before Labor Day, Carol invited Emily in on an apartment she planned to get with Mary Bake, another student, when they graduated this coming June. She was flattered to be included; and since Lillian wasn't expected back for over a year, she agreed. In the meantime she began looking for a teaching job for the following September. She got her résumé together and sent it out to various schools, particularly targeting private ones, which didn't pay as well as the public schools but her trust monies would make up the difference and the students were better and the classes smaller. Then, as the fall semester got under way, she met Nelson Curry.

Nelson struck her as a poet if ever there was one. He had that look—wild-eyed and woolly. He was ranting about Dylan Thomas when she first got wind of him, standing near her booth at The West End with his hair a red storm on his shoulders, shaking his head, gesturing emotionally, quoting *A Child's Christmas in Wales*—this huge bear of a man in uncombed locks, dressed in suspenders, baggy trousers, a shirt with the top buttons missing. He had twinkly green eyes, an impish grin, and Ireland was all over his face. It wasn't long before she added her opinions to his; and after midnight Nelson walked her back to the dorm.

From then on they were together almost daily. Carol found him uncouth and tried to discourage her attentions. But Emily was taken by Nelson's verbosity, his down-to-earth manner, the fact that he said he liked strong women, that he was restless and into barhopping. He had a temper that she saw occasionally, but his heart was kind. And on a deeper level, there was a certain feyness he possessed that touched her, a wounding of spirit. Nelson was the first man Emily ever shared her poetry with, the first man who ever encouraged her to write. They spent Christmas at his cousin's in Connecticut. And at a New Year's Eve party he kissed her. He had never done that before, and it seemed to take them both by surprise, which only endeared her to him more. That brought up something else. Much more than Carl, Nelson was reserved about sex. Fine. She wanted to go slow too. She began thinking if she had been born a man she would have wanted to be like Nelson Curry.

The résumés she sent out netted results in January, and she received invitations for personal interviews. She met with three different administrations; and her pick was Sloe Academy in White Plains. It required a one-hour commute, but she had already decided to get a car when she finished Columbia. In a February follow-up meeting, Sloe hired her as a senior English teacher, pending her M.A. And on the train back to the city that afternoon, she decided to celebrate.

Now it bears mention that Emily's fascination with Greenwich Village had continued unabated all this time. Once she had even taken the subway down there alone, gotten out at Sheridan Square and walked around, as curious as any cat in a new house to see what might be in store. But if she expected a queer to fall out of a tree in front of her, she was disappointed. She decided they must be drinking in the bars; however, she wasn't about to go in one alone. Twice she asked Nelson to take her. She didn't say to a queer bar. She just suggested the Village would be a fun thing to do one night. But Nelson said he didn't like the Village, and she thought if she pushed it would look strange. Tonight was an exception, though. She had seen an ad in *The Village Voice* about a nightclub near Sheridan Square that featured female impersonators; and she resolved to take Nelson there as a treat.

Back in the dorm, Dot Cash, who lived on her floor, said she had gotten a phone call earlier from someone named Joan, who would try to reach her tomorrow. Emily didn't give that a second thought as she left to meet Nelson for dinner.

She told him she had a surprise place to show him, but she refused to say where even though Nelson persisted. Around eleven they boarded the South Ferry local for downtown, and all was well. Once the train pulled out of Thirty-fourth Street though, he asked tentatively, "You're going to the Village, aren't you?" It didn't take an Einstein to figure that out since at this point the destination most likely would be there, Chinatown, or Wall Street. She nodded and smiled enigmatically, pleased with herself. But he made a face. "If it's the Village, I already told you I don't like it there. I never go."

"Well then," she teased lightly, "I don't go either. We'll be tourists. It's my treat, so relax."

"I'm no tourist," he sniffed. "I've been to the Village before."

"Well, I haven't really."

"So where're you taking me?"

"Nelson, why spoil my first surprise ever in this relationship?"

"I want to know."

"Then hold on to your horses and you'll soon find out. You might even have fun, perish the thought."

"What's the name of it?"

"The Circle Three."

He mulled that over. "Where's it at?"

"Seventh Avenue."

"Where on Seventh?"

She pulled a piece of paper out of her purse grouchily. Why was he making such a big deal out of this? "Two twenty-one South Seventh, near the subway," she answered.

"Where'd you hear about it?"

"The *Voice.*"

He dug his hands into both pockets of his army jacket and stared silently out the window. She sensed a mood change. "If I didn't know you better, Nel, I'd think you didn't want to go." She put a foot on his boot and kicked his ankle playfully. He didn't respond, so she tried another tack. "Come on, don't be a sourpuss. It's my big night out. We always go where you want to go."

That seemed to loosen him up, and he halfway smiled. They were just pulling into Sheridan Square; and when they got out, Emily took his hand and together they ran up the stairs onto the street; they crossed Seventh Avenue and walked north following the numbers. In about five minutes they saw a canopy with CIRCLE 3 in lights. She broke off to dash to the marquee with Nelson right beside her. "Is this it?" he asked. He didn't sound particularly overjoyed.

"Yes. Look!" She pointed to a picture of a woman with short hair, in black tights and tux jacket and holding a whip. Tootles Boot, the name said. Next to that was a reed of a young man with Valentino-style hair and a pout. His name was listed as The Rare Montclair. Above those was a glossy of eight men in women's clothes with their wigs off. "Come on," she entreated, dying to go in. Nelson, visibly hesitant now, didn't move. From the rear two men and two women approached just as the door to the bar opened. And in the rush of people about to enter and others departing, Emily and Nelson found themselves inside. Her heart was doing a tap dance, she was so excited. The people who had come in too found a table across the room, leaving them to face a few empty bar stools just ahead. Her eyes swiftly took it all in. On the wall there were American flags surrounding a dollar-bill-studded mirror beside a picture of Bette Davis and a bosomy nude with a gaze approaching beatification. But Emily's attention was riveted on two men at an adjacent table. One looked like your everyday banker—business suit, tie, the whole bit. His companion, however, was something to behold: powder-caked face, thick rouge, dangling rhinestone earrings, purplish nails, blood-red lips, cleavage in a skintight shockingly pink gown. A slit up the side revealed a large hairy leg. Definitely male. Now he stuck his friend's fingers in his mouth, sucking and licking them while smiling wickedly. Behind her, Nelson muttered ominously, "Let's get the hell out of here!"

But she was already at the bar ordering two beers. "How much?" she asked breathlessly when they came quickly.

"One fifty."

Recklessly she placed two bills on the counter, told the bartender to keep the change, and yanked at Nelson's sleeve. Jesus, she thought, what's eating him? As if reading her mind, he lowered himself to the stool and sat with his drink between his hands like a dog guarding a bone. After minutes of intolerable tension, she pleaded, "Nelson, would you kindly tell me what's going on so I can enjoy my drink."

"I told you. I don't like the Village. And I don't like it *here.*"

"What's to like? It's just a place to go. We're not moving in."

"It's a fag place. I don't like fags."

"Oh, grow up." Since ordinarily they got on famously, Nelson's behavior took some getting used to; and at first Emily couldn't read the signs. Deliberately she turned away, trying to forget him. The man in the gown was on his friend's lap now, kissing his neck. "Jesus!" Nelson snarled.

Emily didn't respond.

He kept it up, "Jesus! Would you look at that. That makes me sick."

She glanced at him nervously, "Oh God, Nelson. What's it to you?"

"Fags," he muttered. "If one of them so much as lays a hand on me, I'll . . . " He banged his bottle for emphasis.

"Are you crazy? They're not going to bother you."

He threw his hands up in disgust, "They bother me. They bother me, okay? They bother me by breathing the same air. Come on; drink up."

She gestured toward the two couples who had come in behind them. "Why can't we be like them and just have a good time? What's the harm? I thought you were a . . ."

"A *what*?" he interrupted fiercely. "A fag!"

"Shhh, would you keep your voice down?"

"Well, what did you mean?"

"Nelson, I can't believe this. Of course I don't think that."

"So why'd you think I'd want to come here, of all places?"

The juke box cut in and she tried to climb into the music now, away from Nelson's unpleasantness. She wasn't going to let him ruin this for her. She felt young and vibrant; and she wanted to be an Observer. This was really living, her mind said. Big time life! Looking around, she saw mostly men with their arms entwined and a sprinkling of women at the end of the bar; but since it was smoky, it was hard to really see their faces. Down the way the curtains opened, and a blast of music filled the room as the record faded. The floor show! She had to see it. She poked Nelson in the ribs and tried to make him laugh. "What do they call a man with no arms or legs who's lying under a pile of leaves?" Nelson wouldn't even look at her. "Russell," she hooted. She put her fingers at the corners of his lips to turn them up; and when he pulled back, she said, "Oh come on, big guy. Give us a happy." He pushed her hands away, but she persisted. "What do they call a man with no arms or legs in the water? Bob," she answered her question just as someone tapped her on the shoulder. She gazed up to a head that didn't belong to its body. A woman's body, for she could see the contours under the jacket. But it was as though the head had been stuck on the neck by some distracted inventor who, forgetting it, had gone on to other business. The face was as plain as oatmeal. Heavily lined brow. Haircut like a Marx brother. Bulky hands full of rings, holding a long ivory cigarette holder. And when the voice asked if Emily and her friend were here for the show, the sound was almost tender; and the smile that went with it exposed the whitest teeth Emily had ever seen. "Yes," she answered before Nelson could refuse, and started to rise.

The smile wrapped itself around the woman's ears. "I'm Micki Ross," she offered.

"I'm Emily Stolle. This is Nelson Curry."

"Emily," Nelson groaned. "Don't give out our names."

She heard that, but she didn't care. She was fixated on seeing the show. Micki turned to motion the two couples to follow her, saying the same to Emily, who whispered to Nelson, "Please, it's my special night. I promise we won't stay long." Tensely, Nelson got up. And presently all six were filing through the curtains into a small room with a partial stage. At the first table, Micki pulled chairs out for Emily and Nelson before going on with the others. As soon as they sat down, Tootles Boot came up in a black bikini with matching knee-high boots. This time Emily didn't introduce herself, she just ordered two beers and tried to forget Nelson's mood.

In a short time the drinks arrived, just as the lights dimmed and a tall thin man slithered onto the stage. "Ladies and gentlemen," a voice boomed from the rear. "Straight from Fire Island, Hollywood, Provincetown, the sensation of New Orleans and gay, I mean *gay-y-y* Paree, the one and only, the *sin*-sational, the *sex*-sational Rare Montclair!"

Limp as a rubber band, wiggling like a Hawaiian dancer, an extremely effeminate, lipsticked male laced himself with the cord of the mike, his long silky fingers caressing it as he brought the mike to his mouth so closely it appeared he might eat it. The word "honeysuckle" crawled through his lips and he began to strip. "Honey-*suck*le," he warbled (pump pump pump, rubbing his crotch). Off went the "honey." "*Suck,*" he moaned, hips rotating; the "le" bit the dust. He stopped, waving his tongue at the audience like a finger up to no good. Now he caroled "suck-suck-suck," holding the mike closer to his mouth as his fingers seduced the top part, "You stir my sug-uh"; in sweet compliance his hips ground a slow clockwise motion and he seemed on the verge of mounting the microphone.

You're going to *suck*le
I'll *suck*le
You *suck*le
Let's us *suck*le
Bay-bee *our* sweet sug-uh makes my tongue go howdy
Over *suck*le your r-o-o-o-se.

"That's it. Suit yourself, but I'm out of here!" Nelson shot up from the chair; and with a quick look at Emily, he was gone. Miserable with embarrassment, she put some bills on the table, waited a minute, and then followed him outside. He was in the street waving at traffic. "What are you doing?" she bawled, coming up behind him.

"What does it look like I'm doing? I'm trying to get a goddamn taxi."

"Oh, you were just going to leave me there, huh?"

"I knew you'd come. Don't worry about it."

"Why don't we take the subway?"

"They're too goddamn slow at this hour."

It was when she tried to get a smoke that she realized she didn't have her bag. She began patting herself frantically as if it might be hanging on some invisible part of her body; but the awful truth was she had left it inside. God, but she couldn't go back in after leaving like that. Now she begged Nelson to get it. It had everything in it, all her ID. He refused. She got angry. He still refused. She yelled it was all his fault. If he hadn't pulled that stunt, it never would have happened. No dice.

"Go to hell!" she shouted, and marched back in, back to the darkened room where the show was still in progress; but the table had been cleared. She searched the floor by the chairs. Nothing. In the dim light she waited for the waitress; and when they spotted each other, Tootles Boot made a just-a-minute sign, disappeared, and shortly was back with her purse. Apologizing profusely, Emily tipped her five dollars and returned to the street; but Nelson was nowhere in sight. Two off-duty cabs rolled past, their headlights making small mist-pies in the light drizzle. What a fink to just run out on her like this! She started toward the subway; then, realizing it was too late to ride alone, and since all the taxis seemed to be off-duty, she decided to call a private service.

There was a phone booth at the corner, and she headed toward it only to be met by a loud cry some fifty yards away. Looking in that direction, she saw Nelson lunge from an alley holding a man by the collar and shaking him hard. She ran over in fright. "Stop it, Nelson! Cut it out! You're going to hurt him!" The man was struggling and yelling that all he had wanted was a match. Pow! right in the kisser.

And then Nelson had him on the ground with the man still

trying to cover his face with his hands. "Match my ass, scumbag!" He kicked him. The man rolled on his stomach.

Emily grabbed Nelson's sleeve, but he brushed her aside as if she were merely a winged thing on a petal. She stumbled, steadied herself, tried to block his foot again and again. A car light neared the curb. She raced over calling, "Help! Please! He's going to kill him!" The driver noted the action, shook his head, rolled his window up, and sped off. She dashed toward the bar but then veered back thinking they would only call the police and she didn't want trouble. Nelson had the man on his feet when Emily got there, and he was slapping him in the face. She then beat on Nelson with her bag, distracting him enough so that his grip loosened and the man was able to escape.

Emily quickly followed, shouting "Stop, wait, let me help you!" But after a few blocks the dark had gobbled him up and he was gone. Out of breath, she staggered to a building and leaned on it, panting heavily. And then slowly she retraced her steps. In that time of approximately ten minutes, Nelson had changed drastically. No longer the fighter, he was now sitting on the curb cradling his head in his hands and sobbing loudly. Torn between anger and concern, Emily went up to him and touched his shoulder. "Nelson," she said urgently. "What is it?"

"Where is he?"

"I don't know. I lost him."

"Is he okay?"

Is he okay? Was this a joke? For a moment sarcasm got the upper hand. She really didn't know how he was, she snapped. She hadn't had a chance to engage him in conversation.

He ignored her tone and shuffled to his feet. "Well," he said, wiping his eyes. "You better go on now."

"I better do *what*?"

"Go home."

"Back to the dorm you mean? You're telling me after this to leave, to go back to the dorm just like that, nice doggy, roll over. Is that it, Nelson? Are you drunk? Nelson, say something. Who was that man? What was that all about?"

"Come on," he answered wearily. "I'll help you get a cab."

"Where are you going?"

"I'm staying at a friend's on Canal Street."

Had he lost his mind? That was the only explanation that made sense of this. Surely she would wake up and be in her own safe bed, and this would all have been a dream. Except it wasn't a dream. Nelson was really standing here playing the role of the fine gentleman preparing to escort her to a cab. "Forget it!" she barked. "I'll get my own ride." She started on, but he was after her, saying she couldn't be on the street alone so late. Without breaking stride, she answered she didn't want his noise, calling him a Jekyll and Hyde.

"Just a minute," he said. She gave him a withering look and picked up her step. Never had she been so enraged, so disappointed. He grabbed her arm and she tried to reclaim it. "Let me go, Nelson. You're hurting me." But he had the other arm now, a big guy whose strength she couldn't match. Rashly she egged him on, "Oh, okay; why don't you hit me too, you maniac."

"Look at me!"

She didn't flinch.

"I said look at me."

"I'm looking. I'm looking. What do you want?"

"I want you to see me. You look, but do you really know who I am? Maybe I'm not who you think I am."

She rolled her eyes in disgust. "Oh, for pete's sake, Nelson. Will you save it for your next novel." She tried to move on, but he was in her path. She attempted to go the other way, but he blocked that too. She stepped to the right, then the left, with him imitating her back and forth, like birds doing a little jig, and then he had her by the shoulders again. "Listen to me, goddammit. I'm not just a fucking lunatic. There's reasons for what happened tonight. Don't you get it?"

"Get it. Get what?"

"That guy," Nelson lost his voice. In a moment he found it way deep in his throat and brought it out where it clung to his lips, pale and quaking as a man dangling from a great height. "He's me. I'm no better'n him. That's me I was hitting on."

"I don't understand."

"Sure you do. Why do you think I didn't want to come downtown?"

"I don't know. How would I know?" she said with exasperation.

"Use your head, goddammit. You're not stupid. Don't make me spell it out." But when she still seemed bewildered, he sighed, "He came on to me, Emily. Okay? You want those words. Fine. He came up with his stupid-ass match question, but he wasn't after a match; and I blew it, man; I lost it." Her head slanted to the right like a dog listening to a high note. "You want me to draw you a picture, Emily? Listen. I know that guy. I mean I don't know him–know him; but I know him. Don't you see? I know where he's coming from. I've been in that boat."

Something was beginning to click in her head. In growing astonishment, she said, "What . . . what are you saying?"

"I'm saying he made a pass at me."

"And?"

"And I know how it feels because I've done that too."

"You," she gasped. "Are you . . . ?"

"Yes," he exhaled quietly.

"You!"

And then the point of her question stabbed Nelson on the tongue, and now it was his turn to gape dumbly.

"Nelson," she repeated his name as if it were a foreign substance. "You're a . . ." She was absolutely incapable of saying the word.

So he said it for her. "Queer? Yes, I am. Like a three-dollar bill."

No. It couldn't be, she thought. She had to leave. She didn't know this man. He was an imposter, a phony, this whole thing was absurd. She didn't want to hear. She said that. "I don't want to hear. Shut up!" She tried to scream, but he put his hand on her mouth and then she tried to cover her ears but he took her hands in his; and she broke down crying.

There on this isolated block of Seventh Avenue he told about being caught by a priest in Catholic school with another boy, and for weeks and months his daily penance had been to run soap over his tongue, which the priest had said could break from the weight of its own dark and unnatural passions. He had graduated and come to New York and lived with a guy not far from here but it about did him in: what he felt, what he wasn't supposed to feel, living like two enemy camps were in him throwing darts at each other. So he walked out one day and never came back and made a vow to be celibate. That's why he never came to the Village. It was too much down here, too much temptation, too many memories.

Then he had met her and felt what he had never felt for a girl before, it was like they had had this instinctive connection. He thought she could fix him, make him feel what he was supposed to feel. And then that miserable SOB had come up to him and tried to touch him and he saw himself in his face. He was afraid. Afraid of what was still in him. Didn't she wonder why he never had gotten fresh, he asked. He was afraid if he did he wouldn't want her and then he would know for sure.

"You're lucky, Emily, 'cause you do know who you are, 'cause you've never had to live some dirty lie of the mind!" With that he let go her hands and began striking himself in the face.

She watched in horror with the thought of running away. But how could she leave him like this? She understood him. She knew his expression—crazed; and she knew her own: she was Sheila looking at herself. "Stop it!" she yelled, trying to interrupt his arms. But as before he was too strong. So she backed off and then with all the energy at her command, she lowered her head and charged like a bull into a red flag yelling, "Stop it! Stop it! Goddammit Nelson, I can't take it anymore!"

It worked. His hands fell lifelessly to his sides. It was after three now, and cabs looking for last-call revelers were beginning to appear. One flew down from Fourteenth Street. Then another. All available. But she couldn't move. She hurt too much. Nelson, standing helplessly before her, broke her with his matted hair, his chest heaving, his shirt damp and messy, his face filled with hurt. At that moment there came to Emily, how would she ever forget this, a longing to hold him, to embrace his pain closer than she had ever touched anything, to feel it press into her, merging her own dark terrors with it, then to love him for all the grief she knew he felt, and for her own too, to forgive them both. She started, but then fear rose in her heart, bringing anger with its lack of charity. And a harsher need prevailed. She would never be able to accept what Nelson's life said about *her*. I'm not what you are, a voice inside her declared firmly. I never was what you are. And how dare you smash my dreams!

The force of this sentiment shook her. It was not a simple thing, being pulled in opposite directions at once. She heard him say with uncharacteristic timidity, "Don't turn on me, Emily. Please. I need a friend." A sudden tenderness engulfed her, but then she closed down again.

Two blocks away another cab was pulling out from the curb, and she chose that time to survive. He should see a doctor, she said, and leave her alone. It wasn't her problem. She never wanted to see him again. She couldn't deal with the depth of his sickness, she said. Then she was hurrying up the street as the cab approached. Wings. It stopped, and she got in. The last she saw as the cab wound south before turning right to the highway was Nelson staring after it like a small boy watching a wagon train leave.

A dream woke her. She was running down a long corridor that kept unfolding like a rug pulled at the other end. She bolted up in bed. Across the room the blinds wrung out the remnants of evening. Six-thirty. Troubled, she fell back on the pillow. Then like a snapshot coming into focus, the edges of memory sharpened around Nelson's face. She closed her eyes. Her head hurt. In a minute she drifted off.

An hour later a tennis ball was banging in her ear. "Rise and shine, beetlebrain!" It was Carol rolling up the shades; and then day slammed into the room like an armored truck. Threads of pain stitched the back of Emily's head. Her stomach felt like a war zone. "Someone's on the phone for you, sweetheart." Carol leaned down and mussed her hair playfully. "Says it's important."

Nelson! She might have known. "Tell him I'm asleep," she grimaced, pulling the covers over her head.

"It's not a him; it's a her."

Lillian? "Who?" Emily peeked over her red and white quilt.

"Now how should I know?" Carol's white socks and trim athletic skirt bounded to the door radioing vigor and good health. "Gotta go," she called over her shoulder. "I've got a match at eight. I'll just say you're hung over and to try back later!"

"No, wait!" Emily sat up, shielding her eyes from the light. Maybe it really was Lillian. "Thanks, Carol. I'll be right there." She grabbed her robe on the chair and in seconds was in the phone booth. "Yes, hello. This is Emily."

"Emily!" a distinctly un-Lillian voice responded. "It's *me.* Joan!"

Joan? Who the . . . ?

"Joan. Joan Franke. Joanie-Frankfurter, idiot," the voice broke into her confusion happily.

Now memory pushed the image of her former sorority sister through the fog. Crap, she thought. I'm not up for this. But she had to be. "Joan," she said with as much warmth as possible. "Where are you?"

"New York City! Five minutes from your dorm and on my way to get you!"

"What?"

Laughter. "No. No. Relax. I'm at my aunt's over on Lexington Avenue, about to leave for the airport."

"The airport?"

"I'm off to Dallas. I'll tell you about it in a minute. I'm sorry to phone so early, but I didn't want to miss you." She went on at a rapid clip, explaining she had had to get Carl's number from Information to find her, and he had said he thought she was in the dorm but didn't know the name, so Joan had ended up calling the English department and here she was. "How's that for persistence?" she added.

"Are you who called me yesterday?"

"That's me. I didn't leave a message. I wanted to surprise you."

There were some general comments about Joan modeling for JCPenney and being based in Dallas. Needling Emily too for not writing. But the heart of her message was: she was coming back to New York May twenty-eighth to see her aunt and uncle off for Europe, and she was throwing a party to reunite as many of the girls as she could round up. "Coco's coming from New Jersey," she chimed breathlessly. "Luckily Millie Cox will be in Boston at a buyer's convention, and she's going to fly down. Oh and Lu; you probably know Ralph landed a big job in Germany and they're sailing out on the *Queen Mary* Memorial Day. They've already got Broadway tickets around then, so she promised she'd make it. Sally Lace will too. And Midge Somer. Sue Beth said she'd do her damnedest, and you know what *that* means! Did you know Sue Beth had twins? Emily. Emily, are you *there*?"

"Yes," she answered as the stone of Lu hit her squarely in the gut. Lu coming to Joan's party! Panic temporarily eased her headache, and then Nelson crowded out everything. She had to get off the phone. She couldn't handle any more. So with Joan saying to puh-leeze put the party date on her calendar, and Emily promising not to forget because she had orals the eighteenth and it would be something to look forward to, they said good-bye.

She hung up and walked back to her room. The initial pangs about seeing Lu faded because it was so far off, but Nelson was here and now. Fully awake, his face last night began to torment her. How could she have left him like that? A wave of pity engulfed her. But that was followed by resentment. He had tricked her. It wasn't right. And what was wrong with her anyhow to have attracted someone like him? What if he had killed that poor man and the police had come and it was smeared all over the papers? Glumly she dressed and went out. She wasn't up to seeing anyone. It was like she had this monster on her back that she couldn't run away from. To even have imagined Nelson might be someone significant in her life and then to find out he was queer! Now whom could she trust? She felt betrayed.

The end of Nelson changed the balance of the semester for Emily. She quit the West End and submerged herself in her studies. When asked why she wasn't dating him any longer, she said he had just gotten to be "too much," and let it go at that. And as the days went on, her anger was replaced by a silent disgust at herself for having been so cold. There were times when she was even tempted to contact him. Yet too many buttons had been pressed, and she feared if she saw him, she might become too emotional. Orals were coming, and her master's thesis was due. She couldn't afford to stew. Once she thought she saw Nelson on the street, but then he was lost in the crowd. Days later she heard he had moved.

The only bright star on the horizon was Carol, who was fast becoming something of a role model to Emily: on-her-toes, savvy, infectiously witty, goodhumored Carol Coin whom people just seemed naturally to gravitate to. From time to time she found herself acting like Carol. Using the word "fabulous," which Carol said at the drop of a verbal hat, wearing similar jackets and skirts. Greenwich Village seemed far away.

In April, she, Carol, and the other student, Mary Bake, found an apartment on Central Park West ten minutes from Lillian's old place. She wrote Lillian: "I'm definitely going to move in, Lil, 'cause you won't be back you say until sometime after Christmas and it's easier to share a place. Anyway, I'm just around the corner, and you'll really like Carol. She's going to work at the UN." That last impressed Emily. Already she could see herself hostessing the little cocktail parties Carol talked about a lot, and meeting diplomats from around the world. What a life awaited her when she left Columbia. She nearly wrote Sheila to show how successful she was, what an exciting life she was having in New York, and did send a note to Aunt Francie, who had closed the Newport News house and was spending most of her time now in Hawaii.

While all this was going on, Joan Franke's party was getting closer. Frankly, Emily hadn't given it much thought until Joan called in May; then two weeks later a formal invitation arrived in the mail. There it was in print, making everything definite:

SISTERS UNITE!

AT JOAN FRANKE'S DOMAIN

FRIDAY, MAY 28, 7 P.M.

386 LEXINGTON AVENUE

NEW YORK CITY

555-5698

"Don't RSVP, Emily. Just come, dammit!" Joan had scrawled in big letters. Her throat tightened as Lu's face came to her clearly. Maybe she shouldn't go.

But then any thought of not was canceled out by all the good things in Emily's life. Why shouldn't she be there? Why should she give Lu so much power? Wouldn't it be great to let everyone see how well she was doing? She had a wonderful job waiting in September. She was moving into an apartment with one of the best-liked girls in the dorm. She had passed her orals with flying colors and gotten "outstanding" on her thesis. So what did she have to fear? Wouldn't this be a good test of her recovery? Emily felt almost boastfully confident that afternoon as she got ready for Joan's party.

The minute she got into the taxi for the ride to Lexington Avenue, the driver was talking up a blue streak. "Castro's too big for his britches," he reflected at the first light. "You'd think he'd be a little 'preciative for what we've done for him. That's the trouble with these guys, you know, they get themselves a little real estate and we give 'em a pat on the back and then they bite the hand that feeds 'em. We never shudda let the SOB in New York in the first place." He grunted, pleased with his vision of the world.

Emily lit a cigarette, trying to calm her nerves, her earlier confidence all but shattered as the cab wound south on Amsterdam en route to the party. She hoped she looked okay. She took her Violet Fuchsia out of her purse and gave her lips another coat; then she stared out the window for a moment wondering how Lu felt about *her* coming. Hey, she hadn't thought about that. Well, surely Lu knew, Emily told herself, surely Joan would have said she was going to be at the party so maybe Lu wouldn't even be there herself. Great. That's just great. She could feel the driver's eyes again, and she looked away, determined to be optimistic and wishing he would zip up.

He was saying he knows people like Castro. Take his brother-in-law. His brother-in-law's got a mouth like the Grand Canyon, you could fall in and get lost, ha ha, always telling you what to do, how to do it. What his sister sees in that jerk he can't figure but women are funny, like his wife's always mouthing off he should lose weight and then whaddaya think she does? his eyes walked over her face again. She shoves pizza in his mug. So how's he supposed to deal with that news, huh? His hands waved in the air to make the point and he half turned in his seat. Well, he don't understand women, that's for sure. Once more his eyes toasted her in the mirror; a big grin dug two dimples in either cheek.

"Bet you got lots of boyfriends, don't you, nicelooking girl like you? Oh I get it," he went on, honking at a car that cut him off. "You don't wanna talk, right? I don't blame you. My wife's always saying I'm a motormouth, she bets people pay me just to shut me up. I don't know. Don't ask me nothing about women!" Emily smiled slightly and rolled the window down. At Ninety-sixth Street he slowed for two joggers, which reminded her she should exercise more. "So how you like New York?" he broke into her reverie. "Me, you can have it. What I want is a little place on the Island, you know. New York's no good for kids. You got kids?"

She shook her head and mentally practiced what she would say to Lu if she were there. Hi, Lu. How's it going? How's Ralph? You two having a good time? So how's it feel to be going to Europe? I'll bet. Well me, I couldn't be better. I just finished my master's you know, I did it on Hopkins, right, and I got this super job, so it's all working out. I'm going to be living with this girl who works for the UN. Yeah. I'm meeting lots of famous actors and poets, and New York's stupendous. Well, good luck to you. Tell Ralph hi.

A sudden cramp seized her foot. She removed it from her shoe and rubbed it vigorously. At that moment the driver announced: "I get it. I was trying to label you. You're a college girl, right? You got brains instead of kids. Is that it? Me, I never sat still for no college. I got married. That's my first mistake, ha! My wife she's always saying I got the green grass disease, you know that's when you're always thinking the grass is greener on the other side. But she should talk, my wife; she's never satisfied. Know what I mean? Always wanting this and then she gets it and she don't want it no more. Get off the streets, you bums!" he snarled at two men pushing a cart across Seventy-ninth Street. "Where they going?" he jerked his head at Emily as if she had the answer. "What they think they gonna find when they get there? Always running around like ants. That's what New York is full of, a bunch of wacko ants. Makes me crazy, you know I should have it nice like you, college girl." When she didn't respond, he persisted. "My name's Al. Al Giero. What's yours? Emily? Emily what? Emily Stolle. Hmmm, that's a nice handle. English, I'll bet. Sure. I go for them birds all right. They're real smart if you ask me. But who's asking? Right?" At this he emitted a belly laugh and twirled his hand in the air as if directing an orchestra.

Now they were whizzing through Central Park, almost at Joan's as he expounded his views on General MacArthur, who he said he took his hat off to. "You understand that, don't you, college girl?" She felt his eyes once again and shifted to avoid them. "You know maybe I should come up to that fancy school of yours someday and give my brains a wax job, study Shakespeare or something, ha: roses are red and violets are blue, now that's *my* idea of a poem. So what you think, college girl, seeing ol' Al here huffing into one of your classes. Hey!" he turned and gave her a bold wink, "whadda they teach you kids up there anyways?" He crossed Madison Avenue toward Lexington and then he was stopping at a green awning with a uniformed man who opened the door. She paid the driver, uttered sentiments about having a nice day, and then she was staring at the skyscraper like a child lost. I don't know if I can go through with this she thought as she entered the building.

The instant she saw Lu whatever was left of her confidence vanished. She was in the living room with a drink and cigarette talking to Millie Cox, clad in navy blue with a matching scarf. Her hair was longer, and she appeared somewhat fuller. A ringing came to Emily's ears, but then Joan was hugging her, Coco was shrieking, "It's Emily! Just look at *you*!" and firing more questions than the mind can tolerate. But when the view was cleared, Lu was still seated, her hands clasped tightly in her lap, her smile fixed as a performer's as Emily started over for the mandatory greeting among females: a hug. She felt the withdrawal as she lightly brushed her cheek, inwardly pleading, dear God, don't give us away. "How are you?" she managed as she stood aright.
  "Just fine," Lu answered smoothly.
  "And Ralph?"
  "He's just fine too."
  "Do you like New York?"
  "Yes. It's very special."
  A few more sentences, correct between them like with Sheila at her sister's wedding. But who was listening? Lu looked wonderful: same shiny spot on her nose, skin pink and soft, lips— ah, facts know this: she had kissed that mouth. Later she would remember Lu's eyes that seemed to say: *I don't know you, Emily Stolle. I have no memory about that semester at school or whatever madness we carried in our hearts.* But suddenly Joan was beside her, joking they shouldn't monopolize each other as they

used to. Christ! Why did she have to say that? Lu looked ashen. I've got to get out of here, Emily thought. I never should have come. Turning too quickly, she fell over a stool and landed on the floor; her skirt coasting up her bare thighs left her humiliated and foolish, reminiscent of their first meeting at Carolina. That brought Joan running over.

"Oh Emily," she teased, "you'll do *anything* to get attention, won't you? Come on." She pulled Emily to her feet, along with Lu from the chair. She put Lu's hand in Emily's. She took Emily's other one in her own. "Okay, everybody! For old times' sake!" Joan kicked the stool out of the way. "Join hands and make a big circle, babes! Let's hear it!" At once they were all screaming:

> I'm a Tarheel born
> I'm a Tarheel bred
> And when I die
> I'm a Tarheel dead,
> So it's rah rah, Carolina, Lina,
> Rah rah Carolina, Lina,
> Rah rah Caro-li-i-i-nuh!

By now the only part of Emily with feeling was her hand holding Lu's, which seemed as cold and lifeless as a dead bird. Lu's hand lay between Emily's fingers, a blunted arrow of memory, an emotional bullet that still scarred her heart. Only later would she explore the depth of her pain then, or what it had meant to be strangers when her mouth had once traveled the private geographies of Lu's body. Unthinkingly, she squeezed Lu's hand. Damn! She hadn't intended to do that. Horrified, she broke away and began kicking higher than anyone and leading the rest in cheers. She had to convince Lu she didn't care, that squeezing her hand had been an accident. Soon after, she told Joan she had to get back to school to study for an exam; and when she left, she barely told Lu good-bye.

She took a cab directly to her dorm. In her room she got a beer and sat staring out at the lights nesting in a row of trees.

In a while she went to her bed, pulled a box from beneath it, and found her Carolina yearbook. Leafing through that, she came to a picture of her sorority; and there was Lu bright and shining. Until tonight she hadn't even looked at it.

She closed the yearbook and put it back in the box; then she went over to the window and stood there thinking about everything. Touches of the past stabbed her, and she felt abandoned all over again. She thought of the party and seeing Lu, when the breath had almost gone from her. No sense fooling herself. The excitement she had felt when she saw Lu had been greater than anything she had ever felt for Carl or Nelson. And those emotions were sick, sick, sick. She hated them. She began to cry, which was how Carol found her later: sitting by the window with her head in her arms, sobbing.

"My God!" Carol called in alarm, running to her. "What is it, Emily? What's wrong?"

Oh Jesus, didn't I lock the door, Emily thought, burying her head in her arms. "Nothing," she finally answered. "Just leave me alone."

"No. I'm not going to leave you alone. Talk to me. What happened?"

"Carol, please, I can't talk about it."

"You must, Emily. You'll feel better."

At that, Emily sobbed harder and Carol squeezed her shoulder, begging her to say something.

Again she repeated, "No, please. Just go away."

"Is someone dead?"

"No." Emily's voice broke. "Yes," she said slowly. "In a way."

"Nelson?"

"No. Not Nelson."

"Has someone hurt you?"

"No, I don't know, I can't say it."

"Try, Emily; you've got to try."

"Carol, I can't." She began crying harder. "You wouldn't understand. No one understands."

"Try me," Carol said softly, putting her arms around her.

"That's what friends are for. You can trust me. Whatever it is it doesn't matter. My God, we're going to be roommates, Emily. Let me help you. Please."

Her voice, so tender and compelling, broke the dam, stirred something out of her fragile wounds, came at a time when she felt most vulnerable; and so she did something that amazed her when she thought of it later: she spoke of Paris and losing her virginity to get over women; she didn't mention Mattie, but she talked about crushes she had had on girls before, particularly one, and that that had evolved into the great love of her life, Lu, that she had lived with Carl to get over her and actually thought she had until tonight when it all came back. When she finished, Carol, who had said nothing during this whole outpouring, patted her awkwardly on the shoulder, said things would look better in the morning, and that she must go.

Emily, too self-involved to give that much thought, eventually fell asleep in her chair. She woke up stiff from having sat there so long; and when she walked to her basin, she found this note shoved under her door:

May 28, 1956

Emily:

    I've tossed and turned trying to compose this letter in my head and hoping I am able to say what is imperative.

    Of course what you told me will forever be sealed in strictest confidence. But surely you understand why it's necessary that I reassess our plans. Frankly, I'm not able to live with a homo; and after long and serious thought, I've decided we can no longer be friends. I'll make up something to tell Mary Bake so you needn't be concerned about that. Now I know this looks like I'm running out on you in your hour of need, but try to put yourself in my shoes. I have to consider my life and how it would look if anyone knew my roommate was a homo. Anyway, how do I know what you might do to me if you got desperate? Please believe this isn't a cruel heart speaking, but rather the logical mind attempting to express what must be stated. I'll close on that note, trusting you'll get the help your soul cries out for. I realize this is a lame letter, but what else can I do?

Sincerely,
Carol Coin

She read that letter over and over. It was like a car wreck, horrible but fascinating at the same time. She kept going back to it as if the repetition of the words would make the message untrue. But it *was* true. And eventually, as its impact took hold, she gave in.

She gave in because she was tired of the struggle, and she couldn't take it any longer. It didn't help that she was pretty, that a penis could get inside her, that she was unaffected by most girls and liked men fine and was large-breasted besides (somehow it seemed large breasts proved she was normal). What mattered was she still had a dark, unnamed thing in her, maybe a virus caught in the childhood's affliction of Mattie. And the only way to kill it was to let it run its course, to meet a girl like Lu and be with her long enough for it to die on its own, like a germ exposed to the air. In fact, if she and Mattie had kept seeing each other, that probably would have happened and there wouldn't even have been a Lu. But she had been stopped before she was cured with both of them; she had been left stranded on an emotional turntable. And the only way to get off that turntable was to see this thing through.

Sitting in her room now, surrounded by all the trappings of success—her job confirmation letter from Sloe Academy, her thesis, the books she knew so well—the clearest thing in Emily's mind was the truth of Lu. But this time, unlike in North Carolina, she would face the music. And where better than in Greenwich Village. She would go there and stay for as long as she had to, to get over this. She would never see Carol and those people again. As for Lillian, she wasn't due back until after Christmas and she would write her and say her plans had fallen through and she had decided to live around artists.

That made sense. After a while, she dressed; then she cautiously opened her door. Seeing the corridor was empty, she hurried to the stairs and once outside walked to the subway. She took the train to Sheridan Square and found a realtor. To impress him, she said she was a teacher, she had a master's degree from Columbia University and was going to be teaching at Sloe Academy in the fall. She added she wanted a place with atmosphere and was eager to move in right away because she was working on some important projects and had to leave the dormitory.

The realtor took her to a partially furnished apartment off Houston Street in the wings of Greenwich Village. It was a five-story walkup with a tub in the dining area, a bedroom roughly the size of a phone booth laid flat on one side, a fire escape with cats that stared through the window, a fireplace that worked on whim. It wasn't the Taj Mahal, but it was fine for a bohemian; and the neighborhood was homey, full of pizza parlors, small bakeries, mothers sitting on their front steps tending their children. A huge Catholic church was on the corner. This was Little Italy, the safest area in the city, the realtor told her, and at fifty-five dollars a month a steal.

Thus it was here that Emily came to live that June of 1956.

GREENWICH
VILLAGE
AND GONE
MAD

Part Two

WOMEN

She had to stay busy. She couldn't dwell on the past or wallow in self-pity. She must remember she had a master's degree from Columbia, a good job waiting in September, that she was the same person she had always been, once looking for a man to make her normal, now looking for a woman for ultimately the same thing, but still Emily Stolle from White River who had pledged a good sorority, been popular, was kind and intelligent. She had to get on with her life in this strange continent of Greenwich Village. She had to find a girl she wanted to have sex with. The sooner she did, the sooner her disease would play itself out. And now with almost three months left of summer, she had time to adjust before Sloe started in September. All this was what Emily kept telling herself as she prepared for her new life. Lacking confidence, lonelier than at any point in memory and with Carol's rejection ringing in her ears, she maintained herself on one pep talk after another.

Her first priority was to fix her place up for when she brought someone home. The apartment came with a bed, end tables, and other pieces of furniture; but it needed style. Using her trust monies, she bought rugs, a picture of a running elephant with its front foot raised, a lamp shaped like a rooster, a wagon wheel, an antique trunk, a neon mouth-shaped light that turned bright red when a button was pushed, a carousel horse she had to pay the cab driver to help lug home. She named that horse Horace for no particular reason and set it at the foot of her bed hoping it and everything else would make her look bohemian (she had decided to call herself that since it seemed a more inclusive term than "artist"). Her final purchase for fifteen hundred dollars was a black VW Beetle from a dealer on Houston Street. All this helped her spirits.

Within the first week she found time to write Lillian. "Carol got married at the last minute," her letter said in part, "which shot the Central Park West plans to hell and back. So here I am in Greenwich Village. I got wind of a great apartment down here—227 Spring Street—at fifty-five dollars a month and I figured why not. You know I've always wanted to be around artists. And they're all over the place, Lil. There's two right here in my building. I've already met one. We go to poetry readings and stuff and maybe I'll even perk up my own writing. I couldn't be happier!" That same day she signed up at the New School for a drama class about to start. The half-hour walk from her apartment to there would give her a real feel for the area, she thought, as well as something constructive to do with her spare time.

When all this was accomplished, she set about learning the neighborhood. She introduced herself to people in her building. She shopped on her block, letting the merchants know she was a teacher. She soon discovered power in Little Italy was three-pronged. First were the priests, all very saved, Catholic, and God-knowing. They shared their authority with the men-in-dark-business-suits who stood out like gold thumbs mainly because they were rich, immaculately attired, they parked their long, black, shiny Cadillacs where they pleased, got their shoes shined almost daily, always waving, smiling, and talking in soft tones. No one dared mess with them. Besides those, there were the mothers. Their power, while not as overt as the men's, came from having borne Italian sons. The mothers were the eyes and ears of Little Italy, the chorus in a Greek tragedy who knew the comings and goings long before they happened, and what they didn't know they interpreted down to the last nuance. In the warm days of summer, in the white tongues of early morning, in the settling dusk, they held forth on the front stoops of their buildings, their power base, cackling about husbands, children, sin. They planned the summer festivals when the statue of the Virgin was paraded down Sullivan Street and the faithful rushed to pin money on her gown. Approval from the mothers virtually guaranteed a stranger such as Emily would be left alone. Thus she went out of her way to be polite to them and let them know she was a teacher. Italians respected education.

As for women—as Emily considered this most vital objective, she decided she needed a breaking-in period. In other words, she couldn't just expect to run out and meet someone like Lu. She needed practice first. And the best place to start would be in the only queer bar she knew, the Circle 3. Surely after all these months no one would remember her.

It was a Tuesday night, and the traffic was racing around Sheridan Square. Emily parked her car on Charles Street and walked north on Seventh Avenue. Soon she was standing near where Nelson had had his fight on that sad, scarred evening months ago. She had on new jeans, a knotted neck scarf under a blue shirt, and white leather boots, the sort she had observed on various women in her walks around the Village. She had almost bought sandals for this occasion, the reputed shoe-code for bohemians; but she hated her toes. She pulled her mirror out for one last look and put on a fresh coat of lipstick. Now, having inhaled four beers back in her apartment and carrying a worn copy of *War and Peace,* she walked up to the door of the Circle 3, opened it, and went in, heading straight for the rear. There a tall man with a receding hairline asked if she was alone. She nodded, and he led her to a table. She sat down and placed her book on the white cloth near the candle, making sure the title showed so she would appear smart. She saw the waitress come up that she remembered as Tootles Boot. Tonight Tootles was wearing a lavender blouse, orange toreador pants, and a long gold chain. Glad she wasn't recognized, Emily ordered a beer and eased back into the seat, barely hearing the piano. She was trying to get up the nerve to pay for a woman. That's what she had decided to do because it made it seem easier, as if to pay meant she couldn't be rejected. And if she pulled it off tonight, she would never have to do it again because she would have experience. She began rehearsing in her head: Look here, she would direct to the waitress, could you get me a woman for tonight? Then quick she would fork over the loot. Yeah, but what if Tootles laughed or threw her out or, for God's sake, what if the woman Tootles found looked like Tootles! She hadn't thought of that. But she did now, watching her approach, the square, boxy face, short hair, resolute features, laughless eyes—nothing that even remotely interested her. Oh well, hope for the best! Tootles set the drink down just as Emily whipped a cool ten from her pocket as gangsters do when they want a special table, and crammed it into her hand, swallowing hard, blurting out, "I, you, listen, could-you-get-me-a-woman-for-tonight?"

Tootles's hand lay in the air as if resting on an invisible shelf. Then as her fist slowly embraced the bill, as the meaning of Emily's words sank in, a big smile bit off half her face. If this seemed an extraordinary request, it didn't show. "You want a girl?" she repeated.

"That's right."

"For *all* night?"

Well, sure. "Yes, if that's possible."

The eyes gave her the once-over. "Wait here." Emily didn't breathe until Tootles came back saying she had someone but it would cost her. "For the girl I mean," she explained when Emily appeared puzzled.

Don't be a cheapskate! "How much?"

"Thirty should do it."

She gave that to Tootles, who disappeared again, leaving Emily full of doubts. Something about having to pay *the girl.* But too late now. She picked up *War and Peace* just as Tootles came up with a young woman in her early twenties. She was sparrow-thin, with brown hair piled atop her hair that loaned her features a hard edge. She seemed stiff, a trifle sullen; but she looked okay. Emily turned her book toward the girl, then put it back on the table wondering in panic, does she like my looks? What if she doesn't! She stretched her smile as close to her ears as possible, but the young woman barely glanced at her. She was carrying a purse, a lit cigarette, and her drink. "This is Melanie. Melanie, this is . . . What's your name, honey?" Tootles directed to Emily.

"Emily. Emily Stolle." She started to get up.

Tootles shooed her back down. "Well, Emily Stolle," she chirped festively, "here's Melanie. Melanie, here's Emily Stolle. You kids have fun!" One conspiratorial wink and she was off, as Melanie sat down next to her.

Emily felt a thigh. Now what? This girl's thigh was beside hers. Should she move over? No. That was the point. You start with a thigh and go from there. But she couldn't just sit here feeling Melanie's thigh. She had to get a conversation going. But how? She didn't seem to have a word left in her brain. "You want a drink?" she managed shortly.

Melanie held up a full glass and rattled the ice cubes.

"Oh, I see. You came prepared." Dammit, she thought immediately. Now why did I say *that*?

But Melanie didn't appear to notice. It wasn't that she was rude. It was as if she were with herself. Period. She pulled a mirror out and began playing with her hair, running her finger down her lips the way women do when they line up their lipstick. Emily couldn't stand the silence. "My name's Emily," she offered.

"I know." Melanie put her mirror back and snapped her purse shut. "You already said that."

"Oh yes, so I did. And you're Melanie."

"That's right."

"Melanie who?"

"Just Melanie." Her eyes narrowed.

"Oh. Okay. Were you already here?"

"Where?"

"The Circle Three?"

"Yes. Out in the bar."

"Oh. I didn't see you when I came in."

"Well, I was there."

"You come here often?"

"Sometimes."

"You a friend of hers? Tootles?" she added when Melanie's face went blank.

"Yeah. Sort of." Melanie put her cigarette out and took a deep sip of her drink, giving no indication of interest in this line of talk.

There followed a brief exchange about favorite brews. Melanie didn't like beer so much, she declared. At that, Emily asked if she wanted another drink.

"Maybe, when I finish this. You in some kind of hurry or something?"

Sensing she was doing something wrong, Emily leaned back and said no, of course not, that she had all night. The pianist was about to take a break. Emily commented on how well he played. Melanie agreed. Again they fell silent. Emily caught herself obsessing about Melanie's thigh, imagining pressing her lips to hers. She zeroed in on Melanie's mouth. The lips were too thin, yet exaggerated by lipstick; and they didn't appeal to her, she couldn't imagine kissing them. But she had to, she reminded herself, she had to want to. She decided she should first get to know her. "What do you do?" she wondered aloud.

"Do?" Melanie, swishing a little stick in her drink, quit swishing and acted as if she had never heard that word.

"Yes. Do," Emily reasserted. "Where do you work?"

"On Wall Street."

"Wow! Wall Street! That's something. Where on Wall Street?"

With just a trace of wariness, Melanie replied, "In one of those places down there."

Like a mole underground, Emily burrowed on. "I see. Well, do you like it?"

"What's to like? It's a job." Melanie stuck a cigarette in her mouth. "You got some fire on you?"

Emily yanked a lighter from her pocket, and Melanie leaned into it, bringing a truck of perfume with her. As she did, her thigh pulled alongside Emily's. Well, she must like me, she concluded, or she wouldn't keep it there. She felt almost jaunty when she inquired, "Is Wall Street fun?"

Melanie's eyebrows arched. "Fun?"

"I mean does it satisfy you?"

"I don't know. I never thought about it."

"Have you done it long?"

"Done what?"

"Your work. Wall Street?"

"Not really."

"So what'd you do before?"

Now Melanie was looking at her oddly. "Different things," she finally answered.

Emily pondered that. Suddenly she was overcome with curiosity, but Melanie seemed to have withdrawn. Why? What was wrong with trying to get to know her? She picked her book up and said, "Well, I don't know squat about Wall Street. I'm a teacher. I'll be starting at Sloe Academy in the fall. That's the one in White Plains," she finished proudly.

Melanie's eyes widened. "You're a *teacher*?"

"I will be. I just got my master's in English at Columbia."

"English, huh?" Melanie made a face, and she sank back in her seat. "I never did too good in English."

"Well don't feel bad about it. You should see me in math. Bet you're good in that, aren't you?"

Melanie just shrugged her shoulders and then she asked why she had that book like that.

Emily was holding *War and Peace* with her arm propped up on the table. "Oh that," she acted as if it had been forgotten. "I wanted you to see what I'm into. You ever read this?"

"No," Melanie grunted. "What's it about?"

"Russia."

"Well I don't know anything about Russia. I got New York to worry about, you know what I mean?"

Emily said of course she did. And then they talked a bit about living in New York. Emily asked her where she was from.

Melanie said Jersey.

She asked if she drove over to the city.

Melanie said no, she took the tubes. No big deal.

She asked if she knew where Little Italy was.

Melanie said sure, over by Houston.

She said she lived there, trying to work up the courage to get her home, trying to find Melanie's face interesting; but when the light showed, she looked tired and there were dark circles under her eyes. "You ever been to Little Italy?"

"Not lately. I don't have a lot of time."

Emily started to suggest they leave, but instead inquired about her family. Did she have any sisters or brothers?

"I got one sister."

"You close to her."

"Man!" Melanie exclaimed. "You sure do ask a lot of questions!" But she sat back up, bringing her thigh close. Before Emily could defend herself, a comic came onstage joking about this broad in the garment center who always wore black panties 'cause she'd buried so many men there, ha ha ha. Then, drawing some imaginary lines in the air, he said he was a mute having an orgasm. More ha-ha-ha's as his body jackknifed in appreciation. But Emily, truly high now, was only conscious of Melanie's thigh. Given the number of beers she had had tonight, Melanie was about the nicest thing going.

Now Melanie turned and said, "I'm hungry. You got enough money on you?"

"Sure. What about a steak down at the corner?"

The last thing she remembered as they walked out was Tootles's grin. It hung in the air like a Goodyear blimp, blocking out the stage, the tables, everything.

Over a London broil Melanie got positively chatty. She told Emily she wanted to be a singer, which was why she hung around the Circle 3: she hoped to get her first big break there. Then she was going to Hollywood. She knew she could make it in the movies. Everyone said so. You just have to know the right people. Didn't Emily agree?

Emily was trying to follow the conversation, but each tick of the clock was bringing her closer to a vision. The vision was a bed, waiting for them. It was as if that bed was a bear's mouth, and they were tied on a mechanical belt heading into it. But she couldn't think like that. She had to get down to business. She had paid money, done that desperate thing to succeed tonight. And it didn't matter about her feelings. She wasn't able to go through this again. So at a point she took the plunge and asked Melanie to stay over.

Okay. But she had to have cab fare tomorrow.

"How much you need?"

"Twenty dollars."

"Twenty dollars for a taxi!"

Melanie's eyes narrowed. "I got some pickups to do, and you have to tip."

Oh hell, she didn't care, she had the cash, over a hundred dollars. She suddenly felt reckless, almost cavalier; she fished a twenty out of her pocket and in no time they were driving to Houston Street. She found a parking space near her building, and soon they were starting the climb up. Glad no one could see them, Emily had already decided to show off Horace, let this girl see how unusual her mind was to have a horse by her bed. They would talk a little, put on some music. And, you know—

But the minute she opened the door, Melanie ran into the toilet; and when she emerged, her face five pounds lighter with the gunk off, she started to undress right in the living room. She didn't need pajamas she said. She hated them. With that, she began stripping down to the law of her body—a skinscape of ribs and hips, flat stomach, breasts that appeared nippleless. Seeing her naked, a massive futility hit Emily. How could she touch this formidable being? What was she to do in bed? Was there anything more fearsome than even attempting to go through with this?

"What're you looking at?" Melanie asked sharply.

She mumbled something that didn't even sound like her.

"The bedroom in there?"

Emily nodded.

"You coming in?"

"Yes. I gotta go to the john." She waited for Melanie to comment on Horace as she walked in, but the only sound was the bed squeaking. She turned and went to the toilet; and when she was finished, she came back to the room. Melanie was under the sheet, her eyes shut. Emily stood beside her horse as if waiting for a command. Then, impulsively she grabbed the stirrups and hoisted herself up in the saddle. She couldn't get into that bed now, she needed more time. But she couldn't let Melanie fall asleep either. She would impress her. In a firm, clear voice, she began:

> Give me my Romeo; . . .
> And cut him out in little stars,
> And . . . make the face of Heaven so . . .

Melanie shot up in bed, her breasts wiggling furiously. "*What* is going on?" she erupted, her eyes wide in astonishment.

"That's from *Romeo and Juliet.* Isn't it beautiful?"

"Are you crazy? Yes, you're crazy. It's fucking three o'clock in the morning, and you're . . . I *never* met anyone like you in my life. Will you get off that stupid thing and cut the light out? I've got business to take care of tomorrow!"

Compliantly she slid off and sat on the edge of her bed, catching the moon from the open window. The moon highlighted the veins in her hands, and unaccountably she thought of her father. A feeling of great sadness overtook her, and then Melanie moved and the bed shook. Don't forget: you have a woman in your bed, bringing you even closer to the defining moment of your sexual existence in Greenwich Village! Go on, she urged herself. Kiss her.

But Emily just sat still, thinking now about Lu and how there had been nothing in that motel room that night but Lu, there had been nothing in her backyard that afternoon but Mattie. But with Melanie she was conscious of the lamp, the green ashtray on the bureau, the blunt edge of the chair, Horace's white teeth washed in the moon, her boots that hurt her feet. She took them off and moved with all her clothes on under the covers. Lying there and lying there. Should she talk about her feelings? Get to know this girl better?

"What're you doing?" The question broke the bubble: Melanie was waiting for action. Emily didn't feel like action, she didn't want to kiss this stranger. She said to Melanie she'd like to get to know her better and that this was the first time she'd been in bed with a girl since college. She spoke of Lu a while and Carol's letter. She described how hard it had been to move here but that she hadn't had anywhere else to go. The more she talked these strange rare words, the more she felt she had been in jail all these years, a jail with no window or light, no friends or human comfort; but now, talking about her true feelings, it seemed a weight was leaving, a rock on her chest had been lifted and she was able to stand and move about her cell. The words came easier, and she began to have warm thoughts even toward Melanie. She asked her if she wanted to see a play sometime. When Melanie didn't respond, Emily suddenly realized she had been doing all the talking. She pulled herself up on her elbow and gazed at her silent bed partner. The moon had parted Melanie's hair, softened her features. Her eyes were shut, her mouth slightly ajar, her body breathing in sleep's dance: she hadn't heard a word Emily said.

Crushed, she lay back down and eventually traveled the same route.

Nine A.M. "Holy shit! I'm late!" Melanie bounded from bed and rushed into the toilet. Startled awake, Emily at first lay there hearing the rapid back-and-forth steps of her "guest," a shoe hitting the floor, water running. She ran her tongue over her lips and blew out the taste. Sour. She realized her scarf was still on. She took it off and flung it across the covers, trying to decide what to do. She decided to get up. Melanie was just putting the final installment on her attire when Emily entered the living room. She looked older, harder, her lips exaggerated from too much paint; the colors of her blouse and skirt clashed.

"Good morning," Emily said politely. "You want some coffee?"

Without looking at her, Melanie grunted, "Can't. Gotta run."

She watched her smooth her skirt out, then take a comb and start to work on her hair. "You going to Wall Street?" she asked shortly.

This time Melanie glared at her. "Jesus, woman! Is that all you do? Ask questions? That's all I remember from last night! I got a headache from it! You better get it through your skull you don't go around asking stuff that's none of your damn business!"

Her obvious irritation threw Emily off. What was she so sore about? After all the money spent on her last night, what right did she have to be so rude? She started to ask; but Melanie, with a seeya and a slight wave, opened the door and was gone, her heels making a racket down the hall. She closed the door and sat down wearily, disgusted with herself. She went over all the details of last night, telling herself she had to have been smashed to have brought home someone like that, someone who didn't even know what *War and Peace* was. She could just hear Melanie back at the bar: "Remember that jerk I left with last night, Tootles? You know what she did?" Then would follow the whole rotten story of Emily's questions and Emily sitting on a horse in her bedroom quoting poetry.

Oh God, now she longed to move out of here. She didn't

know how to be queer. She didn't know what to do with a girl. She didn't know about small talk with someone you pick up and what's expected of you when you get her home. It wasn't like with a man when he makes the moves. It was like being herself when she's with a man except she's the man but she really isn't; and if that isn't upside down, what is? She tried to put herself in Melanie's shoes. That made her want to throw up.

Suddenly she looked at Horace and hated him. She went into the bedroom and moved him to a dark corner in her hall and then she gave herself one of her famous talkings-to: She was here, she had to stay here, she had to let the virus run its course. And no sense trying to kid herself. By definition, she was queer. Mattie and Lu had gotten married and fixed themselves, but she didn't like sex with men that much, she liked the sex she had had with them, which alone made her queer. But she didn't have to stay that way. She just had to burn this sick thing out of her. And now, the-morning-after-Melanie, she repeated what she had told herself so many times before: that if she could have been with Lu for any length of time, or with Mattie either for that matter, her feelings about them would have died from the weight of their own disease. So she should learn from Melanie what *not* to do: Don't ask so many questions with a girl. Don't climb up on Horace and show off at some unholy hour. And if you bring one home, touch her.

This made her feel better. She showered and around noon went outside. It was a sunny day, and Mrs. Cordello who lived on the first floor was on the steps. She and Emily had talked before about how hard moving was. Now Mrs. Cordello smiled and said hi, sweetie, extending her hand, a gesture so kind it almost brought Emily to tears.

"How are you, Mrs. Cordello?" she responded, sitting down beside her.

"Oh, good, good. You gotta your place all fix now?"

"Yes. It's coming along fine."

"So listen, you get some lucky fella he go crazy such a nice girl make him dinner. Huh?"

"I'll try, Mrs. Cordello." The old lady's warmth lifted her

spirits. She stayed a while chatting, and that afternoon walked to the New School to buy a book for her class starting tomorrow.

A bar named Pandy's sat on Greenwich Avenue like a big frog on a water lily, and it snapped Emily up a few days later.

She knew women were inside. She had seen them as she walked to class, she had heard the music and once, curious, had even pressed her face to the window and watched. So one night, still smarting from Melanie, she went in. And there she sat for several hours, a living antenna meshed in the wires of Queer, picking up the sounds and nuances of the women who drank here, studying their dress, manner, reactions. Pandy's appeared to be a neighborhood bar with that sort of intimacy, steady talk, laughs, shouts of recognition when someone new came in, a bartender who called everyone by name. There was a pool table at the rear, a juke box by the door, a lace of tiny bulbs that trimmed the large mirror like the one at the Circle 3, and a German shepherd named Max who roamed freely. A few people smiled at her. The bartender was friendly. Soon she began to relax and, before leaving, had been included in some conversations. Thus it was that Pandy's would become a near daily event in Emily's life in Greenwich Village, the place where she would meet most of the women she got to know, including her earliest sexual encounters.

The first of these was a short, sandyhaired, fortyish, pugnosed, intense woman who came in one evening, took the stool next to Emily's, and asked for a light. Unusually forthcoming, she soon was giving Emily her name: Lorraine; her job: real estate; her marital status: married (but her husband was out of town a lot, like tonight, she threw in); her hobby: horseback riding. She had been coming to Pandy's since '52 maybe three or four times a year, depending. She liked it because you could hear yourself think here; but she had never seen Emily before, her eyes narrowed. Oh, Emily was new. I see, Lorraine said. And she was a teacher. How nice. Lorraine liked teachers. She liked Emily's eyes too. Very deep. Did she know the Greeks said eyes were the windows to the soul? Or was it gateways? Lorraine couldn't remember. Oh, windows, right, Lorraine agreed with Emily. Well, maybe a trite quote, but there was a world of truth to it she thought. Weren't those Greeks something? Sounded like Emily had been to college. Where? Chapel Hill. Bet it was nice down there. She had a sister who used to live in Raleigh. Oh, and Emily had gone to Columbia? Really! For what? English! Well I'll be darned, she said; English was her favorite subject; when she was a kid she used to write poetry up a storm; then she wanted to be a brain surgeon but that took too much time so she had gone into real estate—on and on.

She seemed nice enough, and Emily was wondering if she might have found a new friend just when Lorraine asked if she wanted to have a drink at a wonderful German bar near her apartment on Sixty-eighth Street. They could split a cab if she didn't have a car.

So that's what they did. More talk followed; then Lorraine invited her up for a nightcap. She just lived around the corner, she said, that big building with the doorman in front. Now up to this point nothing in the dynamics had suggested anything but sociality, but as soon as Emily walked into the apartment living room, things changed. Saying she was horny and her husband couldn't get it up, Lorraine began disrobing as Emily, dazed by these unexpected developments, watched silently. In seconds Lorraine was down to her bare minimum—pubic hair, hips, hungry breasts. She grabbed Emily's arm, feeding her hands to each breast, cooing as she did, rubbing Emily's fingers over the nipples as Lorraine pulled her into the bedroom. There, still holding her, she got on the bed, grabbed Emily and brought her on top of her. Spreading her legs, she pushed Emily's mouth to her crotch, from which exuded a tantalizing perfume. Vagina.

A wicked power seized her. And before she knew it, her tongue was opening Lorraine up like the petals of an exotic flower.

And when it was done, when Lorraine lay melted, all passion gone (passed out or seeming that way), Emily felt all manner of things. Surprise, for one, that this had happened, emptiness for another, that she had absolutely no emotions for this stranger, loneliness beyond the telling, as if she were stranded in some forlorn nation, not knowing the language or customs, having no guide to direct her, no map to take her where she belonged. And out of that came a confusion that would dog Emily for years with women—her role. She didn't know what to do now. She hadn't felt this with Mattie or Lu, and between men and women the sexual strategy is clear—key into the keyhole: explosion. But this was different. Wasn't she supposed to be touched too? Yet even if Lorraine had tried, Emily wouldn't have known how suddenly to reverse her position, to become vulnerable, open, ready. And what about her breasts? If she had let Lorraine touch them, wouldn't that have been embarrassing? Hers were larger than Lorraine's. Didn't that make Emily more womanly? Yet she had been the one who was aggressive. Oh, it was too complicated! So eventually she succumbed to the one lover she could trust—sleep.

An empty bed greeted her the next morning. After getting her bearings, Emily washed her face and went into the kitchen area. Lorraine was seated at a table drinking coffee and reading a paper. She looked cross and barely acknowledged the hesitant good morning. Emily stood in the doorway feeling like an intruder; then taking the hint, she left without even a good-bye. All day she felt used and cheapened by what had happened. But in the months to come, she would see there were many Lorraines who came into Pandy's on one kick or another. Greenwich Village women blew in the dust—here one day, gone the next. Case in point: when she ran into Lorraine months later, she acted as if she had never met Emily. That was troubling.

Not long after Lorraine, Wendy happened during an evening when Emily had had quite a bit to drink. Wendy was tall, slim, longnecked, sweetfaced, a creamyskinned natural redhead with big green eyes and a likable whimsy. She too sat down near

Emily at Pandy's; and when the girl between them left, they began talking. Among the first things Wendy wanted to know was Emily's sign. Told Leo, Wendy almost jumped for joy. Her sign was Pisces, she exclaimed eagerly; and the two were compatible.

Wendy was an avid astrologer and in two days was moving to California because California was an Aquarius state and Wendy's moon would be going into the eleventh house with Pluto rising on the cusp of Jupiter-ascending, which meant this was a good time to travel.

Well, okay. Emily didn't know astrology from a hole in the sun; but she liked Wendy's looks. And even though she was about to leave New York, the attention was flattering. So was what Wendy said about her palm. She picked Emily's right hand up, turned it on its back, and studiously traced Emily's lifeline from wrist to fingers. Then she announced she had a yod. A *what*? A yod, that's a gift from the gods bestowed on the rarest of people, Wendy said solemnly, adding that she sensed Emily was a magical presence.

Ten sheets to the wind, Emily sensed magic too: having a yod and everything! By last call, Pandy's had turned into an escalator, and Wendy was looking like Rita Hayworth!

Wendy, never the shy one, asked to go back to where she was staying—at a friend's who was out of town for a few days.

And what she would remember later was trying to find Wendy's breasts which, along with everything else, were spinning around the room. When that happened, she was in bed playing Dick Tracy to a naked Wendy. She found Wendy's nose, mouth, her hand dropped past Wendy's chin toward her fleshy twin peaks, which was when nausea clubbed her. Forget breasts! She barely made it to the john before vomit was everywhere and she had surrendered to a series of dry heaves before an absolute dark. When she came to, she was lying on the floor inches from a huge cockroach that was twitching its whiskers in her face. The stench of suppers past was on the floor, walls, even her hair. Mortified, she got to her feet and cleaned up as best she could. She left without a word, thankful that Wendy was zonked out on the mattress and, even more, that she was moving to California!

It was during this period she met Nina Sams, a handsome, rosy-cheeked Amazon of a woman with curly blond hair that framed the most cherubic face Emily had ever seen. Nina was that rarity, a woman faithful to another—Faye Black—with whom she had lived for years. No one at Pandy's had ever seen Faye because she didn't go to the bars.

Faye and Nina were antique dealers in New York. Successful, rich, devoted to each other but giving the other much independence, they owned a shop on Lexington Avenue, another in London where Faye was from, a luxury brownstone off Fifth Avenue, and a house in Connecticut where Faye stayed a great deal, riding horses. Often they traveled on buying trips, sometimes to Europe. Nina frequently spoke of their living in England someday.

Nina came to Pandy's regularly when Faye was out of town. And one July evening when Emily was already in her cups, that's what happened: the door opened and in came this tall, striking woman radiating cheer, blowing kisses and hellos, and setting the bar up all night. In the daze of music and more and more rounds of drink, she and Emily fell into conversation. And from that a new alliance was formed. Emily liked Nina's warmth and generosity. Nina, fifteen years older, found Emily a true innocent. In the ensuing months, a warm camaraderie was established, one based on a common love of night life, beer, and talk. Nina took an active interest in Emily's various flings that never lasted, Emily would lament when they were together. She would confide in Nina that she didn't know what to do when she got a woman, she didn't know how to keep her interested, she got scared. How had Nina and Faye lasted so long? That's what she wanted. But she didn't know how. All that touched Nina, brought out her Dear Abby side. Nina would become the closest thing to a friend Emily had in Greenwich Village, though their relationship was limited to the bars.

After Labor Day Sloe began, and it was then that Emily's two lives took shape. By day she was a true professional in heels and skirt, staying late with her students, tough, demanding, skilled, caring, a teacher who obviously loved her job. But at night she was a bar hound in pants and boots chasing an illusion of some Miss Goodbar from one club to another. She made up so many stories at school about her personal life—for what is more fascinating than a single young woman? and questions *were* asked—that it got hard to keep track of them. She said she had been married twice, first to a fellow from high school whom she had divorced after eleven rocky months. No children thank the Lord! The second had been the love of her life, a boy from college who had died in a traffic accident. Coincidentally he had had the same last name as she, Stolle. Emily said that because it was easy to remember when she used "Mrs." (Before school started, she had purchased a solid gold wedding band that she wore from time to time for "sentimental" reasons.) And she always told the other teachers she went out with exciting men from the city. In the muddled route of mendacity, she sometimes lost her way; but the road became so well traveled, the scenery so familiar, that increasingly she told her tales with confidence. And after a while she could almost believe she had been married twice, she could almost feel tears in her eyes when she spoke of her dead love, she could exude genuine emotion when she spoke of weekends with this man or that in New York. Her double life excited her. Her secrets made her believe she was fascinating. And never did any of this affect her job. For, blessed with remarkable energy, she could carouse all night and be fresh as a daisy for school the next morning. Her students were drawn to her, the parents thought their children fortunate to have such a demanding teacher. Even so, as Emily became more and more involved with women (and less and less absorbed in finding out whether she had a virus or not), the real potatoes, the hot potatoes, the meat and gravy served up with those potatoes, were the bars!

THE BARS

. . . The bars! Let me say they offered—you'll forgive me if I add nothing has really changed—plenty of women to choose from. In the 1950s women rattled in from the main streets of middle America, from rural New England and Alabama—lots of Catholics, Jews, southerners. Some were your typical English majors who romanticized pain. Along the way they might have read *The Well of Loneliness* and never gotten over it, or had a crush on a female professor and never gotten over that either. Often they were part of that quotidian series of younger women who moved to California to "find themselves," then got lost and ended up back in Vermont making rock gardens and stained-glass windows. Eventually they drifted into New York to *live.* There were also the gladiator types with mikes for mouths, and softer damsels painstakingly shy. Still others—how can I put this—were the older queers who had been around forever it seemed, who, like midlifers everywhere, had made the compromises and thus held a certain resignation in their eyes. In other words—and not to sound preachy—there was no such thing as an Everyqueer.

Queers came in all shapes and colors and sizes, and were not, in my opinion, any more sensitive than anyone else, or given to a greater or lesser intelligence. Certainly in Greenwich Village, that unpadded cell of emotional liberation, no one called the police or honked or went leaping if a queer walked down the street, which is why so many lived there.

Queers could be rich or poor; smart or stupid; ugly or good-looking. Some men queers strapped their cocks and padded their breasts (others were quintessentially macho). Some women queers padded their crotches and strapped their breasts (others were incandescently feminine). There were queers who hated being queer; there were queers immensely gratified by their lot. There were queer alkies, queer teetotalers, queer whores and celibates. Some queers were monogamous; some were sex machines; some were anonymous; some hung out on Fire Island sucking dick. Queers could be academicians or plumbers, bums or bankers, hairdressers or Republicans; preachers, teachers—I'm talking about the owned and the owners of this planet, people who, like everyone else, are exquisitely mortal. And the truth is there is no single truth: queers are facts exaggerated by myth.

The female queers I knew, like drinkers everywhere, were insecure, yet full of an endless boast. The tougher ones stuffed short black combs in their rear pockets. They hustled drinks and conversation in the catacomb dark of their favorite haunts. They wore ducktails, sturdy shoes, ran their hands over their genitals, inched up their shoulders like marines, played Very Serious Pool, and used the juke box as a third leg. They seldom made eye contact. When they walked, their separate body parts, as if congealed to some bulk of physical gravity, seemed to move not so much singly as in one thickness. Some (Nina told me once) made love with cucumbers and carrots or fashioned male-looking "tools" with feathers attached to the end. One exceptionally attractive woman I knew, a college professor, sold domesticated penises—eight inches of a taut, flesh-colored rubber complete with dangling balls, that she used as bookends when not in service. She wanted me to try one. "Come on," she urged, fastening it through a stainless steel aperture hooked to a leather stirrup. "This," she pointed to a strap that slid between the buttocks, "keeps it in place. And this," she humped the air with the whole thing, "does the rest."

No, no, I remember thinking, utterly flustered. How would I make it secure? Stick it in? Position it in front? What if it came off? What if I saw myself in the mirror? Suddenly the thought of wearing that contraption obliterated my childhood.

But some were not complete without one. Those were the Al Capone types who came into their element in the bars. Outside they might drive cabs or clean cages at the vet's or, in the endless vacuum of New York factories, work a night shift. But inside the bars they had their egos by the tail, and made out in the restrooms where they whittled out their little ballads of love and pussy:

Want to lick you, baby!

or

Selma sucks twat!

My favorite was "Carole, I'm just a hobo on the trip of love," plus that other emblem of enduring passion found in nondiscriminating toilets everywhere:

the initials varied

The more urbane women I knew—college graduates, aspiring college graduates, admirers of college graduates—engaged in what could only be described as Meaningful Dialogue: women's rights, Freud, Ezra Pound versus the Jews, vivisection. Some could quote Dylan Thomas until the cows came home. Some affected accents, preferably British. Some were drunks. And some were the power-trippers. They'd blow into Pandy's as Lorraine had done, looking for sex. But there the comparison ended. These women were into dominance. Females, through moods as contradictory as desire, had filtered in and out of their lives for years. But who would have known for the way they lived in the world? On the job they mimicked the males, called their secretaries "honey," told dumb blonde jokes, belted a few down after five with some of the loudmouths from work who didn't know how to take them, except the women were good at their jobs; thus the men tried forgetting they were women, which meant, in a manner of speaking, they were no one. Socially they adored faggots. Played bridge with them, laughed at their jokes. And they hated women, hated what their lust for women said about them. How do I know? Oh, from Nina, or I'd hear it on the grapevine, that mythic cord running through the bars that connected us all symbiotically.

A definite wariness pervaded the bars of my memory. As Melanie said, you didn't readily give your last name or number out—these being the hangover days of McCarthy when every vote-chasing official had a leg up for queers was one reason, these being the days when the FBI recruited queers to turn in queers for one reason or another, these being the days when New York's finest raided certain dance bars that hadn't paid off. Queers who were caught were hauled off to the Women's House of Detention, an imposing, funereal-looking establishment not far from Pandy's, where male officers routinely strip-searched females for contraband. I never saw that happen. I was never in a raid. But I heard about it.

The men who frequented the bars were mainly two types: the regulars, and the ones who waited. The former, for whatever reasons, found places like Pandy's nonthreatening and viewed the clientele as their pals. But the men who waited were another matter. These were the self-confessed saviors, the men with penises they deemed large enough to unqueer the queers. Sometimes they came in looking for a threesome. And if they found some girl down on her luck, they could score. Hence the process of delusion, like regenerative cells, went on and on.

Pandy's, where I mainly hung out, was a talk bar. But there were flashy places where you could dance. A popular one was near Fourteenth Street, hostessed by a poor man's version of Zsa Zsa Gabor. She was blond, bosomy, and tunnel-visioned. Her job was to keep the glasses full, to control the women who pawed each other openly or ducked into the johns for sex (sometimes getting into vicious fights), and to enforce the rules of general order. Around NYU a similar bar distinguished itself by a female whose job was to sit atop a stool outside the restroom dispensing toilet paper based on the size of a customer's buttocks. Even raunchier was a place on Nineteenth Street. Set amid abandoned warehouses where rats scuttled from alleys and the moon was used as a lamp, you were admitted only if approved; and if that happened, you stepped into a world turned upside down: men dressed as women dancing with women dressed as men, assorted drag queens, butches in various stages of machismo escorting beehived femmes with enough cleavage to sink a ship, bored housewives, model types from uptown—a dance zoo of grinding pelvises, tongues, roving fingers, women kissing as if they were leaving for Korea at dawn. And when all these closed at four A.M., the beat could be continued at any of a number of after-hours clubs. Like desert flowers all the queer hangouts came and went, deepened many an official pocket as they did, teased many a sexual dilettante. But Pandy's outlasted them all!

Let me add there were plenty of queers who didn't drink, who never set a foot in Pandy's. I just didn't know them. I knew the bars. To me they were like the merchant marine: the past was dead, the future was another drink, and *now* was a minute hand stuck to the next affair. I had my share in those days, women dotting the wicked *i*'s of my libido. And after a while I quit thinking queer was a virus. Somewhere under the dark stone of my guilt, on the subliminal banks of my consciousness, I believed queer was wrong, I hated myself. But I didn't think about that and (unless recovering from some romantic fatality) I had a ball. My double life quite frankly intrigued me. So did my cronies. Lillian always said she wanted to see the world. Well, my world was in the bars, plugged into the live wires of the universe. There we all were hatched on our stools, cranking out our little tunes of love and need. For it was in the bars where I played out the significant rhapsodies of my life then. I liked thinking I was hip, the bartender bringing my Bud the minute I walked in, the bouncers admitting me without fee. I tipped like I was buying a ship, was unfailingly polite, brooded over my suds like I was Plato or something, always searching for my ship of love—we were all looking for that ship—believing if I sat there long enough, bought enough rounds, squeezed enough poems out on my napkin, some heat of female luminosity would tip my heart. I gave my last name out, my number, because I was an innocent, you might say. But even if I hadn't, it was easy to find me—on my throne at Pandy's running my mouth. And understand, it was not so much the drinks that propelled me as the sense that when I was riding my bar stool, I would never die. Every moment was anticipatory; every woman coming through that door possibly *the* one!

In the small village of White River where I grew up, the trains trumpeted through the quiescent countryside like a thousand alarm clocks. How they thrilled me. How I fantasized their passengers, the mysterious ports to which they were bound! How I yearned to ride their backs as a circus performer her two stallions, one foot on each train as they plummeted me into the very nerve centers of creation!

Denied that, I came to Columbia by plane, then on to Greenwich Village, where I rummaged about my dreams like a cat in heat. But dream I did! I can still see myself barhopping along Eighth Avenue, the shop awnings fluttering into small tents, the newspapers rippling across the street like abandoned dogs. I can see autumn caught in the trees of Washington Square as I sailed from one shining pub to another. I was a sort of loner in those days. I liked it that way. I liked thinking of myself as a secretary taking down the dictation of this solitary life. I liked talking to people in bars, sitting with a drink in my hand, my eyes trading places with the wallpaper and listening to music until it burned out parts of my brain. And I loved Pandy's. I should mention that a number of women I knew there, even with their hard and constant features, had a sort of Colleen Dewhurst majesty, a sort of magnificence to their physiques, a strength, even a nobility in their jaws, and a handy weight to their grasps. Many were handsome as the day was long. On mustardy afternoons, and with names like Lonnie, Rene, Babbit, they scattered themselves about the room, full of a drinker's brag and (when their guard was down) an astonishing fragility. I salute them!

I was actively saluting them that winter of 1957, almost ten months from when I first moved to the Village. That was when Lillian got back from Peru, right as I was in the first of two major love affairs. Her name was Reena Dee . . .

Ripe. That was the word to describe Reena Dee. A walk out of a wet dream. Legs that kept on going when you closed your eyes. Full bosom with nipples prominent beneath the skinhugging blouses she favored. Wide brow, black hair, a Hedy Lamarr twin under the paint, a seasoned Gretchen Stryker over it. And she just appeared one autumn's afternoon at Pandy's amid rumors that Pandy had known her before, that she had been with a girl from Jersey who had split for Florida. But Reena was stingy with details except to say she had had a bad marriage and was staying in a rooming house downtown. Also, she liked to draw.

Reena soon proved an able replacement for the previous bartender. She was quick, witty, she could make a mean cocktail; and, to repeat, she was ripe. But Nina thought she was a phony. She based that on Reena's makeup—lots of powder and rouge, hair so permed it wouldn't have moved under a fan, double lashes she was always teasing with a little brush. If Emily bought her line, Nina sniffed, she would end up choking on it.

Ah, but what did Nina know? She didn't understand how much Emily wanted to find someone, or how thrilling it was when Reena kept an extra-cold beer waiting in the ice when she came in, calling her baby when she left: "Seeya later, baby," she would say as Emily went out the door. It was enough to make her skin shake. And after Reena learned she was a teacher, she started asking her advice on different matters. In October, some five months from when Emily moved to Greenwich Village, she invited Reena to dinner.

From the outset it was clear that Reena viewed this like a woman-man date: she waited for Emily to light her cigarettes, she asked Emily to order for them both and made no move to help on the check, she walked farthest from the curb, preceded Emily when they entered and left the restaurant, and openly flirted with her. It was that very seductiveness, so conspicuously coquettish, that intimidated Emily. So that she began to feel awkward about her own femaleness. This was a first. Never had she been shy about putting on lipstick around a girl or combing her hair; but she was now. And that had to do with how Reena looked, with what Reena's actions toward Emily implied, and with sex, that old bear: sex rattled between them so loudly that night that back in the car Emily kissed her. What else was she supposed to do? Reena had almost climbed on her lap, and Reena's mouth was a magnet. My God, but Emily had almost forgotten the hunger of sex with a woman. Reena's tongue slid under hers into the soft ready of Emily's mouth, sucking gently. Emily's hands dropped to Reena's breasts; the nipples hardened. "Ah" sprang through Reena's lips, her arms tightened around Emily's neck. Emily's spine turned into a noodle; her brain filled with steam. At that moment had the car been a bed, she would have performed her lover's tasks and done them well. For the mission was clear; and the music she heard issued from some ancient memory of Lu and Mattie. But the bed was locked in her fifth-floor apartment blocks away.

And how is fever sustained through traffic lights? Thus nothing ultimate happened that evening. But there were more dinners of that kind. And finally Emily took Reena home with her, taking pains to be discreet. (As this occurred more frequently, she would insist they enter and leave her apartment separately if it were a warm day and the neighborhood women were out and about. For in the Village, if seen with the same woman too often, unless a man or child were present, you could be thought queer.)

Beginning with that first night of sex, Emily kept a tee shirt and underpants on and, as with Lorraine, wouldn't allow herself to be touched. (Reena never tried, either.) As with Lorraine too, she couldn't bear Reena seeing her nude. Somehow the thought of having breasts, especially if her breasts were larger than those of the woman she was making love to, never fit with the aggressor mold. She didn't know how to explain this to herself, and she didn't try any more than she had with Lorraine. It was just a feeling. But that feeling didn't matter since her goal with Reena was to satisfy more than Reena had ever been satisfied. Sex was the tie that binds, Emily believed. And Reena was responsive, completely uninhibited. She made Emily believe no one had ever made love to her so well. Orgasms seemed to flow from her body, one after another in uninterrupted sequence. More nights of wild sex were to follow. Emily started coming to Pandy's after work. She would wait for Reena to finish her shift. They would have dinner, then hit the sack. The sack was a burning bed of thighs and Reena's dark hair sprawled everywhere. Emily got into sex. Really into sex. Into the little mole on Reena Dee's neck. Into the dimple in Reena Dee's cheek. Into Reena Dee's nipples that stayed flat no matter how much Emily caressed them, hungry nipples wanting tongue, sucking them as Reena's flesh opened into a forbidden city of pleasure. Do it to me!

Emily did it. Her own orgasms came from fantasies of power. They had not the orgiastic fervor as with Lu or Mattie. They were more a ticktock, a second's flame. But she didn't care. She was too caught up in thinking herself a big cheese to have scored with the bartender at Pandy's. Reena made her look good. She didn't read, as Lu had. She had never even finished high school and her soul was charged on clothes, makeup, gossip. But she was sex, a drug, and Emily got addicted. By the third week it was just do-it-to-me-baby, all going down and coming up, tongues here, there, Reena moving under her tongue, wet, fingers entering, sucking, fucking, do it, "Ah, no one has *ever* made me feel like you do, Emily." Within that first month, she was showering Reena with gifts and money. And bit by bit Reena was moving in. Her apartment became so crowded she had to stack linens on Horace's saddle.

By Thanksgiving Reena was living with her full-time and rent-free. By way of explanation, Emily told Mrs. Cordello (who had a big mouth) that Reena was going through a hellish divorce and she was helping her get on her feet. She told the same thing to Lillian when Lillian happened to call one night from Peru and Reena picked up the phone. "You living with someone now, Stollie?" Lillian had asked innocently as Emily's heart hit the floor. No, she answered, going into her song and dance. Lillian said she would be coming back sometime after Christmas and would let Emily know so she could pick her up at the airport. She had a flicker of anxiety as she hung up later about what she would say to Lillian when Reena was still living with her. Well, she would just have to cross that bridge when she got to it. The same with Mrs. Cordello.

Soon problems began to surface. One of these was Reena's tendency to flirt. In the beginning, her eyes had been just for Emily. But after she moved into Emily's apartment, she started acting friendlier with the butchy women who swarmed around her at Pandy's like moths circling a porch light. Even more unsettling was her play to men. For example, one night at a local eatery she and Reena were having dinner when a man came up to the table; he stood there ogling Reena like a male dog getting a whiff of something; then he pulled up a chair and sat down with his back to Emily and proceeded to tell Reena she should be in the movies. Reena of course ate that up with a shovel while Emily just sat there feeling like an ant. It took Reena way too long to get rid of him; and when she did and Emily expressed annoyance, Reena became angry and accused her of being too possessive. That scene happened more than once; and each time Emily would try to appear oblivious: she would sit at the table forcing herself to think of poetry or some deep philosophical subject so she could feel mentally superior to Reena and this intruder. She would remind herself of Carl's former devotions and boys who had liked her in college. Yet she hurt all over. She didn't know how to compete with a man. She couldn't exert her rights with Reena because she didn't have any. And she didn't know how to translate her aggressions in bed to the outside world. She just had to smile if the man deigned to glance at her lest she be called a sourpuss, or worse.

Another problem was Reena's job. Shortly after she and Emily began living together, Reena announced her shift had been changed to the last one. Henceforth she wouldn't be finished until four A.M.; and then, she said, she needed to unwind at The Urge, an after-hours club that opened when the regular bars closed.

At first Emily tried to keep up. She would rest after school, meet Reena before four and go to The Urge. She would leave there at six-thirty to be at Sloe before eight, changing into her heels and skirt in the car. But after a string of days of this schedule, she was almost falling asleep at the wheel and had to stop. The result was they barely saw each other during the week.

But on the weekends that changed, which soon developed into a problem too. On Friday and Saturday nights, Emily would accompany Reena to The Urge. She would sit at the bar with her drink; Reena would be next to her thinking she was Ava Gardner. The butches would be trying to elbow in between or strutting about like roosters. Reena would bat her eyes at them and blow kisses. Ooooh bay-beee wails from the juke box. Odors of booze and human sweat. Gossip bouncing from one rosy mouth to the other:

Peg-was-splitting-with-Kathy-who-used-to-go-
with-Sue-who-was-hitting-on-Liddy-who-had-just-
broken-up-with-Judy-who-was-still-nuts-about-Sally.
And-didya-know-Heidi-and-Lorna-were-on-the-outs-
again . . .

On the dance floor everyone was looking for love: Hips grinding into hips as they searched, hands grabbing buttocks, quick feels in the you-know-wheres, mouths sucking necks. And what about love-love-love? the juke box would sing to their deepest aspirations.

Emily got tired of it. Tired of Reena thinking she was Ava Gardner. Tired of the butches looking at Reena as if she were sirloin steak and hating her (Emily) because she had her and they didn't. She was tired of the hangovers too and her stomach feeling like a fish tank. Tired of what about love-love-love. *I. Want. Out.,* she told Reena more than once. There was just no sense living together if they never saw each other.

When that happened, Reena, realizing she had pushed too far and knowing a good deal when she had one, would start coming home right after four, sliding next to Emily in bed when she got there, naked, whispering in Emily's ear that if she would just be patient she would be going back to her earlier shift at Pandy's soon.

Sex greases many a rusty heart. And that's how things went with them all through Christmas.

In January Emily heard from Lillian.

> Grand Turk, the Bahamas
> December 27, 1956

Dearest Em,

Season's greetings from the land of sun and surf. I've tried calling you but couldn't get through and once when I did no one was there. Where were you on a Saturday night at four A.M. *your time*???? Anyway, it's best to write to see how this looks in print. First, thanks for the camera and hope you got what I sent. Now for my Big News—I'm in love!!!

I'm sitting here in paradise watching the dolphins and the
boats and wondering if I really said that. But I did.
Remember I told you about Bob Baxley when I called a
couple of months ago. Let me refresh your memory: He's
that great guy who's been on my dig team in Peru and
teaches archaeology at Miami Institute. I told you he has a
cottage here and I might be visiting with some other people.
But I intentionally downplayed his importance, maybe
because I couldn't bring myself to believe I might be falling
for him. But I have. It's now Official—we're quote-unquote
"together." It must come as a shock since I always said I'd
be the last holdout but I feel like I've known Bob all my life.
You've *got* to meet him! Outside you, he's the only person
who's ever supported my dreams. What's so great is he has
the same ones. And we have plenty of time to think things
through. When I get back to the States, he'll be in North
Africa, then Egypt for a year and a half, which is about the
same amount of time I need to finish up my courses plus
three teaching classes I still owe GAI. So I'll have my hands
full. But as it stands now, when I get my Ph.D. I'm going to
Miami Institute, where he can get me a job, and then we
plan to work and travel together. It's such a great chance
that I have to pinch myself to make sure it's real. Which
brings me to the second part of this epistle:

You told me you could pick me up whenever I got there
and I'm making it easy on you. I'm not arriving at dawn or
even midnight. I'll be at La Guardia at eight P.M., Pan Am
flight 287, January twenty-first. That's a Friday so you can
sleep late after we're up all night!!! Greta's gone, and that
student I rented your old room to will be out by then so
we'll have the whole place to ourselves.

So that's it from this end. How's school? Are you still
dating that Dick you told me about? I can't wait to get
caught up on everything.

I love you, Stollie,

Lil

Like it or not, Lillian's return threatened discovery. And that
was gnawing at Emily as she drove out to La Guardia the

evening of January twenty-first. For the first time the anonymity of New York seemed compromised. That's why she felt so anxious now. For what if Lillian just happened to see her coming out of Pandy's one night with her arm around Reena Dee? What if Lillian inadvertently learned that Reena Dee, that sexy-looking tomato, was the woman who had answered the phone when Lillian called that night? What if Lillian ran into Emily on Eighth Street with some faggots, or in the company of some dykey-looking women? It wasn't likely, but anything was possible. Certainly Lillian's apartment on 113th Street, a thirty-minute subway ride from Little Italy, was closer than Peru. The more she obsessed the more her most punishing fantasies had turned Lillian into some giant presence towering over the skyscrapers, about to tap into Emily's black and furtive misdeeds!

Miles past the Triborough Bridge she reminded herself to stay on her toes about Dick Fields. Dick Fields was supposedly the man she was dating. She had told Lillian about him for months, making him a lawyer instead of an artist because lawyers traveled and she planned to use that as the reason why Lillian would never be able to meet him. She had already told Lillian that Dick Fields was getting a divorce. His wife was paranoid and had hired a detective to follow him around. If the detective caught Dick with Emily, the wife could sue him for every last penny. For that reason Dick didn't want to be seen in public with her, or to meet any of her friends. In time this might change. But that's how it was now. She had written this, plotted and planned it hoping it sounded logical and intentionally making the story extreme because she didn't want Lillian just popping in without phoning. Even if Reena Dee moved out—an increasing possibility—who knows what other woman Emily might have staying over. She wasn't ready to stop being queer *yet* just because Lillian was back in town!

Pay attention! A car cutting across the lane almost hit her. And then she saw LA GUARDIA: 3 MILES. In a few minutes she began following directional arrows to Pan Am. It was nearing eight. A half mile later she turned into a lot and parked. She put a celebratory bottle of champagne in the trunk with her overnight bag, then rushed into the terminal and up the stairs to the reception area where passengers from flight 287 were just beginning to trickle down the corridor. In seconds she spotted Lillian's familiar jeans and windbreaker and then, putting aside all that junk about Dick Fields, she was screaming her name: "Lillian! Lillian!"

Lillian saw her. Picked up speed. And shortly they were wrapped up in a hug, shrieking and pounding each other on the back. She looked great: tanner, hair longer and lighter, a bit heavier. They decided to have a drink before getting her luggage and soon were in the lounge, where Emily found herself talking comfortably about Dick when she had to. Mostly though she tried keeping the conversation away from her. Lillian said she hoped to be with Bob this summer in England, where her mother was living now. She was dying for Emily to meet him. Wild horses couldn't drag him to New York after he had been mugged here twice in one week four years ago, so Emily should plan on coming to where they were at some point, et cetera, et cetera.

It was after ten when they finally left the airport. Back in Lillian's apartment, they killed off the champagne and Lillian gave her a map she had made of her travels. Emily finally went to bed that night filled with nostalgia. This was her first visit to the area since Columbia, and some of those memories invariably returned. She fell asleep thinking about Carol and Nelson.

Anxious to get it over with, and arranging to do so when Reena was safely at work, Emily had Lillian down to her apartment as soon as possible, taking great pains to say she slept on the bed and her roommate had the sofa in the living room. She felt more relaxed after that, and soon their contacts had settled into a routine that would last the balance of Lillian's tenure in New York. As expected, Lillian was quickly overwhelmed with her own commitments; but they managed to get together a few times a month, usually at a steak house called Kelly's Grill on West Eighty-sixth Street. And they talked on the phone practically every day.

In February not long after Lillian's return, a man named Jim Spane moved centerstage into Emily's relationship with Reena. Jim owned a bar on Macdougal Street called The Naughty Angel. The Naughty Angel was like the Circle 3 (that had been shut months ago because it hadn't bought enough protection). But Jim paid through the nose, so the police left him alone. Jim was a tall, sandyhaired Gary Cooper type carved out of a straight stick. He had drifted into town from somewhere out west and made the Angel into what it was—a lure for drunks, street people, queers. Those last, especially the women, were Jim's favorites. He called himself their good buddy. He loaned them money when they fell on hard times and played Cupid if the need arose. Rumor had it Jim was a cokehead. But that didn't give anyone a heart attack.

Jim and Reena were friends and often saw each other at The Urge. Sometimes when they did they talked so privately it was like a moat had been dug around their bodies and the bridge pulled up. If Emily chanced to be around and Jim caught her eye, he would wink as if they shared some understanding. That about drove her bonkers; and as so commonly happens in the jungle of love, she got jealous. That very jealousy rekindled her flagging interest in Reena at a time when she was close to asking her to move out. So when Jim offered Reena a bartending job, Emily began thinking she was back in love. And during her midwinter recess, she decided to give her affair one more shot. She asked Reena to go off with her for a few days to think things over before she made her job decision. She knew Reena was torn about this. Pandy's had made her the night manager, which was clout in the bar world. But The Naughty Angel paid more. Emily offered to make up the difference. She also appealed to Reena's love of the ocean. She said she knew a place in Tidewater, Virginia, called the Chambers Hotel and she would like to take her there. To sweeten the pot, she threw in a strand of real pearls.

Reena wasn't crazy about going, but she loved the pearls, and she had time coming from work. Those facts, and Emily's coaxing, won the day. Before Emily left, she called Lillian and told her she and Dick were going off during her school vacation and she would meet her at Kelly's the next Monday night for dinner. About seven, she told Lillian.

And so she went to Virginia. She went back to the hotel where she had slept with Gary, back by the same highway they had driven for her night of sexual malfunction, back to The Old Bay Line, the seagulls, the smells of the Tidewater, back to memory's feet. And when she did, something enlivened her relationship with Reena, for, once out of New York, Reena seemed the simpler girl Emily had always envisioned under the makeup. Her hair stayed loose, her clothes were plainer, she didn't overburden her face with paint, and they actually related well. The weather was part of that—blue skies and at night the mooncrossed sea under the heavens: God's bookends.

They went to Williamsburg and Norfolk. Emily took her to Newport News and pointed out Aunt Francie's house. Aunt Francie was still in Hawaii, but she mailed her a card making up a story as to why she was back.

And then the last night everything changed. They were just finishing dinner at a little place near the hotel when two sailors came in feeling their oats. The sailors spotted them across the room and sauntered over to ask what were two pretties doing out by their lonesomes on a Saddynight. With that, they pulled up chairs and made themselves at home as if they belonged there. The restaurant was attached to a bar where a band was playing, and there were a few couples on the other side of the room. One of the sailors decided he was Fred Astaire. He jumped to his feet and executed some jigs. His friend followed, and then they invited Emily and Reena into their arms. Both declined, but the sailors took no for yes. This kept up with the heat rising in Emily's head and no help in sight. Reena told her to cool it. Emily ignored that advice and told the men to get lost. That didn't sit well.

One of the sailors grabbed Reena's arm. The other diners

began to gawk, but no one offered any help, and the waitress, who looked like she wasn't sure of her name, was nowhere in sight. That got Emily to her feet and she ordered the men to leave them alone. One of them, with a grin holding his chin up, yelled they must be dykes because they didn't like guys.

Goddammit! To her surprise, Emily flung her drink at him, stunning him, the other sailor lunged at her, backing Emily into a table, the force of which sent flatware and glasses clattering to the floor. That brought the waitress in with a manager someone had dug up, and there was great commotion over restraining the men as Emily held a chair up for a shield.

Reena ran out screaming. The battle ended with the manager telling Emily the dinner was on the house and why didn't she just leave to calm things down. Obviously the military buttered his bread, and he wasn't about to jeopardize his business. What could she do? She left for her car where Reena waited, livid with rage. A big argument was next. Both of them yelling at each other. Reena blaming her for everything. On and on. At the hotel Reena went to bed, Emily took to the lounge and got loaded. Next morning the drive to New York was a nightmare as Emily silently cursed her life: nothing, it seemed, was working out.

When they drove into the city, Reena split, Emily went home thoroughly demoralized, never wanting a relationship again. Reena hadn't returned when she left for school the next day. Screw her. By noon she was so shaky and felt so bad the headmaster told her to go home and when she did all Reena's clothes and sundry articles were gone: no note, nothing. She called Pandy's, Information Center of the Universe, and was told Reena had quit and was working at The Naughty Angel and living with Jim in his apartment above the bar.

That did it. All the money and things she had bought her were down the tubes. Plus pride. It wasn't that Reena Dee had been the love of Emily's life. It wasn't that she had come close to Mattie or Lu or, in his way, even to Carl. It wasn't that Emily hadn't sensed a gold-digging quality, as Nina would say: Reena

Dee was a born fake. But losing her was yet again losing, was having something snatched from her grasp when she was still starved, was a reminder. And that reminder, what Emily perceived as another failure coming on the heels of a reasonably good time in Virginia, made things doubly painful, made it easy to smear herself with Reena's accusations. Thus all her sorry self-opinions became magnified. And that old devil, jealousy, reared its head: Emily kept seeing Reena and Jim make love.

But she had to do something. Fortunately she reached Nina, who already had heard the news—the Village grapevine being what it is—and they arranged to meet at Pandy's. She then called The Naughty Angel, not to get Reena back, she never wanted to see Reena again; but to finish this, to play the drama out. Jim answered. There were words. Reena butted in. Emily demanded to know why she couldn't *at least* have extended the common courtesy of saying good-bye in person. Reena said, Oh, fuck off, and banged the phone down. Infuriated, Emily called back. Again the phone slammed in her ear. She called back. Now in a spiraling of verbal warfare in which each hurled accusations at the other, Reena told her to quit bugging them or she'd call the police. She said she and Jim had been involved before she even went to goddamn Virginia and she had been phoning him the whole time when Emily wasn't around. Furthermore, the only reason she had gone was to fucking pay Emily back, and on and on.

Later at Pandy's as Emily sang the blues, Nina's practical response was, Good riddance. "I told you but you wouldn't listen. It's like with a kid. You let the kid stick his finger in the socket so he won't do it again. You burn and you learn, Emily."

Back at her apartment, unpleasantly inebriated, she called The Naughty Angel once more, figuring that having the last word would provide the solace she needed for one of the most blatant mistakes she had ever made. Working the late shift, Reena picked up. Emily screamed, "Go to hell," and hung up. Satisfied, she then took the phone off the hook and zonked out.

She awakened to a loud banging a little after nine A.M. "Let me in, Emily!" she recognized Lillian's voice. "I know you're in there! I can hear the radio!"

She sat up dazed and unprotected, trying to halt a pounding between her ears. What was Lillian doing here? "Hang on," she called. "I'm coming. Just let me get to the john a second."

When she opened the door, Lillian marched in looking none too cheerful. "Are you dead?" she asked.

"What?"

"They said you were out sick at school."

"When did you call there?"

"This morning. They said you left yesterday sick and weren't coming in for a couple of days. Where were you last night? Why didn't you call?"

"When? What for?"

"We had a date for God's sake."

"We what . . . oh," the light was dawning. "At Kelly's?" she asked weakly.

"You got it."

"I thought that was next week."

"We made it right after your vacation, Monday, last night. I waited and then I called and then I got pissed and then I kept trying and it went from no answer to busy so I had the operator check and she said the phone was off the hook." At that, Lillian looked around the room. There it was—dead on the floor. She walked over and put the receiver on the phone and returned to confront Emily to her face. "Are you sick? You look awful. Jesus, this place!" she waved her arms in the air. "It looks like a war zone. Where's Dick?"

"Dick?" she muttered groggily. She wasn't up for this.

Lillian snapped her fingers in Emily's face. "Get with it, Emily. Dick. Your boyfriend. Remember him? Didn't you two go to Virginia?"

"Yes, of course," she sat down fumbling for a cigarette. "I got food poisoning."

"When?"

"When I was there. I was sick all the way back."

"So where is he to leave you like this?"

"He had to go to work. He's not here all the time."

"Where's your roommate?"

"Uh . . . she went back with her husband."

"When?"

"When? I don't know when," she repeated the word with some annoyance. "You want the exact hour?"

"Oh shit, Emily. I was worried. I didn't know if you were dead or what the fuck was happening." She went over to the refrigerator now and opened it up. Inside was a jar of pickles, beer, a quart of milk that proved sour when she sniffed it. She said, "I'm going over to that deli across the street and get you something to eat."

"No, wait," Emily cried before she got out. "I don't want anything."

"Have you seen a doctor?" Lillian studied her face carefully.

"Yes, of course, that's right, I went to a doctor. I told you I have a little bit of food poisoning. I'll be fine. Wait a minute." Now she did feel sick so she ran into the toilet. When she emerged, Lillian was holding a picture of Emily she had given Reena Dee a few weeks ago. It was still in the living room and she had forgotten about it. On it had been written, "To Reena, all my love, Emily." She panicked. Then she walked over and calmly took it from Lillian's hands with no explanation whatsoever, immediately launching into a furious depiction of last night as she lived it in her head at this moment. She said she and Dick had been here when out of the blue his wife had appeared at her door with a hired detective and there had been a horrible scene. That was why Dick wasn't here and she was sorry about forgetting their dinner. Things were just nuts. As she got into her story, she began to cry. She cried for all the stories she had ever told, for her life in the muck of this apartment, half-smoked cigarettes everywhere, empty beer cans littering the floor; she cried for that worthless photo she had given Reena and for all the things she couldn't confide, all the pain for which she had no vocabulary, all the language in this foreign country of her life that she could never share. And as she did,

Lillian was beside her, holding her in her arms and saying, "It's okay, Stollie. Whatever it is, it's going to be all right."

. . . I don't know what Lillian knew or didn't know. We never spoke of that experience again. Soon my ego was restored and I vowed to keep my emotions on a shorter leash. Not long afterward, I replaced Dick Fields with Clark Preston. I don't know why I named him Clark; I guess I just liked the way it sounded. Anyway, Clark had Nelson's personality, Gary's looks; I made him a pilot so far as Lillian was concerned, which explained why he too was gone so often.

Nearly sixteen months from the day Lillian returned to New York, she received her Ph.D. and joined Bob overseas. Our friendship thrived through letters I received from all over the globe. We frequently spoke of a reunion, but invariably something would come up, usually on my end, sometimes on hers.

And now time must pass. I had arrived in Greenwich Village, a greenhorn, June of 1956. From then until 1962 when I tried men again, I lived high on the hog of emotion, playing musical beds with a variety of women—a psychologist, a belly dancer, two nurses, an actress, an officer in the Israeli army, an insurance agent, a scattering of teachers, sundry women of no fixed address or occupation. Sloe went on. Pandy's went on. Life went on. One Christmas I met Aunt Francie in Newport News when she returned to put her house on the market. Sheila and I, perhaps in homage to something that didn't exist but which we thought should, went through the motions of exchanging cards over holidays. And one fine May day the Sloe yearbook was dedicated to me for outstanding work with my students.

The night before my Easter vacation, 1962, I met that second female who actually moved in with me. Coincidentally, she came into my life hours before I was to fly to the Bahamas as a wedding present to Lillian and Bob. (They had recently tied the Big Knot, and I was to be their gift.) It was a sorry thing I did, missing the plane like that . . .

One night Nina and Emily decided to try out a new bar called Nookies. Emily was leaving for the Bahamas next morning as a wedding present to Lillian and Bob; and Nina was about to join Faye in England, where her mother was ill. After that those two were planning to move to Cape Cod and open up an antique shop there. Emily was already wondering what the Village would be like without her best drinking buddy.

They had dinner at the Ninth Circle and then walked over to Nookies. And that's where she met Landy Camp.

Landy Camp was dancing solo when she and Nina sat down at a table, and the eyes of the room were stuck to her body. She looked and moved like Rita Hayworth, barefoot, bending the floor around her body as if it were a blanket, her dark long hair matting her brow, her skin olive and damp. Her blouse was undone on top and her eyes were half shut. She was inside the music so deep you forgot she was separate from it. Flushed, sexy as hell. "Cut in, Emily," Nina coaxed.

"Oh, sure."

"Go on. I dare you."

Beer took the challenge. Beer stood up, stepped to the floor, caught the girl in Emily's arms, whirling her about as Emily the Dancer did her mighty thing, whispering in this creature's ear, "What's a girl of quality like *you* doing in a place like *this*?"

By last call Landy Camp went home with her. And to make a short story shorter, they had sex. The sex was so good and Landy Camp was so gorgeous and Emily was so proud to have won such a trophy that she missed her flight. And when she tried to reschedule, all seats had been booked through the week. She then had to call Lillian with a fiction that she had fallen down the stairs and broken her leg. Yes, she felt guilty. No, she couldn't help it. Landy Camp, sweet and twenty-one, was an airline hostess temporarily based in New York, and she had the curiosity of a sexual kitten. Everything about her was an intoxicant!

263

For almost two months life was a party. Landy, who had been staying at a hotel with two other stewardesses in midtown, moved in with Emily. Never having been with a woman before, she was obviously swept away by the adventure. Things ended when Emily caught her in bed with her cousin who was visiting Landy from South Carolina. She (Emily) had arrived home unexpectedly one afternoon. The radio was on so loud no one heard when she entered the bedroom. And there was cousin Tom sitting naked on Landy's face as she sucked his penis.

The upshot was Emily kicked them both out. And that day, sitting dejectedly on her bed reviewing the last six years of her life, she decided women were not for her. She had tried and look what she had to show for it. Someone like Reena Dee. Someone like Landy Camp. Someone like any of the other women she had gone after, though she had always started a sexual union thinking it might lead to more. She wasn't attracted to that many women, but she had felt she needed experience. And maybe she didn't have the virus anymore. She thought about that. She thought about Pandy's too and that she was getting bored with it. She told herself she had seen enough of the games women played, and she wasn't getting any younger. Clearly it was time to go back to men.

PROVINCETOWN

Part Three

The man she selected was Philip Randall.

Divorced and in his early forties, Philip was a history teacher at Sloe. And by the time Landy Camp had bit the dust, he had already asked Emily out. One afternoon in May she took him up on it, and they went to a movie.

In the looks department, Philip was a C-minus. He was short and eggshaped with strands of brown hair strategically placed to thatch a premature balding. His eyes were blue and ordinary; his face genial, though plain. But his red Jaguar lent him a sporting air, and he was bright and unpretentious. He was also impulsive, game to hit the bars at a moment's notice; he liked jazz and politics and he could talk endlessly on a variety of subjects. Most important, he was a man and completely non-threatening. As to those who might wonder why Emily suddenly was going out with someone from school, she just said she enjoyed his company. What she didn't say was that Philip

Randall would be her bridge back to the real world, her passage from Pandy's, proof that she had finally completed a destructive period in her life: she was no longer queer!

She went to bed with him after the third date. He lay on top of her in his Scarsdale apartment, gasping, panting, telling her she was dynamite. She kept her skirt on, but let him remove her bra and play with her breasts. It was the first time they had been touched since Carl (was that possible!), and she came like a comet, redhot, brilliantly intense, but as quickly extinguished. Afterward she fought the deadness that always plagued her following sex with men: she couldn't stand further intimacy; she needed to be by herself. She dealt with this by telling Philip she had to be home by midnight for an important phone call.

Over the next weeks they went to bed several times. Quick tosses in the saddle because that's all she was into, surrendering her mind to one dirty movie after another to make it easier and always being sure Philip was satisfied before she stopped the sex. She didn't know where this relationship was going. That wasn't important. She was just glad it wasn't with a woman.

With the introduction of Philip to her life, Emily quit Pandy's and was even thinking about moving out of the Village once her lease expired. She started socializing with some female teachers at Sloe and signed on to teach summer school. Once during this time she heard from Nina, who wrote that Faye's mother was still ill so they were staying longer in England. Then in June Philip invited her to a cocktail party. Shortly after they arrived, his stockbroker pulled them into a discussion on investments. Emily soon got bored and wandered over to the hors d'oeuvres table. Standing there was a young woman in her early thirties whom she had noticed earlier because she was exceptionally attractive. Now they smiled and exchanged pleasantries as Emily began sampling some of the food. As she did, the young woman held up a string bean wrapped in garlic bread and said, "Have you tried these? They're wonderful."

Emily tasted it and agreed. "What are they?"

"Dilly beans they're called. I saw them advertised at Altman's."

"Hmm, what's in them?"

"Dill. Lots of red pepper."

They talked a bit about food, just general comments, and then the woman introduced herself as Anna Rubin and held out her hand.

Emily took it and smiled. "I'm Emily Stolle." About this time she caught Philip's eye and they waved at each other.

Anna said, "You came in with him, didn't you? I remember seeing you."

"Yes. He teaches in my school."

"Oh, what do you teach?"

"English. At Sloe Academy," she added proudly.

"Sloe. That's a good school. We have a lot of students who went there."

"You teach too?"

"Yes. In fact I work for the man who's throwing this little shindig. That's why I'm here. I'm not really much of a cocktail person," she laughed at that.

"Dean Hopkins you mean, at Hunter?" Emily asked.

"That's right. I'm assistant professor in the French department."

Emily studied her a moment. "Well," she said. "You're certainly young to be a professor. You look like a student." Indeed. She was wearing a long skirt, a high-buttoned blouse under a pale blue cardigan. She was tall and rather elegant looking: a narrative of dark skin and hair, with eyes that told their own tale of reserve. Something about her reminded Emily of Mattie, perhaps the way she fooled with her hair, twisting the ends when she talked or throwing it over her shoulder. They were soon into a lengthy discussion about education and books, discovering a lot in common. And as they went on, it seemed they had carved a little island for themselves in this room, all the while people coming and going around them. Hi. Hi. Nice to see you. And so on. Clink of ice cubes. Smoke clouding the wooden sky of the interior amid a surf of rising and falling voices.

Philip came over with some banter, and Emily introduced

him to Anna. He left, asking her to join him, but she didn't want to talk about stocks. She was beginning to enjoy herself. She liked this woman, this Anna with the inquisitive eyes and the way she listened with her whole being. In time the conversation turned personal.

Anna asked if she had ever been married. She said no, that she had lived with a doctor in Chicago for a few months but it hadn't worked out, which was really fine because she prized her independence. Anna agreed. She had just gotten divorced some months ago and was beginning to unwind from that. A nice fellow, she said, living in Europe now, but it had been a mistake from the get-go.

"Funny," she went on, "you can think you know someone to a T, and then when you start living with them you discover you don't at all. With us there was a passion that was missing. I don't mean physically. I mean something much larger than that. Goodness," she started, "I can't believe I'm saying all this."

"It's okay. I understand."

"But I barely know you," Anna protested. Just then Philip came up and rested his arm lightly on her shoulder. For some reason she felt a safety in that. She caught his hand, glad he was there but then not sure why she was glad. The three stood chatting amiably until Anna excused herself. By then she and Emily had agreed to get together at a future date.

A few days later Emily was really pleased to make arrangements for dinner. For all her time in the Village, she had nothing to show for a real friendship except Nina, and she had been mainly a drinking companion. But here was a serious person to do things with who didn't live in the bars. And what a fine time they had that evening. After that, Anna and Emily began seeing each other regularly, meeting with colleagues of Anna's at Hunter, having supper together. Anna gave her a spare key and often Emily on her way back from school would pull off the West Side Highway and wait for her in Anna's apartment. It was becoming apparent that Anna was helping

Emily as much as any man to heal the past, notably: by fall Emily had quit dating Philip Randall. And then something happened that deepened their friendship. This revolved around the death of Aunt Francie.

For months Emily had known her aunt had lung cancer and that to be near a prominent physician in Washington she had left Hawaii and moved in with Sheila. This necessarily had reopened communication because Emily, in phoning her ailing relative every so often, would have to talk to Sheila. In September, Emily sent her aunt roses for her sixty-eighth birthday. That was a Monday. On Tuesday the florist contacted her with the news that the flowers had been undeliverable because Francine Stolle had passed away a week ago. Emily, truly hurt not to have been informed, immediately called Sheila for an explanation. They discovered a total breakdown in information. Sheila thought Sam had told Emily; Sam thought Sheila had. The apology she got was mollifying, but old wounds had been reopened. Emily took those wounds to Anna that same evening and over supper for the first time mentioned estrangement from family. Of course she didn't go into the root cause. She just said everyone she loved was dead and she and her sister were distant forever. She stayed over at Anna's in the guest room, and they sat up late talking about Anna's failed marriage, her own parents, both deceased, and broken dreams of childhood. The next morning on her drive to school Emily was wearing one of Anna's skirts and happier than she had been in a long time. Never would she have admitted this, but what was really beginning to matter now, the single most important thing she looked forward to, was her growing friendship with Anna Rubin.

At the height of the autumn season, Anna asked Emily to the vacation home of some old friends in Wellfleet, Massachusetts. When they got there, however, the house was locked and empty. And when Anna called the Sterns in Boston, she found out to her chagrin that she was expected the next weekend. With nowhere else to stay, she and Emily went to a Holiday Inn.

Déjà vu. A motel. A woman she already felt close to. One bed rising like a phoenix from the ashes of North Carolina.

Thus it was that here in this motel that October's night Emily once again experienced whatever it was that made her an alien in this world: to want a woman who lay in bed beside her, and the want of that bigger than the nonwant, and the desire for that larger than the fear of that desire. Surely it had been there all along lurking in the tall grass of their friendship until at the proper moment it sprang like a cat from a hot roof eager and dancing and clattering when their guard was down. So many similarities with Lu.

And it wasn't as with the numberless girls before, when she and Anna first kissed that night. It wasn't having power over Anna, needing power to feel secure. It wasn't worrying what to do with her own breasts under the moon's full eye. It wasn't as with men, letting them do the wild thing to her breasts and fuck her so she would be in harmony with nature. It wasn't planned or plotted or deliberated or defined. None of that. It was just light riding a wave to the crest. Passion was the boat.

Sex carries the seeds of its own destruction. It is the stone gone mad, drunk on itself and its spinning destination, stones of the flesh that become the darker ones of love—stones of jealousy, possession, temperament. Sex is the final brutality, the ultimate affirmation. All that, Emily and Anna took back with them to New York after their night of revelation.

Their week was wonderful, and Emily could only marvel at how easily and naturally Anna accepted this new affair. Here, as with Lu, was a woman who had never been with a woman before. Yet she seemed to have no problem adjusting to it; she made no secret of her unabashed enjoyment in Emily's company. And though Emily kept waiting for the worry, guilt, and anger she thought sure to come, Anna just said she was happy. After all, they had been close before that night, and to her what had happened only cemented things. As a result, Emily had never felt so wanted. The extremes she had gone to with Philip

Randall seemed unreal. The next weekend, however, returning to Cape Cod for the original date with Anna's friends, Martha and Ray Stern, the first draft of cold air blew through.

Martha Stern was a tall, imposing, beaknosed intellectual who years ago had been a dancer, performing all over the world to some acclaim. Retired now, she still maintained the flair of a performance artist. She wore loud scarves, walked with a brisk, no-nonsense carriage, gray hair bobbing in a ponytail behind her, which made her face longer and more severe. Her husband, Ray, was shorter and much more passive, and was like an echo chamber to his wife. Both described themselves as liberals, but apparently that word had limits that became painfully evident about an hour into the visit.

Emily had been told they doted on Anna and asked lots of personal questions. These questions weren't to be construed as meddlesome; it was just their way of showing affection. This affection, though, led to tension. They were having a drink in the den when Martha started on about whom Anna was dating. Anna had come prepared with the name of a man in her department and she offered that, but Martha wanted to know more. She kept bringing up the subject of marriage and hammering away that Anna should be thinking about it again because the biological clock was ticking, she had no children, and it was a shame to waste such brilliant genes.

In the midst of this, Anna got up from her chair, walked to the window, stood with her back to the room, then bearing a brave little smile and glancing briefly at Emily as if for support, she told them she cared too much about them both to lie and that the truth was Emily was her lover.

The silence that came from that was so intense you could hear a pin sitting on the table. And then the word lover began reverberating in that room like a balloon running out of air. You could almost see it enter the brain cells of Martha and Ray Stern and light up their minds like pinball machines. Lover: two women naked and doing things to each other. What's in a word? Queer. And once again Emily lost her name. Right there in that room all that was she dropped like autumn leaves. No longer was she Emily Stolle, teacher, poet, whatever; she was queer: flypaper with everything scummy sticking to it. From a great distance she heard Martha clear her throat and say, My, how interesting, her voice betraying nothing. Emily forced herself to look up and was cut by Martha's eyes with their fine, moral points. To her right Ray Stern sat studying his shoelaces. And suddenly Emily felt they blamed her for Anna's corruption. Anna was talking about how they had met but all she could think was she was the person ruining Anna's genes. There was a brief moment when the Sterns left the room and Anna, realizing her discomfort, apologized, saying she hadn't meant to spring this on her but it had just popped out.

They had dinner and played cards, but Emily retired early. She and Anna had been put into the guest room with two beds, but now she felt self-conscious, as if her hosts would be listening through the walls. And when Anna came up shortly after, they talked about what had happened. Anna said, "I just heard myself, and I got sick of what I was saying. It just happened."

"Well, you better get used to lying. You can't go around telling everyone as you did tonight. You've got to know that."

"I do; but I don't have to like it."

"No one says you have to like it. You just have to do it. You have to get used to it. Sad but true."

"But these are my friends. They care about me. It's wrong to lie to them about something so important."

"No it's not. It's selfish to tell them."

"Why? All they want is for me to be happy."

"Oh Anna, you're so naive. Don't you realize no one wants you to be like this? I don't make the rules. I just know you set them up tonight."

"For what?"

"For what they'll see every time they look at you. I don't care how long they've known you or what you've been to them. This is what will stick from now on."

"I don't believe that. I'm the same person."

"Not anymore you're not."

"Well, I can't live that way around people who are supposed to be my friends."

She didn't understand, she said, how Anna could be so accepting of herself. Where had she learned that? Didn't she worry what people thought? How could she act so unconcerned? And Anna said she wasn't saying it was easy, but it was a principle to her.

"Remember Lillian," Emily replied. "I've told you about her. Well, she's like family and there have been plenty of times I wanted to tell her, but it would kill her. She wouldn't know how to take it."

"How do you know?"

"I know."

"Maybe you underestimate her."

"No I don't. It's the way it is. To some people there's nothing worse than this. I told you about Carol."

"She was narrow-minded."

"People are."

"Then that's their problem."

"No. It's your problem, my problem, if we want someone particular in our lives."

"But you said you wanted me to meet Lillian."

"I do. But as my friend. That's all."

"Are you ashamed of me, Emily?"

"No."

"Are you sure?"

"Anna, I told you; I don't make the rules." And she looked away, feeling she was dishonoring something, overcome at this moment for the limits she was putting on Anna. "Listen, I need to tell you something I've never told anyone." And that led to the story about Mattie. "Lillian would die," she concluded. "You see. You see what I mean."

All Anna said now was, "That must have really hurt. Where is she now, Mattie, I mean?"

"I don't know."

"Oh Emily, what a thing to bear for all of you. But maybe if you told Lillian it would deepen things."

"No. No it wouldn't."

"But how do you think she'd feel not knowing you're who she thinks you are?"

"I'm the same person she's always known."

"That's what I said about me and the Sterns and you said I was setting them up."

"Yes. And that's what I'd be doing with Lillian. I am the same person, but she wouldn't see me like that."

"But you're hiding something so essential. How is that right?"

"She doesn't know. What she doesn't know won't hurt her."

"But you know."

"So what. It doesn't bother me."

"It has to. Somewhere. It's cheating. It's like rust, it spreads and it rots the core. That's what I feel. I see that wedding ring you wear at school and I think how sad that you feel you have to do that. It's like an air bubble. You're drowning and you stick your nose in that bubble for one last breath of air. And that's your business if that's how you have to live in the world. I recognize that, and I'll do it too when I have to. But we're talking about supposedly real friends here and who I am is their business if they're a friend. That's the point. You make the world too small, Emily."

"That's not true. I can live in two worlds easily. It's easy to love you and lie about my life."

"But why lie more than you have to?"

"Oh, come on. Get real, Anna."

"I am real, Emily. I'm the realest person you'll ever have. There's just a limit to compromise."

She went to bed unpersuaded and messed up in mind and spirit. The handwriting was on the wall, and she would lose Anna like everyone else in her life. People like the Sterns would take her. The world would take her. It was inevitable. Thus the messenger of insecurity moved into Emily's heart after that visit to Wellfleet. The messenger of insecurity moved into Anna's apartment too, which was where Emily was spending most of her time. She began to drink heavily. She needed constant reassurances. She called Anna at work to make her say over the phone that she loved her and would never leave. In some contorted way, she was determined to create the very thing she feared; and at length she succeeded.

On a night during the Christmas holidays, she tore Anna's blouse in a drunken rage, and Anna left. They had been invited to the Sterns for New Year's Eve, those two now having made efforts to reach out to Emily. The party was on Cape Cod, where they were staying for the winter; but Anna, in deference to Emily's wishes, had declined. Now though, she decided to go alone. She had a month between semesters and she needed time to think. She wasn't saying she was going to break up, but she wanted to be alone. It was their only chance. She wouldn't even let Emily drive her to the Cape.

Emily stood outside the house in Wellfleet hoping to catch Anna's silhouette behind the shade. To her that house was the shape of her own defeat, a fortress sealing Anna inside it with guns trained to her head to keep her away. But here she was fresh up from the city after Anna had told her on the phone not to come. She had to though. She was in too much pain. All she wanted was five minutes.

She took a deep breath and started to the house. And when she knocked, Martha Stern herself opened the door. Her expression told the story. She was obviously displeased.

She stepped in before Martha could do anything and just stood numbly in the hall. She didn't care what Martha thought. She was beyond that. She said she wasn't here to make a scene, but she had driven from New York and she wanted to see Anna for about five minutes. She kept saying this until finally in a fit of exasperation, Martha said wait a minute, and left. In a short time Anna came down in a red turtleneck and steely expression. She barely glanced at Emily. "Come on," she said tersely. "We can't stay here."

She followed her across the street until darkness ate them. It was barely snowing, and she could see she was enraged. Anna started, "Why are you here? I told you not to come. You're ruining everything. This isn't my house."

"I love you."

"Bullshit. You don't love me. You want to own me."

"No, please, I'm sorry for everything. Look what I have." She fished a Bulova watch from her pocket, gold with a black face.

"Emily," Anna recoiled in disbelief.

"It's eighteen-carat gold."

"I don't care. I don't want that."

"But you said you needed a watch. It's a Christmas present."

"I don't need a watch. I need to be left alone."

"Don't you love me, Anna?"

"Love. You keep using that word. Don't you know love isn't everything?"

Emily dropped to her knees and kept saying, I love you, I love you. Anna in exasperation told her to get up, that she couldn't stand this. Emily rose obediently but kept repeating she loved her. Anna said she was sorry and she was going back into the house. "Take care of yourself, Emily."

"What does that mean?"

"It's not working," Anna said simply. "Don't you see? It's not working."

"I'll change," Emily started to cry.

"No. I don't believe that anymore. You can't even leave me alone here. You want too much. I'm sorry. I'm sorry about your pain. But I can't make up for everything that's ever hurt you."

Emily grabbed her and tried to kiss her as Anna pushed her away and said to quit making a fool of herself. Then, leaving Emily there, she walked into the house as snow fell through the branches. In the distance a foghorn blew its poem to sea. And sailing through the air came Emily's voice over and over, "I love you, Anna! I love you!"

Almost at the foot of the stairs, Anna turned back and then after a slight hesitation she went up to the porch. Emily stayed in the snow, looking at that house with all its people inside, and at the houses next to it with their warm families inside. Then she started toward her car. It had quit snowing, but it seemed colder. As she walked, she dug her hands inside her pockets, which was when she realized she still had the watch. She held it in front of her for a moment. Then, as on those millions of light-years ago, it became Mattie's little stone, and she threw it as far as she could until it vanished into the night. This was it, she thought, moving even faster toward her car. It was over.

. . . I headed back to the city that night. I drove like a bandit though the roads were icy. I drove as if I were chasing something or being chased. I ached for Anna. I didn't care if the car slid off the road or not. I didn't care.

Somewhere on I-95 I had a stir of hope. Anna's expression came to me as it had been that night—disappointment more than rage. I saw her hesitate before going into the Sterns'. I remembered all the times we had held each other, all the times she said she had never loved like this. Anna wasn't a fake. Maybe when she got back, we could try again.

From then on I tried to be a saint. I moved all my clothes back to my apartment and left her key on her table. I threw myself into my teaching. I didn't get drunk. Then at the end of that month I called. I got no answer. This went on for several days with no results so I ended up phoning Hunter. The secretary, recognizing my voice and assuming Anna and I were friends, told me that after New Year's Day Dr. Rubin had requested her sabbatical be moved up to the winter term to work on a book for the department. She was staying on Cape Cod until next September. I hung up in shock, all my dreams out the window.

And so booze moved in with me that February in 1963. A patient lover, it waited for me after work, it kissed me on the lips when I was tired, it sat with me as I wallowed in Joan Baez, night after painful night getting smashed and playing sad tunes and getting more smashed and mooning over Anna's picture with her smile like a torch. Dying. Booze went with me in my winter's search for women, back to the bars where loneliness had honeyed thighs. Booze came in the shape of all the women who were not Anna, Anna ruined my desire for other women. A dozen letters I started to her but never mailed. Once, thinking I saw her on the street, I ran up. But it wasn't Anna. It wasn't even close to Anna. Pity the lover. Pity the beloved. Pity.

Enter the dream: the dream began after New Year's Eve and came regularly thereafter. It was always the same: I was on a street across from a crowd. A face appeared in thin air. It was brooding and dark and it hurt me, seeming to be the face of everything I had ever lost, stirring memory in the hot coals of memory, suffusing me with warmth and tenderness. And I ran to it, reached to touch it just as it vanished like smoke only to reappear and float over the crowd like a balloon on a long string. Again I nearly touched it, but once more it disappeared. And this time, filling me with an unaccountable sorrow, it woke me up. I would then lie in bed and think about Anna. She was like my dreams of Mattie as a girl. Yet with Mattie at least I had my little stone. And now I had nothing. Plus I was older. It's always harder when you're older . . .

Emily started going back to Pandy's after she and Anna ended. And it was there that she got news of Nina, who owned a shop now in Provincetown with Faye, called Memories. Actually, Nina had sent her a card, but she had never gotten around to answering it. And then when she and Anna parted company, she didn't have the heart to write. She just figured Nina was gone too.

But that changed one April afternoon when she came into the bar restless and out of sorts. It was nearing summer, and she didn't know what she was going to do except she didn't want to teach or stay in New York. It was too hot here.

Suddenly, as the door closed behind her, Nina was swooping her up in a big hug. She had been on a buying trip to Atlantic City and on impulse had stopped in, hoping to find her. "I was just talking about you," she said, leading Emily over to the bar. "Guess who with?"

"I give up," Emily answered, sitting down on the stool and waving at someone across the room. "I don't know anyone in Provincetown."

"Anna Rubin."

"Anna!" She put a cigarette in her mouth unsteadily. "When did you meet Anna?"

"In the shop. She's living in Provincetown."

She took the cigarette, still unlit, out of her mouth and stared at Nina in shock. "What do you mean she's living in Provincetown?"

"That's what I mean. She took a place until Labor Day right near the shop."

"What happened to Wellfleet?"

"I don't know for sure. I think the people there went back to Boston. But you want to hear something? Faye had her for French at Hunter two years ago. She thought she was fantastic." At that Nina went on about how much she had loved her shop.

"Was she with anyone?" Emily interrupted.

"No. She was by herself," Nina smiled broadly, which Emily ignored.

"So how'd my name come up?" she said after a few drags.

"She asked me if I knew you."

Unbelievable. "She did *what*?"

"We were talking about New York. Hey, Audrey," she called out to the bartender. "Bring us a couple, sweetie. My friend here's about to have a heart attack." Nina thought that funny and started laughing.

"Come on, Nina," she prodded impatiently. "What happened?"

"Nothing happened. We started talking about New York and she asked me if I had ever been to Pandy's. I said yes, and she wanted to know if I knew you. That's all."

"So what did you say?"

"I said forever."

"And . . . ?"

"I told her you hung the moon."

Emily laughed good-naturedly, "Oh hell, Nina."

"I did. The ol' moon. I said you just stuck it right up there between the stars, that you were the only one who could handle the job."

She felt the wind knocked out of her suddenly. Anna's name cut, and she hadn't expected to hear it when she came to Pandy's. Yet there was hardly a time when she wasn't thinking about her in one way or another, plotting how to arrange to see her when she came back to the city this fall. Her reaction must have shown, because Nina quickly changed her tone and said almost confidentially, "I'll tell you something if you give a shit, and I can see you do: I think she's still sweet on you."

Now that didn't make any sense. "How?" the word squeezed through Emily's lips like a newborn.

"Just a feeling I have. All her questions after I said I knew you about how long had we been friends and what were you like before and when had I last seen you. Stuff like that. I didn't catch on at first. I thought maybe you two had known each other in teaching. She thinks you're quite a writer, you know."

"Oh don't give me that."

"I mean it. Christ." She gave Emily a little pat on the shoulder. "Nothing changes, does it? Here I am once again watching you come unglued over some woman."

"She's not *some* woman," Emily responded heatedly.

Nina grinned. "What if I told you she asked me to keep my mouth shut if I ran into you this trip?"

"So what?"

"So don't you get it? It's a game. She wants to know all about you, but she doesn't want you to know she does."

"Why?"

"Oh, Emily—how can you be so smart and so dumb at the same time?" Nina took a deep drag on her cigarette and exhaled in Emily's face. "Because it ruins the mystery. That's what it's all about, with men and women and two women, all of them; it's the same difference."

Emily stared glumly into her suds.

"And you come on too strong. I always told you that when you were running after that fool Reena Dee. You don't leave any blank spaces."

She turned to Nina urgently and gripped her arm. "Nina, we were friends. *Friends,*" she repeated, as if this were a revelation. "There wasn't any game. We weren't like that. I don't want a game."

"So what happened?"

Emily turned her attention back to her beer. "You know," she muttered.

"Sure. You blew it."

"Yep. 'Fraid so."

"With your thousand and one questions."

"And drinking and stuff and," she sputtered in disgust, "I got carried away. She'd never been with a woman before either."

Nina digested this quietly. "Well, she's not like those other ones you've picked, that's for sure. She impressed me as a real grown-up, you know. She's her own person, right?"

"I guess so."

"And you scared the hell out of her. You do that with someone like her and forget it."

"I know."

"But it's her first time. That's what you've got going for you. The first time is special. I'm telling you: she's still interested. You want her back, don't you?"

Of course. And Emily said so. At which point Nina volunteered, "So why don't you come up and get her?"

This caught Emily by surprise. "Do *what?*"

"Come up to Provincetown and play it cool."

"I don't follow."

"Spend the summer up there. Let her know you've got your act together."

"How?"

"How?" Nina rolled her eyes and spoke to the wall. "I don't believe this woman."

"But, Nina, I can't come up there. I've never been to Provincetown."

"So that's all the more reason you should come. It's wonderful." Now Nina was warming to her subject. "Unless you've got some big plans over your vacation you can't break, like coming here every fucking day."

"But wouldn't she know why I was there?"

"Not necessarily. That's up to you. Everyone goes to Provincetown from here. You just arrive and keep your nose clean and it'll work out. I'll be there to keep you out of trouble."

And when Emily wondered aloud why Nina was so interested, Nina replied she liked stray cats. Then she gave Emily a hug. "Here." She scribbled some numbers on a piece of paper. "This is the shop phone. And here's the one in Truro. Think about it. If you decide to come, let me know. I've got a friend in real estate who can find you something right on the water. So what's to lose? Even if you don't get her back, you'll be in God's country. It sure beats hanging around this hell hole. Trust me."

And so.

AND AFTER THAT

It would come later—the Age of the Sword. In the 1980s the Plague would bring the young men back to Provincetown to die.

On beaches where waves rode in like horses to bend their necks at the shore, the waves would ride out carrying the mourners. Up from Florida they would come—parents, friends, lovers. Up from Georgia and North Carolina—sisters, brothers, cousins. Back from Minnesota and Los Angeles they would ride the wooden barges, boats of death, pausing on the swirling plate of the Atlantic to pay tribute, scattering the remains. Farewell glad son, proud friend, apple of my eye—farewell. All but ashes now, death's feed. In the 1980s skeletons would walk the streets in Provincetown, stiffgaited, pale, their eyes like dried leaves in standing water, fingerwidth limbs, stick-armed, leaning on canes, half blind, torturously summoning breath for one more step. Their time had come, and they knew it. Soon they too would float seaward into the bleeding horizon, into the sun's last squirt beyond the rim. Float to oblivion, young men turned old, men who in the summers of their youth, in the bright mornings of their passion, in the red marrow of their sexuality, had come to Provincetown to find out who they were, young men now to rest permanently where once they had relaxed. That would be the 1980s.

But when Emily arrived two decades before, the town was full of life. And always beautiful. Long before, the pilgrims had developed it by the sea. They spun paths on its natural elevations. They erected houses on those paths as quaint and picturesque as boats carved inside bottles. Their ships fed on the harbor like pups nursing at an earthen teat, bringing in a harvest of seaweed and ocean, smells of fish. They traveled to a light that artists would call the purest in the land. They became fishermen who took the sea as their mistress, who felt that mistress up in their imaginations, who entered that mistress with their dreams of plunder, who lay with her at night under God's jewelry, a million stars. Then, as now, the fishermen are everywhere. So is the fog. In Provincetown, fog drools over the pavement, backs up in alleys, squats on rooftops from which it leaps like a ghostly feline, builds like smoke in cramped quarters winding bayward from Hyannis through Orleans, Eastham, Wellfleet, Truro, flowing between the sandtears of dunes that weep across highway 6. In winter, Provincetown sleeps. In summer, it rings with dance. Artists come. Families come. So do the queers. Provincetown is yet another bead on the string that connects the empires of Queer—Ogunquit, Fire Island, Greenwich Village, Key West. In the 1960s queer was in the thighsoft sands, inside the singing of the surf, the wet and lonely ringing of the wind where egrets ran, where men were eager and women were independent. In the shothot summers of the 1960s, Provincetown was one long party. Everyone was invited, including Emily—or so she wanted to believe.

It was decided that Nina would be the Love Agent. When school was out, Emily would come to Provincetown and the strategy would be cat-and-mouse. She would do the exact opposite of what Anna would expect. She would not call or leave notes. If she saw her, she would pass on by. As for Nina, she would find out all she could about Anna's doings and tell Emily. Nina had already set the stage, for Anna trusted her. Soon after Nina returned from New York, she told Anna about running into Emily and described Emily as having looked great, as being sober, and as not having any particular reaction when Anna's name came up. Funny, but Emily was coming to Provincetown too. Wasn't that coincidental?

This had upset Anna. She had gotten a place here for peace and quiet and to do some work. She didn't want any complications. Nina assured her there would be none. She made her believe that Anna had nothing to do with Emily's decision, that Emily had wanted to get out of New York, and anyway lots of women came here over the summer. It was then Anna had told how their relationship had ended. "She wants independence, Emily," Nina said over the phone one night. "If you can't give her that, if you can't stay out of her hair when you're here, forget it. You've got to make her think you don't give a damn. But if you play your cards right, it'll work."

In June, and having significantly eased her drinking, Emily arrived in Provincetown with a full deck. She moved into the one-room beach house Nina's real estate friend had found. It was rustic and cloaked by trees that obscured it from the street. By night she could hear music from a nearby men's bar. By day she could watch the seagulls flip in the sun and the sailboats playing host to the wind. Her landlords were two teachers from Boston, Ben and Jack, who had been coming here for years. Their summer place was directly above hers, and they knew everyone, including Nina, to whom they had promised they would look after Emily. So from the moment she hit town, she had a ready-made social life. She also met Faye and liked her. And she took the Grand Tour with Nina. That tour included driving by Anna's house, gray and set back from the road. The door was open and it hit Emily to be so close yet so far. But she took Nina's advice. She stayed away from the shop in the mornings, which was when Anna dropped by, and she avoided Anna's neck of the woods. Soon she had melted into the breezy life with Ben and Jack's crowd: afternoon cocktails, poker, local clubs at night. But always she hoped to see Anna. In the swarms of tourists that clogged Commercial Street, the main drag, she would find herself searching for Anna's face to rise above the crowds like the slickly groomed tail of a black cat. And when it didn't happen after the first week, she became discouraged. Nina kept her on track though, feeding her carrots of wisdom: be patient. Telling her about Anna's being impressed that Emily hadn't bothered her, that Anna had gotten Nina to tell her where Emily was staying, that Anna had asked several times how Emily was doing. Then toward the end of that month, Emily had the first of three "sightings" in almost as many days. Fate?

The first was early one Saturday morning at the A & P when she spotted Anna talking to a young couple in the produce aisle. She hadn't seen her since New Year's Eve, and initially she was stunned. Anna looked leaner, darker, prettier, long hair brushed back, wearing a simple white skirt under a loose green blouse. Who wouldn't have fallen in love with her? Why wouldn't the vegetables have done a dance? She heard her name float over the potatoes: "Emily!" Anna's head jerked about. Their eyes met. Janet Brown, whom Emily knew from Ben and Jack's, was coming happily toward her. But Janet also knew Anna's friends, and suddenly all were together being introduced. At a point, Emily and Anna had to say they knew each other. Awkward. As soon as possible, Emily left. As she was pushing her cart away, she accidentally rammed it into a fruit stand sending a plethora of apples and oranges piled on top of each other plummeting to the floor. Goddammit! On her knees getting them. Anna's familiar laugh. Anna beside her doing the same thing. Thanking her and stumbling off distressed by this dismal turn. What an ox she must have looked! And she hadn't any lipstick on! If she had had any idea she would have seen Anna, she would have, plus she would have donned the blue shirt open at the neck that Anna used to say was sexy! Too bad

Nina was in Boston until tomorrow. She had no one to talk to. Miserably she went home and stayed in her cottage all the rest of that day.

Came the next day. Emily arrived at the shop in a slight drizzle, anxious to see Nina. Someone in a giant-sized raincoat was on the landing bent over and struggling to open a black umbrella. It was unusually windy, and suddenly a sharp gust lifted that umbrella and pitched it over the railing and up the street. Without thinking, Emily raced in pursuit. She got it and started back, which was when she realized the person on the landing, who now had stepped down one stair, was Anna with an expression of mixed emotions. Emily's knees buckled; she felt weak. This can't be! I just saw her! But there Anna was, bigger than the town of Provincetown, bigger than the cars or sun out for a brief stroll among the clouds, bigger than a man shouting at some hapless driver about to illegally park and a woman carrying out her trash. The rain had matted her hair; drops stood boldly on her cheeks. Emily was soon at the foot of the steps, and her breath left her body. She looked up at Anna, who looked down at her. She had this sensation, as she had the first time they met, that they were alone dancing to some lingering refrain. Anna's mouth seemed to travel toward her, Anna's face seemed that of the dream, like a balloon attached to a long string, and Emily felt a reaching inside her soul to catch that face and press her lips to it: kiss. She felt herself moving up the stairs riveted to the glue of Anna's presence just as the door to the shop opened and an elderly couple emerged. As that happened, another customer approached from the rear. Because the passage was narrow, Anna and Emily had to move. When they met midstair, Emily handed over the umbrella. Thank you, Anna said, her eyes not leaving Emily's face. It's okay, Emily murmured softly. She got to the landing and turned around. As if having expected this, Anna was waiting on the street, smiling before she walked off. She got a short distance and turned around. Emily was still rooted in front of the door, restraining the wildest urge to run after her. But she heard a tapping. It was Nina at the window, who had seen much of this. She was gesturing furiously for her to enter. Reluctantly, Emily did, only to be told she had done the right thing. "You want her back, don't you?" Nina cajoled. "Well then, don't be making an ass of yourself. Leave her be. It's not time yet." Emily's head was reeling. It was still reeling two nights later when she saw Anna yet again after a play. And once again the world shrank to a stage of two.

They were both in an arcade surrounding the theater when it happened. Emily was talking to the women she had come with and preparing to join some others at a local bar. Anna, nearer the street, was speaking animatedly with two men Emily didn't recognize. The whole place was mobbed. She decided to throw caution to the wind. "Wait here," she told her friends. "I'll be right back." With that, she started toward Anna from an angle to avoid detection. She wanted the element of surprise, to catch her unawares. She was relying on how Anna had looked at the shop two days ago, warm and glad to see her. She was counting on whatever it had been that had made Anna drop to her knees at the A & P, and she was just doing it with a nothing-ventured-nothing-gained sort of logic. She didn't know what Nina would have advised, but she was about to ask Anna to have a drink.

She saw a man named Ted, a friend of Ben and Jack's, but, indicating she was in a rush, she went on. She saw a heavyset blonde run over and put an arm around Anna's shoulder, saying something that made them all roar. She stopped dead in her tracks with an awful fear that maybe she and Anna were involved, but surely Nina would have told her. Just then a car honked and the four started toward the street. *"Anna!"* the word broke out of her mouth.

And the dear girl turned with that Look again. Don't go, Emily was pleading silently. Then the fat woman, who had walked off, came back, tugging on Anna's sleeve. Emily could hear, "Come on. We're going to be late."

Anna shrugged, looked confused momentarily, and then as if to say what can I do, she waved at Emily and started toward the car. That was a dagger in the heart. Emily stood watching the Buick move off, feeling cheated and let down. It wasn't fair. Why stay in Provincetown and be hurt like this? Why not go back to New York where at least she wouldn't have to see Anna? Nina's predictions weren't worth a plug nickel.

In that mood she rejoined her party. Around midnight she left the Spades Bar to walk home by the bay. It was a glorious night, the waves giddy with freedom, the moon drawing a long yellow hall in the water—so quiet it seemed the world had stuck its head in the sand.

At a path by an inn she started toward the cottage and was just about to enter when she heard her name. It came, and it was eerie how it came, floating and soft like a feather from over by the bushes. She turned quickly and there was Anna running toward her from where she had been waiting. Emily stumbled in her eagerness to reach her, but then Anna was in her arms; there was a huge oak in the middle of the yard and they backed into it, sliding down the trunk onto the wakeful grass as the night with all its baggage curled around Anna's body.

And then in the paling lights through the paling trees with the branches spreading their knees to the wind, Anna turned her into a lake of fire. And they were rising, rising, licking the fire with their tongues: Sex, delicious thing, you make me into flame, into a running light!

. . . Now if I can adequately describe what was to come:

After that night we picked up the pieces and went on, Anna and I. There were, as I recall, some mighty big ones to carry: in particular my insecurity—that hot stone that maddens the soul. It bore no particular weight in Provincetown. But back in New York that September it still caused problems. Anna, smart girl, forced me to develop control: on this, our second time around, she restricted our visits to weekends. And when I ranted and raved, she refused to see me.

It worked. Why? Well, like Plato said once: love is a divided body searching the world over for its other half. Not to sound corny, but maybe that was our genius: on the most basic level, we fit. Who can make sense of these things? We come into this world naked, leave it naked, lie with our lover naked, looking to heal our wounds. Our souls in their jails of skin reach through the bars of our own fear and vulnerability for the other's truth; only fleetingly do we touch. Men with women, women with women, men with men—it's all the same. Born strangers, we live as strangers, except at moments. And then what glory!

You ask: has it been simple with Anna all these years? No. Yes. We took off I suppose where Mattie and I stopped. And we loved each other.

Thus that spring of 1964 we found our own apartment in New York and moved in together. She remained at Hunter; I at Sloe. And the cat of time got fat. As for the outside world, of course we danced to its drummer. Only when we were alone were we honest.

Each summer we returned to that same cottage in Provincetown until we bought our own place there, which is where I am now, trying to complete this dark odyssey about Lillian.

You see tonight, July 15, is her birthday. I always used to send her cards. Often unsure where she was, I'd write "forward" on the envelope and mail them to the university in Florida. She always got them.

Now I sit in my cottage in Provincetown. In the next room, Anna sleeps. Outside, the moon wraps itself in the pillow of a moving cloud. It is midnight. Lovers abound under the eyes of a flashing sky. Nothing changes. Everything changes. Tonight memory is my mistress. Lillian still haunts, and the strange walk of our souls since Mattie Hurst.

Understand, I give her all the credit. It was Lillian who sustained our friendship—letters from Charata in Argentina, or Manta in Ecuador, or Moyobamba in Peru. Cards from the Far East, Near East, Russia. "Hi, Stollie," her squeak of a Yankee accent would romance my ears, and then we were off and running on our "umbilical cord" as we called the telephone. After I met Anna, she became "Andy" Rubin, so I'd mention his name to Lillian as Anna made faces. On one of our talks,

Lillian said she and Bob had separated and then gotten back together and that things between them had never been so good. Ironically that had happened about the same time as my trials with Anna, but I never said a word.

In 1971 I flew down to see her in Miami, where she had some rare school business that brought her to America. And what a great reunion. The next few years we were bound by calls and correspondence. Always she would try to get me and "Andy" to visit. But Anna refused to go and lie to my best friend. This raised a thorny issue, but I didn't give ground. Anna's point was it was wrong to fool someone like Lillian. But to me the subject was closed. The result was I never visited her, nor did I meet Bob. I just felt too guilty about lying with Anna harping on the subject. So I told myself eventually Anna would relent and we would visit Lillian on *my* terms.

Then in April of 1977 I got a letter from Lillian. It sounded all right on the surface. But I was to learn later that something dark and foreboding was between the lines . . .

NEW
YORK

Part Four

LILLIAN
_____

April 3, 1977

Dear Emily,

Sorry I haven't written for so long, but it's been crazy
here. Anyway, the Big News is I'm coming back to New
York on a combination business-pleasure trip. The business
end is to see a lawyer referred by Mom's attorney in England
about some family property and then go to Gunther (they're
using my work in Peru for a research project, and I've
agreed to help on a couple of things). The other is to go to
Vermont and, last but not least, see you. I've something
important to tell you and want to do it in person. I was
thinking maybe we could meet at Kelly's Grill (assuming it's
still going strong) on Thursday, April 27, at seven P.M. You
can let Bob know when he calls; and if it's no longer there,
then come up with another place. Let me give you now a
quick rundown of plans: We land at La Guardia that
Monday the 24th, coming from either Paris or Germany.

There won't be time to phone, and don't even think about coming out. I'm not sure of flight numbers because of the uncertainty at this point about where we leave from. As soon as we finish customs, Bob is taking an immediate plane to Miami, and I'm off to Boston to rest up and then I have an appointment in Cambridge. From there it's Vermont, to White River, specifically. Not to see anyone, but just to get back to my old roots once more. I'll explain all when I see you. I'll be in New York the twenty-seventh and for one night only. I don't know arrival time, but expect to see the lawyer that day. I'm staying in an apartment of a friend who's in Spain. It's near the old place so that'll be interesting and works out well cause it's so much closer to Gunther. I'll be at Gunther all the next day and then am leaving that same night, the twenty-eighth, to join Bob in Miami. I'm not going to call you because the schedule is obviously jampacked but there's a time factor involved and it's the best I can do. Anyway, it'll be nice for us to have our first contact at Kelly's.

Bob will be calling to confirm this on Sunday the seventeenth and will try to get through between eight A.M. and noon *your time*. I won't be able to be with him then, so he's doing the honors alone.

Did you get the Peruvian dolls I sent???
How's Andy?

Can't wait to see you. Much love,
Lil

P.S. Try to get us our old booth if we're meeting at Kelly's!

At 6:40 on the evening of April twenty-seventh, Emily was at Kelly's in the booth Lillian had specified, with a full view of the front of the restaurant. She had taken the subway, her usual mode of travel in the city for it was cheaper and there were no problems with parking. But the express had been faster than expected, so now time weighed heavily. She sipped her beer and tried to relax. She checked the Dom Perignon in the bucket of ice beside the booth and looked about. Not much was different for all the years since she had been here. The bar was longer.

There was dancing in the rear on Saturdays. But the decor was unchanged; the waiters were still friendly, though she didn't recognize any. It was here she and Lillian used to meet regularly after Emily first moved to the Village. They would sit for hours talking and drinking while Emily lied about all the men she was dating. In those days a porterhouse was five dollars; now the price was doubled. She lit a cigarette and kept watching the door. She was tense. As eager as she was to see Lillian, something didn't feel right. For instance, why when Bob called had he sounded so funny when she asked about Lillian? They had never met, but she had talked to him on the phone enough to be familiar with his voice. And what was this big thing Lillian had to tell her? Oh well, she would find out soon enough. Anna said she was worrying too much.

A little after seven the door opened, and there she was. Emily rushed to the front; and in the excitement of greeting, she didn't really get a close look at Lillian. But once seated in the glow of the small candle the waiter had provided, she was shocked at her appearance. Age it seemed had set up housekeeping on Lillian's face, run its errands around the lips and lower cheeks, dumped garbage near the eyes. She was bone-thin, thinner than Emily remembered, her expression wan and peaked. Something cautioned Emily to avoid questions; and at the start, her curiosity was drowned out in a flurry of comments about White River, Lillian's trip, being back in New York, catch-up talk on Bob and Andy. Champagne finished, they ordered shrimp cocktail, steak, salad, and beer. Lillian was wearing a short-sleeved blouse; and when she took her jacket off, she looked even skinnier. Was her hand shaking? Emily reached over and covered it with her own. "You okay?" she asked softly. She felt Lillian pull back, and with growing alarm demanded, "Lillian, what is it? What's going on?"

The waiter chose that moment to bring the shrimp. Lillian took one, dunked it in the sauce; then in a voice as calm as if asking for the salt, she said the words that sank terror in Emily's heart, "I've got cancer, Stollie. It's terminal. That's what I've come to tell you. I wanted to do it in person and not over the phone." She put the shrimp in her mouth, then pointed to her bosom. "They took both of them." She made a small chopping gesture over her left breast, chuckling drily as if still amazed at the irony of the situation. "All those years stuffing my bra to look like Marilyn Monroe, right? Well, guess you can't miss what you never had!"

Oh Lord, she's so young, was Emily's first reaction, as mental hands grabbed her own breasts to feel for lumps. She pushed her plate away and stared in disbelief as around them the world continued its normal pace: waiters scurrying by with trays, sounds of laughter from a nearby table, a clatter of dishes. "I don't understand," she finally managed. "When? When did you find out?"

"About a year ago."

"A year ago!"

"Yes, but I didn't know for sure. I mean I knew but I wouldn't let myself believe it."

"Where were you?"

"Africa, taking a shower. I felt this hard thing. I could almost put my fingers around it, and I panicked. Then I just ignored it, which was pretty stupid considering Mom and Mom's two sisters died from the same thing. But I kept thinking if I left it alone it would just go on its own. Bob noticed it, and I told him it was nothing."

"Oh, my God!"

"Then it got larger. By the time we checked, it had spread; so we went to Miami for the operation."

"You had the operation in Miami?" Emily gasped.

"That's right."

"When did all this happen?"

"About seven months ago."

"That's why you haven't written?"

"Yes, I . . ."

She interrupted, genuinely hurt, "You were in Miami all this time and you didn't let me know!"

"I didn't know how. Even if Mom were alive, I don't know if I could have told her right away. I was too ashamed."

"Ashamed? Ashamed of what?"

"Having cancer. It was like I'd failed or something. That probably doesn't make sense, but it's how I felt. People can't handle it. They don't know what to do. They look at you like you're going to drop dead, and you end up having to take care of them. I didn't want to go through that. I didn't want to deal with someone else's guilt that I had it and they didn't; so I just kept it as my dirty little secret and Bob's."

"But I'm not like that. I'm supposed to be your best friend."

"You are. That's why I'm telling you."

"But look at all the time we've missed, Lillian. I could have been with you."

"Emily, I've been trying to get you to visit for years. You've never even met Bob."

She groaned, "I know, I know. But this is different. I would have come at the drop of a hat no matter what was going on with me."

"No, no; there was nothing you could do. I've been sick as a dog. I took chemo and radiation. My hair fell out."

Emily's eyes darted to her head. Yes, the hair was shorter; but she had thought it just a cut. Lillian caught the glance. "Some of it isn't real," she said very quietly.

"Oh, Lil."

"Is everything okay?" The waiter was at the booth filling Lillian's glass with water. Emily nodded, aware of the absurdity of his question. He left, and she asked slowly, "What do you mean terminal?"

"That's what I mean. It's too late."

"But how? They've made all these advances. My mother died of breast cancer. If she'd had it now, she'd still be alive. I know that."

"Emily, listen to me. I'm trying to tell you something. I refused any more treatments."

"You did what?"

"I refused."

"What do you mean, you refused."

"That. I made up my mind I wasn't going to do it anymore,

I wasn't going out like Mom. I never told you the whole story on that, but it was awful, it was terrible at the end. When they got finished with her, she weighed seventy pounds. Seventy pounds!" Lillian shuddered. "Think of it! Do you have any idea what seventy pounds is on a grown woman? It's bone and rag, that's what; it's a skeleton. It's a cruel and inhuman finish to any life, let alone someone you love. She was so doped up with so much poison in her from all the treatments, she didn't know who she was or what was happening. She thought I was her mother. I'd go visit her in that hospital in England and climb into bed with her and hold her and the roles switched. She was the child and I was the parent." Now for the first time color marked Lillian's face, and her eyes brimmed in memory. "In a way that whole passage of time and going backward with her in it brought me the deepest peace. It's hard to talk about it, but I vowed I'd never become a victim like that."

"But don't you want to live?"

"Yes, of course. And as fully as I can with what's left of my life. But I want it to have quality. There's something to be said for that: the quality of living, the quality of dying."

"What does Bob say?"

"It's my decision. That's the way we are. Like this trip. He would have come, but I told him it was something I had to do for myself, to go back home where it all started, to come here and go up to school and then see you. I couldn't share that with anyone now."

Emily took a bite of shrimp but barely tasted it. Then, after a lingering few minutes, she asked the question she no longer could bear, "How long?"

Lillian didn't blink. "A year, probably less."

She leaned over the table jabbing her fork slightly, "Who says that?"

"Everyone. Me. You know something like that."

"How?"

"You just do."

"You're saying there's *nothing* out there that works in this day and age? You've got to keep fighting, Lillian. You've got to fight and fight."

Now Lillian blinked with a look of pure will, even annoyance, "What do you think I've been doing? Bob and I have been living like pack rats, like cancer junkies going from one so-called cure to another. That's what I was doing in Cambridge. I quit my job; he took an extended leave. Thank God, we've saved some money. And we've just been all over. You name it, I've tried it: meditation, diets, injections, seeing the tumor in my head—they call this imaging—as a piece of cheese that the rats are nibbling on. I've gone the whole nine yards except for Lourdes and I'm tired. Bob's tired."

"But I was just reading in the *Times* about this doctor in Mexico . . ."

"Yes, I know," Lillian cut in. "I know about him. Don't you see—I've passed that mark. It's got me now, and I have to come to terms with it. It's invasive. I can feel it pressing on my nerve endings. There's a tumor growing in my chest. It's called lymph node involvement. The lumps came back after the mastectomies, after all the treatments. That's why I said to hell with it while I have some strength left." She stopped as the waiter brought the main course. When he left, Emily said with evident emotion, "I just feel so bad you didn't let me know so I could have been with you."

"You *are* with me. You always are. And this is where I want us to say good-bye."

"Say it *where*?"

"Here."

"At Kelly's!"

"Yes."

"What about tomorrow? I'll call in sick and spend the day with you."

"No, I wrote you: I have to go up to Gunther."

"So I'll pick you up there."

"I don't want that. I don't want the pressure. I don't know what time I'll be finished, so I'll just get a cab."

"But I'm taking you to the airport, aren't I?"

Lillian shook her head. She didn't want to be driven to the airport, she said. She didn't want some emotion-packed good-bye with a plane in the background, like in *Casablanca*. She wanted to leave New York the way she had come in, anonymously by cab, no fuss, able to have her own thoughts. And besides, wouldn't it be best to remember each other right here over a drink? She hated good-byes; why drag this one out? And when Emily pushed her to stay longer, Lillian declined that too, saying she and Bob were traveling and she had to keep to the schedule.

But Emily couldn't let go; she couldn't imagine this being their final time together. "Let me come too," she cried, feeling desperate and close to tears. "Please, Lil. We can spend a little time together. I'll meet Bob. I can take some time from school."

"No. It's impossible. We've . . ."

Emily interrupted. "Then at least let me come to where you're staying tomorrow. I won't even bring the car. I'll take the subway. That way there'll be no hassle about my driving you to the airport."

Lillian didn't respond.

"You've got to. You can't just come back and turn my life upside down like this and then leave."

"But won't it be the same tomorrow night? It'll be just as hard then."

"I don't know. But that's what I'm going to do. I'm going to come up before you leave."

Lillian looked at her a moment. Then, almost inaudibly, she stated a fact. "I love you, Stollie. I want you to know that before I leave. You've been closer to me than any sister could ever have been; and you've helped me through this. I've thought a lot about how you would have dealt with my situation. It's made me stronger."

Emily, never having considered herself inspirational, could only react in wonderment. "Why? What did I do?"

"You haven't let them break you."

"Who?"

"Life, you know, you've kept your spirit intact. That's one thing you've given me."

"I don't understand."

"It's how you carry yourself. I've always sensed you had this huge pain inside."

"What pain?" Why did she feel so defensive? "I don't have any pain."

"Emily, I'm not attacking you."

"I don't feel attacked. I just don't know what you're getting at."

"I'm trying to clear the smoke tonight, to be honest like we've been all these years. I'm telling you I've felt your strength even though you didn't know I did, and I'm grateful. And when I say pain, I'm talking about a feeling I've always had from the day you went off to that school in Connecticut when we were kids. I knew you were going through hell, but you'd never talk about it."

Emily shifted uneasily. "I told you, my folks were getting divorced. Why're you bringing this up anyway? Why're we raking over the past?"

"We're not raking over anything. People need to tell each other these things before it's too late." She began cutting her steak and motioned Emily to eat. "What I'm trying to say," Lillian continued with a trace of fatigue in her voice, "is you're a fighter. I've seen that in you all through school whenever we had any connection; and when you were in New York there was something, I didn't get it all, but something in you," she paused as if to find the right word. "You seemed so unsure and yet you struggled with that, you struggled to get your life going the way you wanted it to. And you didn't give in. I told Bob that. I said you handled your problems like a pro and if you were in my shoes you'd fight the hell out of this thing just like you've fought your own battles, which I don't pretend to know about. I've always thought you were so brave."

Dammit. She didn't feel brave. She felt just the opposite. And she didn't want to get into any talk of the past. "Oh God, Lil," she cried. "You were the brave one."

"No braver than you. You took risks. You dreamed big."

"I did *what*? What in the world did I do?"

"You wrote your dreams. Every poem you wrote was a dream. Even the ones that went on forever that I'd find all over the apartment when you lived with me, the ones about freedom and independence, all that stuff you'd say you talked about with your students, and having the courage to be who you were—well, it was something for me to just know you felt that too. Outside Bob you were the only person who ever backed what I wanted no matter what it was. Remember that time I said I wanted to be the first woman on the moon?" She laughed, but Emily didn't. She was too caught up in sadness, doubt, all that. "You know, I really meant that. All the Muskateers were saying they wanted to get married or do this or that, and hell, I really wanted to go to the moon."

"I know," Emily agreed quietly.

"Well, it meant everything to me the way you felt. What you gave me was a confidence I could do whatever I tried to do. And now I think I'm on the right track. In a way cancer has freed me up, strange as that might sound." And when Emily asked how, Lillian answered that she and Bob had bought a boat called *The Raven;* and when she got back to Florida tomorrow night, they were setting out.

"For where?" Emily swallowed hard.

"Wherever."

"How?" She was dumbfounded.

"Remember that day on my aunt's boat in Maine, Stollie, when we ran out of wind?"

"Yes, of course."

"It was like a call. I'm not trying to sound dramatic, but when I've thought about it, as I have a great deal, it was a really spiritual experience. I'm talking about going to sea, that what I felt that day had to be what some truly religious person feels, that there's no other way for them, something they can't even figure out is speaking to them. And for me, nothing's changed since then. Except for when I held Mom before she died, I've never had such peace of mind as that day. It was like going home, as if the water had taken shape and was beckoning me. I knew then that that was what I wanted even though girls didn't pursue stuff like that. But it was in me to go a different way. I remember Dad told me once he wanted to be a sailor when he was young; so maybe that rubbed off. Anyway, I had to grow up and Mom was on my back to do something important that was serious, so I went into archaeology as a compromise. You've heard all this. Don't get me wrong. I've had a great time, and I met Bob. But I've always had that nagging suspicion I had sold out by being part of a system with all the system's egos and politics and petty b. s. Even though I was doing things a lot of people only dream about, I was still playing a game, still squandering part of my *soul* for lack of a better word. I guess this makes me a purist. But there it is. Does this sound too corny?"

"No. Not at all. I only wish," Emily stopped.

"You wish what?"

"I wish," she answered truthfully, "I could feel like that. I mean that I could be absolutely certain about something."

"You will."

"Maybe. I don't know. Sometimes I don't think I have any real convictions."

For a while they ate without comment, though Emily had lost her appetite. Then Lillian said, "You know what I think it's all about, Stollie? It's about making the right connections. It's about getting down to the basics, being naked on your haunches, feeling the flow of creation, like Thoreau said. If I ever had any doubts about that, I don't anymore. That's what I mean about being free now. Cancer is rude, it doesn't have any manners, it comes in and takes over. But it's forced me to really face myself. So, to make a long story short, we're sailing into the sunset toward some islands in South America; and when it's time, Bob knows what to do."

"What do you mean?" Emily's voice broke.

"You know what I mean. I've always counted on you to know what I mean."

"But . . . how?"

"That's not important. We've talked about it a lot."

"Are you scared?" she dared ask.

"Of what?"

"I don't know," Emily looked about helplessly.

"Death?"

"I guess so." She didn't know how to say these dreadful words.

"No. Not anymore. I'm past that."

"How?"

"I just am. It comes."

"Will I hear from you?"

"No. That's part of what this is all about. Breaking away."

Smells. Voices. Busboys with their white napkins tucked in their aprons. A child's excitable squeal up ahead. Laughter from the bar. Emily's throat constricted, and she took another bite of steak. She washed that down with beer and took another sip. That sip hardened like a marble in her throat, and she had the sensation it wasn't going down. But when it did, it hurt her chest, and she felt the tears. She bit her lip and strived for a measure of control. Out of the corner of her eye she saw the waiter approaching, a nice young man doing his job, but she didn't want him to ask if everything was all right, because everything was rotten and she didn't feel like lying; so she dismissed him with a gentle wave and he veered off. After what seemed an interminably long time, she heard Lillian ask, "Do you love Andy?"

"Yes," she started, caught off guard.

"You going to marry him?"

"I don't know. I can't think about him right now."

"I wish you could have met Bob."

Silence.

"I really do."

"Me too, Lil." She looked directly into Lillian's eyes.

"Emily, I just have to ask this. How come you never visited us? Were you ashamed for me to meet Andy?"

"Oh God, Lillian! What a thing to say!"

"Then why? You'd never even let me talk to him on the phone when I called."

"He wasn't there," she tensed up.

"But you never let me meet any of the men you went out with."

So now what, she thought in panic. So now I'm supposed to get down on my fucking knees and pray for some way out of this? So why not tell her? Look at her, so white and small and brave, and my God the relief to say the truth! Anna's face suddenly floated over that table, clear and strong and vibrant. And Emily cried out, "Lillian, I was so royally screwed up then. I didn't know what I was doing. It had nothing to do with our friendship. I can't say what it meant to me, what it means now, all I can tell you is that it held me together lots of times just knowing you were in the world when I felt lousy or all alone. You've been like family, you know; you're the only person I've kept in touch with all these years." She took a deep breath. "I love you so much right now I don't know how to talk anymore." She choked up, and this time it was Lillian grabbing her hand. They sat like that without saying a word. After a while Lillian took out a piece of paper and scribbled on it. "Here," she said, "is the name of my friend where I'm staying. Pat Prouchie. 620 West 116th, right at the corner of Riverside Drive. I can't remember the apartment number, but it'll be on the roster. Come up at six tomorrow night, and we'll have an hour. The plane leaves at nine, and I want to be in the cab no later than seven. You know how I am about being on time."

Yes. Emily remembered that.

"Bring Andy if you want."

She made a face. "I can't. He'll be in Philadelphia."

Okay. Now it was time for a mood change. With a touch of her old verve, Lillian told a joke about a man lying in the desert with a huge sword through his chest. His skin was ripped and blistered. His eyeballs bulged. His tongue was swollen and black. After a few days a soldier rides up on a smart, white horse. He looks down at the guy on the sand and asks, Does it hurt? The fellow on the sand coughs up blood and sputters, Only when I laugh.

Vintage Lillian. They finished their meal, intentionally staying clear of more morose conversation. Then it was time to leave. Yet all Emily could think about was death. Death sat between them at Kelly's moving not muscle nor hair. Waiting. It stood with them as they embraced on the sidewalk just before Lillian got into a taxi. It watched as the taxi drove off with Lillian waving from the window. It huddled next to Emily on the subway home. And when she couldn't find her mirror, death loaned her his.

It was after midnight when Emily got home. She undressed and went to bed, sliding next to Anna, who was already asleep. "Anna," she whispered, shaking her shoulder urgently. "Anna, wake up! Lillian's sick!"

"Wha . . ." came the muffled response.

"Lillian's got cancer! She's dying!" She began crying softly. This brought Anna around; and after telling the whole story, Emily fell asleep in her arms.

A dream carried her back in time. She was in her old room in White River trying to decide whether to slip out and meet Lillian or not. A brilliant moon painted the sky; and around that, millions of stars lit their matches, enabling her to see her front yard, her bike, the tall familiar tree that guarded her window. Then rapidly the scene changed to Lillian's street. Emily was running up and down frantically trying to find Lillian's house; but where the Jackson home had once taken over two entire acres, now there was only a dirt field.

She woke up thinking about death and wondering if she had made a big mistake in insisting on seeing Lillian again. She felt like she was going to a funeral. A wave of despair swept her. She was sad, and sick of herself at the same time. Last night Anna had offered to be with her as moral support. She would take the train with her at five-thirty, then wait somewhere as Emily made her final good-byes. Or, if Emily wanted, she would go with her to the apartment and do the "Andy's sister" routine, a gesture all the more generous given her feelings. But Emily, though she could have used the comfort, had declined. It seemed wrong to bring Anna under any pretext at a time like this. She lay in bed thinking about it all. She knew how concerned Anna was, and she was ashamed of her feelings, ashamed that in her most private thoughts she would be humiliated if Lillian knew she was queer, particularly Lillian. It was a sorry conflict. On the one hand, she was deeply proud of Anna. Before Lillian became ill, Emily would have delighted in introducing someone so smart and attractive and interesting as Anna. But if Anna had agreed to visit Lillian, would Emily have really brought her? Right now she wasn't so sure. A part of her felt she might have been diminished and that to avoid any temptation of the truth, Anna mustn't get anywhere near Lillian—even though at a point last night she had ached to tell her. Yet how could she have dealt with the shame that Lillian would then be privy to—Mattie, the whole bit? Because in a way, wasn't telling Lillian telling everyone? Well, that was it: she couldn't. It was too embarrassing, no matter how much she loved Anna.

Six A.M., the clock said. She better get moving. Mary Silk was riding with her this week. Mary taught history at Sloe, and her car was in repair. Good. Mary talked incessantly, and that would keep her from having to dwell on Lillian. She got up and went to the toilet. Her eyes were swollen and red from crying, so she wiped her face with a damp rag. After showering and getting dressed, she walked to the window. It was raining. Dammit. On impulse she dug a picture of Lillian out from her desk drawer. There she was, bright as the morning sun, standing on a boat in Costa Rica clad in shorts and pointing with pride to a three-hundred-fifty-pound, six-foot bull shark she had just caught. Memories of last night overcame her. She heard Anna call. Putting the photo away, she went into the bedroom and stood at the door.

"Come here," Anna said. When Emily approached the bed hesitantly, Anna asked, "How're you doing?"

"Okay."

Anna pulled her down beside her. "I'm still ready to go if you want. I can meet you here, and we can ride up together."

"No. That's all right. I'm better."

Anna traced Emily's face gently with her hand. "It's really okay my being with you tonight, Emily. I know what you're going through. Don't worry. I wouldn't do anything to give us away."

"No, no really," she said guiltily. "It's all right."

"Poor baby," Anna murmured.

"Why?"

"No reason. Just poor baby."

She felt a lump in her throat and stood up. "I gotta run."

"What time will you be leaving?"

"I'll catch the five-thirty express."

"Well, call me before you do."

"Okay," Emily ruffled Anna's hair. "I love you."

She left and got Mary Silk, who kept up a steady line of chat all the way to White Plains. In class she lectured, so she wouldn't have to think about Lillian that much, and she made it a point not to be alone all day. After school she drove Mary home and was in her own apartment by four.

She called Anna and reassured her she was fine. But she wasn't. Now that she was by herself, a dark depression was setting in. Exhausted by scant sleep and anxiety, she lay down on the couch to watch TV and unintentionally dozed off.

She awoke later than expected and ran around crazily trying to get ready. In short order she was running (in what promised to be quite a rain) the one block to the subway; and there close to five-thirty she descended into the subterranean environs of the IRT ticking through the vast pit-hole of Manhattan. It was the start of rush hour, when the express came regularly, and she would be at 116th Street in roughly fifteen minutes—from 34th to Times Square to 72nd to 96th—bingo. She got her token and joined the crowd. When nothing happened, she went to the edge of the platform, peering toward the plumbless dark of the tunnel, and was just beginning to get worried when she heard the train. It was a local. Damn! Locals were much slower and stopped everywhere. It was now 5:40. She paused, not sure what to do, until the conductor yelled through a loudspeaker that due to technical problems there was no express service northbound on the Seventh Avenue line tonight.

She got on to a sardine pack of people jammed together in a pinch of heat and odors, wedging herself into the belly of the car, where she stood upright like a bean in a vertical pack. That's when she first felt someone looking at her. Turning slightly, she gazed into the dark eyes of a pockmarked, swarthily built man with a large crucifix around his neck. Immediately she averted her face. The doors closed and opened, closed and opened with the nervous rapidity of a blinking eye. Finally, they clanged shut, and the train went into labor. It moved a few feet, then died. She saw the man still watching. Her first thought was to stare back, but Anna always said not to give a creep the satisfaction of response; so she purposefully kept her attention somewhere else. Looking around, she saw at the rear of the car a small cubicle, two seats on each side separated by a narrow passage like the neck of a bottle. To the right of that was a door connecting this car with the one after it. To the left of the cubicle was the exit door, and sitting next to that was a woman who appeared to be leaving. At the upcoming stop she did; and Emily took her place beside another woman, across from a nun and a well-dressed gentleman whose briefcase and crisp pin-stripes conveyed the demeanor and haughty authority of, say, someone in banking. It was stuffy, so she removed her jacket.

The man, the pest, had taken her former spot, which was diagonally across, and Emily could feel his eyes swarm over her like a mess of ants. Her wedding ring that she had removed because she was seeing Lillian was in her purse; but now she slipped it on for as long as he would be on the subway; then she rested her hand in her lap hoping he would understand she was spoken for and leave her alone. It didn't work. Deliberately she looked him full force in the face. What she saw repulsed her. He was leering and licking his lips and there was no mistake that he was staring at her. Once again she turned aside, praying he wouldn't be getting out at her stop and wanting only to be left with her thoughts about Lillian. At the next stop the woman beside her got out and was quickly replaced by a young, college-aged woman carrying a Vanderbilt University notebook. With more riders also boarding, the man was eclipsed.

It was getting on to six; and for the first time it occurred to her that she might not have a full hour with Lillian. Suddenly she wanted that hour desperately. The force of her want made everything else unimportant. Idly she wondered if she should get off at Fifty-seventh Street. But then it was raining, she remembered, and she would never get a cab, so she tried calming herself by thinking about something neutral. She looked around at the poster ads, Miss Subway smiling down at humanity, Prudential Life and the good times it promised, Chemical Bank and savings accounts, Arthur Godfrey and his joyful recommendations for coffee. The train jerked and started up just as her attention was drawn to a young couple seated in the middle of the car. The woman had an arm around her companion's shoulder and, leaning against him, was buttoning his shirt with her free hand as he stared contentedly ahead. She was doing this as if she had done it hundreds of times before, as if she had memorized his body, knew the exact distance between his nipples, as if, simply, she could read him in the dark. That familiarity, the man's trusting acceptance, struck Emily as one of the most intimate things she had ever seen. It spoke the language of lovers, it spoke a solidarity to the world. It spoke nonverbally what she and Anna could never say publicly. And it reminded her of two weeks past in Central Park.

On a gorgeous Sunday afternoon they had gone there to celebrate their thirteenth anniversary of living together. And as they were strolling in a secluded section of the park, Anna, who usually frowned on public displays, suddenly reached for Emily's wrist. Today was special, she said, and why not hold hands. Emily accepted the hand as if it were a hot potato. It made her nervous, but she did it, assuring herself that French women did the same thing quite naturally. Before long they noted a couple advancing toward them, perhaps a city block and a half away. Her intimacy with Anna then became a dare. The couple was talking animatedly, giving them no heed at all. But as they neared, Emily felt Anna's arm stiffen; and at that point they became as two drivers speeding toward a cliff, challenging the other to break off first. Closer and closer the four approached. Then about half a block off, she and Anna pulled apart simultaneously. Until this moment Emily hadn't given that a second thought.

Fifty-seventh Street now. Again the doors failed to open in timely fashion. When they did, the car thinned and the man became newly visible. She ignored him as Lillian's face came to mind. She didn't want to think about him; she resented the intrusion. The train began inching into the Seventy-second Street station. As that happened, the man, apparently leaving, moved toward the exit. He got right to it and stood there. Emily, sensing his presence, fixed her eyes on her bag, but his eyes drew hers up and she saw his tongue move inside a gaping smirk. Then he was out as the doors fluttered apart. She looked over at the college girl in distaste. She was writing in her notebook. The nun's eyes were closed. The so-called banker was reading his paper. He's gone, she counseled herself. Just think about Lillian.

Just then the door between the two cars opened, and a teenager stalked in with a loud radio. "I'm *me*, muthafucker!" his attitude menaced. "Get outta my face!" The banker scowled and pulled his legs in. The nun's eyelids fluttered. The girl beside Emily quit writing. The teenager, his buttocks under his tight jeans shaped like hard, round basketballs, shuffled through the car and vanished as a child on its mother's lap clapped to the beat.

After six now. She thought of Lillian and began rehearsing her words: "I love you, Lil. I'll always love you. You've been the best friend I . . ." The tears came, and she bit her lip. How was she to get through this? The train had pulled away from 72nd Street now and was proceeding north. Creeping, creeping. In and out of 79th to 86th. There the door yawned open like a huge mouth that wouldn't close. It was after 6:20 now. No way was she going to have that much time with Lillian. Jesus! The door closed, and the train wound its way into 96th. Creeping, creeping. Out of there to 103rd. Only two more stops! Somewhere before 110th Street, though, the subway completely lost power. Five, seven minutes passed. By now the banker had quit reading. The nun had quit resting. The girl beside her had quit writing. People were talking busily at the other end. She caught the girl searching her face as if she, Emily Stolle, could decode the mysteries of the New York transit system. Finally she asked, "Is it always like this?"

"No. Not really," Emily murmured.

At that the banker, overhearing, volunteered that last week his wife had been stuck on an East Side subway for more than an hour. The nun smiled. The girl responded in a southern accent so thick you couldn't have sucked it through a straw, "Well, that's sure sorry. I don't see how y'all stand for it!" She went back to her notebook. In the meantime Emily was in a panic. To begin with, she bordered on being claustrophobic. She hated elevators, high rises, planes, anything she couldn't get out of in a hurry. It was the feeling of powerlessness that got her—being trapped, walls pressing inward, suffocation. Now the door between the cars opened, and a conductor passed through the train announcing there was a problem ahead with one of the switching signals, plus some debris was on the track. They had to wait for a part. How long? He didn't know. They were doing the best they could. He continued on to the next compartment as Emily shook her head in frustration.

And suddenly with all her heart she missed Anna, missed the elegance and safety Anna gave her life. Why, she raged silently, hadn't she let her come, she could have used her support. Well, no use crying over spilled milk. She checked her watch. It was nearing six-thirty. She couldn't stand the way she felt. She stood up as if that would start the train; but then, not eager to draw attention, she sat back down and stared gloomily out the window. In the distance she could see flashlights and make out figures. She heard the college girl beside her grumble it was a darn shame they didn't make these trains better. That stated, she directed the following to Emily: she was from Nashville, Tennessee, and they had *buses* down there, why she wouldn't have one of these stupid things if they gave them to her; her boyfriend was going to be scared silly because she was late; she was going to Vanderbilt and she had come to New York for a teaching interview but now she felt like telling them to go fly a kite. Emily responded appropriately. But the river in her mind, the steady drumbeat between her ears was Lillian: would Lillian think she wasn't coming because of her cancer? Oh God, Lillian knew better than that!

Around this time the conductor reappeared. Someone shouted, "Hey, man, let's get this show on the road!" The conductor said it shouldn't be too much longer; then he turned on his heel and left. The train lurched; and after moments of just sitting idly, the four in the cubicle began a few tentative comments to pass the time. The nun said she was on her way to Columbia Presbyterian to visit a friend. The man, it turned out, was indeed from Wall Street. The girl repeated what she had earlier told Emily about being in New York for an interview. And when Emily explained she was a teacher, the girl turned into a question box: what was it really like in the schools up here? Oh, she exclaimed when Emily said she taught at Sloe, what was that like? Where was it? Why a private and not a public school? On and on and yet the wire still stringing all Emily's emotions together was Lillian. You'll make it, she encouraged herself privately. Just hang on. In the midst of all this, the girl, apparently having seen Emily's wedding band, asked that question females have put to each other since time was young: "What does your husband do?"

This came when Emily was so tense, she felt like fizz in a bottle of hot soda. She heard the question, but it didn't really register until the girl, after an awkward pause, restated it. The banker and nun had quit talking. And now it seemed they too were waiting for her response. In Emily's confusion she might have exaggerated this perception. But her anxiety was real. She started, "He's . . . a . . . uh . . . he's . . ." and her mind went blank; for the life of her she wasn't able to conjure up a male or even vaguely imagine having a husband. All her lies about Gary and Carl, the usual males she compared her husband with, went dead as the subway. Something lay naked in her. All of a sudden it hit her with such force that this was how she lived in the world, with this hunger she could never feed. Not knowing who she was, split at her most fundamental core, she strived externally to be what others would expect her, an ambition all the more urgent as she matured. A husband, or any masculine pronoun, he, him, his, protected her. She started up once again, "He's a . . ." and stopped.

"Yes?" the college girl interjected with a puzzled expression.

"He's . . . he *travels!*" And at that moment Emily felt she was breaking down. Her eyes welled with tears. She heard voices outside. She was conscious of a strong light against the train, the sound of metal striking metal. Please, Lillian; please wait! Now in the dimlit corridors of memory, Lu was running to her, a ghost, a haunt of the girl she had tried to anesthetize with Carl's body.

And thus it was that in a place as mundane as the New York subway, Emily's repression began to unravel. All the shame and guilt and error she had stored up in some room in her brain, a room airless and dirt-laden and unused, a room of cracked and peeling paint and broken furniture that smelled of neglect and age: such was the room of her inhibition. And now that room, that tight knot of denial, was coming untied by the girl's innocent question, by the vulgar manner of that man on the train, by the thought of Lillian herself. For a moment her entire life seemed to unfold—the priest Carl had taken her to so many years ago. And Jean Battle. The loneliness she had felt with men. For the sparest second a tenderness stirred in Emily for her own being. She felt the tears streaking her cheeks, and she faced these three in the cubicle who were watching her in astonishment. Thinking: *All my life I've wanted respect. I've wanted people to pay attention to my words, to look up to me, to treat me nice.* Central Park came back, and the need for clarity as Lillian had described last night. *I'm human,* she thought. *I bleed. I know the mechanisms of dreams. Lillian said I was courageous!*

The train jerked, and suddenly she was on her feet rushing to the pole in front of the cubicle. She grabbed it as the train began to move, and hung on to it while the car exploded in a frenzy of clapping and yells of "Way to go!"

And then Emily was crying so hard the nun stood up too, reaching her hand out, softfaced nun, "My dear," she said in concern. "What is it? What's wrong?"

Nothing, sister. Everything, sister. Lillian's dying. That's all Emily knew. Lillian her love, her loss, her touchstone. She had to get to her, she had to tell her the truth which maybe she already knew, but she couldn't think about that now. At this moment giving Lillian her honesty was the most important thing in her life. Perhaps that's what Lillian had been trying to tell her all along. It was after seven. But maybe the plane was delayed or Lillian was still waiting; and if not, she would get a cab to the airport. And with that, fear left Emily's eyes; something else moved in. She pushed off from the pole and came closer to the college girl, saying to her in a clear, firm voice, "I don't have a husband. I lied to you." Then, including the nun and the banker, she finished, "I'm not married. I live with a woman. I love her. We've been together for over thirteen years."

Never would she forget their expressions.

The train was in and out of 110th within seconds, roaring on to 116th. And she was in the center of the cubicle just as Lillian might stand on her boat, she was holding on to the pole as the train raced through the tunnel, the wind might as well have been in her hair for the freedom she felt. She had this smile on her face. She felt it. It had wiggled loose from some dark burial place inside and floated upward, grabbing the light of her lips. A butterfly worked free of the grime.

116th. Doors opened. She was out. 7:20. Please, please let her be there! She bounded in the rain across Broadway, past Convent Avenue to Riverside Drive at the corner, 620 West 116th. She asked the doorman, "Can you tell me where Pat Prouchie's apartment is?"

"Pat Prouchie. Oh," he said. "You looking for a Lillian Jackson?"

"Yes. Yes I am."

"She's left."

"When?"

"Before seven. She said to tell you if you made it she couldn't wait any longer because of the weather and to give you this." He went over to the table and picked up an envelope. "She told me to be sure to tell you to read this over a drink." With that, he gave it to her.

"Thanks." She raced back to Broadway. All the cabs she saw were filled. She was jumping, running into the street trying to flag one down. Finally one stopped. "La Guardia," she gasped. "I've got to get to the airport for a plane leaving at nine-fifteen."

The driver shook his head dismally. "No way. Traffic's backed up at the Triborough. It's soup out there."

"Please, look here. I'll give you an extra twenty dollars. Anything."

He turned almost sternly. "Miss, it's no go. I'm telling you. Traffic's blocked up solid as a brick. It's on the radio. It'll take us over two hours just to drive out and then you've still got to get in the terminal. No sense taking your money. Believe me."

The cab shook in the wind, and Emily sat a moment looking out the window. She had never seen so much rain.

. . . I left the taxi and walked three blocks to my old stomping ground, The West End bar. I hadn't been back since Columbia, and I couldn't help thinking about Carol and Nelson and some of my regular drinking buddies as I got a beer and sat in the back listening to the Beatles and reading Lillian's letter. It said in part:

What I am trying to tell you, Stollie, is that this disease in
what has been a very eventful life is only a short episode. All
turning points are such. They may stand on the graph of life
as special peaks, grotesque or beautiful—it matters not, if
they lead to growth. For that is the point of being alive. I
am not writing this as an instruction, for you already know
that. And what I want you to understand is that beneath the
surface I am fine, as I have always been. My layers of pain
will harden, and I will adjust. Right now I have to allow
myself latitudes even if I don't like it, for that is part of the
flow of life, and it makes it easier to adjust to radical change.
As for you, I'm enclosing a copy of something given to Bob
that you might find of some relevance to your life.

"They come in small family groups, practically naked, and
stand shyly at a distance. They are beautiful. We give them
clothes donated to the mission and then they look awful.
They come here and get baptized, then to the Catholics,
where they are baptized again, then to the Presbyterians, and
then to the Baptists; and each time they get gifts of clothes
and pots and pans to entice them to stay in a community. I'll
swear that if all the reports from the various missions were
totaled up about baptisms and new converts to Christianity,
it would show British Guiana with five million Indian
converts each year and there's only one hundred thousand
here. But I love them.

"When I first came here, I gave them the whole story
about religion and love and God. A week later I was walking
through the village, and I saw a fire with a wild pig on a
spit. Now I know we have to bend a little because wild
peccary is a mainstay of the Indians' diet. But anyway, I
said, 'Jonathan, you're cooking a pig and I told you that to
eat wild pig, meat of the cloven-hoofed animal, is forbidden
by the church and if you want to be a good Christian and go
to Heaven you must not eat pigmeat.'

"He said, 'But sir, this is not pigmeat; this is fish.'

" 'But Jonathan,' I said. 'I can clearly see that it's a pig.'

" 'No, sir. When you first come to village, you take us to
the river and you put water on my head and say, "Bicharu,

you are name Jonathan." I take this pig to river, and put water on him and say, "Pig, you are now fish." So I am cooking fish, not pig.' "

As told to Bob Baxley on the
Kamarang River, British Guiana, 1956, by a
Seventh Day Adventist Missionary

That was it. I never saw Lillian again, or even heard from her. Ten months later some stuff came in the mail from Bob: artifacts from Haiti, pictures of us when we were kids, a photo of her as a drum majorette in high school. Bob's letter said her ashes had been distributed on the Turks and Caicos islands over the North Coast Reef and a sunken freighter that at one time she had operated as captain. She was dead.

It is years later and I stand here in my Provincetown cottage overlooking the bay, restless and filled with my ghosts. Outside the moon lies in its black pie of the sea. Moon, as legend says, the repository of broken vows. For me I've one vow to keep for my days—to have Lillian close on her birthday. Tonight, as on each of hers that rolls around, I reread that letter. For years I puzzled over why she had left it for me and what it meant. And what I keep going back to is that maybe she knew all along. Maybe that was the message of Jonathan: that it didn't matter what name I gave myself—she loved me as I was. What a gift; what a memory to keep before she left. Knowing how I still hide from the world, it staggers me what I did. For on that subway I had my place in the sun, my moment of exquisite certainty. Lillian's bravery had compelled me to be brave too. And when I fall short of whatever it was that emboldened me that evening—courage, or perhaps for one glorious moment a splendid indifference to everything but Truth—I remember that ride. I was then as Lillian would have liked me: I was on *my* boat as I can see her on hers, hanging on to the mast of my pole as I forged new tracks, filled with the same rhythm of creation that she had talked about at dinner—and surely for that time at some peace.

About the Author

JACQUELYN PARK, relocated Southerner, lives and
teaches in Connecticut. This is her first novel.
She is currently at work on a second book
set in Vermont, Virginia, and California.